PRAISE FOR
THE HOUSE WITH THE G

T0028933

"Harper is unflinching in her description o.
the hypocrisies of the men who use them. . . . As vivid, unsentimental, and
compelling as *The Wolf Den*."
—*The London Times*

"Elodie Harper's . . . gripping sequel leaves the down-market milieu of
the fleshpots to depict its protagonist Amara's new and luxurious life as a
courtesan. . . . Harper's recreation of this ancient world continues to thrill."
—*The Guardian*

"The rare sequel that's as good as its predecessor."
—*Paste* magazine

"A beautiful, heartbreaking story of a woman who would do anything
for the people she loves, and for her own survival; *The House with
the Golden Door* is absolutely stunning, and kept me glued to the pages
until I was done."
—Hannah Whitten, *New York Times* bestselling
author of *For the Wolf*

"[Amara is] a beautifully flawed heroine in an agonizingly compelling story.
Friendship, love, lust, power, hate, and betrayal coalesce into a scintillating
novel full of tragedy, triumph, and female resilience."
—*The Book Reporter*

"Beautifully written with great heart. . . . Addictive reading."
—*NB Magazine*

"Richly evocative, and reeling with drama and the determined passion and
conflicts of its unforgettable heroine, this is historical fiction at its most
thrillingly entertaining."
—*LoveReading*

"A spell-binding novel that brings Pompeii back to life and explores
enslavement in all its forms."
—Anna Mazzola, author of *The Clockwork Girl*

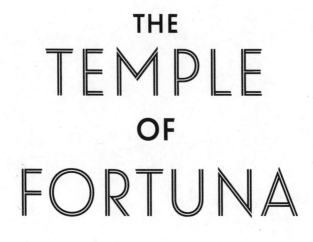

THE
TEMPLE
OF
FORTUNA

THE
TEMPLE
OF
FORTUNA

ELODIE HARPER

UNION
SQUARE
& CO.

NEW YORK

**UNION
SQUARE
& CO.**

NEW YORK

UNION SQUARE & CO. and the distinctive Union Square & Co. logo
are trademarks of Sterling Publishing Co., Inc.

Union Square & Co., LLC is a subsidiary of Sterling Publishing Co., Inc.

ISBN 978-1-4549-4664-9
ISBN 978-1-4549-4665-6 (e-book)

For information about custom editions, special sales, and premium purchases,
please contact specialsales@sterlingpublishing.com.

Manufactured in Canada

2 4 6 8 10 9 7 5 3 1

unionsquareandco.com

Original cover illustration and design by Holly Ovenden
Cover typography US/CAN edition by Melissa Farris

To Andrea Binfor, for a friendship spanning decades,
taking us from teenage laughter in the park to the streets of Pompeii.

Love you always.

ROME

SEPTEMBER 79 CE

1

"Berenice was at the very height of her power. . . . She dwelt in the palace, cohabiting with Titus. She expected to marry him and was already behaving in every respect as if she were his wife; but when he perceived that the Romans were displeased with the situation, he sent her away."

—Cassius Dio, *Roman History*

The night air is heavy with the scent of oleander, the sweet poison that Amara always associates with Rome. She stands with the other women, facing the high arched windows that overlook the moonlit city, caressed by a breeze that is still warm from the sweltering heat of the day. From up here on the Palatine, the noise of the streets is faint, but still the Empire's capital never rests. Carts rumble and clatter over the stones at all hours, and down there, below the Imperial Palace, Amara knows the smell is fetid, not flowery.

Torchlight ripples over the marble floors and across the painted walls, illuminating the gold, making it look liquid. The wealth surrounding Amara is a different world from the darkness that shaped her in the Wolf Den, but for all the splendor here, there is still pain. Queen Berenice is before them, her dark hair unbound, black kohl in streaks down her face. The Queen of

Judea has always excelled at theater, scarcely anything she does is without calculation, but Amara knows that tonight her tears are unfeigned. Even the most powerful woman can be broken by love.

The room reverberates with the low murmur of weeping, as wailing maids crowd around the queen, clinging to her clothes. Amara watches them with a cold eye, wondering how many are truly sorry to see their mistress go. There are fewer influential people here to take their leave of Berenice than she expected. Perhaps Titus will not change his mind after all, perhaps this time his lover truly *is* banished. He has promised to get rid of Berenice so many times, then found himself unable to part from the woman who is, in all important respects, his wife. Amara is certain that the irony will not be lost on Berenice; the moment she reached the pinnacle of Fortuna's wheel, when her lover became emperor, is also the moment that Titus was forced to let her fall.

The line shuffles forward. Soon it will be Amara's turn to take her leave. She tries to memorize all the faces she can see here, silently counting them off. Her patron, Demetrius, will expect the most detailed report. It is why he sent her. To get some sense of how likely it is that Berenice will return. Amara tells herself she would have come to pay her respects in any case; she does, after all, deeply admire the queen. But she knows in her heart that if Demetrius had asked her to stay away, she would have done so.

Amara is squinting to see the newest arrival in the hall—is it a senator's wife?—when she realizes the woman in front of her, who had seemed as if she would never tire of clutching Berenice's jeweled hand to her bosom, is finally about to leave. Amara steps swiftly forward into the queen's embrace.

"*Plinia Amara. You came.*"

It seems impossible that this is the last time she will hear the queen's deep voice. Amara looks into Berenice's eyes, which are smudged with tears. The woman who stole Titus's heart is nearly fifty, already at an age when satirists are decrying her decrepitude, but their mockery cannot dim Berenice's beauty. Even now, after a night of crying, she is still one of the most striking people Amara has ever seen. Not that this is why Titus chose her. The emperor loves Berenice for the same reason her enemies hate her: she is a powerful woman, of formidable intelligence, unafraid to speak her mind.

"He will send for you again," Amara says impulsively, forgetting the bland words of flattery she had rehearsed. "When he has ruled Rome for a year, when his position is secure. I am certain of it."

"So they all say," Berenice gestures at the waiting line. She sniffs, standing straighter. "But perhaps *I* will refuse to come." Amara meets the queen's gaze until Berenice smiles. "Or perhaps not." Berenice looks weary then, and Amara understands the pain of her lost pride. That she should be left hanging on the whim of a man, even the most powerful man in the world. "I shall miss hearing you read," Berenice says. "The admiral did not lie about your voice."

"You are too kind. But I am sure you will have many skilled secretaries in Jerusalem."

"None with your wit. Or your keen mind," Berenice's voice has taken on an edge, the way frost sharpens grass in winter. "I suppose I should draw greater comfort from *your* visit, Plinia Amara, than from any other. My return to Rome must be assured. You have never been one to step onto a sinking ship."

Amara hesitates. Berenice often does this; offer a compliment that risks the recipient giving offense in return. "Your eventual triumph is not in doubt," she says. "But nothing would have kept me from you this evening."

"Then I will not say goodbye, since we are so sure to be reunited." Berenice holds out her hand for Amara to kiss. Amara bends her head and the queen turns, as if already anticipating her next audience. There is a beat, as Amara waits, expecting a more formal dismissal that does not come. She tries to catch the eye of one of the maids who are still weeping softly, clutching at the hem of their queen's gown, but the girl slides her gaze to the side. There is nothing for Amara to do but leave.

She walks backward, head still bowed, not wishing to show disrespect, then skirts the room as silently as she can, heading for the stairs. The palace feels suddenly oppressive, weighed down by the queen's grief and the emperor's absence. It takes all Amara's effort to resist the urge to run down the marble steps like a child. Instead she walks solemnly past the waiting slaves who waste their lives keeping watch, past the gilded statues of Augustus, Livia and Caesar, before passing underneath the hanging oil lamps that circle above like the constellations, and escaping into the night air. Her litter is waiting for her.

The swaying ascent, as the slaves lift her from the ground, makes Amara feel drunk. She reclines against the cushions, the fabric soft against her skin, and resists the urge to grip the sides. She can never quite get used to allowing others to carry her; the slightest stumble leaves her imagining they will drop the litter. Her own feet feel much more reliable. She brushes the curtains enclosing her with her fingertips, opening them by a sliver—enough for her to glimpse the outside world as it passes without being seen. They are leaving the compound of the Imperial Palace, with its fountains and flowers, and heading into the streets. Amara's pulse beats faster. She never likes being out in Rome at night.

They make their way down the slopes of the Palatine, the shops clustered at the skirts of the Imperial estate all shuttered up for the evening, before reaching the Vicus Longus. The rocking movement of Amara's litter is often interrupted, as the road is crowded with cartloads of masonry, rumbling their way to the colossal Flavian amphitheater. She peers out as they pass the building site. The arena rises against the night sky like a ghost, its pale stone arches framing the darkness inside. Vespasian's theater of death, the source of so much noise and hammering and dust, is almost complete.

The road home is direct from here, Amara could almost walk it in her sleep. Demetrius lives on the Vicus Longus, near the Quirinal Hill, where his former master Vespasian had long-standing family roots. The new emperor's move to the Palatine is one of the few ruptures Titus has made from his father's rule, and Amara hopes her own patron's physical distance from the palace will not mark a similar drift from his place of influence. Gone are the days when Demetrius could return from an audience with the emperor within moments; now it is a slower, noisier route back, though at least a broad, well-populated one. The city's dangerous, twisting back streets hold an especial horror for Amara.

Rome's nighttime world passes in glimpses through her sliver of curtain. A wealthy man walks close by on the pavement, surrounded by slaves and torches. He ignores a prostitute chancing her luck from an archway. Amara watches the woman curse him silently after he passes, her thin hand shaking. There is something in the dejected way the woman stands that tugs at the threads of Amara's memory, unraveling it, until the stranger disappears and she can see Cressa, her long-dead friend from the brothel in Pompeii. Then she is gone, lost in the shadows.

Wafts of incense herald the nearby shrine of Febris, the halfway point in Amara's journey, long before her litter reaches the goddess of fever's painted altar and its smoking offerings. Amara makes the sign of the evil eye. The Italians' devotion to Febris is alien to everything she was taught in Greece, where her doctor father—who dealt with death all his working life—assiduously avoided any mention of Hades. Why draw the attention of Death or Sickness to yourself? It makes no sense. Amara's mood is not lightened by the flashes of graffiti she can make out, daubed over and over again on the walls. *Upstart Cleopatra, Eastern bitch, Jewish whore.* Hatred of Berenice seems to be everywhere.

Amara closes the curtains, shutting herself into the dark, a sick feeling in her stomach. Foreign harlots are not popular in Rome; perhaps it's safer to stay hidden. Who knows if a jumped-up Greek courtesan might find herself attracting the violence the graffiti writers wanted to inflict on the banished queen? Rome has always had an edge, unrest smoldering under the surface like hot embers ready to burst into flame, but never more so than now. Ever since the death of the Emperor Vespasian four months ago, Amara has felt afraid. It has been so long since this city saw a peaceful transition in power.

Even cocooned in the darkness, Amara recognizes the approach to her own home, the bump in the road that the litter bearers have to navigate before stopping at Demetrius's door, the reek of incense from the nearby temple of Fortuna the Hopeful. The men lower her from their shoulders, helping her step outside.

The porter, Salvius, greets her in the hallway: "He is waiting for you."

Stepping over the threshold of the house, Amara experiences a familiar feeling of calm. It is the sense of belonging she once took for granted on returning home in Aphidnai when her father was alive, although the atrium here is infinitely grander than her family home in Attica. Amara uncovers her hair, letting the silk fall to her shoulders as she walks across the marble floor. The walls are not painted but covered in shimmering mosaics of glass, their colors unnaturally bright even in the lamplight. Demetrius commissioned the scenes many years before he met Amara, but their audacity always makes her smile. Where other wealthy homes have scenes of the gods in all their glory and power, he has chosen to celebrate cunning. Fables written by Aesop, a lowly Greek slave, are picked out like priceless gems. Guests to Demetrius's house find themselves watched by a glittering congregation of foxes, wolves, mice and crows. When he first brought her here, Amara had asked him what he meant by it. Demetrius only laughed. *My darling, be proud of the things others despise. Who cares that you were once a whore and I a slave? Look where we are standing now.*

It takes some time to cross to the other side of the house, where the rooms encircle the garden. The door to her patron's bedchamber is ajar, a young slave standing guard outside. Amara nods at the boy as a sign of dismissal. Through the gap in the doorway, she can see Demetrius has dozed off while waiting for her. He is propped upright on the couch, his eyes closed, his jaw slack. She shuts the door loudly enough to wake him, knowing he won't want to acknowledge the weakness of his age, then takes her time adjusting the latch, giving him a moment to compose himself while her back is turned.

"How was Berenice?"

She turns around at his voice, crossing the room to sit beside him. "Everything you might expect. Heartbroken, angry, proud. I think he really intends to banish her this time. There was a sense of hopelessness."

Demetrius sighs. "Pliny says much the same. Titus is resolved—incredible as that may seem. Who else did you see there?"

Amara runs over the list, counting off on her fingers toward the end, to make sure she has not forgotten anyone. "And he has dismissed all the musicians and performers from court."

"*All* of them?" Demetrius raises his eyebrows. "I had heard that he banished the dancers, but not the singers too. The court will certainly feel rather different."

"Perhaps you and I will be the most dissolute couple there."

Demetrius does not smile, ignoring her invitation to levity. "There is always an appetite for courtesans, as long as they are not seen to hold too much power." He lowers his voice, even though they are completely alone. "Look at the emperor's brother. He refused to kiss Antonia Caenis, his father's concubine, yet thinks nothing of keeping his own." Tension takes hold of Amara like an unwanted embrace. She knows where this conversation is leading. *Domitian.* The emperor's volatile younger brother, whose disappointment at the lack of power sharing with Titus on the death of their father is an open secret, and whose ambition and cruelty are a source of constant anxiety for her patron. Rumors of murder follow him, though none would dare accuse Domitian publicly. Demetrius watches Amara closely. "No need for that sour face, my darling." He rests his hand on her knee in a half-hearted gesture of affection, although she scowls at him.

"There's every need. It's obvious what you are going to ask me next."

"The trouble is, *Kalliste*, you are too good a spy not to use you."

"How flattering," Amara says, not softening at his use of the Greek endearment.

"Well, you can either be cheerful about it, or sour, as you please. But I still need you to visit Saturia tomorrow."

"The girl is infuriating." Amara shifts so that he has to move his hand. "And besides, she never has anything useful to say. I don't think Domitian is spending his time with Saturia for her political insights. I doubt he tells her anything at all. I wouldn't. She's an absolute fool."

"Men always let something slip to the women they are fucking. It's inevitable."

"But don't you think Domitian might suspect you have sent me to spy, if I'm seen with her too often? Or worse, what if his wife thinks he's fucking *me*, as well? Domitia is hardly an enemy we need to acquire."

"All anyone will see is two pretty little courtesans spending time together to discuss the latest fashions. Sometimes my love, there are advantages to other people underestimating your intelligence. Even if *I* never do." Amara thinks of the fables on Demetrius's walls. His homage to cunning. She knows it is one of the reasons he values her so highly and sniffs, not wanting to let him know his flattery worked. "I only ask out of the great respect I have for you, Plinia Amara." Demetrius continues with his charm offensive, slipping an arm around her waist. Her mouth twists with the effort of continuing to look displeased. Sensing victory, he leans forward to kiss her lightly on the lips.

"Very well," she says, in the tone of a woman making a vast concession. "I will go."

"Pliny is also eager for you to cultivate Saturia's friendship, if that makes it more pleasant for you."

It is not lost on Amara that Demetrius would choose to tell her this only after she has agreed to his request. It is one of the few signs of jealousy she has ever seen in her patron; his insecurity over whether her loyalty to Pliny, the man who granted her her freedom, is greater than her loyalty to him. "It does not make it more pleasant," she says, with a false show of petulance. "How disagreeable of you both to order me about." From the corner of her eye, she can see him smile. "And now, I suppose, you will expect me to stay the night," Amara kisses Demetrius again, to take the sting out of her tone, and make it plain that she is not averse to the idea. In truth Amara feels absolutely no desire for Demetrius, and never has. But she is fond of him, and sometimes finds it comforting to be physically close, if only because this is when her patron is relaxed enough to show her true affection.

"How could I refuse such a gracious invitation?" Demetrius kisses her back, his own desire real enough. He stands up, taking her by the hand to lead her to bed. "Though I can't have you stay the whole night. I need to get some sleep afterward. And you never leave me any room."

Against her will, Amara thinks of Philos. Of what it felt like to be with a man who held her as if he never wanted to let her go. Whose love she never doubted. She crushes the memory, instead smiling at her patron, pretending she doesn't feel the ache of loneliness in her heart.

2

"We are so subject to chance that Chance herself takes the place of God; she proves that God is uncertain."

—Pliny the Elder, *Natural History*

The maids flutter around Amara like bees to a flower, except they are coating her in nectar, rather than extracting it. These days it takes a full hour to make her presentable. The white powder itches as one of the girls brushes it over her face and neck, giving her skin a pale, glistening sheen. Amara insists on using marl out of respect for her doctor father, even though it is less fashionable than lead. Timaios often lectured her on the metal's poisonous properties and she cannot bring herself to use it now, even though Demetrius rolls his eyes at her fastidiousness.

Iris purses her own lips as she applies the red to Amara's mouth, deepening the bow with small, deft brushstrokes. When she has finished, she steps back and encourages Amara to pout. Demetrius paid a fortune for Iris and Daphne, the two women whose lives revolve around making his mistress beautiful. Another fortune is spread out on the dressing table in the form of perfumes and cosmetics, among them a shell, full of bright green malachite. Amara closes her eyes in anticipation of the flash of color Iris will lay above the lines of kohl she has already drawn. The gentle touch of the brush on her eyelids is soothing, as is the silence. Behind her chair, Daphne is carefully dressing her hair, so softly she can scarcely feel it. Amara knows very little about either woman, preferring to be left to her own thoughts while they work.

After they have finished, Amara does not even have to lift the mirror to view herself. Daphne holds it up for her, a large highly polished disk of silver with a woman's profile engraved on the back. Amara stares at her reflection. Her eyes are perfectly symmetrical, the green tapering at the corners, making them look larger. Her mouth, which has always been her most striking feature, looks even fuller with its deep shade of red. It is her face, as much as her intelligence, that has led to Amara sitting at this dressing table, owned by one of the richest men in Rome. She thinks of her friend Dido, who was even more beautiful, imagines how she too might have been transformed with the help of a Daphne or an Iris, and finds she doesn't want to look at herself anymore.

"Thank you," she says, smiling at Daphne, who sets down the mirror. Iris brings over a wooden box, inlaid with two mother-of-pearl nymphs, dancing. The silver clasp is cool under Amara's thumb as she presses it, releasing the lid. She takes a moment to enjoy the riches inside. A priceless cameo from Demetrius, with her own face engraved as the goddess Pallas-Athene, gold and silver bracelets stacked in a pile like the cheap glass ones she used to see on sale in Pompeii, endless rings, and most precious of all, a necklace of gold and pearl given to her by the late Emperor Vespasian on the Kalends of March. She can still remember Demetrius's pride when she was singled out as one of the women to benefit from the emperor's annual act of generosity. They had discussed whether Vespasian might want to take her to bed too, and Demetrius had made it plain this was one act of infidelity he would allow. Amara could never tell whether he was disappointed or relieved when his master did not request a night with his lover. Knowing Demetrius, she expects it was both.

She selects the cameo, a pair of gold earrings and several rings, including two she always wears: one of amethyst and bronze—which she bought for herself—and the ring Demetrius gave her when he first brought her to Rome. It is solid silver, stamped with a leaping hare, the symbol of sexuality and fertility. *Perhaps you might give me a son in return*, he had remarked when she thanked him, his tone light, as if it meant nothing, but she had seen the hope in his eyes. Three years on and they have no child, only two early losses, which neither of them ever discusses.

The two maids step back as Amara rises from her chair and Daphne picks up the silk mantle from the bed, laying it reverently over her mistress's head and shoulders. It is blue, to match her chiton, stars embroidered on it in threads of silver. Amara leaves Iris and Daphne to tidy away the dressing table and walks out into the garden, passing her patron's bedchamber that sits next to hers on the colonnade. Demetrius will not be there at this time of the morning. Instead, he will be in his study meeting clients and conducting business on behalf of the emperor. The expensive scent of cinnamon mingles with that of the oleander as she makes her way to her usual spot by the fountain. A slave is waiting with sweet buns and figs, offering them to Amara as she sits on the bench, which is warm from the September sunshine.

When Amara is settled, the slave woman holds out a sealed tablet. "This came for you, Mistress."

Amara almost drops the food in her haste to take the letter. It is from Pompeii. Her hands shake as she breaks the seal, her eyes darting to the top.

Greetings Mistress, all is well with your daughter

Amara lets out a shuddering breath, overwhelmed with relief. Philos always starts his letters this way to spare her anxiety. He knows that she is terrified of bad news, so many small children die, their parents not even permitted to mourn them fully until they pass the age of ten. Amara reads on, hearing every word in Philos's voice, with its musical Campanian accent.

Rufina continues to excel in everything she does. She is cheerful, polite and loved by all who know her. At the age of three, not only has she already mastered her alphabet—as you know—but she can now also write over twenty words, which I am told is prodigious. The toy bird you sent is rarely out of her hands and stays each night beside her bed. She sends her beloved mother a kiss, and keeps you close in her heart.

Tears sting Amara's eyes and she is forced to pause. There is a knot in her chest where all the love for her daughter is kept trapped and hidden. Rufina. It is so much easier not to think of her, not to think of Philos. To forget the family she left behind. All the money Demetrius gives Amara is securing her daughter's future, yet she knows it will never bring back the years she is losing.

Julia and Livia continue well. They wish the blessings of the gods upon you. Your businesses continue to thrive, although we have incurred some costs from an unexpected quarter. Britannica has been chosen to lead the games in October, an honor for your entire gladiatorial company, which continues to succeed under your sponsorship. I have no doubt she will lead them to victory.

*I trust all is well with you in Rome, Mistress, and I remain
your obedient servant,
Philos*

The last line hurts, even though the words are nothing but a formula. It is not as if Philos can admit his true role as Rufina's father, or as Amara's lover. *Former lover*, she reminds herself, setting the tablet down in her lap. It is years since they lay together, or shared any of the intimacies that make up her daily life with Demetrius. Perhaps Philos now loves someone else. The thought is not a comforting one.

Philos's letter is only a few lines long and yet it brings a backwash of painful emotion. The stone bench grows colder underneath Amara as she sits, unable to eat, longing not only for her daughter, but for all those she left behind. Britannica, her most loyal friend, whose exploits as a gladiator in the arena fill Amara both with pride for her strength, and terror for her safety. Julia and Livia, whose company and wit she misses dearly. It was Julia who provided Amara with a permanent home in Pompeii after Rufus left her, and Julia who is now ensuring that Rufina has a loving childhood in that same home, within the walls of her estate. One of the most formidable entrepreneurs in the town and a friend of Pliny, Julia Felix is the closest Rufina has to a mother in Amara's absence, even helping persuade Rufus to keep his slave Philos on loan to Amara, to oversee their child's education. *Philos*. It is impossible to think of him without sadness. She has grown to care very much for Demetrius, but still, it is an affection that cannot compete with the passion she once felt for Philos, the man she chose for herself.

She re-reads the letter in a calmer frame of mind, and this time another line strikes her: *we have incurred some costs from an unexpected quarter*. It seems an innocent enough phrase, but the ambiguity now makes her uneasy. Philos is always plain speaking unless he cannot be, unless he is perhaps hinting at Felix, the blackmailer who still haunts their family. Even here in Rome, in her patron's beautiful villa, her old master from the brothel still manages to cast a shadow. Amara stares at the tablet, willing it to make sense, while the fountain murmurs beside her and the slave stands in silent attendance.

The walled garden where she sits no longer feels as safe. There is no mansion stout enough to keep out her past. Her former life as a brothel whore, and later as Rufus's concubine, are facts well known to her patron; it is impossible for a woman to have been enslaved and to have lived virtuously. But the secret that could destroy her is one she knows Demetrius would not be able to forgive. The father of Amara's daughter is not Rufus, but Philos, Rufus's slave. To have betrayed a patron with his own servant is not only a fault of character, it is illegal, and could forfeit both Amara and Rufina's freedom. This is the secret Felix holds, the secret he has written into his will, and the reason she is still forced to pay for his silence each month. It is a secret that was betrayed to him by Victoria, who was once Amara's closest friend, but is now Felix's wife. The tablet is solid in her fingers as Amara grips it, wondering as always, what unpleasantness might one day come for her from Pompeii.

Eventually she puts the letter down. Stewing in fear will not make the meaning any clearer, and if her family were in serious danger from Felix, she knows what words Philos would have said. They have already agreed on the code he would send if she needed to return urgently to Pompeii, or if she were at risk of imminent discovery. Amara finishes her breakfast, without speaking to the woman whose presence she had momentarily forgotten. It used to bother her, the way her first patron Rufus did not *see* the slaves who served him, anticipating his needs and moving around him like moths dancing attendance on a candle. But now she and Demetrius are much the same, in spite of both having endured enslavement themselves.

Voices from the other side of the colonnade draw her back into the present. Some of the household servants are discussing the preparation for Pliny's visit later. Amara looks up. The sky has lost the rosy tint of the morning and is deepening to the clear blue of a hot September day. The visit to Saturia can no longer be delayed. She rises, without speaking to the woman who served her, and makes her way across the garden to the atrium. The villa in Rome is large but not as enormous as Demetrius's luxurious estate in Stabiae—as a freedman, he does not want to attract too much envy among the capital's elite.

A line of mosaic ants watches Amara as she passes her patron's study. The obsidian insects are hard at work while a yellow grasshopper sings, wasting his day in idleness. It is very like Demetrius to have commissioned a fable on the importance of remaining diligent, right outside his own place of work. She pauses at the door, hearing the deep murmur of his voice, speaking Greek. The sound is comforting. Amara wants to slip inside, to wish him well before she leaves, but suspects this might annoy him. Whatever affection Demetrius feels for her is unlikely to offset his dislike at being interrupted with a client.

A litter is waiting for her at the door. The master has already issued instructions for how his lover will spend her day. Amara sits upright, holding on to the post as the litter bearers hoist her onto their shoulders, and then they are off. Rome's streets are transformed by the daylight. Even the most vicious graffiti loses its sting, people call loudly to one another in the street or from the windows, pavements are packed with those trying to buy and sell. Amara leaves her curtain open, enjoying being carried above the crush of the crowd. She remembers having to fight for every inch of space in Pompeii, the hems of her tunics constantly soiled by dust and dirt.

Saturia lives in a fashionable street in the Campus Martius, not as grand as where Demetrius has his villa, but more glamorous and youthful. Or at least this is what Saturia has often declared to Amara. The courtesan's house is visible the moment Amara's litter sways into her neighborhood. The bright yellow building stands out from its plainer neighbors, with the love story of Eros and Psyche depicted in a series of roundels on the first floor. Psyche's naked form is twisted into a succession of titillating poses and bears a striking resemblance to Saturia herself, though the artist clearly chose a less inflammatory subject than Domitian for the winged god Eros.

One of Demetrius's litter bearers, a Gaul whose name Amara can never pronounce, orders his fellows to stop. Amara alights carefully, knowing the close attention Saturia always pays to the appearance of other women, and adjusts the silk over her hair. Incense wafts from the house into the street as Amara steps into the cool, dark hallway. The porter is obscured by shadow, his oiled beard gleaming in the dim light. He bows. Amara is fast becoming a familiar figure at Saturia's home. She follows the man into the atrium, which is painted in the latest style, the walls creating a false sense of depth, illusory green curtains draped between painted columns, deceiving the eye. A marble tiger prowls around the edge of the pool at the room's center, its striped reflection rippling in the shallow water.

The porter claps his hands and a young maid hurries forward. "Tell the Mistress that Plinia Amara is here." The blonde girl scampers up the stairs, light-footed as a rabbit, leaving Amara and the porter to enjoy a moment of awkward silence.

The maid returns, looking flustered. "Mistress is having her hair done, but she will see you."

Amara follows the girl up the steps, then along the tiled corridor toward the sound of voices. The door is open, welcoming them into the bustle of Saturia's beauty routine. It is a very different scene from the gloomy atrium. Two windows look onto the garden, letting in the full light of the morning sun, and the air is full of laughter, as four maids fuss over their mistress. Amara cannot see Saturia's face, only a cascade of golden-brown hair being curled, and a limp hand, held out to have the nails painted.

"My darling, so sweet of you to come!" Saturia does not turn, leaving Amara no choice but to walk around to face her instead. Domitian's young mistress is illuminated by sunlight, her hair a halo of fire. It is impossible not to be struck by her beauty. A gloss of white lead has been smoothed over her skin, making her look like a doll. Her wide-set eyes are an unusual shade of blue, which she always accentuates with a matching line of color, and her cheeks have a childlike plumpness that allows her to lay claim to being seventeen, even though Amara is certain she is closer to twenty. But whatever Saturia's exact age, she is younger than Amara, a fact she rarely allows her to forget.

"You look radiant," Amara says, treating Saturia to her most ingratiating smile, the one she learned at the brothel, the one her pimp Felix would wear when he wanted to charm difficult clients.

"I wish you would let me give you some of this," Saturia gestures at the lead. "Marl can be so aging. Powder shows up even the tiniest little lines." Amara does not allow her smile to falter, only raises her eyebrows as if with interest. "Although your patron is so *old*, isn't he? I suppose that does have its advantages.

Even when you are long past it at forty, you will still look like a slip of a girl to him—he will be so very, very ancient by then."

"Demetrius has the energy of a much younger man." Amara is stung into defending her lover, trying not to picture him as he looked last night, tired from waiting up for her. Instead, she wills herself to see him at work in his study, conducting the emperor's business. Her fate is bound up with his, and it is fear as much as affection that makes her dread age weakening his grip on power.

"How sweet of you to be fond of him," Saturia says, wiggling her fingers in the air to set the color on her nails. "I'm not sure I would be able to overlook his past, myself. Is it true that when he was a slave, he was obliged to pleasure his first master's wife?" She shudders. "The idea of a man serving a woman is too unnatural."

Amara inwardly curses Demetrius for sending her here. Saturia is immensely irritating. Although at least now she can repay her patron with a small act of disloyalty, as a means of gaining her target's trust. "It is entirely true," she says with a sly smile, reigniting a rumor that has long dogged Demetrius's reputation. "He *was* obliged to serve his master's wife. Though I cannot say a man learning to pay attention to a woman's pleasure is such a disagreeable state of affairs. Besides, he told me once that the wife was young and pretty, so it was not such a trial for him to endure."

Saturia gasps with feigned horror, then laughs. "I'm sorry darling, but I've met Demetrius and the whole idea is too ridiculous. The idea that anybody ever lusted after him! Although I guess we are all young once."

"Of course we cannot all be so fortunate in our lovers," Amara replies, not quite daring to name Domitian, but hoping Saturia will. Instead, the girl just smiles with infuriating smugness.

"I don't think you are doing too badly, darling," Saturia says. "He has a lovely house, doesn't he? That must make up for rather a lot."

Amara tries to see herself through Saturia's eyes. An older courtesan with a dubious past, whose patron—for all his wealth and influence—is a mere freedman. Perhaps Saturia imagines Amara is insecure or envious of a seventeen-year-old who is bedding the emperor's brother. "Of course," she says, attempting to sound humble. "At my age, I'm lucky to have him. And at least he is always gentle and kind."

To Amara's surprise, Saturia seems to take her remark as a dig, rather than self-deprecation. Even through the lead paste, she can see Saturia's cheeks flush red. "How nice for you," she sneers. "To have somebody *kind*." Saturia raises her chin, looking defiantly at Amara. "I don't know what you've heard, but I'm perfectly happy and perfectly capable of looking after myself. Men are only gentle when they're too old and doddery to be anything else. And who wants *that*."

There is a moment's silence. The maids glance at each other, and the girl painting Saturia's last fingernail is now completely still. "I meant no offense." Amara holds up her hands. "I swear I have heard nothing, and if I had, that is the last thing I would ever use against another woman. You must know enough rumors about *my* past to believe me." She watches Saturia who is now scowling at the floor, her lower lip quivering. Amara is reminded of her former friend Victoria, her fellow whore at the brothel, who would hide her fear of Felix with anger. And then she understands. *Saturia is afraid of Domitian.* "You cannot possibly imagine I have anything but admiration for you," Amara says, speaking to Saturia gently, as if she were a frightened child.

"People say Pliny picked you up in a brothel," Saturia sniffs, taking Amara's bait to save face. "Is that true?"

"I doubt the admiral has ever set foot in a brothel. But it is certainly true that I have."

"Then I suppose you have done very well for yourself," Saturia flicks her hand at the maid, gesturing for her to finish the fingernail. "In your position, I too would be pleased to have landed Demetrius."

This is as close as Saturia ever comes to paying another woman a compliment. Amara bows her head. "You are too gracious."

Saturia pauses, watching the last touch of red paste coat her little finger, then she stands, waving the maids away. "I was planning on seeing the new statue on display at the Temple of Fortuna Huiusce Diei this morning. Everyone is talking about it. Perhaps you will join me?"

The temple to the goddess Fortuna in her guise as "the luck of the present day" is more art gallery than religious sanctuary, and one of the most fashionable places to be seen in Rome. Amara would have preferred a more private meeting at home; if Domitian does not already know of this friendship, he certainly will after they have taken a turn around Fortuna's rotunda. At the same time, she can hardly refuse. "What a lovely idea," she exclaims, taking Saturia's outstretched hand. "I would be delighted."

The temple is only a short walk from the house, but Amara soon regrets their decision not to take the litter. Sharing a pavement with Saturia is not easy. They are followed by a fresh gaggle of maids, and Saturia complains constantly about the noise, the smell and the dirt. At one point Amara is obliged to help hold up Saturia's chiton, which she suspects is a deliberate form of power play, to let any onlookers know who the more important courtesan is of the two.

After yet more dithering outside a fabric shop, they reach Fortuna's temple. It stands behind Pompey's Theater, which Demetrius once told her was the site of Julius Caesar's murder—an irony given the dictator's lifelong devotion to the goddess of chance. Amara gazes at the elegant round building that sits atop a flight of white marble steps. It reminds her a little of the Temple to Hera in her hometown of Aphidnai, and she stands for a moment, lost in memory, imagining the sound of her parents' voices, calling her. Then she notices Saturia is shifting from foot to foot in a childish gesture of boredom, the way Victoria would fidget when she was restless. Again Amara feels a flicker of compassion. The girl is irritating, but it is unpleasant to think of her being abused by a powerful man like Domitian. Amara smiles. "Shall we go in?"

Saturia nods and the pair of them climb slowly up the steps to the Temple sanctuary. At the top, Saturia pauses, ostensibly to straighten her head scarf, but Amara can tell it is to strike the most flattering pose. When Saturia is happy with her appearance, they enter the sanctuary.

Even in the dimmer light, Fortuna's statue commands immediate attention. Towering up toward the domed roof, she is a monstrous figure, making it easy to believe in the deity's power to crush men and their empires underfoot. Looking up at the goddess, Amara's head does not even reach her knee.

"They didn't make her very *pretty*, did they?" Saturia whispers to Amara, squeezing her arm.

Amara wants to laugh but doesn't dare. "No," she says solemnly. "I suppose not." It is true there is nothing overtly feminine about this Fortuna; her face could almost be that of a man, and her lips are parted—not with desire but indifference. Her bronze torso verges on being flat chested, making her even more androgynous, while the heavy cornucopia that she holds could double as a weapon. Amara stares. Fortuna looks a little like her friend Britannica. She smiles at the thought. The ability to grant good luck on the day seems a fitting gift for a gladiator, and Amara offers up a prayer to the goddess of chance for Britannica's safety in the arena, on this day, and every day.

"I've never been inside here before," Amara says, glancing around, her eyes adjusting to the gloom. "It's beautiful."

"You've never been?" Saturia is aghast. "I suppose as a Greek you wouldn't know what's culturally important in Rome. It houses some of the best artwork of the city. I think that's the new statue, over there." She starts to walk around the rotunda, forcing Amara to keep pace. The walls are covered in paintings and sculpture showing the power of Fortuna over the lives of mortals. The goddess stands astride cities, both raising them up and destroying them, while armies fight at her feet, their victory decided not by might but by Fate. Fortuna's expression in all these scenes is the same; she appears equally unmoved by joy or suffering.

Saturia pays scant attention to the frescoes, peering at the statues instead. Even Amara, who knows very little about art, can tell that they are superior. She lingers at a beautifully realized version of Pallas-Athene, and touches the cameo at her neck that Demetrius gave her. The goddess of Attica—Amara's Greek homeland—rests on her spear, scanning the horizon for the enemy, her lips curled in an enigmatic smile. The head of Medusa is pinned to her breastplate, the snakes so real Amara almost expects them to move. She would like to spend an hour going over every detail of her patron goddess, but realizes she is ignoring Saturia, the reason she is supposed to be here. Amara joins her at the base of a tall nude, a young man carrying a sword.

"Is it wise to stand just here?" Amara asks, raising an eyebrow, hoping to draw Saturia out with teasing. "People might wonder why we are staring at him."

"Well darling, I can see why Demetrius might be jealous," Saturia smirks. "Though maybe this is how he appeared to his master's wife, all those *centuries* ago when he was in demand."

"And does *your* patron have cause to be jealous?"

"Never of my loyalty." Saturia is still gazing at the naked young man, at the weapon clasped in his hands. Her voice, when she speaks again, is barely a murmur. "And I do believe he is capable of rising higher than this." Amara looks swiftly at her companion. It is the closest Saturia has ever come to a political comment. Saturia looks back at Amara and for a moment there is an unmistakable edge to her expression, but then she smiles, placing her fingers coyly to her lips, as if all she intended was a lover's compliment.

3

*"What a splendid comrade you were when
we were on active service together!"*
—Pliny the Elder to Emperor Titus, *Preface to the Natural History*

The Admiral of the Roman Fleet is perched on a bench outside Demetrius's dining room, while a slave boy washes his feet. Pliny has his familiar air of restlessness, as if even pausing for the most basic preparations before dinner is time wasted. He is grayer and heavier than when Amara first met him, though his wit is just as sharp. She and Demetrius sit opposite their guest, having their own feet toweled dry by another attendant.

"So she has left at last," Pliny rises from the bench as soon as the slave has finished drying between his toes. "The queen set off for Judea this morning."

Amara pictures Berenice as she appeared the night before, desolate and alone. "Did Titus visit her to say goodbye?"

"No. And it's for the best. I liked her very much, as you know. But the people would never accept her. It is hard enough to govern, without enduring daily insults about one's choice of partner. It risks eroding respect for the emperor's position." They walk through to the dining room and Pliny lowers himself onto the central couch, while Amara and Demetrius take those on either side. Demetrius never expects Amara to recline next to him when guests are present, as if she were a plaything. She is afforded the status of a wife instead. "You might not like me for it, Amara," Pliny continues, "but I'm afraid I strongly advised Titus *not* to see her again. It only prolongs the agony and we cannot afford for him to waver."

"Titus is fortunate to have your counsel," Demetrius says, accepting a glass of wine from the slave hovering beside him.

"He has little need of it. We could not have hoped for a better exchange in power after the death of your late—much mourned—master. Vespasian and Titus prepared well for this moment, over many years, and their efforts have proved worthwhile. It was what I always admired about Vespasian: his pragmatism and his commitment. Rome is worth more than the life of one man, even the emperor. He understood this."

"Especially after what went before," Demetrius remarks. There is a moment's silence when Amara suspects both men are reflecting on the tumultuous reign of Nero and the civil war that followed. In Greece, she was barely conscious of the chaos raging here ten years ago at the seat of power, more concerned instead with her own family's painfully upended fortunes. It is hard to imagine Demetrius as he must have been back then, a loyal servant to Vespasian who was not emperor but only a general in the Roman army, his claim to power far from secure.

"May Fortuna grant that we never see such days again," Pliny says, raising his glass. "To the long life of Emperor Titus." The three of them drink.

Slaves from the kitchen set out the meal on small silver tables beside their couches, and the smell of boiled goose, seasoned with cumin and thyme, wafts from the opened dishes. Beneath the slaves' bare feet, the floor is covered in a mosaic of fish bones, symbolizing scraps left for the *lemures*, the spirits who lurk in the dark corners of every house. "I fear the goose is not as good as the birds from Germania," Demetrius says to Pliny as he tries the meat. "But we had it prepared as your cook advised."

Pliny nods his approval. "I used to eat this dish with Titus, on campaign. I wonder if he still remembers. He was always the most delightful company as a young man. We saw less action than expected that season. Though enough, I suppose. Germania was a brutal front to fight on."

Amara still finds it hard to see Pliny as a soldier, even after all these years she has known him. Although she does not find it difficult to imagine the hours he spent during campaigns noting down the customs and wildlife he encountered. Last year Pliny gave Demetrius a draft copy of his *Natural History*, as a token of their friendship, but it is Amara, not her patron, who has read every word.

"As long as Rome herself is free of fighting," Demetrius says.

"Indeed." Both Pliny and Demetrius glance at Amara. "You visited the Temple of Fortuna today, I believe," Pliny says to her. "With your new friend."

"Saturia was most struck by a soldier in the sanctuary," Amara says, as if delivering a casual remark. "Though she felt her patron might rise higher."

Pliny is staring at her, as if trying to read Saturia's meaning on Amara's face. "I suppose that might have been nothing more than a courtesan's innuendo."

"Perhaps. Though I am starting to think she is less foolish than she appears. I believe she is afraid of him."

"Not all patrons are as indulgent as yours," Pliny says, gesturing at Demetrius. "It can be perfectly natural for a woman to fear the waning of a man's affection."

"I don't believe this is what she fears." Amara does not have to say more. Even though Pliny himself has written a book praising the Flavian dynasty, including Domitian, they all know the rumors about the emperor's younger brother—about his cruelty to animals, servants and women.

"I'm sure as a good friend, you pay attention to all Saturia tells you," Pliny says pleasantly, turning back to his goose. Even within a trusted circle like this, Amara is used to political conversations being a little cryptic. Pliny and Demetrius might treat slaves as if they are invisible, but they still know they have ears.

Demetrius catches the arm of one of the servers. "Send Hermeros to me. Then the rest of you may leave us for a while." The boy nods and goes to fetch Demetrius's steward, who Amara knows is entirely in his confidence. She also trusts Hermeros, although given her own forbidden relationship with Philos, a steward who betrayed his master Rufus by sleeping with Amara, she takes nothing for granted. Slavery creates a shadow world, with its own secrets and loyalties.

When Hermeros enters, closing the door behind him, Demetrius drops his guard. "Has Titus decided what power to give his brother?"

Pliny swills the wine. "None."

"Nothing? No office at all?"

"Ceremonial only. Though with the promise of more in time."

"Is that wise?"

"It is a dangerous balance. Whether it is wiser to keep your enemy close or at a distance. I think this is a means of biding for time, and watching how Domitian responds." Pliny smiles at Amara. "Which is what makes your new friendship so helpful."

"I'm not certain Saturia knows anything," Amara replies feeling both flattered and uncomfortable at the admiral's attention. "I think Domitian only beds her, nothing more."

"Not like his father with Antonia," Demetrius says, his fondness for Vespasian obvious in the warmth of his voice.

Pliny laughs. "Vespasian's most important counselor. The times I would be called at dawn, only to see Antonia Caenis in the bed too, advising him on the business of the day before I had even had a chance to cross the threshold."

"Her death was a heavy loss. I don't believe my master ever recovered."

"He took enough other women to bed to get over the heartbreak," Amara says, waspish.

Demetrius laughs. "*Kalliste*, a man may appreciate women for many different reasons. It doesn't mean the one he values best is replaceable."

"In Domitian's case that woman would be his *wife*, Domitia," Amara declares, spearing a piece of goose. "I don't think he values Saturia at all."

"Well, who knows? People might look at you and mistakenly believe I value you solely for your beauty."

"I rather doubt that," Pliny says, looking between the pair of them with amusement. "Not when she has my name."

Demetrius throws up his hands in mock surrender. "Whose side are you on?"

"I only mean Amara's friendship with Saturia may need to be exploited quickly, in order to be useful," Pliny says. "It is true Domitian might start to suspect Amara's motives. The man is no fool—he knows she is your woman, and he knows where your loyalties lie."

"Amara will be accompanying Saturia to watch the funeral," Demetrius says, referring to Vespasian's last procession through Rome. "In all the excitement of the day, the girl should be inclined to gossip. Then we might learn something more of Domitian's plans."

"You must be relieved that preparations for the funeral are almost finished," Pliny says, perhaps deciding from Amara's peeved expression that it is wise to change the subject. "I was surprised by the choice of the actor Favor; he's rather vulgar, though I suppose he's popular with the people."

"The entire procession is for the people. The emperor certainly cared nothing for such extravagance when he was alive. But I believe it amused Vespasian to think of his death being marked like this, so at odds with the way he lived," Demetrius smiles and Amara wonders which memory he is reliving about the man he served for so many decades, the master who gave him his freedom. She knows her patron's painstaking attention to the detail of the funeral has personal as well as political significance: it is his last act of service.

"I will be returning to Misenum after the rites are complete," Pliny says.

"Oh! So soon?" Amara is too taken aback to hide her disappointment. "We will miss you."

"It's only for a few months. I can't abandon the fleet forever." Pliny turns to Demetrius. "I will be sure to send some of my men to visit your estates at Stabiae, if you would like an independent update on the harvest."

"You are most kind," Demetrius smiles warmly at his friend. If he was jealous at Amara's expression of regret, or Pliny's earlier claim to her, he does not show it.

Pliny does not stay late. Amara suspects that he has several scrolls lined up to be read aloud before bedtime, and is glad her own voice will not be made hoarse by hours of recitation for the admiral. The days when Pliny was the object of her wide-eyed devotion are gone, but even so, a deeper understanding of his flaws has done nothing to lessen Amara's fondness for the man who is responsible, above all others, for rescuing her from the Wolf Den.

In Demetrius's chamber, her patron lies propped on his elbow, watching her as she gets ready to join him on the bed. Amara knows her body and her beauty have the comfort of familiarity for him now, and getting undressed is companionable rather than anything else.

"You seemed a little tense earlier," Demetrius remarks, running his hands over her shoulders when she slips in beside him.

"I have a bad feeling about spending time with Saturia," she replies, leaning against him. "I can't fully explain it."

"She does sound rather irritating."

"It's not only that. Maybe it's the thought of what might be happening behind closed doors. The price she is paying for all those paintings, and the servants and the tiger."

"Tiger?" Demetrius stops caressing her, surprised.

"A marble one. By the pool in the atrium."

"Well. Some people have no class." They both snort with laughter, aware of the absurdity of two foreign former slaves mocking a freeborn Roman woman. Demetrius kisses her neck. "I'm sorry you will miss Pliny so much."

"He is like a father to me."

Demetrius laughs. "He's younger than I am."

"That's not the point," Amara says, not wanting to hurt his feelings by explaining that a gap of thirty or forty years is so vast, a decade between him and Pliny makes little difference. They are both old men to her. "Although I do wish you weren't walking the *entire* funeral procession." She turns around and puts her arms around him, unable to keep the anxiety from her voice. "Won't it be very exhausting?"

"Don't be ridiculous. You do *fuss*," Demetrius disentangles himself, as if stifled by her embrace. It is one of the many contradictions Amara has learned about her patron—that he enjoys her affection but not too much of it.

"Don't I have a right to fuss over your health?" she says, pretending to pout. "Who else is going to keep me in all this luxury if anything happens to you? I might have to move to the Suburra if you die, which would be *unbearable*."

Demetrius smiles, more comfortable with being teased than loved. "Always so tenderhearted," he says, drawing her closer again, so that her head is tucked under his chin, her face resting against his chest. She listens to his heartbeat as he falls asleep.

4

*"Even at his funeral, the leading mime actor Favor, who was
wearing a mask of his face and imitating the actions and speech
of the deceased during his lifetime, as is the custom, asked the
procurators how much the funeral and the procession had cost
and, hearing that it was ten million sesterces, exclaimed that they
should give him a hundred thousand and throw him into the river."*

—Suetonius, "The Deified Vespasian," *Lives of the Caesars*

Amara stands beside Saturia at the very edge of the colonnade, nothing but air between the two courtesans and the space where the procession will pass. The stones are bleached bone-white, reflecting the harsh brilliance of the sun. Amara's eyes water to look at them. The road has been cleaned of its usual filth, so nothing will sully the emperor's final passage to the Campus Martius. The same cannot be said of those now crowding the streets, whose stench is worsened by sweating in the heat. She is aware of the crush of people behind her, of how easily they could surge forward, pushing her down into the gutter. Her privileged view is also a precarious one. She glances at the man to her left, part of a ring of guards that encircles both her and Saturia, protecting them from the common people at the back.

Amara's feet ache from standing so long, forcing her to shift on the pavement to ease the discomfort. She hopes her own heavy makeup is not smearing in the heat, although looking at Saturia the signs are not encouraging. On the opposite side of the street Amara can see other minor functionaries of the Imperial court. A fellow courtesan briefly catches her eye. The woman's name eludes her, but the pale face, with its high arched brows, is familiar. One of the dead Emperor Vespasian's many lovers.

"What's that bitch doing, making faces at us?" Saturia nods at the woman opposite. "Gaia, isn't it? She must be at least thirty. I wouldn't acknowledge her if I were you."

"I had forgotten her name. Wasn't she one of Vespasian's favorites?"

"Hardly. Or even if she *was*, she's a nobody now." Saturia sighs loudly. Standing in the heat for hours has done nothing to improve her temper. They are not important enough to have been granted a place to view the main funeral ceremonies in the Forum, or the cremation in the Campus Martius; the best Demetrius could secure was a decent view of the procession toward the end of the emperor's journey.

"Can you hear that?" Amara nudges her. "I think they might be coming."

Saturia stiffens, instantly at attention. Noise is growing above the chatter of the crowds, like the hum of bees swarming. More people become quiet, straining to hear, until the street is almost silent. The funeral procession must finally be approaching. They wait as a rising crescendo of wailing and piping reaches them, even though the road is still empty. It is an approaching river Amara knows will soon burst through the channel of the Via Sacra, contained by banks of high buildings. An answering murmur goes up from the spectators as the weeping and screaming grows louder, and then the professional mourners are upon them.

The first women stagger, exhausted, onto the stones, but somehow they still have air left in their lungs to scream. Blood streaks their faces where they have torn at their own skin in a grotesque display of grief. One mourner stumbles too close to the pavement, her eyes vacant as if drunk, and Amara instinctively steps back at the sight of the raw, bloody patches on the woman's scalp where she has ripped out tufts of hair. Saturia clutches her arm, and Amara holds her closer. The keening builds from those standing behind them as well as from the procession in front. Hysteria is catching, spreading through the crowd like fire. Across the road, Gaia flings up her hands, covering her eyes, her shoulders shaking. Amara feels tears prick her own eyes too, though not for the dead emperor. The women's cries bring back memories of her father's funeral, her last sighting of her mother, and worse, of Dido dying, opening Amara's old wounds to the point of pain. Next to her, Amara can feel Saturia trembling and wonders who the girl is crying for.

Flute players weave between the mourners, their shrill piping giving a savage rhythm to the sobbing and screaming, and then, just as swiftly as they arrived, the wailers have passed, and the noise is receding. Next come the emperor's freedmen, a sober, grim-faced parade after the women's wildness. Amara anxiously scans their ranks for Demetrius and finds him near the front. He had arranged where she should stand and Amara holds her breath, willing him to find her, aware that he must be looking for her too. His eyes alight on her face. They hold one another's gaze, briefly, then he passes.

"Your old man is holding up well," Saturia sniffs, evidently recovered from her tears. "I'm amazed someone his age could manage a walk that long."

More musicians follow the freedmen, and the mood of the crowd shifts again. Amara can hear people laughing behind her. They all know what is coming next. The drumming and piping take on a livelier tone as the mime actors arrive, cavorting across the stones. Many are dressed as soldiers but no real warriors ever moved like this. It is like a dance, the way they wheel and bow, flimsy helmets half covering their faces, sweat making their painted armor stick to their chests. They are Vespasian's armies, conquering Jerusalem. The men playing the Judeans have masks that gape in fear, cringing and leaping from the blows of blunted swords. It is no accident that the new emperor, Titus, has made the conquest of Judea so prominent in his father's memorial: it is also an honor to himself, given they both fought in the campaign. Perhaps too, he intends to remind his people of the queen he gave up for Rome. Amara thinks of Berenice and feels a pang, wondering if Titus truly loved the woman who shared a decade of his life, or if she was also partly the spoils of war.

"I suppose it's as well that ridiculous Berenice isn't here to see this," Saturia says, voicing Amara's thoughts. "She was so full of herself, with no shame at all in being a Jew. Though you liked her, didn't you?"

"She was an impressive woman."

"She would have been even more impressive if she'd managed to hang on to the emperor. I cannot imagine fumbling it at the last moment, if *I* were that close to power."

"Do you think you might be?" Amara asks, her tone playful. But Saturia pretends not to hear.

The celebration of Vespasian's deeds seems endless. More men troop past, carrying models of the dead man's grandest building projects in bronze and wax. Amara catches the heavy scent of beeswax from the giant amphitheater, which is starting to soften in the heat, in spite of its bearers' efforts to keep the structure steady. There are mutters as some of the more ostentatious theatrical props are carried past, representing looted treasures from the Temple of Jerusalem. A voice yells from the back *"What about a pisspot?"* and several others jeer. Amara stiffens. Demetrius had a hand in planning Vespasian's infamous tax on urine, which earned the late emperor the undying hatred of tanners and laundrymen and everyone else who needs it for business. The tax filled the imperial coffers, but was hugely unpopular. She had pressed Demetrius on it once, asking what he really thought of the levy, but he had only repeated the emperor's own words: *money has no smell.*

A ripple of cheering builds from further down the road. Favor, the lead actor, the one honored with the task of representing Vespasian himself, is nearly upon them. She and Saturia stand on tiptoe, straining to see, and then suddenly he is on the road, so close to Amara she could almost touch him. His disguise leaves little trace of the beautiful actor underneath. It is unnerving, seeing Vespasian's face superimposed onto another man, the small darting eyes looking out from behind the death mask, encircled by hollows of wax. Favor is much slighter than the late emperor, and his imitation carries a hint of mockery. He has mastered his subject's barrel-chested stride, but it is exaggerated, becoming an ostentatious swagger rather than the blunt soldier's manner Vespasian always affected.

Saturia looks sidelong at Amara, her eyes wide with mischief and amusement. "Do you think they knew he would play Vespasian like that?"

"Demetrius told me Vespasian himself chose Favor. I guess the emperor must have known how he was likely to behave, but didn't care."

"I suppose it's an emperor's duty to entertain the masses," Saturia says, her tone lofty, as if she were not also part of the eagerly watching mob.

More musicians follow Favor, their piping harsh and solemn, heralding the arrival of the Praetorian Guard. Rome's real soldiers, as opposed to the actors who passed by earlier, quiet the high spirits of the crowd. The men march in formation, row after relentless row, a reminder, if any were needed, that the world's greatest city is upheld by violence. It is surrounded by his soldiers that Vespasian's golden funeral bier finally arrives. The emperor's real body was burned in a private ceremony months ago: the wax effigy now on display exists only to mark his apotheosis as a god. Amara lowers her eyes, rather than gaze at the figure, as Demetrius instructed. There is total silence in the crowd as Emperor Titus himself rides past. Titus does not look at his people, his gaze is trained instead on his father's bier, his expression as much a mask as the wax face Favor wore.

Domitian follows him, also on horseback. Unlike Titus, his eyes flick over the watching crowd. Amara wonders if he is nervous, looking for enemies who might attempt an assassination. His gaze rests briefly on her and Saturia, making Amara's stomach clench, but then his eyes slide off so quickly, she wonders if he even registered who they were. Surely he would have more important things to notice than two whores on the day of his father's funeral. She looks at Saturia whose hands are clasped so tightly her knuckles are whiter than the lead on her face.

"You must feel very proud," Amara murmurs.

Saturia startles. "Of course," she says, without looking at Amara or relaxing her hands.

When the last of the guards have passed, the crowd begins murmuring, noise and movement returning as people contemplate the trek back to their homes, or to other street celebrations. The state is providing free food and drink for the city today, at a price that makes Demetrius fret for the Imperial coffers.

"I hope we get back home in time to see his spirit rise," Saturia says, as they watch people jostling. Saturia's street is only a short distance from the square where the emperor's funeral pyre will be set alight; it should be possible to catch a glimpse of it burning from her upper windows. Across the road, Gaia has already managed to slip away. "Why can't people move themselves more quickly?"

Amara lays a reassuring hand on Saturia's arm. "Demetrius said there is another ceremony first; we should have plenty of time."

"It was decent of him to secure us a place to watch," Saturia says, in a rare expression of gratitude. Amara glances at her, looking for sarcasm, but sees none.

They shuffle painstakingly along the street, their hired guard ensuring they are not mauled by the crowd, eventually reaching the bright yellow façade of Saturia's house. On the upper floor, slaves have set out refreshments on a balcony that overhangs the street, ready for them to watch the ceremony. The very top of the emperor's pyre is just visible above the red rooftops. Demetrius took Amara to see its construction yesterday, proud of the work he spent so long supervising, pointing out its various aspects. At the bottom sits a chamber of logs, sweet-smelling herbs and bundles of sticks, then the chamber where the bier and wax body will lie, built like a temple and surrounded by columns and tapestries, then on top of this are piled further rooms of painted wood and ivory, each carved with Vespasian's exploits, all of them diminishing in size as the tower ascends. To Amara's eyes it resembled an enormous glittering lighthouse. Her first thought had been regret at the waste of burning so many treasures, any of which she would have given an eye for during her days at the Wolf Den, but she kept this to herself. She knows Demetrius well enough to suspect he will have had similar misgivings, although he cannot admit any criticism of his former master, even to himself.

Now only the last chamber of the pyre is visible, its gilded walls catching the light of the sun, making it flash like a beacon. Saturia stretches out her legs, wiggling her toes where they have gone numb from standing so long on stone. She leans over to take a fig from the table, peeling it with a sigh. "What would they do if the eagle breathed in too much smoke?"

"That won't happen," Amara says, although this idea had occurred to her too. She asked Demetrius to explain the mechanism by which the bird is released when the pyre is lit, anxious about how safe it might be.

"Your piety is admirable," Saturia says with a smirk. "Or is it faith in your lover's ingenuity? I don't suppose Demetrius would last long if *that* happened."

"As you've said many times, he has lived unscathed to a very great age. I do not fear for him."

"You must forgive a little teasing my darling," Saturia laughs. "It's too adorable how you always leap to his defense. I think it must be your servile nature, it's hard to erase, especially for Greeks. Though you weren't always a slave, were you?"

"No." Amara turns aside, feigning interest in watching people pass on the street below. Saturia's jibes don't hurt, but she is annoyed at herself. She had believed she gave nothing away, including her affection for Demetrius. Saturia is sharper than she looks.

"That's hardly an answer." Saturia is still intent on her fig, licking her fingers where the pink pulp has stuck. "Tell me about yourself."

"Such as?"

Saturia waves a hand. "Who are you?"

The pyre must still be unlit. Amara stares at its summit, hoping it might bring a distraction, wondering how best to stop this conversation veering off course. "Very well. But only if you return the favor afterward."

"That's rather bold."

"Boldness is an asset in a courtesan, don't you find?"

Saturia raises her eyebrows at Amara's decision to place them on an equal footing. "Fair enough."

Amara picks up a fig too, giving her fingers something to do, while she measures out her words. "I was born free, in Attica. My father, Timaios, was a respected physician. On his death my family became destitute and I was sold into servitude to ensure my survival." She carefully lays a scrap of the fig's purple skin on the table, before digging her nails into its flesh to peel off another strip. "After that, I ended up in Pompeii and became the concubine of Placidus Rufus, whose uncle is a dear friend of the Admiral. Pliny granted me my freedom, for my services to him in researching his *Natural History*. And through Pliny, I met Demetrius."

"You missed out the brothel."

"Out of respect for your decency. Some places are corrupting for a freeborn woman even to hear about." Amara smiles, taking a bite from the soft white fruit, knowing Saturia will have difficulty pressing her further after such an answer. To her surprise, Saturia does not huff in annoyance—she is not even looking at Amara, instead she is inspecting her fingernails.

"And what of Demetrius?"

In the brief time Amara has known Saturia, she has never seen the girl take such an interest in anyone else's life, still less in someone beneath her. Understanding hits Amara, as abrupt as a sudden stumble on the pavement with its lurching fear of a fall. *Perhaps*

Domitian has asked Saturia to turn spy. "What of Demetrius?" she shrugs. "You've met him yourself. There's not much to say."

"You must know more about his life than that!"

"He is old and rich. That's all that interests me."

"Oh, come now." Saturia throws her hands up. "You've told me how very *kind* he is. And he's Greek like you, isn't he? Your kind are forever chattering. Why not tell me about him?"

"I cannot imagine why you find my lover interesting. Not when your own is so much more impressive."

"But we're friends, aren't we, darling? Of course I'm interested."

Amara tries to calculate how little she can tell, without seeming evasive. "Demetrius is from Olympia, the sacred city. Perhaps it is a part of Greece that is familiar to you? The Temple of Zeus there is famous." She reaches over to take a sip of sweet wine as if waiting for an answer, but Saturia says nothing, obliging her to continue. "Demetrius was born enslaved but he was highly educated, to increase his eventual price. He passed through several hands as a youth, including the hands of one master's wife—as you know—until at the age of twenty, he became a servant to Vespasian, who later made him his freedman in recognition of his loyal service."

"That's nothing more than I knew already," Saturia pouts.

"If you knew Demetrius, you would understand how little he likes to talk about himself. Even if he *is* Greek." Saturia's lips are parted, ready to ask another question, but in the distance, a loud blare of flutes and drums signals the lighting of the pyre. Amara seizes Saturia's arm. "I think it's starting!"

Both women jump to their feet, instinctively wanting to be higher up. Amara squints to see the gilded apex of the pyre, waiting for the moment the eagle is released. There is no trace of smoke when the bird at last takes flight. This far off the creature is little more than a black smudge, though Amara can just make out the beating of its wings as it propels itself away from the heat, before soaring over the rooftops.

"It's headed for the Palatine!" Saturia exclaims, twisting to watch.

Amara tries to track the eagle's flight but fails. The bird that represents the soul of the dead emperor—ascending to the heavens for his apotheosis as a god—is quickly lost against the bright blue of the September sky.

"I can't believe how straight it flew! As if it knew exactly where it was going! Do you think Vespasian wanted to see the palace, one last time?" Saturia's eyes are round with awe, and she looks suddenly like a credulous young girl.

"Yes," Amara replies, her face solemn. She turns back to face the pyre. It is shimmering now, not yet alight, but wavering through the haze of heat and smoke. It is impossible to tell from this distance if the roaring noise comes from the watching crowd or the invisible flames below. Then, so suddenly she almost misses it, the pyre vanishes. One of the lower levels must have collapsed, sucking the top downward. But even though she cannot see the fire, Amara knows it is there, burning in the heart of Rome.

5

"Domitian hated [Titus and Vespasian] because they had not supplied all his numerous and unreasonable demands, as well as because they had been held in some honor; for he regarded as his enemy anyone who had enjoyed his father's or his brother's affection."
—Cassius Dio, *Roman History*

The shops that line Quirinal Hill near Amara's home have only been standing for a few years. Demetrius told her the old slums were destroyed when Vespasian set up his court in the neighborhood; the emperor might not have chosen to move to the Palatine, but he still didn't wish to see—or smell—abject poverty on his doorstep. The pavements here are wider than on some of the older roads, and the stores have a pleasing symmetry, their fronts completely open onto the street, with pretty mosaics marking each threshold from the other. She glances down at them, passing a dolphin, two fighting cats, and an optical illusion of receding squares. Above each shop is a single window, letting in the light for the family's small living space.

Daphne accompanies her, walking a little behind on the pavement, carrying the basket so that Amara's hands will not be burdened. There is scant trace here of last night's street celebrations to mark Vespasian's ascension to the heavens, the shopkeepers have been busy scrubbing up. They will have to do it all again tomorrow morning, too. Free food and wine will flow for the next two nights, an investment by Titus to buy the people's goodwill. Amara knows Demetrius does not entirely approve, although he sees the logic of it. Amara herself is not entirely convinced of the wisdom of Titus's other decision, either—to give his brother no official power. Pliny once told her that the two have long been semi-estranged; they were not even raised together as boys, so lack the shared history of siblings. And while Titus has proved himself time and again in military campaigns, Domitian has never shown any aptitude, or at least has never been given the chance to do so.

Amara wonders what the man is really like. Saturia is obviously afraid of her patron, and yet she also seems loyal. Certainly Domitian has been generous to his young courtesan. And even if he hadn't, Amara could hardly ask her about the more lurid rumors that swirl around the emperor's overlooked younger brother—that he tortures animals for pleasure and is cruel in bed. His enemies, however, do seem to have a habit of dying rather suddenly. Amara thinks again of Saturia's uncharacteristic interest in Demetrius last night, followed by her eagerness to see Amara again today, and feels uneasy. With nothing to keep him occupied, surely Domitian is more, not less, dangerous. He has no shortage of spare time to imagine conspiracies and spies and enemies. In the case of Pliny and Demetrius, his suspicions would not even be wholly illusory.

She stops for a moment, her attention caught by a store selling beautiful glassware. The shopkeeper, a woman of a similar age to Amara, looks her up and down, taking in the rich fabric of Amara's tunic, the glittering veil that covers her hair, and smiles broadly.

"You must come in, Mistress!" she exclaims. "I can see you have a discerning eye."

Amara had not intended to buy any luxuries today but she is drawn to the glass statuettes of the gods, like a wasp to honey. There, on the highest shelf, is an exquisite figure of Pallas-Athene. The goddess's face is white, and her robes red, shot through with gold. An owl perches on her shoulder. The workmanship is so fine, even the bird's tiny feathers look real. The statuette reminds her of the one her parents used to own in Aphidnai, though the workmanship on this is finer and it must be several times the price. Amara gestures at the figure, indicating that she would like to get a better look.

The woman flicks her eyes at a small boy, most likely her son, as he is too well dressed for a slave, and the child scurries to fetch a stool. It is hard to tell his age, as Amara is unused to children; perhaps he is eight or nine. There is a brief moment when she fears he might knock the figure off the shelf, but the boy is clearly used to working with glass. He hands it silently to the woman who pats his head. Definitely the son.

"She is very fine," says the shopkeeper. "Crafted here in Rome, at one of the best workshops. Even the Flavians buy from us. You can find our glass all over the Palatine. But perhaps you knew that?"

Amara only smiles pleasantly at the woman's flattery, giving nothing of herself away. Then she hands the statue back. "How much?"

"Five hundred sesterces."

Amara raises her eyebrows. "If you bring the statue to my home on the Vicus Longus this afternoon, I will give you three hundred."

"For such a fine piece, I cannot do less than four hundred."

"Three-fifty."

The shopkeeper hesitates. "I can do three-seventy, mistress. But this is enough. I have a family."

Amara nods. "I will pay you three-seventy." She gives instructions on where to find Demetrius's house, while the woman listens attentively. The boy stands behind his mother, shuffling his feet. The hours must be long for him in the shop.

Amara turns to leave, then stops. "You have a fine boy," she says to the shopkeeper. "What is his name?"

"Josephus," the woman says, with a proud glance at her son.

"Josephus," Amara repeats, crouching down to be on eye level with the child. "When your mother delivers the statue to my doorman Salvius later today, there will be a gift waiting for you. I will leave it under your name."

The child looks too stunned to reply. His mother hisses at him, "*Say thank you!*"

"Thank you," he blurts out, eyes widening with anxiety in case the present might be withdrawn. His high, childish voice makes Amara think of her own daughter, several day's journey away, and it hurts her heart.

"You are most welcome," she replies. "Look after your mother."

Amara does not look at Daphne, as they step onto the street. She can feel bitterness following hard on the heels of her pain. Demetrius has never shown the slightest interest in Rufina and has ignored all her suggestions that she bring her daughter to visit them in Rome. The only thing Amara can do for her child is to build her a precious dowry, filled with treasures, like the statue she has just bought. Sometimes she remembers what she once said to Philos, that she would have traded her parents' love a thousand times over for a dowry. Amara is no longer certain she believes this.

She forces down her anger, not wanting to resent the man she has chosen to share her life with, but the feelings, once they surface, are hard to suppress. Amara cannot help but suspect her patron has not told her everything he knows about the powerful man she has been instructed to spy upon. At first Demetrius had promised that her friendship with Saturia was not urgent business, that it was merely useful to keep a foot in Domitian's camp through a casual friendship. But Pliny's suggestion that the friendship be exploited quickly suggests they might know of a more definite plot by Domitian. Frustration sits lodged in her chest, like an indigestible olive stone. It is annoying to feel used, even more so when she is drifting downriver without understanding where the current is most dangerous.

They arrive at the apothecaries, the reason for her outing. Amara wants to stock up on an expensive herbal infusion that soothes the coughs that trouble Demetrius in the colder months. She inhales deeply, taking in the scent of the dried thyme and lavender hanging over the door. Lavender is the scent Demetrius always wears. The image of him comes to her, reclining at dinner with Pliny, and her irritation softens; he is a kinder and more generous patron than Rufus. She tells herself she has much to enjoy about her life in Rome. Most people never know such good fortune. The mosaic by her feet is one of Flora, clutching the flowers of spring. Amara steps over the goddess, determined to count her blessings.

Dinner with Saturia that night is a distracting affair. Amara is mesmerized by the sight of her companion, who appears to have been split into two. The real woman is reclining on the couch opposite, while behind her another Saturia also reclines, this time as a painted version of Helen of Troy. The most beautiful woman in the world is not, perhaps, the subtlest subject for a courtesan's dining room, but the effect is still impressive. Saturia must have commissioned the artist to create this startling optical illusion, for the painting to mirror her posture and her gaze. On the other walls, scenes of Helen's life allow Saturia to show off her own body in a variety of poses. The story starts with Leda's rape by Zeus in his form as a swan—the moment of Helen's conception—followed by Helen's marriage to Menelaus in Sparta, then her abduction by Paris, her celebration at a banquet in Troy, her grief at the brutal fall of the city, and finally her return to Menelaus, unscathed. In all the scenes Helen's body gleams as white as the lead pasted over Saturia's skin, ensuring the eye is drawn to her figure above all others.

The abduction is the most interesting reimagining. In this, Helen's face is inscrutable, her lip slightly curled, making it uncertain whether she is smiling, and she is turned away from Paris, her gaze meeting that of the viewer instead. It is an expression of Saturia's that Amara recognizes, whenever she is asked about Domitian. The painting seems to mock not only Menalaus but Amara's own quest to discover Saturia's secrets.

Amara leans back slightly on the couch, thinking of Felix. All those days she watched her former master draw his debtors out through flattery and questions, somehow managing to charm them, even though his role as wolf was obvious. He is the person she hates most in the world, and yet his skills of manipulation have undoubtedly taught her how to survive. Amara copies one of Felix's most obnoxious habits, which she saw him use against Victoria, and shares seemingly vulnerable details about her own life to coax Saturia into opening up. It is obvious that Saturia is intrigued by the brothel, and so that is where Amara begins. After Saturia has taken a few glasses of wine, Amara is able to move from her own sexual exploits to asking about Saturia's experiences. She nods sympathetically as Saturia complains about the Patrician husband she married at fourteen, whose interest in boys left her neglected and abandoned.

Amara pretends to sip her wine, most of which she has spat carefully into a cloth while Saturia is not looking. Another lesson from observing Felix: never get drunk but try to ensure your adversary does. She gestures at the fresco of the abandoned Menelaus. "Does your husband ever come to see you in Rome?"

"What a ridiculous question. Do you imagine he would welcome being received in this house?" Saturia's cheeks are flushed with wine, her eyes too bright.

"You have done better for yourself without him," Amara nods. "Will you do even better, now, I wonder? With Berenice gone, you might try your chances there."

"You are quick to judge one brother against the other."

"One is the emperor," Amara smiles. "There can be no comparison. A woman is not to blame for being drawn to power."

Saturia laughs. "Is that what you tell yourself when you have to bed Demetrius?" She gestures at the cameo of Athena around Amara's neck. "I suppose you have a hoard of trinkets like that as consolation. Not that I imagine he troubles you much, at his age."

"I know my own limitations," Amara says. "I am not so young as you, nor as beautiful. I am simply curious as to why you would not aim higher?"

"You must think me very disloyal. And in any case, who is to say which man is the most powerful? Fortuna often brings the greatest gifts to those who brave her wheel."

Behind Saturia, Amara becomes aware of the blonde maid, watching her mistress more closely than befits a slave. The sight makes Amara uneasy, and yet she is so close to learning more of Domitian's intentions, she cannot stop. "Is that why we went to visit her temple? Did you beseech her to see your patron rise?" Amara asks the question casually, picking at the bunch of grapes.

"Fortuna was a favorite deity of Julius Caesar. She serves all great men."

Amara thinks of Caesar, murdered within sight of the temple of the goddess he worshipped, but does not say so. Instead she raises her eyes piously to the heavens. "As the god Vespasian has proven."

"Vespasian took power. As did Caesar. As did Octavian. As do all emperors who are worthy of Rome. Perhaps Demetrius would do well to remember this." Saturia is drunk, not only on wine but her own imagined proximity to greatness. She looks at Amara smugly. "He might find the rewards are greater, if he plays the game a little more boldly." The blonde maid slips from the room, so softly Saturia does not hear.

Amara is so close to discovery she cannot help leaning forward. "Should I take this as an offer to my patron?"

It is a miscalculation. Saturia becomes aware of the avidity of Amara's expression, of what she might have betrayed. The blonde maid slips back into the room with another platter of fruit. "I don't understand you," Saturia says, reaching again for her wine. "I spoke only in general terms."

"And yet you said . . ."

Saturia cuts her off. "Enough, Amara! Let us speak of other things." She is clearly agitated, even afraid. "You must promise not to repeat any of my idle chatter. My patron would be most displeased. His loyalty to his brother is beyond question."

There is silence. Amara is aware of the blonde maid, watching her mistress closely, but her expression is not one of concern. It is something colder. "I have no doubt of your loyalty," Amara says. "Truly. It is clear you are nothing but devoted to your patron."

Saturia waves at her to stop. "I said *enough*." Her raised voice causes the servants to glance at one another. Saturia attempts to smile, to lessen the tension. "Tell me more about your life in Greece, the work of your father. How useful it must be for Demetrius to have a woman schooled in alleviating the ailments of old age."

It is surely only coincidence that Saturia would choose to make this jibe the day Amara visited an apothecary for her patron's health, but it adds to her unease, the idea that perhaps she is not the only watchful one. "Like you," Amara begins obsequiously, "I always find it a pleasure to serve my patron." She begins to run down a lengthy list of remedies, talking about the properties of various herbs, wanting to soothe her host with dullness, and Saturia's eyes soon glaze over.

"Perhaps we might enjoy a little music," Saturia says, after Amara has given her a lecture on the various lotions and infusions useful in treating arthritis. She snaps her fingers and one of the women scurries to an adjoining room, returning with a harp. The maid settles herself on a stool in the corner and begins to sing, striking the strings with a plectrum. Amara thinks of Drusilla, her friend and fellow courtesan from Pompeii who plays the harp with infinitely more skill, and feels a surge of longing. Not for the place, but its people. The harp is a siren call, tempting Amara to indulge the memories she usually tries to suppress. She closes her eyes, allowing her imagination to transport her for a moment back to her friend Julia's estate, where she has spent so many hours and which her daughter now calls home. Julia and Livia will no doubt be entertaining favored tenants in the garden dining room tonight, their laughter overlapping with the splash of water that cascades down the wall in a fanciful recreation of the River Nile. Rufina will be sleeping in the apartment Amara rents from Julia, one arm flung above her head in childish abandon, Philos perhaps still at work downstairs, looking over Julia's accounts by lamplight. Amara always loved the way he looked at such moments, lost in thought, a source of calm and quiet focus.

It is not comfortable to linger in memories of Pompeii. Comparisons with a life where she experienced genuine love and friendship only make Amara feel a growing sense of self-loathing for the duplicity she is currently engaged in. She glances over at Saturia, whose eyes are wide open, staring at the harpist without seeming to see her. The blonde maid is still hovering by the door, and Amara likes the slave girl's venomous expression even less. It does not trouble her that a slave would hate their owner, but it is disturbing that the girl makes so little effort to hide it. Amara begins to wish that she might find some excuse to slip away. There is surely nothing else useful Saturia will say tonight, not now she has already blundered. She feels annoyed with Demetrius for continuously putting her in this position, where she becomes the worst, most manipulative version of herself. A slight pause in the song gives Amara hope, but then the harpist starts warbling again. Amara is reaching for the grapes, restless at being kept here when she wants to leave, when the door swings open. She looks up in surprise. A man is standing at the threshold, surrounded by guards. It takes her a moment to understand who it is.

Saturia sees Amara's shock and turns. Domitian, the dead emperor Vespasian's son, is standing in the doorway. Saturia scrambles to her feet. "My love! I was not expecting you, tonight of all nights. Please forgive me, I have nothing prepared."

Domitian holds out his arms, in a theatrical gesture of affection, smiling at his mistress. Saturia hesitates a moment, perhaps unused to this ostentatious greeting, then rushes to embrace him. She turns back to Amara, face flushed with pleasure at such a show of favor. Domitian also turns. Amara has only seen the emperor's brother once or twice, and then at a distance. He is a more attractive man than Titus, especially now, when he seems intent on being charming.

"Who is your little friend?"

"This is Plinia Amara," Saturia says, answering before Amara can introduce herself. "The admiral's freedwoman."

"Of course! And a devoted companion to my father's most loyal servant. I cannot remember a time, even in my childhood, when Demetrius was not at his elbow." Domitian smiles again, even more ingratiating than before.

Amara bows low. "You do us too much honor."

"No doubt I do." Domitian is still smiling, but Amara catches the sarcasm in his tone. Saturia's smile too, starts to waver.

Amara knows that she should seize this moment. The emperor's brother is holding her gaze, in an unspoken invitation to stay. This is an exceptional opportunity to try and charm him, to trick him into revealing some hint of his plans, and so earn Pliny and Demetrius's undying gratitude. And yet all Amara's instincts are screaming at her to leave. In the brothel there were certain men all the she-wolves learned to avoid on sight, in spite of enraging Felix for lost business. Men whose violence was palpable, even when they smiled, just as Domitian is smiling at her now. "I will not keep you both," Amara murmurs, no longer daring to look him in the face, edging away from the couch. "Please forgive the intrusion."

"Without a litter! At this time of night? Unthinkable. I will have my men send word to your master that you mean to return." Domitian does not have to issue the command directly; one of the guards Amara can see in the doorway leaves as soon as he expresses his wish. "Your patron's loyalty to my father was never more evident than at his apotheosis. Please convey my gratitude to Demetrius. I am sure the god Vespasian will look down from Olympus with favor upon his former servant."

"Demetrius will be beyond honored by your words."

Domitian accepts the wine a slave offers him. "Very pretty, isn't she?" he says to Saturia, nodding at Amara. "Lucky Demetrius. Were you a gift to him from the admiral? I'm aware the two have a long acquaintance."

"They are indeed both the best of men," Amara says, laying a hand over her heart in a gesture of devotion, not answering the question.

Domitian laughs. "Lucky little you, in that case." He turns again to Saturia, who is still mute beside him. "Isn't she lucky? With two fine patrons? While you, my poor dove, have only one."

"I am the luckiest woman alive," Saturia whispers, gazing at her lover with what might be taken for devotion if she were not trembling.

The Imperial guardsman returns, nodding at his master. "Your patron must have the most fleet-footed litter bearers!" Domitian says to Amara. "It seems he has sent for you already. Perhaps he anticipated my command."

Amara stands, surprised and relieved. "I am sorry to have troubled you for so long."

"Not at all, little *vicaria*. Mind how you go."

Vicaria. The slave of a slave, the lowest form of human being. Domitian speaks the insult as if it were the sweetest endearment, then turns to kiss Saturia. Amara understands she is dismissed. Domitian's men part to let her through.

It is an effort not to run down the stairs, Amara is so keen to escape the house. Her pace quickens as she crosses the atrium, the marble tiger reflected in the still, black pool as she passes, surrounded by stars.

At the door, the porter does not immediately stand aside to let her out. "Will you not wait for your litter, Mistress?" His face is in shadow, the torch ensconced behind him, and Amara cannot read his face.

"The litter is outside."

"Nobody has sent for it," the porter says, sounding surprised. "I have been by the door all night."

It takes Amara a moment to understand the implications. *Your patron must have the most fleet-footed litter bearers.* The emperor's brother clearly meant to humiliate her. "Please send for the guards my patron hired for the procession. I will have them escort me home."

"Mistress . . ." the porter trails off, embarrassed. "They have all just been dismissed." Amara does not have to ask who made the order. The porter leans closer, his voice low. "I can send one of the servants to your house now, to have your litter brought here."

His face is still in shadow. Perhaps he only means to help her. Perhaps. And yet who knows how many of Saturia's servants answer to Domitian? Amara does not want to stay in this house another moment. The sense of danger that she felt upstairs is only growing in intensity.

"That will not be necessary, thank you. I must return home at once."

"Mistress, that would be most unwise . . ."

"I said *at once*."

The porter nods into the darkened atrium. Amara's heart beats painfully in her chest, expecting the worst, but the only person to approach is a thin slave boy. He creeps up to stand by her elbow, silently holding out her cloak. Amara takes it from him, deftly turning it inside out so that the finer fabric is hidden, leaving the cheaper lining on display, then wraps it around herself.

The two slaves watch as she swiftly takes off her rings and bracelets, stuffing them inside a purse that she has pulled out from where it lay between her breasts, hidden under her clothes. "What?" she snaps at the gawking men as she stows the purse away again. "You've never seen a woman walk a street before?" Amara's sharp tone echoes Victoria, her former friend from the Wolf Den, and she can feel the past merging into the present. In this moment she is no longer Plinia Amara, a high courtesan of Rome, but a she-wolf whose survival depends on obeying her own instincts. "Well?" She gestures impatiently at the door.

"As you wish." The porter turns his back to her, drawing across the heavy bolts with an ugly scraping sound that sets Amara even more on edge. The porter opens the door, averting his eyes from her face as she passes, and Amara slips out onto the street. The heavy wood is immediately banged shut against her back. She pauses, allowing herself a moment to take in her surroundings, trying not to let fear overwhelm her.

In spite of the late hour, Rome is far from quiet. People are out drinking on the streets, shouting and laughing, enjoying the food and wine laid on by Titus to celebrate his father's ascension. Amara sets off along the pavement at a quick, determined pace, her cloak pulled close to her body. Unlike a Patrician woman, she knows how to shrink herself, to move as if she is of no importance. But it is only the appearance of fear that she is able to hide; the blood beats loudly in her ears, driven by her racing heart.

A street performer, standing in the middle of the road blowing fire to whoops and cheers, suddenly swings around and lets out a ripple of flame, a hair's breadth from Amara's face. The crowd laugh but she neither startles nor runs, breathing in sharply to contain her panic. "*Want to feel the heat with me, darling?*" It is a male voice, calling after her, but she keeps walking, not turning to acknowledge that she's heard him, hoping he will be too drunk to follow.

Crowds are fickle. Amara moves her way through the crush of bodies taking care not to catch anyone's eye. The presence of so many people might possibly deter a robber, but she knows that if a man seizes her to rape her, drunken bystanders are as likely to join in the torment as set her free. She keeps going, her legs aching, unused to traveling this far without a litter, but still she never slows her pace, not even when she reaches the outskirts of the Suburra.

The high tenements of Rome's most notorious district lean over the street, the buildings so close together they almost form an arch against the night sky. Amara thinks of Pompeii, of the nights she was forced to walk to get water from the well, when even that short distance carried the risk of violence. *Whatever happens*, she tells herself, *I will endure it. I will survive, as I have before.* For the second time that evening, she thinks of Felix. The fierce, swift walk he adopted at night, the confidence that repelled any attack. Amara mimics his footsteps, twisting her fear to rage, regretful that she is not carrying a knife.

The Suburra is raucous tonight. Prostitutes mingle with the men who spill from the taverns, their clamor louder from the crush. Amara no longer belongs to this world, but even when she did, it still frightened her. She weaves in and out of the heat and press of bodies, ignoring any drunken requests about her price, shying away from the grasping hands that paw at her, hoping that the abundance of women for sale will afford her some protection.

Eventually the road starts to widen as the Vicus Longus ascends the Quirinal Hill. The houses are becoming grander, the crowds thinner. She passes the temple to Febris. Nearly there. Amara keeps going, her leg muscles burning at the climb. The sight of the temple to Fortuna the Hopeful almost makes her weep with relief. Demetrius deliberately made his home near the ancient shrine, said to have been built by the Roman king Servius Tullius who rose from slave to ruler. Incense stings her nostrils as she passes and she reaches out a hand to skim the outer railings in gratitude to Fortuna for bringing her this far, even though the danger is not yet over. She still faces the challenge of persuading Salvius to open the door quickly at such an unsavory hour, when he will not be expecting his mistress to arrive like this, alone and without Demetrius's litter—which is still inside. If Amara sounds too frantic he might ignore her knocking as nothing more than a nuisance caller.

She raps deliberately, three times, and waits. There is no answer. Amara knocks again, louder this time, and again is greeted with silence. She dares a glance over her shoulder, hoping she has not yet drawn attention to herself. Her heart drops to see a man standing across the street, watching her. She is seized with a sudden fear that it is not only the knocking that alerted him; perhaps she has been followed from Saturia's house.

Amara can no longer afford to be discreet. She raps again, raising her voice, praying that Salvius will hear. "*It is your mistress, Plinia Amara. Let me in, Salvius!*"

This time when she is greeted with silence, Amara's nerve starts to fail her. She does not dare look over her shoulder but instead hammers again, even harder: "*It's me, Amara!*"

The door opens, and she falls into the threshold of her home, almost overcome. "Close the door," she shouts at Salvius, although he is beside her, already drawing across the bolts.

"What is this?" Demetrius is standing in the atrium, his expression one of uncharacteristic alarm. Amara flings herself at him, burying her face into his shoulder, her whole body shaking after having braced herself for violence. "Not here," he murmurs, steering her toward his study.

Demetrius disentangles himself from her clinging embrace, bundling her into a chair. "What is this?" he repeats. "What possessed you to walk home alone?"

"Domitian came to the house."

"He threatened you?" Demetrius is gripping the back of the table.

"No, but I could sense the danger," Amara replies, "I think one of the slave girls sent word for him after Saturia spoke about Octavian and Vespasian *seizing* power, as a true emperor should. She said that perhaps Domitian will not always be the less powerful brother, and that you would be wise to mind this. I know this warning seems vague, but it tells us Domitian must be plotting against Titus, or at the very least, seriously considering it. Otherwise, she would not dare be so brazen. That's all I could glean before we were interrupted, but if the slave did indeed warn him what his mistress had just said, Domitian must have been alarmed and angry at Saturia's disclosure."

"But Domitian himself didn't threaten you?" Her patron is frowning. "And you didn't think to stay and talk to him, to see if you could learn anymore?"

"At the brothel I developed an instinct about which men were safe. I *knew* he was not safe. I knew it in my bones." As soon as she has said the words aloud, Amara realizes how ridiculous her fear must sound to anyone who has not experienced life at the Wolf Den.

"The *brothel*," Demetrius repeats and Amara can hear his disappointment in the way he enunciates the word. "This is the reason you fled. Because the emperor's brother reminded you of some violent sailor? Really, Amara, I thought you were more sensible than this. Giving way to feminine hysteria."

"He claimed my litter had been sent for when it hadn't," she protests. Demetrius is silent, and Amara can feel the heat flooding her face, knowing how much he disapproves of her actions. "You think I should have stayed?"

"His prank can't have been pleasant but surely he only meant to humiliate you?" Demetrius waits for her to contradict him, then shakes his head. "All you needed to do was wait a little longer for a servant to reach me, and I would have sent for you. Not indulge this *madness* of walking home alone."

"He had dismissed the guards you hired. It was impossible to know what he intended!"

Demetrius flings up his hands in a familiar gesture of exasperation. "And this is why you chose to walk through the Suburra alone? Some prostitute's instinct that trumps all common sense? I don't believe Domitian would have harmed you, Amara, but it is a miracle you were not violated on the streets. Or worse." He slaps the table, his impatience warming to anger. "You are *not* a brothel whore anymore; you do not rush out into the night without a chaperone. Anything could have happened, *anything*. Do you have no regard for your honor at all? Let alone mine!"

Amara stands, scraping back her chair. "You don't *believe* he would have harmed me? How nice for you, to make that judgment and not have to risk your own skin. And as for *honor*, when did you start to care about that?" Demetrius also rises to his feet, his anger matching her own. "No," Amara holds out her hand to stop him. "Don't." She turns and walks from the room, not waiting to hear the words fall from his half open mouth.

6

*"His cruelty was not only extreme but also ingenious and unpredictable.
The day before he crucified one of his stewards, he invited the man
into his bedchamber, made him sit down beside him on the couch,
then sent him away happy and confident."*

—Suetonius on Domitian, *Lives of the Caesars*

Amara lies in bed, watching pale strands of light on the ceiling widen and brighten as the sun rises. She does not get up. Demetrius designed this room for her, a year into their life together. The patron goddess of her homeland, Pallas-Athene, stalks its walls, presiding over her heroes' legendary deeds. Amara had been touched when Demetrius first led her in here, eager to show her the work he had commissioned, along with the highest compliment he has ever paid her: *may the goddess of strategy bless the cleverest woman in Rome.*

Shortly after that, she miscarried for the first time. They have never spoken of the grief; Demetrius is not a man with whom she has ever shared her vulnerabilities. Opposite her, the goddess of Attica is still in shadow, but Amara knows what the painting shows. Athena is guiding Odysseus, the wiliest of men, sending the North Wind to speed him across the sea. Cunning has always been the virtue Demetrius most admires in Amara, but she imagined their relationship had also grown to include a certain tenderness as well as pragmatism.

Do you have no regard for your honor at all?

The words hurt, lodged like a stone in her chest. She is not even sure why she feels this upset. Maybe she *was* a fool to take off into the night, guided by *some prostitute's instinct* as her patron so scathingly put it. But then, whenever she remembers Domitian's smile, she is certain he intended her harm. Why, after all, should the emperor's brother be less violent than a *sailor* intent on hurting a whore? Demetrius comes again into her mind, his obvious exasperation last night, his palm slapped down on the table. Perhaps what she feels is disappointment; after she saw him in the atrium, when she felt so desperate, she had believed his look of fear came from love. Instead, he had been unwilling to hold her, pushing her into the chair in his study, eager to rid himself of her embrace and her weakness. He only cares for her, so far as she is useful to him.

Amara closes her eyes, even though that brings her closer to the memories she wishes to unsee. Philos. Without willing it, Amara is back in her bedroom at the house with the golden door, Philos close beside her, the darkness softened by lamplight. She is unable to forget what it felt like to be held like that, to feel so certain of another's love. Even now, years later, she does not doubt his kindness, the selflessness with which he is raising their daughter.

"And I left them both." Amara speaks the words aloud, with only the goddess of wisdom to hear her.

There is a soft knock at the door. "Did you call, Mistress?"

Amara shifts herself, swinging her legs out of the covers, placing her feet on the cold floor. She has stayed in bed late, leaving her restless attendants standing outside, forced to wait for her. "Come in," she calls.

Iris and Daphne slip into the room. The three women begin their habitual, silent routine of preparing a courtesan's public face. Amara feels no need to share her unhappiness with her maids. She remembers enough of her own life as a slave to suspect they would, in any case, have little interest in the private woes of the rich.

When Amara is ready, she walks down to the garden. Demetrius is waiting for her, although anyone who knew him or his routines less well would not realize this. He is studying a book of wax tablets, his back to her bedchamber, so that she cannot help but pass him. He looks up at her briefly as she sits on the bench opposite but says nothing. It is impossible to gauge what he feels, whether he is still annoyed, indifferent or remorseful. A lifetime of service means he is never without a mask. Still, Amara has learned to live inside a mask too, and is determined not to be the one to break the silence, instead taking her breakfast from the waiting slave. Eventually, Demetrius cracks.

"I think it would be wise if you called on Saturia this morning."

"Do you?" Amara's tone is placid, as if she never raised her voice in anger last night.

"It is as well you repair any damage done by your sudden departure." Demetrius stands up. "You could have been killed walking home alone. Please never be so foolish again. It is unworthy of one in my service. And I expect you to report back to me as soon as you have called on her."

He stalks off without waiting to see what impact his words have made. Amara raises her eyebrows and sips her sweet wine, as if wearing an unruffled appearance might make her feel as calm inside.

✦ ✦ ✦

The streets, as Amara passes through them in her litter, are still heaped with the debris of last night's celebrations. Dogs and human scavengers pick through the waste, hoping to find something valuable enough to sell. Amara watches an old woman sitting on the kerb, cleaning a handful of cheap hairpins with a rag, and draws the curtain, preferring to cocoon herself within the rich fabric of the litter.

When they reach Saturia's house, Amara is surprised to see a gaggle of people outside the young courtesan's door. She is almost tempted to turn back, but imagines how disagreeable Demetrius will be if she returns home without any news, and gestures to be let out. The Gaul whose name she cannot remember helps her step onto the pavement.

The women in the huddle are tearful, clutching each other and whispering. The sight makes Amara even less keen to elbow her way through to the door and discover whatever lies on the other side. "They'll have to move the body soon," one man, perhaps a shopkeeper, is saying, his tone self-important. "Don't care how rich she is. Can't have a corpse bringing bad luck to the street."

Amara pulls her veil in tighter to her face and shoves past. People protest at her rudeness but let her through. Saturia's tall doors are ajar, with a noticeable gap between her threshold and the street. Even from here, Amara can hear wailing from inside. The sound is chilling, reminding her of the funeral procession she and Saturia watched so recently. She crushes her sense of dread and walks into the atrium, coming face to face with the startled doorman.

"Mistress! You cannot come in, surely you have heard . . ."

Amara side steps him. "Heard what? What's happened? Where is Saturia?" At the sound of their mistress's name, the maids begin to cry even more loudly. Amara grabs the arm of the nearest girl, who gasps in surprise. "Where is she?"

"Dead," the girl says, trembling. "She is dead."

"She can't be!" Amara is too shocked for a moment to say more, clutching harder at the girl, who squirms in protest. "You must be mistaken. Where is she?"

"You cannot see the body—it is polluting. We are waiting to have her moved outside the city walls." It is the blonde slave girl from last night. She stares at Amara, dry-eyed and cold.

Amara remembers the way the same maid slipped from the room, just after Saturia misspoke, the way she hovered by the door, watching. "*Snake,*" Amara whispers. The slave girl sees the rage in Amara's eyes and anticipates the blow, but is not quick enough; Amara smacks her across the face with all her strength. The girl cries out and clutches her cheek, a red mark already rising where one of Amara's rings has broken the skin. The two women glare at each other, fury taut between them. Amara wants to scream at the girl for her disloyalty, for the treachery that she is now certain led to Saturia's death, but does not dare. She cannot have it reported back to Domitian. Instead, Amara looks the slave up and down with contempt. "For your insolence at *daring* to look at me," she says, in case any other eavesdroppers are watching.

The other servants are silent as Amara stalks past, making her way to the stairs, toward Saturia's private chambers. She knows if she shows any fear, it will shatter the brief illusion of authority she just seized through violence.

"You can't go up there!" one of the women shouts, finding a voice at last, as Amara reaches the upper floor.

Amara does not turn around. "*Watch me.*"

The blood is beating so loud in her ears it feels as if she is under-water. Saturia's private rooms sit at the end of the corridor. Sunshine spills through the door, a gift from the wide windows overlooking the garden. Amara steps inside, still able to picture Saturia having her makeup prepared, her hair shining golden, but the dressing table is bare, the expensive box of lead paste sealed shut. Another maid is standing by Saturia's bedroom door, her eyes red and puffy.

"May I see her?"

The woman says nothing, but moves to let Amara pass. It is a room splendid enough to rival any in Demetrius's house, but Amara has no interest in looking at the vivid scenes of Venus on the bright red walls. She is drawn instead to the disarray of sheets and blankets, half strewn across the floor. Saturia is lying on the bed, still clothed.

"How did she die?" Even if she were not a doctor's daughter, Amara would have no need to ask this question; Saturia's body screams the answer. The livid marks on her slender neck.

"Peacefully in her sleep," the maid whispers. "None of us can understand it."

"I see," Amara says, not taking her eyes from the murdered girl's body and the signs of violent struggle that surround her. "Then that is what I will say to anyone that asks me." She moves closer to the maid, who stiffens at Amara's unwelcome proximity. "But now, when it is just the two of us, please do not insult me."

"He was always unkind with her in bed," the woman murmurs. "Perhaps it was an accident."

Amara turns away sharply, eyes prickling with tears. Saturia was not her friend but the girl did not deserve this. To die before she even had a chance to live, her vitality snuffed out by a brutal, selfish man. As if she were less than nothing. Amara blinks, looking up at the ceiling, with its fretwork of painted vines and flowers. This gilded room is worlds apart from the squalor and darkness of the Wolf Den, but she suspects Domitian was just as difficult to endure as Felix. A wave of self-loathing hits her. Amara fully understood what sort of man Domitian was, yet still she pried into Saturia's life, putting her in danger. And for what? To tell Demetrius what he already knew: that the emperor's brother is a treacherous monster.

She crosses to the bedside, standing over Saturia. Gently, she closes Saturia's bloodshot eyes and the dead woman becomes more like her living self, as if she were indeed asleep.

"You will be polluted." It is the maid from the doorway.

"I am not afraid. My father dwelt his whole life between the living and the dead. I know the rites to purify myself." Amara looks at Saturia, wishing she had some words to speak, other than the apology she cannot say aloud. "Saturia," she says, addressing her in Greek. "May you charm Persephone, Queen of the Dead, with your beauty. May you be at peace in the underworld. And may you forgive me."

Demetrius does not immediately admit Amara to his study when she gets back home. Nor does he smile in greeting when she enters.

"Her gift was sent before you reached her," he says gesturing at an expensive scent bottle on the table. "She apologized for the mistake over the litter."

Amara stares at the bottle in disbelief. "What?"

"She must have told you of the perfume?" Demetrius is impatient. "This is Saturia's gift for last night."

"Saturia is dead." If it were not for the horror of the situation, Demetrius's shocked expression would almost be comical.

"Dead?" Demetrius repeats.

"Yes," Amara says, tears springing to her eyes. She takes a moment to control herself, not wishing to cry in front of her patron. "She was strangled in her bed last night." Amara takes the bottle and opens the lid, releasing a familiar scent. "Oleander." She replaces the stopper. "They are not even attempting to hide the fact that the contents are poisonous. Any fool would know. This isn't a murder attempt—it's a taunt."

"You are certain it's oleander?"

"Of course I am!" Amara snaps, angry at his lack of emotion. "Whatever you think of my *honor*, or my whore's instincts, I would hope you trust my knowledge of plants."

"I'm sorry, *Kalliste*."

"For what? Her death? For not believing me?"

"For all of it."

Demetrius looks deflated, seeming to sag with the weight of his contrition. It ages him, making him look uncertain in a way Amara has not seen before. Part of her wants to reassure him, to stop him from appearing like this, but she is too angry. She folds her arms. "I cannot imagine what knowledge we gained from spying on Saturia that was worth this."

"It was impossible for anyone to predict that Domitian's paranoia would be this violent. That he would kill a woman for such a small misstep."

"I *told* you she was afraid of him! How many whispers have there been about him killing those he takes against?"

"This is more than a whisper." Demetrius rubs his eyes, as if he cannot bear to look directly at Amara. "I suppose at least now we have confirmed the extent of his brutality."

"I am sure that will be comforting for Saturia's family."

"It is not Saturia's safety that concerns me now. It is yours."

They both look at the scent bottle. It is expensively made, a mottled shade of green, shot through with silver. In truth the perfume would be unlikely to be fatal unless drunk, but it is the hostility behind the gesture that makes Amara feel afraid. "What do you think we should do?"

Demetrius draws himself upright at her question, recovering his usual posture of command. "Leave me to think about it." Amara rises, understanding herself dismissed, but her patron reaches out his hand. She goes to him and he holds her tightly, kissing the top of her head. Gradually she allows herself to relax against him. "I'm sorry," he says again, but still Amara finds herself unable to reply. Demetrius releases her. "Go now. I will come to you in the garden later, if you wait for me there."

Amara allows herself a backward glance before she steps into the atrium. Demetrius is holding the scent bottle, his shoulders hunched inward.

The sky burns above as Amara waits, the blue deepening, as if she were drifting out to sea. She passes her time sewing, though her concentration is poor, and she often stops to stare into space. Every luxury is laid out for her, the stone bench where she reclines is softened by heaps of fabric, and a slave hovers nearby ready to bring her anything she needs, the moment she demands it. The walls surrounding the garden are as beautiful to look at as the fountains and flowers, covered with a vibrant fresco of plants. Painted pears appear real enough to pluck and winter hellebore bow their heads out of season.

Amara cannot enjoy any of it. She remains trapped in the dead girl's bedroom, and when she closes her eyes, trying to shut it out, the sunlight filters through her eyelids, turning everything red. She feels angry at Demetrius for sending her to Saturia, angrier still at herself for the manipulative games she played. And all they have succeeded in doing is attracting Domitian's animosity, even more keenly than before. She should not have allowed herself to be led by Demetrius and Pliny. She should have asserted her own ideas.

The shade has turned chill when Demetrius finally comes to her. He steps hesitantly, still afflicted with the same uncharacteristic uncertainty she glimpsed in the study. Saturia's mockery rings in her head. *He is old.* It is a fact so familiar to Amara that she realizes she has come to pass over it, no longer even noticing that her patron is an old man. But now, his age fills her with fear. She does not wish Demetrius to grow frailer, less sharp in his judgment, less able to protect her from whatever dangers now lengthen in the shadows.

"You are chilled," Demetrius says, sitting beside her. "I should not have kept you so long."

"It's nothing."

"None of this is nothing." They sit in silence for a moment, watching the water dancing in a nearby fountain, the white curve of its fall mirroring the dolphins whose leaping is frozen in stone. "I should never have asked you to spy, Kalliste. You bear no responsibility for Saturia's death. It is mine."

"It is *his*," Amara says. "He must be mad to have killed her over such a trifling indiscretion. She only meant to defend him! Not to betray him."

"He is a violent man. And perhaps he did not intend to kill her. Perhaps he meant to punish her for indiscretion and used too much force, stopping her breath for too long. It only takes a moment's miscalculation to end another's life that way." Amara thinks of the brothel, of Felix's hands at her throat, of the many times she feared he might kill her by mistake, and shudders. "But if he *did* mean to kill her, I don't believe her death was purely for betrayal. I think it was a warning, aimed at us. Or rather at me for meddling." Demetrius takes Amara's hand, his skin so thin she can feel the bones of his fingers. "I do not believe he would dare harm me directly, for fear of alerting his brother to his ill intentions. But he has just shown us that a courtesan is more expendable. I don't think you can stay in Rome."

Amara stares at him. "You are sending me away?"

"Only for a while. Until his animosity dissipates."

"So you are not . . ." Amara cannot finish the sentence, not wanting to imagine what it might mean if Demetrius intends to abandon her permanently.

"You cannot be my concubine any longer. I think it is safer if you were to become my wife."

"Your wife," Amara repeats, stunned.

Demetrius looks into her eyes, more vulnerable than she has ever known him. She waits, realizing he is about to say the words he has never spoken. To tell her that he loves her. Instead the silence grows and his expression hardens, shuttered by the usual mask. "I think it would be sensible to make you less expendable in the eyes of the world. Given the circumstances." He lets go of her hand. "And it will afford you more protection when I am dead."

Amara leans forward, kissing him lightly. "Don't speak of your death. You know it distresses me." She embraces him, her chin tucked over his shoulder so that they do not have to look at each other, knowing how hard he finds any emotional display. "And thank you. For the highest compliment any man has ever paid me."

Amara holds Demetrius, trying not to think about what this marriage will mean. Trying above all not to think of Philos.

7

*"The only time he took from his work was for his bath, and by
bath I mean his actual immersion, for while he was being rubbed
down and dried he had a book read to him or dictated notes."*
—Pliny the Younger on his uncle, Pliny the Elder

The port of Ostia grows more distant, the tall warehouses of
the quayside dwindling into the horizon, until they are lost
in the sea haze. Hair whips across Amara's face as she stares
out over the waves. She scrapes a flyaway strand behind her
ear, glancing sidelong at the admiral. Pliny is not in a talkative
mood. Nor is he very evidently inhabiting his role as commander, even though it is one of the fleet's ships carrying them
both back to Campania. Instead, he is sitting on deck in the
sunshine, growing impatient with the hapless secretary attempting to read to him.

"You can't possibly be sick *again*," Pliny huffs, as the boy scurries to the side of the boat and heaves over the side. Pliny looks
over at Amara. "His stomach is nothing like as strong as yours."
It is the first remark he has addressed to her since they left Ostia.

"Perhaps I could read to you awhile instead?" She tries not to
smile as she offers, liking Pliny for not asking her directly, even if
his hint was not very subtle.

"Ah yes, well, what a good idea. And I daresay staring about with nothing to do is dull for you, in any case." Pliny waves her to his side. "Read from there. The section on precious metals."

Amara sits beside Pliny, gripping the scroll. The deck sways beneath her, the movement making it harder for her eyes to follow the cramped, spidery script. Pliny stifles another huff, evidently realizing it will not befit him to complain at her hesitancy, not now she is soon to be the wife of Demetrius.

The text is tedious, but Amara plods on, driven by her affection for Pliny and the desire to distract herself from more troubling thoughts. She has sent word to Julia and Philos to expect her in Pompeii in early November, but has no idea if the letter will reach them before she does. Demetrius suggested she spend some weeks in Misenum before visiting her daughter, and to Amara's shame she agreed, not entirely sorry to delay. She longs to see Rufina, yet dreads the moment too. Being close to her daughter always brings home their estrangement. Nor is she certain how to break the news to Philos about her impending marriage. They have not been lovers for years, but the rupture between them remains tender and unhealed. It is not a bruise she cares to press upon.

"You've skipped a line!" Pliny is unable to control his exasperation this time. "Try to listen to the sense of the thing, *please*, Amara."

She resists the temptation to answer back. Pliny is not quite as amenable as Demetrius to being teased out of a grumpy mood. Amara goes back a line, reading slowly, trying to concentrate. The script swiftly sucks her into its dry world, and deciphering it takes up every thought. Time passes and she is so focused on her task, she is not even aware of the dimming light until it affects her ability to read. She stops, realizing she is exhausted. To her intense annoyance she sees Pliny has dozed off. His breathing is heavy, close to a snore. All that effort she made to read, and he must have been oblivious to much of it. Amara finds herself thinking of Secundus, Pliny's devoted steward, who died last year. She knows that Pliny misses him, but still suspects the admiral has little concept of all that Secundus gave. A life of service carries a cost that those who are free cannot imagine.

She sighs—though not too loudly as she has no desire to wake Pliny and begin reading again—and throws back her head to look at the sky. Dusk is falling. The heavens darken, like ink spreading through water. Amara watches the stars brighten against the black, the constellations as numerous as salt spilled on fabric. She traces those her parents taught her: Ariadne's crown, the Great Bear who was once the nymph Callisto, and the vast Dragon guarding the gardens of the Hesperides.

As a child, Amara believed the heavens were the playground of the gods, that the Olympians traced their deeds in stars for mortals to see. Now she is less certain. She remembers the conversation she once had with Pliny, when he told her he did not believe any part of a person survives death. That this life is all we have. He has not mentioned Saturia since her murder, nor the real reason Amara has left Rome. She wonders if he carries any guilt, whether this is the reason for his silence, but suspects not. It seems Saturia was expendable to everyone; even her own family's silence has been bought by a lavish funeral—paid for, no doubt, by her killer.

The air grows colder. Pliny at last stirs beside her. "I think that will do," he says, not acknowledging his slumber. "You will strain your eyes."

"As you wish."

The admiral rises. "You should go to bed, Amara. We have many hours of sailing ahead." He lopes off to join the ship's captain, leaving her alone in the dark.

✦ ✦ ✦

Another day and night pass before their arrival at Misenum. The morning is overcast, a haze obscuring the harbor until they are almost upon it. The thicket of ships is as dense as she remembers, a formidable floating forest. It feels strange to Amara to be back. She has not visited the peninsula since she first met Demetrius here, four years ago.

Pliny seems to shed years as he jumps on shore, eager to greet the commander who has run the fleet in his absence. For Amara this results in a long wait at the quayside, as Pliny forgets to send for the carriage to take her to the villa. She strolls up and down, looking at the vast hulls of the ships, staring out at the bay and listening to the call of the gulls. The captain who sailed them over from Ostia hovers nearby, keeping an eye on her, obviously unable to get on with his business until she is safely accounted for. Amara has brought none of her own attendants from Rome, suggesting to Demetrius that there was no need, given all the servants employed by Pliny and Julia. She did not add—though suspects her patron instinctively understood—that she has no wish for anyone in Rome to grasp the lowliness of her origins in Pompeii. It is one thing for her maids to have heard rumors that their mistress was once a brothel slave, quite another for them to snoop past the Wolf Den to see the place for themselves.

Pliny is, for once, extremely apologetic when he realizes his oversight. "Although I don't see why you didn't come to fetch me," he exclaims, when his contrition is spent. "I hope you are not so meek with Demetrius. You would have been quite entitled to complain at being left alone."

Amara does not like to point out that her betrothed would never commit such an oversight as to leave her loitering among sailors for hours, and only smiles. The carriage takes them up the steep slopes of the headland, toward Pliny's estate. A stout woman, swathed in yellow, waits at the entrance to the villa, gradually coming into greater focus as they approach. It is Plinia, the admiral's sister, expectant for her brother's arrival. A young man stands beside her. Amara realizes it must be Plinia's son, who she dimly remembers as a child from her last visit. Pliny embraces them both, taking his sister's face in his hands and kissing her forehead, his affection touching to witness.

"You remember Amara? My freedwoman?"

"Of course." Plinia politely kisses the air beside Amara's cheek. "Congratulations on your betrothal, my dear. Demetrius is a worthy man." Amara has no idea if Pliny has ever told his respectable sister how he found Amara, or where she came from in Pompeii. Though she suspects Plinia is well used to her brother's eccentricities.

Amara follows the family into the house. The nephew, Cilo, is a gangling youth, as skinny as his uncle is portly. He hovers at Pliny's elbow, clearly eager to grab some of his uncle's attention before he inevitably dives into another book. "There is a passage in Livy I wanted to ask you about, uncle, if you have a moment . . . ?"

Lured by the promise of literature, Pliny accompanies his nephew into a room off the hall, leaving the two women alone.

"Well, that's the pair of *them* taken care of until dinnertime," Plinia says with a snort of laughter. "Perhaps you would like to take a bath? I find traveling by sea so tiring."

"That would be very kind, thank you."

They walk through to the garden that borders the atrium, the first of several that Amara can remember on Pliny's estate. The colonnade is painted with scenes from the Trojan war. Amara sees Helen being reclaimed by Menelaus and looks away, pushing Saturia from her mind. Instead, she gazes at the images of Helen's sister Clytemnestra. The vengeful queen stands over a bath running red with her husband Agamemnon's blood, arms raised in victory. By her feet, a motto is inscribed in Greek. *With the sword he struck, with the sword he paid.* If Amara ever commissioned such a painting, she would have Agamemnon, the king of Mycenae, drawn as Felix.

"I'm so delighted that Demetrius has found a woman who is suitably devoted to him, at last," Plinia says, breaking into her reverie. Amara wonders how many of her patron's previous companions the admiral's sister might have met. "Pliny has told me how very attentive you are. And you must be really rather young? So I am sure you will be a great support to him, over the years."

Plinia's tone is unmistakably kind, and yet Amara is defensive at the suggestion she will have to care for her husband-to-be. "Demetrius has the vigor of a man half his age."

"Of course, my dear." Plinia squeezes Amara's arm, with well-intended yet patronizing kindness. They walk through to the second set of gardens, the ones Amara remembers best, with their long ornamental pond. "Ah, here is Myrtale," Plinia gestures at a maid. "She will look after you now."

Amara follows the barefoot attendant. The baths here are even more luxurious than those at Demetrius's house. She thinks with a pang of what it will be like to be back in Pompeii, without such privacy, obliged to use Julia's public facilities. Amara allows herself to be undressed, and is led to the warm room where she is oiled and massaged, all the sweat and grime of her journey skillfully scraped off by Myrtale. Her immersion in the pool is so relaxing she feels in danger of nodding off. The curved edge of the bath allows her to lie back, resting her head against the tiles. A cascade flows into the water at the opposite end, the sound both soothing and musical. Mosaics of marine life surround her, waves of light dancing across them, reflected from the surface of the water.

By the time Amara is ready to go to the rooms Plinia has set aside for her—the rooms where Demetrius usually stays—all her chests and bags of belongings from Rome have been unloaded. She sits on the edge of the bed, trying to imagine her patron here. Scenes from the legend of the minotaur decorate the walls; above the bed, a sleeping Ariadne lies abandoned on the island of Naxos, Theseus's ship already a speck in the distance. Amara stares at the girl's small, slumbering form. Soon she will see her daughter. She will see Rufina.

Tension returns to Amara's body, so lately relaxed in the baths. She tries to allow herself to feel, to acknowledge the pain that she keeps buried for most of the year. If she did not force herself to forget Rufina, she would not be able to live in Rome. Amara has not felt close to her daughter since she was a baby. Now whenever she sees her, she is already anticipating another separation, knowing they only ever have a few weeks together. Rufina will not recognize her when they meet, nor will she remember the bond there was once between them. How could she, at three years old? Amara shifts herself, kneeling on the bed. She traces a finger over the painting on the wall. Theseus's retreating ship is not much bigger than her thumbnail. Tiny brushstrokes as fine as strands of hair mark the oars; Amara squints at them, then lays her forehead against the cool plaster, closing her eyes. Guilt and longing wash over her. Demetrius is not a man like Rufus, one she endures without affection or respect. Her patron has done more for her than any man living, more even than Pliny. Marrying him will give her the security she has craved every single day since the death of her father. And yet she does not love Demetrius the way she loved Philos. Nor is she any closer to fulfilling her promise to Philos, to find a way to free him.

She jumps off the bed, rifling through one of the bags, trying to find the presents she bought for Rufina, soothing herself by looking at all the gifts she can provide. At least her daughter wants for nothing, even if she lacks her mother's presence. Rufina, unlike Amara, will never face the anguish of poverty. And perhaps one day Demetrius will even be persuaded to adopt her as his heir. A flash of dark red, revealed in the bag, makes Amara pause. It is the winter cloak she bought for Philos. The sight of it unnerves her, again bringing guilt to the surface. She turns abruptly, letting the contents spill to the floor, and leaves the room.

Plinia is in the dining room that stretches out over the gardens, sitting with an unfamiliar man. They are enjoying a platter of figs and nuts, laughing together. Without Demetrius, Amara feels a little shy to interrupt, but then Plinia notices her and beckons her over.

"This is my brother's freedwoman, Plinia Amara," she says to her companion. "Soon to be the wife of Demetrius. And Amara, this is Marcus Decimus, who was in Spain with my brother during his time there as Procurator."

Marcus places his hand to his heart in polite greeting. He is younger than Pliny, heavy set, with a dark beard. "Do you think perhaps your betrothed—were he here—would have more luck in dislodging our dear friend's son and brother from their studies? We have tried to no avail."

"We should tempt him with the promise of Amara's voice," Plinia says, clapping her hands. "Her skills as a secretary have made her invaluable to both Demetrius and my brother." Plinia's tone is bright and determined, not allowing for the possibility of any other past for Amara, whatever rumors Marcus may have heard.

"A delightful prospect. Is Cilo not studying Livy? Perhaps Amara could read him to us at dinner. That might lure the pair of them out."

"If you don't mind, dear," Plinia smiles at Amara.

"I would be honored."

Plinia gestures to one of the slaves, relaying the message she wishes to be taken to her brother. Amara sits at the edge of a couch, not wanting to presume too much. She half expects Pliny and his nephew to refuse to join them, but it seems the admiral is indeed attached to her voice, for he soon comes striding over, trailing his nephew and the slave, who is burdened with a heavy scroll. Livy is unfamiliar to Amara, and she feels a little daunted by the prospect of reading aloud in Latin, rather than the Greek texts Pliny usually gives her.

"Amara does love to be useful," Pliny declares to his friend Marcus, watching as the slave helps her set up the scroll to read. "She has a musical voice. Not too high, which can be annoying in a woman, and hard to endure when you are trying to hear the sense of the text."

Plinia rolls her eyes. Clearly her own voice has been found wanting by her brother at some point. Amara wonders what the pair of them were like as children.

"I do hope that my voice will be as pleasing to you in Latin," Amara murmurs, looking at the script with alarm. The words are crammed together and sprinkled with abbreviations that will slow her down.

"Oh," Pliny says, looking a little disappointed. "Yes, of course. Well, do your best."

"I'm sure you will do a splendid job," Plinia says, providing the reassurance her brother would never think to give. The nephew, Cilo, sits beside his mother, blinking like an owl. He is not looking at Amara; instead his attention is on his uncle.

Amara begins to read from the section the slave indicates, more slowly than usual to try and hide her numerous hesitations. She is too focused on the task to look up at Pliny, but the lack of complaints or huffing suggests he is not altogether displeased. After a while, Livy becomes more familiar to her, and she begins to relax. Pliny has plunged her into the middle of the second Punic war, about which she knows little other than the name.

The narrative confuses her. It is a history of Rome and yet Hannibal seems a better leader than the Roman consul Flaminius, at least in the section she is reading. An evening chill creeps up on the small party in the garden, the gathering dusk made darker by mist rolling in from the sea. Slaves silently light the lamps before dark falls, and although Pliny is not giving any indication of wanting to move, Amara is aware of Plinia shifting restlessly beside her.

Flaminius sets up camp by Lake Trasimene and Amara feels dread as she reads, knowing Hannibal is watching his enemy from the mountains above. The Roman troops are oblivious of their doom, stationed far below alongside the water, engulfed in thick fog, when the Phoenicians descend upon them. "*From the shouting that arose from every side the Romans learned, before they could clearly see, that they were surrounded; and they were already engaged on their front and flank before they could properly form up or get out their arms and draw their swords.*"

Amara pauses for breath and Plinia seizes her chance to interrupt. "Not the most cheerful of tales, is it? And before we are all plunged into a dark as gloomy as poor old Flaminius and his men, I think we ought to break for supper."

"Plinia!" the admiral exclaims. "What are you doing? We were about to hear from the consul! This is edifying for Cilo. His words are worth considering."

"I am sure you can regale us all with what Flaminius said as we eat," his sister retorts. "Enough now."

Amara looks between them, uncertain. "I would certainly welcome your thoughts on what we have just heard," she says to Pliny, hoping to mollify him.

"Oh very well, then," Pliny sighs. "I suppose there's some merit in stopping and considering the text. Let them bring out the supper."

Plinia nods at one of the waiting slaves, who immediately sets off to fetch the food. Amara hands over the scroll to another hovering servant with a sense of relief. She is not sorry to rest her voice for a while. Dishes swiftly arrive. It is roasted moray eel, bred in the Plinys' own pond, served with onion and prunes. Amara picks at the eel's delicate flesh, sweetened by the fruit. As with everything in Campania, it is doused in fermented fish sauce, a taste she still finds a little intense.

"So what did you learn, boy?" Marcus asks Cilo. "What did you think of Flaminius?"

"He was rash to ignore so many omens," Pliny's nephew replies. "And he allowed Hannibal to exploit his temperament."

Pliny nods. "Although he acquitted himself well at the end— which we would have heard, if someone had not been so very eager for eel."

"What did Flaminius say?" Amara asks, wanting to avert Plinia's irritated reply.

"He showed immense courage," Pliny says, closing his eyes while he recites from memory. "He told his men *their position was one from which vows and supplications to the gods could not extricate them, but only their brave exertions: it was the sword that opened a way through embattled enemies, and the less men feared, the less, in general, was their danger."*

"And did Flaminius manage to win against the odds?" Amara asks.

"No. It was carnage. Fifteen thousand men slaughtered in the fog. Flaminius himself was killed by Ducarius, run through by a spear."

"Oh," Amara replies, shocked.

Marcus laughs at her comical expression of dismay. "The battle of Trasumennus is one of the most famous defeats in Roman history. It's a little late to be disappointed now."

"No shame in not knowing," Pliny says, mildly. "Better to admit one's ignorance and learn. Always."

Marcus bows his head, rebuked. "Of course."

"It is true what the consul said though, uncle, isn't it?" Cilo says. "That fear is the greatest enemy."

"Overcoming fear is indeed the battle we all face, every day. Not only in war." Pliny waves a forkful of eel for emphasis. "Imagine all the great feats unaccomplished due to fear, the lives only half-lived. Courage is the truest mark of a man." He glances affectionately at his sister. "Of a woman too."

Dusk has fallen. In the garden, lamps hang by the long ornamental pond, illuminating flashes of water and silver leaves, although most of the outside world has turned black. Their dining room is a blaze of light in the dark, an island in a sea of night.

"So what is the true measure of Flaminius?" Amara asks. "Given he was both brave and foolish?"

"What do you think?" Pliny turns the question on her with a smile.

Amara pauses. In her mind's eye, she sees the consul's long-dead men, terrified in the fog, led there by their commander. She thinks of her life in the Wolf Den, forced into danger by Felix, a man who certainly never lacked courage, only compassion. "I think what he did with his own life, perhaps, was brave. But he was wrong to squander the lives of so many others. This is unforgivable." Amara looks at Pliny, his earnest, well-loved features softened by lamplight. "You told me once that this life is all we have. That nothing comes after. All the more reason to take care, in that case."

Pliny's smile broadens. "I'm glad to see you pay attention." He turns to his nephew. "What is your judgment? Are you as harsh as Amara?"

Cilo had just opened his mouth to reply, when their conversation is interrupted by the rattle of dishes on the small bronze dining tables. Amara gasps, watching the plates judder noisily, but before she has time to feel truly afraid, they fall still again. A minor earth tremor. Everyone looks at each other, not unduly alarmed but watchful, in case worse is about to strike. They wait, until Plinia breaks the long silence, reaching for the wine. "We've had a few of those lately."

"Perfectly normal for Campania," Pliny says to Marcus. "Nothing to concern us." He turns back to Cilo. "So—Flaminius?"

Amara watches the young man as he shares his ponderous thoughts with his doting mother and uncle, trying to quell her sense of unease. The tremor and all this talk of fear has made her aware of Rufina; the lurking danger that her daughter faces in the guise of their blackmailer, Felix. The lines of Philos's letter, his warning about expenses incurred *from an unexpected quarter*, again disturb her. Staying here in Misenum for too long is a form of escapism that might more accurately be called cowardice. What does she fear, after all, in seeing her daughter again? Or in seeing Philos?

The thought of them both makes her feel inexpressibly sad. It is always like this. The nearer she draws to Pompeii, the harder it becomes to ignore all she has sacrificed. Amara presses a hand to her eyes, then realizes Plinia is watching her. "You seem a little tired, my dear," the admiral's sister says, kindly.

Pliny turns to peer at Amara, as if she were a specimen to be examined for his *Natural History.* "The sea can be a little tiring, I suppose, for those unaccustomed to it. When we have read the battle to its end, it might be time for you to retire to bed. I cannot have Demetrius hearing I exploited his bride." He gestures impatiently to the slave bearing the scroll, perhaps fearing Amara will fall asleep before she can finish reading the section he wants to hear.

"She's barely finished eating!" Plinia protests.

"She scarcely eats anything, anyway. You don't mind, Amara, do you?"

"I am perfectly fine to read," Amara reassures them both, aware of Marcus smirking at the scene. Plinia tuts at her brother, well aware Amara could not give him any other answer.

Amara returns to the heat of battle, reading the consul's words that Pliny just recited, and recounting Flaminius's death. Pliny does not make good on his promise to stop there, however, and so instead she is obliged to regale them with Rome's reaction to the defeat, and Hannibal's trail of destruction through Italy toward Campania. A slave with an oil lamp stands beside Amara as she reads, illuminating the text, and crickets sing in the darkness. It is hard to imagine that the quiet fields and valleys of this bay were once ablaze, smoke rising as Hannibal laid waste to towns and villages, killing every man who crossed his path. She stops to cough, her voice growing hoarse after so much use, and Plinia again intervenes.

"Thank you, Amara," she says. "You have read for us splendidly. Now you must rest."

Pliny startles out of the reverie into which Livy had transported him, clearly not welcoming the interruption, but he does not argue. Everyone rises with Amara to bid her goodnight.

"I will also retire," Plinia says. "We may leave the men to discuss matters of war."

The two women walk through the garden's darkened colonnade, servants scurrying ahead like beetles, lighting their way. Plinia stops at Amara's chamber, and the slaves surround them in a bright cocoon. "You may stay here as long as you wish, my dear. I promise I will not allow my brother to have you read for so many hours *every* night."

"It is the greatest joy and honor, always, to stay in your home," Amara says, laying her hand upon her heart. "But it has been nearly a year since I saw my daughter and I will be married in a few months. I feel it is important that I return to her as soon as possible."

Plinia's face is hard to read in the shadows but Amara is aware of the woman's personal history. Demetrius once told her that Plinia left her abusive husband to bring up her only son in Misenum, under the protection of his powerful uncle. "I understand," Plinia nods. "Our children are precious. How old is your daughter now?"

"She is three."

"Ah, they are sweet then," Plinia smiles. "Although Cilo was a mischief at that age. Never gave me any peace. I only inflicted him on my brother after the boy could read. I knew they would have nothing to say to each other before that." The two women laugh, and Plinia leans forward to embrace Amara. "I will ensure you are able to leave for Pompeii to see your daughter at the earliest opportunity." Plinia gestures at one of the waiting maids, indicating that she should stay with Amara. "Goodnight, my dear."

"Goodnight. And thank you."

The admiral's sister walks off to her own chambers, leaving Amara with a silent stranger. The maid points timidly toward the door with her lamp, and Amara opens it, stepping into the cold room. The girl helps her undress, and offers to sleep at the foot of the bed, in case she needs anything in the night. Amara refuses, only asking her to light another lamp before she leaves. When the maid has gone, Amara watches the flickering frescoes on the wall, the shape of the minotaur even more sinister in the gloom. But it is not the monster that haunts her as she drifts off to sleep. It is Ariadne's abandonment that hangs, unseen, above her head.

POMPEII

OCTOBER 79 CE

8

*"There had been tremors for many days previously, a common
occurrence in Campania and no cause for panic."*
—Pliny the Younger, on the eruption of Vesuvius

This is not how she remembers the city. Amara stares at the
ruins. The sensation of the waves on the boat makes her feel
as if she is still swaying, even though she is now standing on stone.
A chunk of the colonnade surrounding the harbor has collapsed.
Smashed statues of the gods lie heaped upon the pavement in an
undignified sprawl, terracotta tiles scattered over them like flies.
A team of slaves is working to clear the mess, but it is a task that
will take weeks.

"What happened?" Amara gestures at the destruction.

"Earthquake," says one of the slaves helping to unload the vessel that carried her from Misenum. "Two days ago."

"It must have been quite severe," Amara replies, thinking of
the minor tremors at Misenum, but the man has already scurried
off. She glances at the other slaves ranged around her belongings,
guarding the chests and bags she has brought back from the capital to keep at Julia's house. The men have been sent from Demetrius's estate at Stabiae to meet her at the harbor. The steward,

whose name she does not remember, coughs nervously. "Will you be taking a litter, mistress?"

"I will walk," she replies, suddenly averse to the idea of traveling in a curtained cocoon, unable to see whatever other damage Pompeii has suffered. The slaves exchange glances, but nobody dares speak up against her eccentricity.

Amara regrets her decision almost as soon as they have left the waterfront. She had forgotten how steep the climb is up into the city, and her expensive tunic is soon sticking to her skin with sweat. Hawkers and sailors stare as she passes, though not with the unabashed leer that she remembers from her time working this harbor as a prostitute. For a moment she is back with the other women from the Wolf Den, fear churning in the pit of her stomach at the thought of having to endure the unwanted touch of a stranger. The image makes her cheeks burn and Amara scowls to deter any man foolish enough to try and catch her eye. The steward stalks ahead. He has an irritating, self-important walk. Behind her the other slaves trail in a long snaking line, red faced under the weight of all her wealth.

They pass under the shaded arch of the Forum gate and onto the narrow street that passes the Temple of Venus. Here too, blocks of fallen masonry lie scattered over the road, though an enterprising street seller has taken advantage of the damage, using a slab near the pavement as a makeshift stall: a collection of tattered baskets rests on its white surface. The man notices Amara watching him and smiles a gap-toothed grin, holding up his largest basket, shouting at her to come over. She quickens her steps, bumping into the steward and forcing the burdened slaves behind them both to keep pace. It is not the street seller but the sight of the destruction that is making her uneasy. If the earthquake hit

Pompeii so recently, she might not have had time to hear the news if Rufina or Philos were hurt.

Amara's nerves were taut even before she heard of the earthquake. It has been a year since she last saw her daughter. An impossibly long stretch of time in the life of a small child. The last time they met, Rufina was two and did not recognize her mother. Instead, she had pulled away, reaching for Philos. He had been embarrassed, prying their daughter's chubby fingers from his tunic, bundling her into Amara's arms. Then he had stood hopelessly, while Amara grappled with a wriggling, bawling child she did not know how to soothe. Rufina had cried for Philos by his name, unaware that the person she loves best is also her father.

The lack of a breeze makes the trudge along the Via Veneria hot and stressful. After Rome, Pompeii seems small and sluggish to Amara, with its low painted houses and dusty streets. She cannot now imagine how the main road here ever seemed wide or grand. The clear up from the tremor's damage makes the place look even more ramshackle. Workmen at a shop are arguing over whether a wall needs to be rebuilt or merely repainted, while the owner looks on, wringing his hands and pleading with them over the price. When they pass Asellina's bar, Amara averts her face. The slave Nicandrus, who once loved her friend Dido, works there. She does not need the embarrassment of him recognizing her.

They have nearly reached the wide portico of Julia's block, when Amara sees a man approaching the complex from the other direction, carrying a small child on his shoulders. It is Philos. She stops. Her eyes shoot upward to the child he is carrying. Rufina looks so different. Before, at two, Rufina still had the softened, unfocused look of a baby, but now she is a sharp-eyed child. Amara sees nothing of herself in her daughter: Rufina is the image of Philos. They are laughing together at something, Rufina pulling at Philos's hair to get his attention. There is so much happiness on his face. It is years since he has been like that with Amara, so unguarded and relaxed. The distance between them feels vaster than that between her old hometown Aphidnai and Rome. Amara's former lover and child walk into Julia's estate, unaware of her presence, disappearing from view. The steward's polite cough alerts her to the fact she is at a standstill, clogging up the pavement.

"You are unwell, Mistress?"

"I am fine," Amara snaps, masking her grief with irritation.

Julia's estate is one of the largest in Pompeii, including a bath complex for the paying public, a whole street of bars, apartments that Julia rents out, and a large, luxurious garden. But even this seems provincial compared to the villas Amara is used to in Rome, and the entrance to her own mean apartment is a further shock. She blinks to adjust to the dimmer light. Then she hears Philos's voice, demanding to know who has entered, and has to force herself to stay quiet while the steward answers: "It is your mistress!"

Philos walks into the room, Rufina in his arms. His eyes meet Amara's and she cannot read the expression in them, beyond surprise. Her lips part, the weight of all she wishes to say pressing against her heart.

"I did not expect you until November," Philos says, glancing between her and the steward, so it is unclear who he is addressing. "Forgive me for the poor welcome."

Rufina is staring over her father's shoulder at the host of strangers with wide-eyed curiosity. Amara glances around, seeing what her daughter sees. The small room is crammed with slaves and expensive chests, a sudden inundation of wealth and people. It feels obscene.

"You may leave us and return to Stabiae," Amara says abruptly. "There is not room for everybody here."

The steward is taken aback. "This is hardly a fitting household . . ."

"It is one to which I am well used," Amara says, cutting him off. "Please go." She stares at the man, cold and direct, until he looks flustered.

The steward claps his hands, venting his anger and humiliation on the slaves under his charge. "You heard her. Move!"

The exhausted group head toward the door, and it is only as the last man leaves that Amara realizes she did not even let them rest long enough to take bread and water. Guilt hits her. She wants to call them back, to apologize, but finds she cannot. To her mortification, she is close to tears.

"I should not have done that," she says, not wanting Philos to judge her for her selfishness. "They were tired." Philos does not answer. He is staring at her, and she sees her own pain mirrored in his face. Amara cannot stop herself. "I missed you both," she blurts out.

"Is that my mother?" Rufina asks, cutting across her parents' distress like a cart on the road. Her voice is loud and imperious, in the way only a small child's can be.

"Yes, my love," Philos exclaims with exaggerated enthusiasm. "Shall we show her all you've been learning? I know you have been longing to see her."

The last remark is surely for Amara's benefit. Longing is not reflected in the suspicious look Rufina casts toward her mother. "No." The child turns her chubby face to the side, hiding it in her father's neck.

"I brought you presents," Amara turns toward the luggage, wishing her voice did not sound quite so desperate to please. It takes her a while to get inside the right bag, the awkwardness of the moment growing due to the pause in conversation. She sees Philos step forward, uncertain whether he should offer to help, then finally, she manages to open the clasp. "For you, my love," she says, holding out a wooden, jointed doll to her daughter. "And she has a whole box of other dresses."

"Isn't she beautiful?" Philos enthuses, while Rufina takes the gift in silence. He gently sets their daughter down, leaving her to inspect the doll. For a moment Amara and Philos contemplate their child, briefly united in their love for her.

"And this is for you," Amara says, handing Philos the red winter cloak. She tries to sound casual, but there is nothing careless about the gift. It is an expensive robe, commissioned from one of the best tailors in Rome, born out of painful memories of Philos standing in the cold in their old garden, dressed only in his tunic.

"Oh," says Philos, taking it, clearly shocked by the obvious wealth stitched into every seam. "Thank you. Though it's too much, really." Seeing Philos holding it, Amara knows he is right. She has given him a gift so rich; he will never be able to wear it. A cloak fit for a free man, not a slave. Philos sees the disappointment in her eyes. "But it was thoughtful of you, Amara," he says. "Truly." Again she wants to say something, but cannot find the words. "I think we should show your mother what you've learned," Philos says, crouching down to Rufina. "You can show the doll too."

"Julia," Rufina replies, still intent on playing with her toy. "She is called Julia."

"Well then, you can show Julia and your mother. Come along." The three of them go into the kitchen, which is even poorer and darker than Amara remembers. She can recall drinking tea at the small table with Britannica when she was pregnant with

Rufina, and feels a wave of sadness for the past. Philos ushers her to a stool.

"Now," he says, turning to Rufina and switching to Greek. "Why don't you tell your mother a story. Perhaps the one about the fox and the grapes."

Rufina is clearly not delighted by the instruction, but obeys her father, growing more confident as she becomes wrapped up in Aesop's fable, recounting the surly behavior of the fox. The pain in Amara's chest deepens. Rufina is adorable, with her theatrical, childish gestures, but her accent is atrocious. Nothing could make Amara feel more estranged from her daughter than hearing Rufina speak her mother's language in her father's voice: Rufina speaks Greek badly, like an Italian, like Philos.

"Wonderful!" Amara exclaims, clapping her hands when the tale is told. "How clever you are!"

Rufina smiles, pleased by the praise, and Amara feels a surge of hope. Perhaps this will not be as hard as she feared. Then the little girl turns to her father. "Is she going now?"

"Rufina! This is your mother's home."

"But she doesn't live here, not really. This is *our* house."

Amara stands up, unable to face her child's rejection or Philos's obvious mortification. "I will go and visit Julia for a while," she says, smiling to hide her discomfort. She touches the new doll lightly on the head, where it sits, clutched in Rufina's hand. "The real one. You stay here with your . . ." she is about to say *father* but catches the look of horrified warning in Philos's eyes. "With Philos," Amara says, and hurries from the room, without looking back at either of them.

In the garden, Amara breathes in deeply. The scent of lavender is heavy here, their purple rows bleached and dry from the sun. It reminds her of Demetrius—lavender is the scent he always wears—and in spite of herself, she has a sudden longing to be back with him in Rome, where the rhythm of her life is so much more familiar. She digs her nails into her palms and walks along the colonnade toward Julia's atrium, announcing her arrival to one of the waiting slaves, who hurries off to tell his mistress. Amara's early arrival in Pompeii was not meant to be a shock, but she realizes that while Pliny informed Demetrius of her change in plans, the message to Julia and Philos must have been forgotten. It makes her feel even more awkward.

Scenes of Pompeii surround her as she stands in the atrium. Julia's home is decorated with everyday images of the Forum, rather than with grand mythological scenes. It reminds Amara of Demetrius and his lowly animal fables; Julia has the same mischievous delight in the unconventional. Amara smiles to herself; there is even the noisy seller of pots and pans, painted in his usual spot, beside the cobbler. Then Julia and Livia's excited voices reach her, and she turns, all anxiety forgotten in her overwhelming eagerness to see them.

"Darling!" Julia clasps Amara's face in her hands, and gazes at her, eyes lit with joy, before enveloping her in a hug.

"How very eccentric of you to turn up like this, after saying you would be staying in Misenum until November!" Livia leans in to kiss Amara on both cheeks as soon as Julia has released her. "Not that we're sorry to see you, but I would have arranged a party!"

"There's no trouble between you and Demetrius, I hope?" Julia lowers her voice, frowning with concern.

"No, no," Amara reassures her. "Nothing like that. In fact, quite the opposite." Suddenly she wishes that Demetrius had allowed her to write to Julia with their news from Rome, but he had been anxious about the letter being intercepted before her safe arrival. "He has asked me to marry him."

Julia shrieks, then both women are upon her again, raining kisses on her cheeks and alternatively clutching her in their arms. "My darling, I knew you were right for each other!" Julia cries, triumphant. "I *knew* it!"

"Yes, quite *extraordinary*," Livia drawls, though she is beaming too. "An older man falls for a beautiful young woman. I have never heard such a tale before."

Julia swats her. "Not today, you terrible creature." She turns back to Amara. "Tell me everything, darling. Every detail."

"He said he wished to protect me. That when I am his wife, my status will be secure."

"And that he loves you of course," Julia says, though seeing Amara's face she hurriedly adds, "or he would never have asked."

"Really, who needs love when you can have *millions* of sesterces?" Livia raises her eyebrows at Julia, who starts to tut. "What? She knows I'm joking, darling. We all love dear old Demetrius but he's hardly one to gush. Even if he were dying of love for a woman, he would never say."

"And when will the wedding be?" Julia asks, ignoring Livia.

"Later this year. Demetrius thought perhaps here in Campania at his Stabian estate, before the Saturnalia."

"I hope you will let us stand in for your parents," Livia says. "You are as dear as family."

"Oh thank you," Amara says, moved by her two friends' kindness. "You have always done so much for me. I can't tell you what it means."

"We're delighted for you, darling," Julia says, taking her hand. "You deserve this. And Demetrius too. How is he holding up now, after Vespasian's death? I imagine that must have hit him very hard."

"It did. Though I think he took great comfort in overseeing the funeral. It was an extraordinary event."

"And Pliny must be a close counselor to Titus," Livia says. "They fought together, didn't they? I hope Demetrius will continue to be as indispensable to the son as he was to the father."

"I'm sure the emperor will recognize loyal service," Amara says smoothly. Demetrius has schooled her to say nothing of the politics back in Rome, even to their closest friends. "But what of the news here?"

"Well, you must have already seen your adorable little Fina," Livia says, leading Amara back out into the colonnade. They wander toward the cool, blue dining room facing the garden, and lie down together on the couches. "I must say she seems to take after your family," Livia continues. "I can't see anything of Rufus in her."

"Rather fortunate, I would say," Julia adds, with a snort of laughter. "That nose would be most out of place on a young girl."

"She has my father's coloring," Amara lies. "Though sadly not his Greek."

"Perhaps Demetrius will let you take her with you, next time you return to Rome," Julia says. "It would surely be good for her education."

Amara smiles but does not answer. She has already asked Demetrius this and knows he is still considering his answer. "I'm so grateful to you both for looking after her, and of course all my business interests, too, while I have been away," she says, changing the subject.

"That was mainly Philos," Livia replies. "He really is a wonder with accounts. I wasn't sure why you decided to invest in those funny little fast-food stores by the theater, but they seem to be turning a profit, even so."

"You make it work so well here at the baths," Amara says. "I hoped to do the same. Though of course I know mine are nothing like as grand."

"The bars are hardly grand, darling," Julia laughs. "Though I appreciate the sentiment. But the baths are something else, I will allow."

One of the slaves arrives with a platter of sliced pomegranates and a jug of water, setting it down on the table. "It is so very good to have you home," Livia says, taking a glistening fruit and picking out the bright red seeds with a spoon. "Though I'm sure you must be missing your beloved already. And he you, of course."

Amara thinks of her last exchange with Demetrius, the way he kissed her forehead, responding to her emotional declaration that she would miss him with a single word: *good*. "I'm sure he will cope," she says drily.

The three women laugh and for the first time since she came to Pompeii, Amara feels lighter. It is a warmth unlike any other, being able to bask in her friends' love, to feel the comfort of being known and accepted in spite of her enslaved past, or the shame of the brothel. None of that matters now. The image of Rufina comes into her mind—the way she turned aside earlier, wanting Amara to leave. Pain lodges in Amara's chest but she ignores it. She reaches over to take a piece of pomegranate, and lies back against the couch, smiling as Livia starts to fill her in on all the gossip she has missed.

9

"Shared danger is the strongest of bonds."
—Livy, *History of Rome*

Amara had intended the visit to her two friends to be brief, and yet it is evening, and the blue peak of Mount Vesuvius has melted into the darkening sky, by the time she returns to her own home. Philos is alone in the kitchen, waiting for her. He must have already settled Rufina into bed. He stands as she enters, moving so that the table is between them. It is the first time they have been alone together like this for years. When Amara last stayed in Pompeii, there was still a wet nurse living in the flat, whose presence added a layer of reserve to all their interactions. Now evening softens everything into greater intimacy, and in the dim light of the kitchen, shadows accentuate the sharp lines of Philos's face. He has always been a strikingly attractive man. Amara is reminded of the moment when she first understood that she loved him, in her study at the old house, on the night of the Floralia. It feels like another lifetime.

"I'm sorry that I missed Rufina's bedtime," she says.

"I know you had business to discuss with Julia and Livia. And I understand it is hard for you, coming back." Philos hesitates as if unsure about whether he has said too much, but obviously understands from Amara's expression that he has not. "I think she will be easier tomorrow. I have arranged to go out early to work for Rufus, so that you have time alone together." The mention of Rufus only deepens the chasm between them, drawing stark attention to Philos's enslaved status, so different from Amara's wealthy life. Rufus still owns Philos, who is merely on loan to Amara to look after Rufina and her business affairs while she is away from Pompeii. Rufus has always refused to sell his steward to Amara, insisting that Philos is too valuable for the work he does in the family business.

Amara walks toward the table, taking the stool opposite him. Philos hesitates then also sits back down. They are so close to one another that Amara could reach across the table and rest her hand on his arm. She pushes the image from her mind. "How have you both been?" she says. "I know you cannot tell me everything in the letters."

"Rufina is exactly as I have described her to you," Philos says. "You have every reason to be proud. You saw her today, reciting the fable." His eyes are bright at the memory. "She brings intelligence and humor to everything she does."

"I'm so grateful to you, for all you are doing for her." Philos does not reply. They stare at one another and emotion fills the silence, making it heavy. "Philos," Amara begins, "there are going to be changes in my life. Demetrius has asked me to marry him. And I have accepted." Amara is not fully prepared for the expression on her former lover's face. It is relief.

"And he will allow you to take Rufina to Rome?"

Amara is stung by his reaction. "Are you so eager to be rid of her?"

"Of course not!" It is Philos's turn to be annoyed. "How can you even ask me such a question? Rufina is my whole life. But this way she will finally be safe. Not brought up by a father whose very existence is a threat to her reputation." He gestures at his face. "Don't you think people are going to start to notice the resemblance? And what power does that give Felix?"

The name brings with it a familiar feeling of dread. "Has he been threatening us? I wondered if he had been causing trouble from your last letter."

"I believe so. Men have been hanging around the stores by the theater lately, demanding protection money. Britannica confronted Felix about it. But he denies any involvement."

"How much money have they been taking?"

"At the moment it's only small change. But if it *is* Felix behind this, the first few demands will likely be a test, to see how far he can push us, before he goes for more."

"I will speak with Britannica." Amara clenches her hands in her lap. "But you and Rufina are safe, aren't you? Felix hasn't been back to the house."

"As soon as you can get her to Rome, none of that will matter anymore."

"That means he *has* threatened you," Amara is about to reach for his hand, then thinks better of it. "Please. You have to tell me."

Philos sighs, knowing Amara is never one to let a matter drop. "Felix approached us the other day in the street. I was outside the wine merchants, placing an order for Julia, when I realized a man was crouching down to speak to Rufina. It was him." Amara clasps a hand to her mouth, eyes wide with alarm. "He never touched her, I promise you. I picked her up before he had a chance," Philos's expression hardens. "If we had been in private, I would have confronted him. But not with Rufina there. Instead, I was forced to make polite conversation until the merchant got restless, and Felix finally walked off. I don't think he is *ever* going to leave you alone, Amara, which means he will never leave our daughter alone either. That's why she needs to go to Rome. You *have* to persuade Demetrius. It's the only way she will be safe."

"But what of you? Rufus still refuses to sell you, every time I ask."

"I made my peace with that years ago. Rufina is what matters now."

Philos speaks without a trace of self-pity and has the calm, stoic look she remembers so well from their life together. It is the mask of a slave, who cannot afford to have feelings. A mask Amara once wore herself. But now she is freed and Philos never will be. Guilt twists inside her. "I'm sorry," she says, knowing no words will ever be enough to atone for the loss Philos faces. "I'm so sorry for all the ways I've failed you and betrayed you . . ."

"That's not how it is," Philos says, cutting her off. "It never has been. I've had years to reflect on it all. The only one who has anything to regret about their behavior is me. I should never have acted on my feelings for you—it was utterly selfish. I thought I loved you, but all I did was risk your life and threaten your future. And now all that matters is that I protect our child. It's the only thing I can do that begins to put it right."

"I wasn't some innocent girl, Philos. I knew what I was doing back then. And I loved you too."

He leans back further on the stool, putting space between them. "Well, whatever happened in the past, it's our daughter we have to think of now. I'm relieved Demetrius will protect you both."

"I don't know for certain that he will agree to let me take her to Rome."

"But surely it's different once you are married?" Philos is incredulous. "What sort of man refuses to adopt his wife's child?"

"Then I will keep asking until he says yes," Amara says, although she feels far less certain of Demetrius's acquiescence than her tone suggests.

"Good." Philos rises. "Rufina is asleep in your room. She rarely wakes in the night. I will let you join her and get some rest."

He turns away, heading to the darkened storeroom without a lamp or backward glance, snuffing out any trace of intimacy between them.

Amara is woken by her daughter early in the morning, in the same room where she once gave birth to her.

"*Where's Philos?*" The question is asked straight into Amara's ear, a chubby hand pulling at her shoulder. "When can he have his bed back?"

"I think he's started work already," Amara says, unable to answer the other question, embarrassed that she has obliged Philos to sleep elsewhere.

"When is he home?"

"I'm not sure. Shall we go get some breakfast?"

Rufina's bottom lip starts to quiver. "I want Philos."

"I know my love," Amara says, swiftly getting out of bed, trying to forestall her small child's threatened tears with busyness. "But he won't be long." Philos has laid Rufina's clothes out ready on the chair, and Amara helps her daughter dress. "How pretty you look!" she says. "And I have brought you new clothes from Rome. Would you like to see them?"

"Maybe."

Amara dresses herself, while Rufina ignores her to play with Julia the doll, her bottom lip still sticking out ominously. "Come on then," Amara says. "Let's go."

They make their way down the narrow stairs into the kitchen. The place feels even darker and pokier than it did last night. Philos has left some bread for them both on the table, along with the soft crumbling cheese Amara associates with Pompeii, with its tang of salt and thyme. Rufina sits opposite her, small legs dangling above the floor, while Amara pours them both a cup of water. "I don't like that bit," Rufina points to the crust. "Philos eats it. I want the middle."

Amara pulls the soft middle out for her daughter, wondering what other indulgences Philos bestows on their child. "A little crust is good for your teeth, though."

Rufina ignores her and carefully picks the small piece of crust her mother has given her off the bread, laying it on the table with a determined expression. In that moment, she does not look like Philos; she looks like Amara.

"You did well with your fables yesterday," Amara says, switching to Greek. "Which ones are your favorites?"

"The one about the mice," Rufina replies in Latin. She studies her mother. "Are you like the town mouse?"

Amara is taken aback, thinking of the story, and the price the town mouse pays for his riches and fine food. Living with a cat. "A little I suppose," she says.

"Are there more presents?" Rufina has swiveled around on her stool, pointing at the storeroom where Amara's bags and boxes are still piled up. The space where Philos must have been obliged to sleep.

"Yes. Do you want to see?"

Rufina nods, sliding off her seat. She trots ahead of Amara, surprisingly swift on her sturdy little legs, Julia the doll clamped firmly to her chest. Love catches Amara off guard. She wants to scoop Rufina up into her arms, to kiss her soft cheek and inhale the scent of her hair, but understands her daughter will recoil if she rushes her.

Instead she sits down by the bag that contains the gifts, balancing on her haunches, giving Rufina space to join in. Amara picks out some of the fabrics she chose for her daughter, rich reds and yellows, an especially fine blue veil to keep for her dowry. Rufina presses close, clutching her mother's arm, wanting to touch everything, eyes bright with curiosity. In the middle of the bag, cushioned between all the material, are the things she has been waiting for: toys. Rufina exclaims with delight, seizing each gift, trying to keep them all piled up in her small arms at once. A wooden horse on wheels, a spinning top, a fabric mouse filled with sand and a clay water whistle in the shape of a bird. Amara gently pries the bird from her daughter's grip. "Shall we go outside to play this? Maybe choose one other toy to take with you, and leave the rest here." Rufina considers her haul, eventually choosing the wooden horse on wheels, silently handing her mother Julia the doll to carry.

It is a relief to leave the dark rooms and emerge into the brighter light of Julia's garden. Rufina reaches up to take her mother's hand as they walk alongside the pond, and warmth spreads through Amara's chest. She squeezes her daughter's small fingers. They stop by the pool's edge and Amara crouches down to fill the bird with water. Its clay body is glazed black, and its beak red. She chose the bird because it reminded her of a similar toy that once belonged to her own mother. A low warble comes from the bird's beak as Amara blows on the tail, a close imitation of real birdsong. Rufina watches, fascinated. "I try!" she says, stretching out her hands, the horse dumped on the paving stones, forgotten.

"Just be gentle, or it won't make a noise," Amara gives it to her, careful to keep the bird upright.

Rufina gives a hearty puff on the whistle, spraying water over her mother. Amara laughs at her child's shocked expression, shaking the drops from her tunic, until Rufina's face dimples into a smile and she laughs too. Then she plumps down, lunging into the pond to refill the whistle, her movements jagged with a small child's impetuosity. Amara keeps a hand on her, to prevent her daughter falling in. They pass the bird to and fro between each other countless times, Rufina never seeming to tire of the repetition. Then she abruptly loses interest, stuffing the bird into her mother's hands, and grabs the wooden horse on wheels. Her feet slap on the stones as she runs alongside the water, the toy rattling behind her. Amara has to dart along to keep up.

One of the paving stones is uneven, its edge jutting out. Amara sees what will happen but is not close enough to grab her child. Rufina trips, falling flat on the ground. She twists around, her face scrunched in outrage, then lets out an ear-splitting wail. Amara rushes to pick her up, heart hammering in fright. Surely, it was only a stumble. Surely, she cannot be badly hurt. Rufina screams as if she is being murdered, while her mother comforts her, checking her over. A scuffed knee is the only visible damage. "There, my love, there, there," Amara soothes, trying to hold her.

"I want Philos!" Rufina shrieks, burying her angry, wet face in her mother's hair. "Philos!"

"Fina!" It is Livia, rushing out of the house. She scrambles through the garden and crouches down beside Amara, on eye level with the wailing child. "What a lot of noise for a tiny tumble!" There is laughter in Livia's voice, but Rufina is in no mood to be placated. "I saw you from the window, Little Frog; it was nothing!"

"It was not nothing!" Rufina screams.

"Do you think Britannica wails like this in the arena?" Livia continues, unruffled at being the target of Rufina's rage. "Think how brave she is! And your mother sponsors an entire troop of gladiators! You're her daughter—you can't possibly cry like a baby over one fall!"

Livia means to be helpful. Amara knows this, but she cannot help but feel exasperated by the interference. "I think the horse fell too," she says, quietly. "Maybe you should check if he is alright?"

"*She*," Rufina says. "Horse is a *she*." In spite of the huffy correction, the distraction works at interrupting her distress. Rufina, Amara and Livia solemnly inspect the wooden horse. "Poor little thing," Rufina says, lavishly comforting the toy, and shooting a filthy look at Livia, whose own attempt at comfort she is clearly rebuking. Amara bites her lip to stop herself from laughing.

"Well," Livia says, "since nobody has died, maybe we will go inside to see Julia?"

"Shall we show Julia, your new Julia, the doll from Rome?" Amara asks, bringing out the toy.

Rufina nods. She holds her arms up, in a sign she wants to be picked up, but it is not her mother she is asking. It is Livia. Amara reaches down before Livia can move between them, hoisting Rufina onto her hip. Her daughter is unresisting but does not cling to her either. The three of them head into the house, the scent of lavender heavy in the autumn sunshine.

Pompeii is at its most relaxing in the early evening, when the heat of the day has passed and yet it is still bright, the air lightened by the sea breeze. Campania has a freshness that Amara misses when she is in Rome. She walks along the Via Veneria toward the theater, two of Julia's servants accompanying her, walking a few steps behind. It is hard to admit to herself the relief she felt when Philos came to take Rufina. Mercurial moods are a part of childhood, she knows this, and yet her daughter's ambivalence is still painful.

They turn into the small, triangular Forum that sits alongside the theater, past the brightly painted Temple of Isis before reaching the gladiatorial barracks. Amara does not recognize the guards at the entrance, although their lascivious stare is familiar enough. Wealthy women are not unknown to visit the gladiators' training grounds for their own enjoyment, to watch the handsome men perform, and maybe for more, if the gossip is true.

"I am Plinia Amara, patron of the Venus Pompeiana troop," she says. "I wish to see my woman Britannica."

One of the guards sets off to fetch Stephanus, the troop's *lanista*, a recently retired gladiator who manages their training and bookings. Amara does not look at the remaining guards as she waits, instead gazing serenely at the street until Stephanus arrives. The guards step aside when he joins them, heads bowed.

"Welcome Mistress," Stephanus speaks to Amara in their native Greek, his hands over his heart in greeting. He is a freedman yet always addresses Amara this way, as a mark of respect for the woman who pays his wages. Broad-shouldered and muscular, his skin is marred by a fretwork of scars and a once broken nose, mementos of the twenty-one fights he survived during his days in the arena. He has the most formidable presence of any man Amara has ever met. It is why she hired him.

"Stephanus," Amara replies, smiling. "I congratulate you on winning a place for us in the October games. Your hard work continues to impress."

"You gave me a wonder to work with," Stephanus replies. "I have never seen her equal. You have come to watch her train?"

"Please," Amara says, as he ushers both her and Julia's two servants into the barracks. She commands them both to wait at the entrance before following Stephanus around the colonnade that encircles the busy training grounds. Watching him, Amara is reminded of the tigers that stalk the arena. He moves silently, without swagger; but although he wears his strength lightly, she has seen for herself how explosive his violence can be. Men nod at him as they pass, either from fear or respect. Some are sparring together with wooden weapons, their shadows lengthening across the sand, while others loiter on the path, swearing and laughing. It is hard to believe that many of these men will eventually kill each other.

One skirmish at the far end of the barracks has attracted a small crowd, which sways with the movement of the fighters. Amara sees a familiar flash of red hair, like flame. Britannica.

Amara taps Stephanus's arm, wanting to approach slowly, to avoid distracting her friend, but he shrugs, perhaps understanding that nothing will diminish Britannica's attention. They join the small group of watching gladiators. A Thracian is crouched low, warily circling the woman who towers over him, armed with her trident. Britannica evades every jab of his wooden sword—so swift on her feet, they might be winged like Hermes. She is taller than Amara remembers, her body lean, the muscles hard as marble. Her hair has been tied back like a horse's tail, or the plume of a helmet, and it swings when she moves, as if she were dancing rather than fighting. Her opponent is broad and stocky, his movements ungainly in comparison. He lunges again at Britannica, who wheels out of the way, striking him lightly on the legs with her trident. It's a playful gesture, but one which would have done untold damage were the weapons real. There is a murmur of approval from the small crowd; the man nearest Amara is grinning. It doesn't seem to matter to anyone here that Britannica is a woman; perhaps they have even forgotten her sex altogether.

Watching her perform, Amara realizes there was no danger of Britannica becoming distracted; the Briton's eyes are trained on the man she faces, anticipating his movements, yet somehow never falling for his feints. Eventually she disarms him with a single flick of her weapon, almost as if she had grown bored of the combat. She steps on the wooden sword as he bends to retrieve it, shaking her head, lips pursed in amusement. Aggrieved, the defeated gladiator flings himself through the ranks of his fellows, swearing loudly, and Britannica laughs. Some of the other men laugh too, nodding their congratulations, before dispersing onto the training grounds. It is then that Britannica sees her.

The two women stare at one another, then, in a couple of giant strides, Britannica is embracing Amara, gripping her by the shoulders.

"You are back." Britannica smiles, revealing the broken teeth she earned not in the arena but at the brothel.

"Yes. And now I find you are second only to Artemis." Amara holds her friend at arm's length, taking her in. Britannica is browner than she remembers, her pale northern skin scorched by the sun, splattered with freckles that have almost turned her arms as auburn as her hair. She is stronger and more alive than anyone Amara has ever seen; the ferocious goddess of hunting does not feel like a far-fetched comparison.

"Yet mortal," Stephanus says, interrupting Amara's admiration.

"I never forget this," Britannica replies, her Latin less heavily accented than the last time Amara saw her. "It is why I am still alive."

"Perhaps we could go to your chambers, Stephanus?" Amara asks, wanting more privacy than is afforded here on the training ground, where she is conscious of the curious, loitering men, some of whom know her as their patron.

Stephanus nods and they follow him to the colonnade, where a doorway leads up a flight of stairs to his living quarters. The study is familiar to Amara. It is painted with scenes of gladiatorial combat; sturdy figures chase one another over the walls, most of them faceless, encased in metal. Above two painted Thracians, a window looks out over the barracks toward the theater, which is now bathed in the pink light of the dying sun. Voices float upward, the gladiator's shouts and laughter almost musical in the evening air.

"Are you here about the games?" Stephanus gestures for them to sit. "Or is it other business?"

"Both." Amara glances at the door. Stephanus takes the hint and walks over to pull it shut.

"You have no need to fear the festival of Mars," he says, drawing up a stool and sitting opposite her. He looks at ease, leaning his weight on one knee. "The troop will acquit you well."

"I have no doubt Britannica will bring us victory."

"There is always doubt," Britannica retorts. "This is why I train hard and strike harder." Stephanus laughs and the two fighters exchange a look of understanding that makes Amara feel momentarily excluded, before Stephanus turns back to her.

"But you are here for Felix?" he says.

"I understand he might be causing problems."

"He is watched," Stephanus says. "My men have no doubt he is behind the threats to your business. The question is, what do you wish us to do?"

Amara knows the men Stephanus refers to are not those training outside. Her *lanista* did not become a gladiator by choice. He was enslaved to the arena as a punishment for robbery and still commands the loyalty of a number of criminals in Pompeii, his own brother Cosmus among them. "We do nothing," she says. "For now."

"No," Britannica says. "Felix takes this as weakness."

"Demetrius has asked me to marry him." Amara is a little irritated by Britannica's emphatic contradiction, delivered with the same expectation of victory she just showed toward her Thracian opponent. "I cannot start a street war in Pompeii."

"No need," Britannica says. "You want to stop a snake biting? Cut off the head."

Amara glances at Stephanus for support, but instead he is looking at Britannica with an unmistakable look of pride. "We can't simply murder a man," Amara snaps, exasperated. "This isn't the arena."

"I agree that *we* can't," Stephanus gestures between them. "But that's not our only option."

"Why you not let me kill him?" Britannica rests a hand on Amara's knee, leaning in close in her urgency. "All these years, it is the best choice. It saves so much suffering."

"*You* are not killing anyone, or not outside the ring," Stephanus declares, with a look of warning at his champion fighter.

"Only a manner of speaking. I trust your brother," Britannica shrugs, though her denial fools neither of her companions. Both of them know how much she would relish murdering Felix, how she feels his death is hers by right, stolen from her by Amara, who refused to let Brtiannica press home the knife at his throat when she once had the chance.

Amara rests a hand on Britannica's arm. "Have you forgotten he has my secrets written into his will?"

"Then we burn down the Wolf Den," Britannica says. "Destroy everything."

Amara exclaims in exasperation, but Stephanus is less perturbed. "I agree that right now this would be too much. But you have to understand Amara, that it may come to this. Felix is extorting money from you, threatening your businesses. Why do you employ me, why keep Cosmus on retainer, if you never intend to show your strength? We are here to protect your family." The former gladiator is leaning forward onto his thigh in the same relaxed posture as before, his apparent calm at odds with all the marks of violence on his skin.

"But the risks," Amara murmurs. "How could we silence all of them? He must have told Gallus and Beronice. I might destroy my family in trying to save it." She does not dare admit her other scruples. The guilt she would feel at taking all those innocent lives, the women who risk being burned in the lupanar. Victoria and her children. The image of Saturia lying murdered comes back into Amara's mind. She does not need more deaths on her conscience.

"No fight is without risk," Stephanus says, mistaking her concern. "We would strike when you were back in Rome. When the chances of it being linked to you are at its lowest. And besides you are a wealthy woman now, under the protection of the admiral. With Felix gone, I doubt anyone else would have the desire to accuse you."

"But Philos and Rufina are here," Amara says. "How could you protect them against retaliation?"

"Felix is feared, not loved," Stephanus shrugs. "His retainers would be too busy fighting each other to take his place to avenge him."

"I never let anyone touch Fighter," Britannica says fiercely, using her nickname for Rufina. "*Never.*"

"There's still Victoria and the children." Amara looks at Britannica, willing her to understand. "You know Victoria would have to die too if we killed Felix. There are no sacrifices we could make to the gods to erase such a crime."

"A family of snakes. Victoria's choice to bear him sons." Britannica shakes her head. "If you let me kill her before, none of this happen. No children born to suffer for such a father."

"My own father dedicated his whole existence to preserving life," Amara says, close to anger. "I cannot just deal out death in defiance of his memory, not unless there truly is no other way."

"Then what do you suggest?" Stephanus's scarred face is, as always, hard to read.

"We tell him to stop. Or pay the consequences."

"You really think he will listen to you?"

"Not to me, no. But maybe to her. He will know she means it."

Britannica smiles, interrupting before Stephanus can object. "When do we go?"

10

"Victoria is unconquered here"
—Graffiti from Pompeii's brothel

Amara and Britannica walk through the darkening streets together, hooded and cloaked to avoid being recognized. Julia's servants have returned to the house, with a message that Britannica will be escorting Amara home later. She already regrets her own suggestion to visit Felix, but the thought of the women and children trapped inside while the brothel burns, keeps her from turning back.

They reach the fountain at the turning off the Via Veneria, the well's white marble face caressed by its cornucopia of plenty, a cluster of people waiting to fill their jugs and buckets. A garland of dried flowers, a memento from the recent Fontanalia festival, is draped over the wellhead. It has been many years since Amara was obliged to queue at a public fountain. She glances at Britannica whose expression is obscured by the shadow of her hood. The two former she-wolves wind their way up the narrow road that runs alongside the Stabian baths, avoiding the bar run by Gallus and Beronice, whose customers have spilled out onto the pavement. The men's voices are loud and they stand blocking the way, as if nobody else deserves any space. One calls out to the two heavily cloaked women as they pass on the other side of the road, asking for a price. Revulsion sits heavily in Amara's stomach. She understands, returning here, where Britannica's violence comes from and her rage that is never far from breaking through the surface.

"No need for fear." Britannica's voice is calm, as if she has heard Amara's thoughts.

They reach the curve of the street where the brothel sits. Felix has added a lantern to the building; it hangs out over the road above the doorway where Thraso, Felix's most brutal henchman, is standing. They do not have to pass him but take the opposite fork in the road. Thraso pays them no notice, not recognizing their shadowed faces at such a distance.

Britannica strides up to the front door of Felix's flat, rapping firmly on the wood. Years have passed since Amara came here, and yet the answering sound of footsteps on the narrow wooden staircase is as familiar as if she heard it yesterday. She braces herself to see Paris when the door creaks open, but instead it is her oldest friend from Pompeii: Victoria.

Britannica shoves her foot in the doorway before Victoria can slam the door shut again.

"You!" Victoria exclaims, eyes wide with fear. She looks back and forth between her two former companions. Where Britannica has grown into herself in the past three years, Victoria seems to have shrunk. Her face is pinched, leeched of its former vitality, and even though Amara hates Victoria for all she has done to put Philos and Rufina in danger, the emotion that almost overwhelms her now is pity. One small boy, barely out of babyhood, is clasped to Victoria's hip, while another, closer in age to Amara's daughter, stands silently by his mother's skirts. He has the sharp features of his father, but with a child's look of innocence. For a moment nobody speaks. The last time the three women were together, Britannica was holding a knife to Felix's throat. They all know Victoria's husband is only alive because Amara did not order his death.

"No welcome for your friends?" Britannica's gap-toothed smile makes Victoria shrink back further, shielding her smallest boy's head.

"Let us in, Victoria." Amara's voice carries the note of command she learned in Rome. "We are not here to harm you."

Victoria does not do as she is asked but instead swivels around to shout up the stairs. "*Felix! Felix, I need you!*"

"How many times have I told you not to shriek like that, you fucking harpy?"

Behind Victoria's shoulder, Amara sees his figure at the top of the landing, face blacked out by the lamplight behind. Felix strides down the stairs, barging Victoria and the children out of the way. If he is surprised to find Britannica and Amara waiting for him, he doesn't show it. His eyes flick Britannica up and down, searching for any evidence of a weapon.

"We want to talk," Amara says. "Nothing more."

For a moment she thinks he is going to slam the door in their faces, but then he smiles his falsest and most ingratiating smile. "Of course. Come in."

The two women enter their former master's home. The place is so much shabbier than Amara remembers. It seems impossible that this man still holds any power over her life. They walk along the corridor to Felix's study. Victoria's steps are the most uncertain, even though she is the one in her own home. She dithers in the doorway, clearly unsure if she is wanted inside, until Felix gives her a vicious shove. "Get in!" he snaps, as she almost stumbles over the threshold. Instinctively, Amara reaches out a hand to steady her, gripping her arm. Victoria stiffens at her former friend's touch, but Amara does not let go. The older boy stays close to his father.

Britannica is the last to enter. She stands near the open doorway, so that she can keep an eye out for anyone coming along the corridor. Her face is as blank as the metal masks Amara has seen the cavalry wear on military processions through Rome, but she knows that Britannica's emotions are as heightened as her own. Memories weigh heavily. All the violence and indignity she suffered in this room. Amara lets go of Victoria, stepping closer to Britannica, their shared anger as palpable as a physical bond between them.

Felix watches them both with his usual arrogant smile, seemingly at ease, even though Amara knows he is surely not such a fool as to be unafraid of Britannica, Pompeii's deadliest gladiator. "What brings you here? Apart from the fond desire to relive old times."

"Why are you threatening my businesses?"

Felix raises his eyebrows. "I am making no threats."

"You have been demanding money from the people who work for me," Amara says. "Don't insult us by denying it."

"Those paltry little bars by the theater?" Felix laughs. "You think I'm so short of fucking money, I would bother myself with those?"

"You stop or we make you stop." Britannica's voice is taut with anger. Amara glances at her. Unlike in the barracks earlier, Britannica looks physically tense, her natural poise sapped by hatred.

"Don't you threaten us, you fucking savage!" Victoria snaps, looking at the gladiator with loathing. Britannica does not deign to reply but Victoria's baby son starts to whimper at his mother's raised voice.

"Can't you keep him quiet, you stupid fucking bitch?" Felix demands. "Or is even *that* beyond you?" Victoria attempts to shush their child, cringing from the contempt in his voice.

"Do you expect your sons will thank you for treating their mother so poorly?" Amara says, making a deliberate reference to Felix's own father, who she knows he murdered. "Or did life teach you nothing?"

Felix steps forward and for a moment Amara fears she has gone too far, but he only rests his hand on his oldest boy's shoulder, drawing him closer. "My sons may have a whore for a mother, but at least their father is not a slave."

Behind her, Amara hears Britannica spit out a curse. "You talk like a man who imagines his words will have no consequences," Amara says, her heart quickening at the insult to her daughter, "which is a mistake."

"You dare threaten me in my own house?" Felix is gripping his son hard. The child gazes up at Amara in uncomprehending fear. She wonders how much violence the boy has already seen.

"I warn you before," Britannica steps forward, all pretense of conciliation gone. "You touch Rufina, you a dead man. You and all who belong to you." She addresses Victoria with unmistakable menace. "Make him understand this. He must leave us alone. For sake of your children. I have no fear to destroy *everything*."

"Get the fuck out of my house," Felix says, his temper finally frayed to breaking point, "or the only words to have consequences will be yours." Victoria glances fearfully at her husband but the two other former she-wolves stay where they are. Felix walks toward Amara, coming so close that Britannica also steps forward, poised to intervene. "I said *leave*."

The only sound is the whimpering of Victoria's youngest son. Amara and Felix stare at one another, their shared hatred exerting a pull neither seems able to resist. Face-to-face with her old nemesis, Amara no longer fears the stain of destroying innocent lives: she wants to burn this place to ash, along with everyone in it. "I have warned you to leave me alone," she says. "You have a family. Don't make them suffer for the sake of your own fucking pride."

"You think just because you painted me as Acteon on a wall, that you can tear me apart?" Felix waves a dismissive hand at Victoria without bothering to look at her. "She showed me the fresco you put up in posh boy's house. The goddess Diana taking her revenge on the man who wronged her. As if a whore like you could ever evoke the protection of the virgin goddess. You are nothing more than some worthless slave who was fucked by any man that cared to pay me. I still own you Amara, I will *always* own you, because I own your secrets." He snaps his fingers at Britannica. "This is the only fucking weapon you have. And her life hangs in the balance every time she steps into the arena. So I don't think *you* are in any position to threaten *me*."

The many times Amara has stood in this place with Felix lie, unspoken, between them. All the pain and degradation he once heaped on her under the gaze of the painted bull's skulls on their black plinths. All the fear she once felt. But the past no longer has the same hold. Her old master's face is flushed with anger and bitterness and in return she gives him the smile he taught her. "You threaten like a small-town pimp," Amara says, looking him up and down with contempt. "Which is what you are. Which is all you will ever be. I have given you fair warning. Heed it or not as you choose."

She turns her back on Felix, trusting in Britannica's protection, and walks from the room.

11

"May the gods make us happy"
—Pompeii graffiti

The marble is warm where Amara leans against the side of the pool. It is the women's day at Julia's Venus Baths and steam rises from the water into the open air. The autumn sky above is bright blue, the sun blazing, but there is a chill that makes the flesh on her upper arms dimple. Amara had hoped to swim, to lose some of the tension still trapped in her body after her confrontation with Felix, but there is little chance of movement in this pool. She is surrounded by a gaggle of obsequious women—other courtesans from Pompeii, desperate to find favor with the former mistress of Placidus Rufus who has made her fortune in Rome.

"You know Queen Berenice? What is she like? How does she style her hair?"

The speaker is a young girl, a Greek like Amara, whose name is Chloris. She is standing far too close, unable to temper her eagerness with deference. Amara's back is already pressed against the side of the pool, and she cannot move further away. "She prefers styles from her native Judea," Amara says dismissively, not wanting to give Chloris her private reflections on Berenice, whose banishment still makes her melancholy.

"And you've seen the Emperor Titus? Is he very fine?" It is a different courtesan this time, an Italian girl whose name Amara cannot keep in her head, although she knows the girl's patron: Quintus. Pompeii truly is a small town. Quintus is the man who first hired Amara and Dido to perform as entertainers in wealthy men's homes; he marked the first step on Amara's laborious, often humiliating climb out of the brothel. This girl's connection to a client from Amara's days as a prostitute doesn't fill her with fondness.

"The emperor bears himself exactly as one would expect of a man who is the son of a god," Amara says, her expression haughty.

"And you actually *saw* his soul take flight for the Palatine?" It is Chloris again, somehow standing even closer, her toe bumping Amara's calf under the water. Something about her childlike face reminds Amara of Saturia, although Chloris has none of the Roman courtesan's guile. Amara pushes herself away from the wall, wanting to escape the press of female bodies, the gaze of envious eyes.

"Excuse me, ladies," she says. "I wish to take a turn in the pool."

Amara swims away from the disappointed courtesans, and as she does, another figure catches her eye. Walking toward the pool's shallow steps is Drusilla. Amara is not alone in staring; it is not only that Drusilla stands out in Pompeii for her Ethiopian heritage, she is also taller and more graceful than every other woman present. A familiar gold bracelet in the shape of a snake shines against the dark brown skin of her arm. Drusilla slides into the water, just as Amara approaches.

"Had enough of your admirers?" Drusilla remarks, raising her eyebrows in the cool, arch expression Amara has always loved.

"My dear friend," Amara replies, embracing her. "I have been longing to see you. Shall we swim for a while, then go warm up?"

"With pleasure," Drusilla says, gracing Amara with one of her most radiant smiles.

The pair of them start to swim leisurely lengths of the pool, side by side. Amara is aware of the other courtesans watching her friend with bitter jealousy. Drusilla is obviously aware too, looking unmistakably smug. Amara does not love Drusilla any less for knowing that her friend's affection has grown brighter the higher Amara has risen to prominence. Drusilla, like Amara, like Britannica, is one of life's born survivors. A woman who understands that being nice will not get you very far in a world that is anything but.

After a few turns in the pool, the pair of them climb out, shivering, and hurry into the bath complex's small, hot room to dry off, before moving to the more relaxing atmosphere of the warm room. The space is crowded, reverberating with the hubbub of female voices and laughter. Attendants slather Amara and Drusilla with oil then swiftly set to work scraping their skin with blunt, curved blades to remove all the grime. The two old friends stand close together, holding their limbs out to be cleansed and caressed, the deft movements of the metal both soothing and invigorating. The slaves work in silence while they chat.

"I suppose Pompeii must seem very dull to you, after Rome," Drusilla says, languidly stretching out a leg to allow the attendant to scrape the oil from her ankles and calves.

"Not at all!" Amara lies. "It is wonderful to be home. How is your adorable son, and Ampliatus?"

"Primus is six now and if I do say so myself, he is an especially clever boy. His father dotes on him."

Amara knows Drusilla is not referring to Primus's *real* father. Ampliatus adopted Primus, Drusilla's son from a previous relationship, as his sole heir. In Drusilla's former life as a courtesan, Ampliatus was Drusilla's patron before he took her as his wife. "This is wonderful to hear," Amara says. "You have protected your boy's future. I hope so much that Demetrius might do the same for Rufina after we are married."

Drusilla shakes off her attendant with a cry, and embraces Amara, whose own attendant tactfully stands back. "My darling! So many congratulations. Marriage to Demetrius! He is quite perfect for you. I always knew you would do *brilliantly* for yourself." Drusilla releases Amara, giving her a sidelong look. "Rather puts Rufus in his place too. Demetrius must be a *hundred* times richer."

"Not that wealth is everything," Amara says piously, and they both laugh. "We're planning to get married at his estate in Stabiae, just before the Saturnalia. I do hope that you will come and celebrate with us."

"But of course," Drusilla says. "I'm sure Ampliatus and Demetrius will become great friends, which will benefit us all."

Amara has her own doubts about how friendly her powerful patron will be to a portly, obsequious wine merchant from Pompeii, but smiles in seeming agreement. "It will be lovely to see Primus and Rufina together too. Although I suppose she will only be a very little child to him."

"How is your girl? Julia dotes on her, you know. Whenever I visit, she is fussing over Rufina."

The attendants are scraping the last remnants of oil from Amara's skin, which is reddened and glowing from the treatment. Their cleansing over, she and Drusilla go to sit together on one of the marble benches that line the room, the wall warm against their backs. "I am grateful to Julia, for all that she does. I sincerely hope, though, that I can take Rufina back to Rome with me."

"Is there any doubt of that?" Drusilla looks surprised.

"Demetrius is considering the idea."

"Darling," Drusilla says, firmly, "you must *make* him do what is best for you. He cannot marry a woman and abandon her child. It simply isn't done."

Amara is aware that Drusilla is enjoying taking on her old role as the courtesan of superior experience, but finds it does not irritate her. The familiarity is even soothing. "I am sure Demetrius will make the right choice. I certainly don't intend to let the matter drop. How did you persuade Ampliatus?"

"Ampliatus was eager for an heir, and my boy is very charming. Little persuasion was needed," Drusilla lowers her voice. "Husbands are tedious, more tedious than patrons if the truth be known. It is not as if you can keep them eager with the possibility of taking flight. But the security your child gains from a father is worth a little boredom."

"Do you miss the old life?" Amara asks, her voice also low.

"Yes and no," Drusilla concedes. "There are freedoms I miss. But really, as one gets older, feeling certain of the future means more than freedom. Ampliatus is dull, darling, but he is loyal and kind. I find these things more agreeable now than I might once have imagined."

"Demetrius is never dull," Amara says. "But he can be a little cold."

"Not cruel, like Rufus though, I hope?"

"No, never cruel."

"Well then," Drusilla shrugs. "If he is cold you can warm yourself in all the fine dresses and furs he buys you. Just as long as he spares some for your daughter. That's all that matters now. You've achieved everything else a woman like us could possibly hope to achieve." She reaches over to take Amara's hand. "I admire you."

"None of it would have been possible without your friend-ship," Amara says, squeezing Drusilla's fingers. She does not want to talk about the time she was nothing more than a brothel slave, but they both know what she means. It was Drusilla who encour-aged Amara to petition Rufus for her freedom, and Drusilla who facilitated his patronage.

"I like to think so," Drusilla says, looking pleased. "Of course, I will expect you to give me a place of honor at the wedding party."

Amara laughs at her friend's shamelessness, only partially dis-guised as a joke. "But of course."

After their bath, Amara and Drusilla spend some time basking in the sunshine of Julia's gardens alongside the pool, warm and relaxed after their soak. Attendants bring them hot wine spiced with honey and sage, which relaxes Amara further. Other women play ball games on the grass, and they watch idly, without feel-ing the urge to join in. The air is scented with lavender, billow-ing from the steam room. Amara has fetched Rufina from Julia's maid, and her daughter runs back and forth, fetching small peb-bles from the garden to show them, piling the stones up in a heap by the bench, her doll tucked under her arm.

"She will come to your wedding of course." Drusilla watches Rufina squat on the grass, poking at a beetle. "That is the perfect opportunity to introduce her to Demetrius. I can bring her, if Julia and Livia are staying in Stabiae ahead of the celebrations."

"Do you think an unexpected meeting is the best idea?" Amara thinks of her patron, of the way his mood can shift from good humor to ice, and wonders what he will make of the sight of another man's child on their wedding day.

"You will be his wife, not his concubine. You have rights, as does your daughter." Drusilla holds her chin high, as formidable in that moment as Queen Berenice of Judea. "Come! We will buy clothes for you both for the wedding." She rises from the bench. "It is not right for Rufina to be excluded from your life."

Amara also rises, sweeping her flowing tunic from the bench behind her. It is comforting to have Drusilla take charge like this, to allow her friend to make decisions on her behalf. In Rome Amara is obliged to be entirely self-reliant, and realizes how much she has missed the love and care of other women. Rufina toddles over when they call, but looks mutinous at the thought of leaving the garden to go shopping.

"I saw the street seller with his tray of sweet pastries earlier," Drusilla says with the practiced ease of a mother well used to bribes. "Perhaps he will still be there."

The suggestion is enough for Rufina to allow Amara to hoist her up onto her hip without protest. She clasps her small warm hands around her mother's neck, then starts to fiddle with one of Amara's curls that the hairdresser at Julia's baths just painstakingly set, yanking it free. The three of them head out onto the Via Veneria, Drusilla guiding Amara through the crowds with one hand on the small of her back. In the other, Drusilla holds Rufina's doll.

They reach the aviary, and Rufina tugs at her mother's tunic, wanting to stop and look. Cages of birds hang from beams and rafters, their shrill chatter spilling onto the street. Some, packed tightly into crates at the back, are destined for the dinner table, but others are for decoration. Starlings, magpies and even a pair of nightingales are on display: the expensive songbirds placed at the center of the shop in an ornate cage. Rufina stretches out to point at a magpie that hangs close to the street, designed to draw in customers with its shimmering blue-black feathers. A server from the shop hurries over, eager for a sale.

"A pet for your beautiful daughter?" the boy asks, picking up a pole to unhook the cage from the ceiling.

"No," Amara says. "We only stopped to look." The boy lowers the pole with a scowl.

"I like him," Rufina says as she continues to point at the bird, who stares back at her, head cocked, black eyes glittering. "Please."

"Maybe later," Amara says. "I will think about it."

They hurry onward, Rufina staring back forlornly at the birds, one chubby arm flapping over her mother's shoulder.

"We should go to Verecundus," Drusilla says. "He sells linen woven with threaded gold. And his felt is the finest in Campania."

Amara thinks of the grand shops in Rome—which sell luxuries infinitely more precious than any in Pompeii—but nods her agreement.

They can see the place long before they reach it; racks of colorful felts are stretched outside to dry, taking up much of the pavement and forcing people onto the steppingstones in the road to avoid them. A pungent smell like the coat of a wet dog wafts from the workshop, where slaves are busy sifting the wool and preparing the material over a furnace. Amara and Drusilla weave through the drying felt, passing the workshop, and make for the shop. The front wall is decorated by a fresco of Venus Pompeiana; the goddess is swathed in blue fabric, standing on the prow of a red boat drawn by four elephants.

Inside a woman sits yawning behind a counter, a wooden display cabinet filled with felt shoes beside her. Her jaw snaps shut as her two customers enter, and she rises, eyes flicking from the gold snake wrapped around Drusilla's arm to her face. She smiles in recognition. "Ladies, please be comfortable," she gestures at a bench facing the counter. "I do hope your dear husband Ampliatus is well? And your fine boy? How may I serve you?"

Amara and Drusilla sit down, Rufina squashed between them, now reunited with her doll. She swings her legs impatiently and Amara has to place a hand on her thighs to make her stop.

"Very well thank you," Drusilla replies. "Our best wishes to Verecundus, as always." She nods at Amara. "My friend Plinia Amara, freedwoman of the Admiral of the Roman Fleet, is to be married. I told her about your skill with gold thread. We will need bridal robes for both her and her daughter."

"Why of course," the woman bows. "An honor." She backs hurriedly away, then slips into a back room where more of the fabrics must be stored.

"Where's the sweet seller?" Rufina is kicking her heels again.

"If you behave well, perhaps we will find him," Drusilla says, crisply.

The shopkeeper returns with an armful of gleaming white linen, laying it out reverently on the counter. "Woven with gold," she says, beckoning them over to look.

Amara and Drusilla run the soft fabric carefully through their fingers. The material glitters as it catches the light, shot through with delicate gold thread. In spite of herself, Amara is impressed. "I will take it," she says, without asking the price. Demetrius has instructed her to spare no expense. "For me and for my daughter. Do you have something similar in saffron for the veil?"

The woman nods vigorously. "And it is decorated with flowers, also stitched in gold." A thud alerts them to the fact Rufina has been trying to reach for the felt shoes displayed on a table near the bench. The shopkeeper smiles to smooth over Amara's obvious embarrassment. "We have saffron slippers too, as your clever daughter has discovered."

Amara scoops Rufina up into her arms. "For you," she says, pointing at the white linen. "You will wear the same as Mummy."

"Shiny," Rufina says, pleased. "Like my magpie."

Drusilla gestures at Amara to hand Rufina over so that the shopkeeper can measure her for her robes. The woman runs the measuring string over Amara's body, while Amara watches Drusilla hold her daughter, bouncing her lightly, the same way she can remember Drusilla once doing with her own child, Primus, when he was the same age. Rufina plucks at the gold snake that digs into the flesh of Drusilla's upper arm, intrigued, and Drusilla laughs. "No, that's not for you."

The words are innocent enough, but Amara, who knows the history of the bracelet, feels a chill. Drusilla was gifted the gold snake by her old master while still a slave, a sign that she was his favorite concubine. A symbol of a life Amara hopes Rufina will never know.

"Now we can measure the little one. Perhaps stand her on the bench?"

Drusilla obliges and Rufina stands solemnly while she is measured, enjoying the attention. Given how much the child's mother is paying for all the fabric, the shopkeeper also indulges Rufina's whim to pretend to have her doll measured too. "You can see an example of our bridal slippers on the table," the woman says. "We also have them made to measure."

The slippers are dyed a beautiful golden yellow. Amara picks one up, bending the supple felt lightly in her fingers. It is the flaming saffron color associated with brides. Marriage is something she has not imagined for herself since childhood, and even then, it held little interest compared to her father's work as a physician. And after her family fell apart, Amara has been driven to survive, to seize whatever she can from life—whether money, love or status—before fate destroys her. Now Demetrius is offering her the safety she thought she craved above all else, so she cannot understand why the present moment does not bring her more happiness.

Amara becomes aware that the shopkeeper is staring, perhaps concerned she does not like the slipper. "It is beautiful," Amara says. "I will take a pair."

The woman nods, relieved.

"I told you that this was the right place to come." Drusilla is clearly pleased to have played such a pivotal role in the wedding preparations. It doesn't seem to matter to anyone in the shop that Amara's status as a freedwoman makes a mockery of all the ancient rites. She is hardly some innocent teenage girl, blushing at the prospect of her first sexual encounter with a man, but a courtesan who has already birthed a child. Still, like most people, the shopkeeper is probably just happy to take the money.

"Everything here is exquisite," Amara says, picking Rufina up and swinging her high into the air, so that she squeals with laughter. "My husband will be delighted with both of us."

Amara and her daughter return home without having managed to find the street seller hawking sweet pastries, much to Rufina's disgust. As soon as Amara sets her down in Julia's garden, Rufina charges off with surprising speed, heading for the orchard at the back. Amara jogs after her, exasperated. She stumbles on the paving stones near the pond, the jolt making her gasp, as Rufina darts through the gate toward the trees. The place is bare after the heat of summer. A few straggling figs are still ripening in the branches, but most of the fruit has been harvested, while the grass is dry and sharp, scratching at Amara's ankles. Rufina runs all the way to the end of the orchard, where the high wall separates Julia's land from the arena and its surrounding marketplace. There at the back, an unfamiliar garden has been dug out, rows of plants bunched together in crisscrossing stripes, flashes of color dotted in the green. A man is working on it, his tunic reflecting the glare of the afternoon sun. He is slim, but muscular. As he stands to greet Rufina, Amara realizes it is Philos. He looks more relaxed than she has seen him in the house, waving casually at her, before squatting down to allow Rufina to help him dig in a plant. Amara gets closer and sees that Pliny's scroll on plants is laid out carefully on a wooden tray.

"What are you working on?" Amara asks.

"I thought it would be good for Rufina to learn something of her grandfather's trade in medicinal herbs," Philos replies, without looking up. "There are several in the admiral's book that I had never heard about." The thought of Philos trying to pass on the knowledge of her own father to their daughter makes Amara too emotional to speak. She watches as he points out a plant to Rufina. "Which is this one? Can you remember?"

Rufina reaches out to touch the dark red leaves. "Black lace."

"Yes, black lace elder. And what do we use it for?"

Amara almost has to stop herself from replying, as she would have done as a child: *to cool a fever.*

"Fruit drink," Rufina says. "I like it!"

Philos smiles. "Well, you *can* flavor drinks with it. Shall we see what it says in the scroll?" Rufina pulls an unenthusiastic face, making him laugh. "No? Go off and play with Primi, then." His daughter darts away, running back to the house.

"Who's Primi?" Amara says, watching her go.

"Primigenia, one of Julia's maids," Philos replies. "She helps look after Rufina." He turns back to dig in the elder and Amara feels like an outsider in her own life.

"I love the garden," she says, squatting down too, so that they are level. "I love that you thought of my father." She wants to say more, but her heart hurts too much. She thinks of the garden she and Philos grew together at the house with the golden door—the place where they fell in love—and wonders if he is thinking the same.

"It's useful too," Philos says, his tone markedly less emotional than hers. "I have been moving some of the plants to Julia's kitchen garden, rotating them, to fit with the seasons." There is silence and he relents. "I know how much your father meant to you, and I know you are not here to teach Rufina everything you would like. But I remember a great deal of what you told me about your family."

"Thank you." She reaches over to look at Pliny's scroll. It has been set to the section on black lace elder—more, she suspects, for Rufina to see, than because Philos has been reading it. "I remember the garden we built before," she says, wanting him to remember, too.

"There's a letter for you in the house," Philos ignores the opening she has left him inviting greater intimacy. "From Rome. I imagine it's from Demetrius. I put it in Julia's study, along with all the accounts for the theater bars. I thought you would want to take a look at the takings and outgoings in more detail."

His tone is polite, even kind, but Amara understands she is being dismissed.

"I will do so," she says, rising to her feet. She walks to the house without looking back.

The atrium is empty save for the steward, who admits Amara without question. The house is unusually silent: Julia and Livia are out today, visiting friends at a villa north of Pompeii. In the study, a neat pile of accounts sits waiting on the desk, the sealed tablet from Rome on the top, just as Philos described. Amara sits down, glancing at the paintings Julia has chosen for this room. Piles of coins, heaped in a tottering mountain, and shelves of accounts. A reminder of the profit that follows hard work.

The tablet from Rome is heavy in her hands. She runs her thumb over the seal that is stamped with the hare from Demetrius's silver ring. A perfect match for the ring on her own finger, which he gave her. Amara breaks the wax to open the letter, hoping in spite of herself, to find some words of tenderness from her patron now that they are to be married. He starts with a formulaic greeting, then plunges into a coded political update. Their "friend" (Domitian) has left Rome, as their worst fears for his "health" (a plot) have been confirmed. *It is hoped time away from the city will cure his fever.* Amara is desperate to know more details—how did Titus react to the conspiracy, who else was implicated, how big a threat does Domitian still pose?—but she will have to wait for all this until she sees Demetrius again in person. He moves into suggestions for the wedding party, urging her to invite whoever she wishes from Pompeii, and to spend generously on the clothes. He says nothing of his feelings about their life together.

She reaches the end of the letter: *I hope you continue to miss me.* From another man, this might read as plaintive, but she knows Demetrius too well. He is expressing wry amusement at the affection she showed him when they parted; affection he was not willing or able to return. His lack of warmth leaves her with a dull feeling, added to her disappointment that he has not mentioned Rufina at all. Amara purses her lips. He did, at least, say she could invite whoever she wanted, so he will hardly be able to complain when Drusilla brings Rufina to Stabiae. Amara tries to picture her daughter not only at Stabiae, but in Rome, wanting to imagine how Demetrius might respond to her wayward, precocious child.

She finds herself unable to conjure up an image of them together. Instead, she sees Philos smiling at Rufina in the garden, his look of love and pride when Rufina recited the fable.

Amara sets down the letter and starts on the accounts. Counting money always soothes her. Ever since she escaped from Felix, it is how she measures her sense of security. The first tablet is tightly packed with Philos's neat script. Everything is in Greek, his written use of her native language fluent in a way his speech is not. Amara reads through his meticulous accounts, detailing all the expenditure and profit that has been accrued in the larger of the fast-food restaurants she owns. At the end, Philos has added his own thoughts about how to increase the revenue: a trial of hiring a hawker to sell food directly to theatergoers at their seats or as they mill about the entrance. The second tablet records similar details about the smaller business. Philos notes that it needs some repairs done to the painting work, which Amara will have to pay for. The last of his tablets is sealed. In this, Amara finds details of the protection money that has been extorted over the past two months, and descriptions of the men making the demands. Amara does not recognize Gallus, Paris or Thraso from the notes, but supposes Felix would not be so foolish as to send anyone she knows. A familiar cloying sense of nausea washes over her, at the thought of her old master. All these years later, he still has the ability to make her feel afraid. She has done so much to distance herself from her past at the brothel, to create the safest possible future for Rufina, and yet there Felix still lurks, a constant threat and reminder of her shame. Even if she escapes to Rome with her daughter, Amara still fears what Felix might do to Philos.

She looks again at the accounts Philos has kept, wondering if it is fanciful to imagine that there is more genuine care for her hidden within all the figures, than in Demetrius's letter. Philos's choice of Greek, his painstaking suggestions, his relentless attention to detail, all show his awareness of what matters to the woman he once loved. She picks up Demetrius's letter again. The expensive wood is sanded to a smoothness that is missing in the rougher working tablets Philos left her. She turns Demetrius's tablet over, running her fingers along the sides. A groove at the edge of the seal makes her pause. Amara peers more closely. There are signs that the seal has been sliced underneath, perhaps opened carefully with a knife before being reset. It was unwise of her to have opened it so thoughtlessly, now she cannot be sure. She sets the tablet down on the desk with an uneasy feeling.

In the atrium, Amara asks the doorman where she might find Primi, the maid caring for her daughter. To her surprise the man does not send her upstairs to Julia's private rooms, but instead points her in the direction of the service quarters, which lie at the back of Julia's complex. It is not a part of the house that is familiar to Amara. Like the veins beneath the surface of her skin, Amara is prone to forget the arteries that serve Julia's business, populated by slaves who keep the baths hot, the rooms clean and the guests served.

The main service corridor runs the whole length of the building, devoid of frescoes and painted in stark stripes of black and white. It is dark compared to the airy rooms that overlook the garden, yet Rufina is still easy to spot. She is playing with a slave child, a small boy who might be a similar age, the two of them racing Amara's expensive wooden horse on wheels up and down the passageway. Harassed servers, bearing platters and jugs to

take to the paying guests, have to dodge the shrieking pair, while
an attractive young woman in a rough tunic trots up and down
beside them—presumably Primigenia. Rufina looks delighted,
clasping the hand of the other child, laughing as he makes the
horse go faster.

Shame hits Amara, hot as steam from the baths. She does not
see two children playing. Instead, she sees her own humiliating
past, the choice she made to bear a slave's child, the hair's breadth
that separates her daughter's life from the boy's, and the hold
Felix still has over her family.

Her pain erupts as rage. "*Rufina!*"

Everyone stops, startled by her shriek, though the servants
quickly resume their tasks, heads bowed, not wishing to attract
the notice or wrath of Julia's powerful guest. Rufina stares at
her mother, mouth open in shock, and the boy cringes. Amara's
shame deepens.

"I have been looking everywhere for you," she says, her voice
gentler, approaching the frightened children and the now stony-
faced slave woman who is standing beside them. "I didn't know
where you were."

"Philos allows Rufina some time to play with my son and the
other slave children of the household," the woman says quietly,
staring at the floor to avoid meeting Amara's eyes. "We mean
no harm."

"Of course." Amara gives Rufina and the boy a forced smile.
"I'm sorry. Of course you should enjoy your new horse."

"You shouted," Rufina says, her lip quivering.

Amara bends down so that she can look in her daughter's eyes.
"I'm sorry," she says, kissing her quickly on the top of the head.
For everything, she thinks. Amara turns back to the slave woman,
noticing again how pretty she is. No, not pretty. Beautiful, with

huge dark eyes, and waves of black hair, pinned artlessly at her temples. Somehow the other woman's striking appearance makes Amara feel even more unmoored. "I will be in the gardens for the afternoon, if you can bring Rufina to me later."

Primigenia nods in acknowledgement, her expression blank, the same emotionless look Amara remembers Philos would give Rufus. Amara turns to leave, conscious of the silent slaves behind her, their judgment following her until she is out of sight.

12

*"How about reflecting that the person you call your slave traces his
origin back to the same stock as yourself, has the same good sky
above him, breathes as you do, lives as you do, dies as you do?"*

—Seneca, *Letters from a Stoic*

Amara waits in the small dim kitchen while Philos settles
Rufina to bed. Her presence downstairs is an admission of
defeat. Rufina had been happy enough to allow her mother to sing
to her, to tell her a story, but when it came to saying goodnight,
she insisted upon Philos and whatever tender ritual is habitual to
the pair of them. Amara can hear the low murmur of his voice
now, but cannot make out the words. A single oil lamp burns on
the table before her. It is glazed red with a naked figure of Venus
curled upon it, the flames gilding the goddess. Amara finds her
mind wandering back to Menander, her first love, a potter's slave
who no doubt still toils in his master's store a few streets away.
The thought fills her with sadness. Perhaps nothing marks the
passage of time as inexorably as the loss of love.

A creak from the stairs alerts her to Philos's return.

"I'm sorry she was so defiant," he says, as he steps down into
the kitchen. "I've been told three is a particularly trying age."

"It's no matter."

There is an awkward pause until Philos speaks again. "Perhaps you will be spending the evening with Julia?"

"Julia is away until tomorrow, but I can spend time with some of the other guests if you prefer." Amara goes to rise from her stool but Philos holds up his hands.

"Please don't leave because of me. I can make myself scarce."

Amara looks around the tiny flat. "How?" She raises her eyebrows in amusement. "By hiding in a cupboard?" Philos smiles, and for a moment, they are drawn closer by the absurdity of their situation. "Please," she says. "Stay with me."

They stare at one another. His gray eyes are steady, never leaving hers. Amara is used to the close presence of Demetrius, a man she cares for deeply but has never desired. Philos is different. He is decades younger than her patron, his physical vitality obvious, while his quiet self-containment exerts its own pull. It has always been this way. Philos is enslaved, and yet he holds himself apart, with a dignity that has never been degraded by the physical power others hold over him. A memory returns to her unbidden: the feel of his chest as she runs her fingers along his skin, and the scarring from the branded words that mark it. *Disobedient.* Amara looks away, fearful of the unexpected strength of her desire. "Please," she repeats. "Stay."

"As you wish." Philos sits opposite her at the table.

Now that Amara's memories have started to torment her, she can scarcely meet his eye. The urge to reach over and touch him, to feel his arms around her again, is so overwhelming that she instinctively clasps her hands together, knuckles whitening. "You always write the accounts in Greek."

"Of course."

"Your script is flawless."

"Unlike my spoken Greek, you mean?" Philos laughs. "I'm well aware I speak your language like a bumpkin."

Amara laughs too at his ridiculous choice of word, as he surely intended. "Well, maybe you don't speak it like a native of Attica." Philos is staring at her again. Her cheeks flush but he does not pay her the courtesy of looking away. "What have you decided to do about Felix?"

"Britannica and I went to visit him."

"You did *what?*"

"We wanted to warn him. If he doesn't stop, Stephanus will have to take the matter into his own hands. I don't need all those deaths on my conscience."

Philos sighs heavily, running both hands over his face. Amara can tell he is exasperated. "You didn't tell Felix this?"

"Of course not! But I had to try, for the sake of Victoria and the children . . ." Amara stops, remembering her former friend's abject unhappiness, the violence Victoria is perhaps enduring now.

"I hope you know what you're doing," Philos shakes his head. "What about your letter from Demetrius? Has he agreed to take Rufina back with you? That would solve most of our difficulties. If she is safely out of the way, Felix matters so much less."

Amara remembers the broken seal and feels a stab of suspicion. *Surely Philos has not spied on her correspondence?* The thought is quickly followed by guilt. *Philos would never do such a thing.* "No," she says. "Demetrius didn't mention her at all."

"But *why?* Does he not love you?" As soon as he has asked the question, Philos seems to realize how inappropriate it is. "Forgive me, I should not have asked . . ."

"I don't know," Amara interrupts. "I don't know if he loves me, or if I am only useful to him. He has my gratitude regardless. And I believe he has a certain fondness for me, at the least."

"Of course. That is not what I meant. It is obvious he has a high regard for you."

"What does that matter? If his regard does not protect our daughter." Amara feels a wave of hopelessness. "What will any of this have mattered, if I cannot make her life better than ours?" Neither of them speaks, aware of the choices she has already made, the sacrifice of their own relationship. "I saw Rufina playing with one of the slave children today," she says to change the subject. "A little boy."

"That would be Servius." Philos smiles, with an expression of unguarded warmth Amara remembers he once reserved for her. "They are always so sweet together."

Amara thinks of the slave woman, the way she averted her face. "His mother seemed very pretty."

"Primi? I suppose she is, yes."

Something in the cautious way Philos says the other woman's name sets off a flare of jealousy in Amara's chest, as sudden as the desire she felt for him earlier. "Do you care for her?"

"What?" Philos is startled by the question.

"You would be entitled to. It's not my business. I didn't mean . . . I wasn't suggesting . . ." Amara trails off, hating herself.

"Do you really think I would risk our daughter's safety by seducing a woman in Julia's household? Is that who you think I am?"

Amara burns with mortification. "No."

"I have already apologized to you, Amara. For my carelessness with your life before. I regret it deeply. Nothing would persuade me to repeat the same mistake with another woman."

"I don't regret it," she says. "I loved you."

"We cannot have this conversation." Philos rises from his stool, ready to leave the room. Amara jumps to her feet, intercepting him before he can escape, catching hold of his hand. He stares at her, his lips parted. For a moment she imagines he will return the clasp of her fingers and pull her in closer, that he will kiss her, but instead he takes back his hand, holding it up in a gesture of denial. "No."

Philos looks like a stranger. Where once she could read his expressions so easily, now she cannot tell if the passion lighting his face is from desire, or anger. Embarrassment floods her body, the scalding heat of it making her blush. "Forgive me." She twists away. "I did not mean . . ."

Philos lays his hand on her arm to stop her from speaking, his touch as gentle as she remembers. "You know we cannot do this. Some things cannot be undone." The kindness in his voice does not take away its sting.

"I know." The words stick like clay to her mouth. Resignation is a weight Amara has long carried, yet it still feels heavy. Why should she expect Philos to love or desire her still, after all she has done? She turns and walks up the stairs, alone, to their daughter.

The sea breeze is sharper in the morning, and the noise of peoples' voices, even the incessant shouts of the hawkers, carries an air of optimism that is lacking in the later heat of the day. Amara pauses on the threshold of the street. Somewhere, a woman is singing. The sound reminds her painfully of Victoria; the singer has the same distinctive lilt to her voice. It could almost *be* Victoria. For the first time in years, Amara is taken back to her mornings at the brothel, the vividness of the memory making her stop. She closes her eyes for a moment, willing the images to pass, but instead she hears the sound of her friends' laughter, remembering how it always brought a glimmer of hope for the new day, however dark the night before. The smell of the oil lamps, the damp of the stone beds, the sense of powerlessness—it all comes back to her in an unwelcome rush.

Amara steps out onto the pavement, pulling her thin cloak tighter over her shoulders, shrugging off the past. She tells herself she is just shaken up from last night. After Philos's rejection she feels an overwhelming need for some time alone outside the confines of the complex, although Julia frowned just now at her refusal of a maid to accompany her. Primigenia comes again into her mind; the girl really is unusually attractive. It is hard to believe Philos has not been tempted, that he has had no lovers at *all* the past three years. Not that it is her business now. He made that perfectly obvious.

The sweet-pastry seller is out on the pavement, and Amara stops to buy a honeyed bun for her daughter. She tucks the treat into the small bag she is carrying, her mood softening. This morning Rufina had climbed into the bed, snuggling into Amara's body, clamping a small proprietorial hand around her mother's neck. Amara had scarcely dared to breathe; the affection was so unexpected. The warmth of Rufina, the baby scent of her hair, took Amara back to the first months of her daughter's life, when such closeness was something she took for granted. Even now her heart feels tight, the memory of love so overwhelming.

She loiters outside the aviary, wondering if she ought to buy the magpie her daughter wanted as a pet. The glossy feathered creature ruffles its wings, seeming to sense it is being watched. It cocks its head to stare back at her. There is a look of unmistakable intelligence in those black eyes. Amara can see why the bird caught Rufina's attention. Though it would make more sense to wait until they get to Rome, rather than try and transport the creature all that way. While she is contemplating the caged bird, Amara becomes aware of someone standing behind her shoulder. She sidesteps, to allow them to get a better view, and the other customer steps with her. Fear makes her pause, then she turns, determined to face whoever it might be. It is not one person, but two. Victoria and Beronice.

The three former she-wolves stare at each other, Amara in her priceless blue cloak, the others in the rough, everyday clothes of working women. Nobody says anything. It is Victoria who finally breaks the silence.

"We were saying what a fine day it is," she exclaims, her voice high and false. "It made me want to sing. Just perfect for three old friends to take a turn around the palaestra, don't you think?"

So the voice earlier was more than a memory. Instinctively, Amara steps back. She had expected Felix to have her watched, but not like this. It is an extra turn of the knife for him to use her former friends against her. She smothers the urge to flee and forces herself to calculate the risks as calmly as possible. Causing a scene would be unpleasant. She has no idea what the other two might start shrieking if she were to accuse them of anything, and at least the Palaestra is a public space. Also, she is now anxious to know what they have to say.

"I suppose it *is* a pleasant morning for a walk," Amara says. Victoria inclines her head in answer, gesturing in the direction of the palaestra, and the three women set off, as if they were indeed all still good friends. "You were lucky to catch me today," Amara says, her voice still light, although her body is tense and ready to fight.

"Oh no, not lucky. We've been watching the place every day since you got back," Victoria says. "We didn't think Drusilla would be as pleased to see us. Nice little shopping trip you two had yesterday. Was that a bridal veil?"

Amara thinks of how much Victoria always loved clothes, and knows how jealous she must have felt, spying on the visit to Verecundus. She ignores Victoria's question. "How strange that I didn't see you."

"Is it though?" Victoria shoots her a glance, and for the first time, Amara sees a flash of Felix.

"I'm surprised Gallus could spare you," Amara says to Beronice.

Her other friend, always gullible, cannot help stumbling into old habits. "Oh yes well, obviously he misses me, but he understands, after all—"

"*Beronice*," Victoria hisses. "Don't be a fucking fool."

"No need to fucking *shout*," Beronice snaps back. "Just because you're married to the boss, doesn't mean you get to lord it over everyone."

The echoes of their former lives, and their former friendships, have soured. Amara thinks of those who are missing, of Dido and Cressa, and feels an overwhelming sense of loss. Her grief is quickly followed by anger. "If you hadn't betrayed me," she says to Victoria, her smile at odds with her bitterness, "we might all have visited the shop together."

"Oh, *of course*," Victoria says. "You'd have taken us to Rome with you! We believe *that* story, don't we, Beronice?"

"I wouldn't have left Gallus, anyway," Beronice says, stubbornly misunderstanding, and Amara feels a surge of exasperated affection. All the changes in the world, and the one constant remains Beronice's loyalty to her worthless man.

They reach the Palaestra, Pompeii's enclosed public park and exercise grounds, and make their way through the arch. Amara's heartbeat quickens. She hopes Felix will not be waiting, that she will have no cause to regret her impulsive decision to come here. Perhaps she should have insisted on stopping at Julia's for a servant to accompany them and keep watch. A gaggle of schoolboys are having a class in the colonnade as they pass, the tutor pointing his cane at one quivering boy, demanding an answer. The women walk by, their soft shoes almost silent on the stone.

"So what is it then?" Amara says, unable to bear the weight of expectation any longer. "Why are we here?"

"We want you to leave us alone," Victoria says.

"*Me* to leave *you* alone?" Amara is so angry she cannot even lower her voice.

"Victoria says you brought the Briton to the Wolf Den," Beronice says. "Why would you do that, after what happened last time?"

Over Beronice's shoulder, Amara can see the exercise ground, young men running circuits on the track. She doubts any of them have the strength of Britannica. Not for the first time, Amara regrets refusing her friend the chance to kill Felix when he lay at her feet. "How else am I to defend myself? When Felix won't leave my businesses alone?"

"He's not asking that much," Victoria scoffs. "You can afford it."

Her goading tone makes Amara so furious she raises her hand to slap her, and Beronice steps between them, anxious to avert a fight. "You *can* afford it, though," Beronice says in a wheedling voice. "And Felix demands much more from most of the other bars he's protecting."

"Why should I pay him a single penny? A man who has done nothing but hurt and humiliate me? Who continues to threaten my child?"

"You act like it was personal back then," Victoria shrugs. "All masters fuck their slaves. So what? You have a richer man to fuck now. Go and enjoy *him* in Rome. You ought to be grateful Felix left you to get on with your life."

"Grateful?" Amara gapes at Victoria, too astounded even for anger.

"Yes, *grateful*," Victoria says, spitting out the word. "Look at you and look at us. How fucking rich are you? Why should you have so much more than we do? You aren't any better than the rest of us. You don't even have to work anymore! Felix barely takes *anything* from you. And you begrudge giving us even that."

All the layers of respectability that Amara has wrapped around herself with as much painstaking care as the folds of her expensive robes, fall away. She is back in the Wolf Den, enraged by any attempt to confine her. "Don't you fucking try that with me," she says, seizing Victoria by the shoulders. "I risked everything to free you, gave you every possible chance. And you betrayed me. If you are in the shit now, it's nobody's fault but your own."

Beronice moves between them again, forcing Amara to let go. "For fuck's sake, people are staring!" Amara glances around. Passersby are indeed giving them a wide berth, noses wrinkled in distaste. In the grip of her fury, Amara can barely restrain herself from shouting at them too. She feels someone take her hand. It is Beronice. Amara looks down at their inter-linked fingers in surprise, the sight jolting her out of her anger. The gesture belongs to the intimacy of their past. "I know this is hard for you," Beronice says. "I know Victoria was a bitch about things." Amara snorts at the understatement, but Beronice plows on. "We all loved each other once though, didn't we? I didn't hate you for buying Victoria, and not me. I still loved you. And you *know* Felix. He's never going to stop. But it's just a pride thing now. He's never going to bring you down Amara, he's not that stupid. Don't you think he realizes that would be the end of him too? Just let him have his pride, let him imagine he's got one up on you. Pay him the protection money, and he won't do any worse." Beronice takes Amara's silence as encouragement and squeezes her hand tighter. "You know that you've won. Felix knows it too. He just can't admit it. And I'm not asking you to do this for him, or even for *her*," she says, jerking her head at Victoria. "But couldn't you do it for me? I have children now too. A girl and a boy. I just want a quiet life with my family. It's all I've ever wanted."

"You have children?" Beronice hesitates at Amara's question, perhaps worried she has made herself vulnerable to an enemy. Her obvious fear affects Amara more than anything else Beronice could have said. "I'm happy for you and Gallus," she says quickly. "Children are precious. I just want Felix to leave *my* child alone. I don't wish harm to anyone else's family."

"I understand," Beronice says, looking relieved. "But you must know Felix won't back down—he never does. So can't you just give us this? You pay him something for his pride, and everyone's family is left well alone."

"How can I be sure he won't act against me?"

"He won't. I *promise* you he won't."

Amara turns to Victoria. It is painful to look at her. There was a time when Victoria's face, now riven with suspicion and spite, was one of those Amara loved best in the world, when Victoria's strength and vitality seemed to be what held them all together in the brothel. Memories return to Amara in a rush: Victoria laughing, her voice ringing with defiance, Victoria managing a customer nobody else wanted to risk, Victoria with her arms around Dido, Victoria killing the man who would have taken Amara's life, Victoria beaten by Felix, the master she could never seem to stop loving, whatever he did. Amara remembers the look of joy on Victoria's face when she first stepped into the house with the golden door and the pain in her eyes when she left. The woman before her is no longer her friend, Amara knows this. Yet she still feels driven to ask the question that has tormented her ever since Felix began his blackmail campaign. "Why?"

"Why what?" Victoria snaps, although they both know what Amara means.

"I understood why you went back to Felix, even if I couldn't forgive you. But to tell him about Philos. To put my child at risk. Why do that to me?"

Amara sees the shame in Victoria's eyes, and for a moment thinks she might be given an answer that will relieve the crushing weight of hatred between them. Perhaps Victoria will say Felix beat it out of her, or even admit that she was jealous as well as afraid. All Amara wants is some acknowledgment of the magnitude of the betrayal. Victoria turns her face away. "He's my husband."

Beronice exclaims in annoyance. "Can't you give her more than *that*?"

"It doesn't matter." Amara turns her back on Victoria, speaking only to Beronice. "I will do what I can to protect you, Gallus and your children. I promise. But if Felix strikes any harder against me, I will have to retaliate, so you need to make sure *his wife* keeps him in check." She leans forward to embrace Beronice, briefly holding her old friend close, then walks off. Amara knows the she-wolves are watching her, their eyes burning a mark between her shoulder blades as she leaves the Palaestra. But she does not look back.

It is the height of the morning visiting hour when Amara returns to Julia's house. She is surprised to find her daughter has taken center stage. Rufina sits perched on Julia's knee, clutching the miniature Julia doll from Rome. A number of tenants are paying their respects to their landlady, milling in the atrium, and Amara's daughter is enjoying the vicarious attention. Scenes of the Forum surround them, the painted figures increasing the sense of a crowd. Behind Julia stands a line of equestrian statues, exactly like those in the colonnade that leads to the fish market, while opposite Amara, a man hands out painted bread, hoping to win election.

A hush falls. Julia is encouraging Rufina to recite one of the fables Philos has taught her. Rufina's piping voice rings out as she makes her way through the story of the foolish grasshopper. When she reaches the end, everyone claps, adding to Rufina's delight. Amara thinks of Demetrius, of the glittering ants, grasshoppers and foxes that line his walls. Fables are the stories of children and slaves; both Philos and Demetrius had the lowliest of beginnings, their enslaved mothers teaching them the homeliest tales, although only one has managed to rise from the gutter into which he was born.

"You must be so proud of her," murmurs the woman beside Amara, pointing at Rufina. It is the painter's wife who rents one of Julia's apartments above the bar. Amara cannot remember her name.

Amara forces a smile, still feeling strained after her confrontation with the she-wolves. She watches Julia shower kisses on her daughter's plump cheeks, while Rufina beams at the affection. "I am grateful to Julia for raising her so well." Amara knows Rufina's father Philos will never receive any credit for all he has done for her. She thinks back to last night and her agitation increases. *How could she have put Philos in that position? How could she have been so selfish?* Shame distracts her, so that she realizes her companion has said something else, without knowing what.

"I said congratulations on your betrothal!" the woman repeats.

"Oh! Thank you!"

The porter is letting in another visitor and Amara turns idly to see who it is. All her senses, which she was trying so hard to relax, flood with panic. Her former patron Rufus is standing on the threshold. He is stouter than the last time she saw him, and his resemblance to his father Hortensius is growing, though he still has traces of the boyish charm that first won her over—before she knew him better.

"Rufus!" Julia exclaims, with a charming smile, as if nothing could have pleased her more than his presence. "What a joy to see you! Oh! You must come with us into the garden." She rises and the tenants fall back, everyone understanding that a much more important guest has arrived. Julia catches Amara's eye, a sign for her to follow, and hoists Rufina onto her hip. The four of them traipse out into the colonnade, Julia guiding them toward the richest room that overlooks the garden, the one decorated with golden figures of the muses. Amara allows Rufus and Julia to walk ahead of her, giving herself a moment to recover before she is obliged to speak to her daughter's legal father. They settle themselves onto the plump-cushioned chairs.

"It is very good to see you," Amara murmurs, lowering her eyes modestly, hoping he will not see her trembling hands.

"The admiral wrote to me with news of your engagement," Rufus says, stiffly. "Many congratulations."

"We're all delighted, darling," Julia enthuses. "What a way to celebrate the Saturnalia!"

"You have not yet borne him children?" Rufus looks awkward, and much as she dislikes him, Amara understands his bluntness is more through embarrassment than unkindness.

"No. Though I pray to the gods they might favor us."

There is a pause while all the adults silently contemplate Demetrius's advanced age and the unlikelihood of him ever becoming a parent. Rufina is standing, clutching Julia's hand and staring shyly at the man she thinks is her father. Her tiny fingers fiddle with her *lunula*, the silver necklace Julia gave her that signifies her freeborn status. Rufus has not yet looked at the child he believes to be his own. "My lovely wife is expecting our second," he says, with crashing insensitivity.

"Congratulations darling, we will all wish dear little Sabina a safe delivery," Julia says.

Amara nods in agreement, laying her hands over her heart to signify sincerity. She has never seen Rufus's teenage bride but Julia has told her enough. A meek, silent creature, somewhat prone to sulking, but rich enough to be treated well by the family.

Julia gently pushes Rufina forward, though she does not let go of the child's hand. "Your Rufina was just impressing my guests with her recitations of Aesop. Would you care to hear her?" Rufina gazes up at Rufus with Philos's wide gray eyes. She looks so like her *real* father that Amara feels herself go cold. How can Rufus not notice?

"Of course," Rufus says, without enthusiasm. He finally looks at the child he believes to be his daughter. His face softens slightly. "Go on, little one."

"Hurry along, darling," Julia says as Rufina stands mute, twisting her skirt between her fingers. "Your father is a very important man in Pompeii, you know."

For the first time Rufina looks to her mother for encouragement, and Amara smiles warmly at her. "Go on, my love. You are so good at it."

Still clutching Julia's hand, Rufina solemnly begins her recitation of the fable, more nervous than she was earlier in the atrium. They all listen, nodding encouragement, and she grows bolder.

"Excellent." Rufus smiles at Rufina before looking back up at Julia. "She seems really rather clever."

"She reminds me so much of *you* as a child," Julia sighs fondly. "Really? I can't say I see it," he says, doubtful. "She looks far more like her mother, I think."

"She's the absolute image of you as a small boy," Julia insists. "I should know, darling; I remember you back then! Oh, the joys of being old!" They all laugh politely.

One of the slaves arrives with refreshments. "I can't stay long," Rufus says, although he helps himself to a handful of figs. Sensing his reluctance to leave, Julia encourages him to talk about his own life—always Rufus's favorite topic—and his hopes for the upcoming elections. Rufina retreats to a corner, away from the adults' attention, whispering to her doll in some imaginary game. Amara says little, but smiles prettily whenever Rufus addresses her. Gradually, he relaxes under the women's flattering attention and even seems to be enjoying himself.

"I had better go," he says at last, after an hour has passed, helping himself to one more fig before he stands.

"I do hope you will visit us again soon," Julia declares, as if bereft at his parting. She gets up to see him out, but Rufus stops her.

"Don't disturb yourself," he says, taking her hand and kissing it. "I should like to speak to Amara for a moment, in any case." Amara rises and walks with her former lover through the colonnade, heart quickening, wondering what he might have to say. "If your husband cares to adopt the child," Rufus begins, without looking at her. "I will have no objection. In fact, it would please me." He frowns, perhaps realizing how cold he sounds. "I don't mean to be heartless. I only mean I am sure Demetrius will wish to build his own family, and it might be easier for him to adopt your daughter and give her his name, than to face reminders of another man's prior ownership of his wife."

"Demetrius is a freedman and I am a freedwoman," Amara says quietly, as they reach the door. "He is not sentimental about my past. Although I appreciate your generosity, as always."

Rufus has the decency to look embarrassed. "Well, the offer still stands." He bows to his former girlfriend. Then he turns and walks swiftly out onto the street.

13

"Here love will be wise"
—Herculaneum graffiti

The road rises as Britannica and Amara head out of Pompeii, under the arch and onto the road that leads to Stabiae. The former she-wolves walk together side by side, a couple of male slaves from the barracks following a little behind, although the slaves are more for show. Amara cannot imagine the gladiator ever needing their protection. Britannica carries herself like no other woman Amara has ever met. The Briton moves as if she has no fear, as if she has never been subjected to violence, or dragged halfway across the world to be penned in a brothel, even though Amara knows Britannica has endured all these things. When the pair of them worked in the Wolf Den and were expected to pick up customers, Amara would always dread "fishing" with Britannica. The Briton's obvious hostility was a threat to their safety, the way she scowled at men, as if daring them for a fight. Now she has lost that outward aggression, and her stride has an easy confidence, but still the threat of her violence remains.

They take a smaller road that branches off toward the river. This stretch of countryside outside Pompeii is full of vineyards and larger villas, their roofs just visible above the high brick walls.

All the grapes have been harvested now, and the vines that Amara glimpses through an open archway are bare of fruit. Men are working among the crop, tying and pruning the vines. A small bonfire burns nearby, its blue smoke rising and clouding the air like incense.

They travel further from the city, the road shaded by umbrella pines. Amara can hear the chatter of starlings in the branches above, and catches a glimpse of their dark, speckled bodies. She thinks of the shop magpie in its cage, with nothing but a dusty street to stare at. The image makes her feel melancholy, or perhaps it is another memory that taints this walk with sadness. It is not the first time the two former she-wolves have walked this road. They came here once before, to celebrate the Nemoralia. Only, that time, Victoria was with them.

"Beronice has a good heart," Britannica says. "Even though she is fool."

They have been talking of Amara's meeting with her old friends the day before. Britannica's harsh judgment is wholly unsurprising.

"I don't know that her advice was so foolish," Amara replies. "I have been thinking that maybe she has a point about Felix, that he will never give up. It could be safer for everyone if I continue to pay. As long as that is where it stops."

"True that he will not give up. Only his death will free you."

Amara sighs heavily. "Killing Felix is like burning down the prison that traps you inside. You might never escape what you've started."

"You have too much fear."

"And you have none," Amara laughs. "Between us, perhaps there is a balance."

"I am often afraid," Britannica says. "Fear is like an enemy you see on the road. You raise your hand to him, you greet him, and you continue on your way."

"You don't fight him?" Amara asks amused. "That's unusual for you."

Britannica smiles, exposing her missing teeth. "Sometimes I fight him, yes. I know *you* fight him many times. In the Wolf Den." Sensations of her life at the brothel return to Amara. Its violence, its fear, and above all her rage, which burned white-hot in the darkness. "*This.*" Britannica seizes Amara's hand, gazing at her with understanding. Something of Amara's anger must have shown on her face. "This is what will save you. Always."

"Anger?"

"In my language, it has another word. It is fire that burns within. I use it in the arena when I fight."

Amara does not let go of Britannica's hand. "What is your country like?"

"Home," Britannica says. "It is home."

In her mind's eye, Amara sees her old street in Aphidnai: the well at the corner, the overhanging balcony of her parents' house shading the pavement below and the potted plants trailing around the doorway. *Home.* It is both unbearably vivid and impossible to reach. "I understand."

"Also, it has better weather," Britannica grimaces. "More rain, less sun."

"You like the rain?"

"I like the fog. When it is rising, the enemy not see you. Here, everything too hot, too bright, no gray."

Amara thinks of Livy's description of the battle of Trasimene. The men slaughtered in the mist, unable to see the hoards that descended on them. It is not difficult to imagine Britannica embroiled in such a scene. "Were you a warrior, back then?"

"My whole family is fighters. All dead now. I am the last. My brother, the older one, he teach me what to say before battle." Britannica murmurs something in her own harsh language, then frowns, obviously trying to think of how to say it in Latin. "It not end here," she says, although from the dissatisfied look on her face, something must have been lost in the translation. "He means you not die *now*. One day you die, but you tell yourself, not *there*."

Amara nods, understanding the gist, disappointed that Britannica's words have lost some of their meaning and their power.

They arrive at the shrine to Diana, the reason for their visit. Diana, Artemis, Lucina—the merciless goddess of many names who triumphs in the hunt and guides women through the violence of childbirth—is standing by the river. Her statue seems diminished in the blazing sun, perhaps, as a moon goddess, her potency is better felt at night. Amara had Diana painted on the wall of the house with the golden door, wearing Dido's face, the goddess's finger pointing in vengeance at Acteon, the unfortunate man who had dared to see her naked. In Amara's imagination Acteon became Felix, enduring the revenge she longed to inflict.

Britannica walks toward the riverbank, carrying the offering she has brought to ask for victory in the arena. It is a clay figurine of a stag representing the opponent she wishes to defeat. She lays it at the feet of the goddess, while Amara ties a written prayer to the branches of a nearby tree, where it joins the other rolls of fabric that flutter in the breeze. They are a strange fruit. Some have rotted in the rain. Amara squints up into the branches, wondering if her own prayer, or that of Victoria, still lingers here from their long ago visit.

At the statue, Britannica is still standing with her head bowed. Amara glances down the road, where the slaves are waiting, then back to the gladiator. It is so unusual to see Britannica with her face down, the pose is uncharacteristically vulnerable. Fear strikes Amara then, as sudden as lightning. *What if Britannica dies in the arena?* Amara makes the sign of the evil eye, visualizing the thought burning to ash, not wanting to bring any bad luck to the site of her friend's prayers.

When she has finished, Britannica turns to leave, but Amara stops her. "Shall we wait awhile? We have so little time together these days."

Britannica nods and they go to sit at one of the marble benches facing the shine, a spot for travelers to rest under Diana's protection. "We come here when you carry Fighter," Britannica says, patting her own stomach. "The goddess make her fierce. She likes to watch me train."

"Philos takes Rufina to the barracks?" Amara is a little surprised.

"To see me, yes, he brings Fighter," Britannica says. "You not take Philos to Rome?"

"I can't."

"He is loyal to you. I not meet the other one. The one in Stabiae."

It takes Amara a moment to realize that Britannica is comparing Philos to Demetrius, as if there were a choice to be made between them. "I am not free to serve any other man than my patron," she says, a little annoyed at the implication that perhaps *she* is not loyal, unlike Philos.

Britannica shrugs. "As I say, I not meet him. Maybe a good man to raise Fighter, maybe not."

Amara glances again toward the slaves, still standing a safe distance away on the road, the roar of the river ensuring they are well out of earshot. "Philos is enslaved. I have no choice."

"I always like him. Loyal."

Britannica is staring at the river with a stubborn look on her face. She can be infuriating in this mood, but Amara is determined not to have a row so close to Britannica's time in the arena. "I hope he will be safe from Felix, when I have left." She cannot bear to add *when I have taken Rufina away from him.*

"As long as I live, he is safe."

"Thank you." Amara reaches over to take her hand. "When you are victorious, we should come back here, to give thanks."

"Yes, we come," Britannica says. "Also, I am promised to worship at the Temple of Fortuna. The day of the fight."

"I said a prayer for you, to the Fortuna in Rome. She looked like you, I thought."

"Like me?" Britannica grins. "How?"

Amara smiles. "She was holding her cornucopia of plenty as if it were a weapon. To knock down anyone who annoyed her."

The two she-wolves laugh, their voices carried out toward the sea on the rush of the river.

14

"Methe, slave-girl of Cominia from Atella, loves Chrestus.
May Pompeian Venus be dear to them both and
may they always live in harmony."
—Pompeii graffiti

Julia and Livia's dressing room is filled with early morning sunlight. The sound of birdsong and the scent of lavender, wafting in through the open window, soothe Amara's senses. Her makeup is being applied by one of the household maids. The girl is not as skilled as Daphne or Iris in Rome; she is dabbing on far too much of the malachite eyeshadow. Amara watches her stab the brush into the carved seashell full of powder, sending out puffs of green, grateful it is not her own brush the woman is ruining. The girl styling her hair is not much better, though she has the opposite flaw, barely touching Amara's curls, as if the tresses might burn her. Not that anyone would guess Amara's discontentment from her serene expression. She is far too polite to criticize her friend's servants.

"I love that look on you, darling," Julia remarks. She is relaxing on a couch with Livia, the pair of them already made-up for the day. "Much more youthful than all those tight curls piled on top like a beehive."

"I'm amazed any of the women in Rome can hold their heads up," Livia agrees. "A ridiculous fashion." Nobody could accuse Amara's two friends of fussing too much about their appearance; they barely cover their skin with paste. Neither seem to have any angst about aging in spite of the cruel judgments heaped on any woman who dares to pass the age of thirty-five. It's as if they do not care for men's opinions at all.

Out of the corner of her eye, Amara sees Livia take Julia's hand. It is a common gesture of affection between women, one she has shared with friends countless times, but Amara has long suspected the love between Julia and Livia is something more. It would be typical of them both to make no effort to hide a forbidden relationship, and rely instead on the slow wits of men. Although perhaps nothing is safer than facing down the risk of infamy and social exclusion by keeping your "crime" in plain sight. After all, Amara lived openly with Philos for a while. The thought makes her feel sad for herself, yet love her friends even more.

The women's companionable silence is broken by Julia's steward, who calls out to his mistress from the doorway.

"Come in," Julia drawls. "We are all quite respectable."

The man steps inside, bowing to Amara. "The dressmaker from Verecundus is here with your robes, and a request for payment."

"Please tell the woman I will be down shortly."

"How exciting, darling!" Livia exclaims. "I hope you will bring them upstairs to show us."

"Of course." Amara gestures at the girl to finish pinning her hair. The other maid holds up the mirror for Amara to see. She blinks. The green really is too much. Amara wipes her index finger hard over each eyelid, then stubs it on a cloth to get rid of the green. The line of kohl is now smudged, but at least she does not look like a parrot.

Amara touches Julia affectionately on the shoulder as she passes. "I will be back in a moment."

She walks through the colonnade to her own flat, squinting at the sudden darkness. The place is empty. Ever since her foolishness the other night, she and Philos have been avoiding one another. The chest in the storeroom where Amara keeps her money is locked, its key hidden in a pot in the kitchen. She rummages in a cupboard for the pot and then tips the key out onto her palm. Not the most original hiding place, but it is hard to imagine robbers breaking into the sanctuary of Julia's complex. Amara opens the chest, counting out the money she agreed at the shop into a cheap cloth bag.

On her approach to the atrium, Amara sees a small crowd has gathered near the half-open door. Rufina is running around the woman from the dress shop, reaching for the wrapped-up clothes, and with her is Servius, the slave child. Philos and Primigenia are standing together, trying to calm the children. Amara stops. The sight hurts more than a physical blow. They look like a family.

"My mommy is going to be a bride!" she hears Rufina shout. "And I have a pretty dress too!"

"Rufina! Behave yourself!" Amara's voice is cold, cutting across the warmth of the scene. Everyone turns to her. Primigenia's expression is blank, the studied indifference of a slave, though her son cowers into her skirts. Philos looks embarrassed. As if he has been caught out.

"But I want everyone to see the clothes." Rufina is seemingly the only person unaffected by Amara's tone of command. She tugs at Philos. "I want *you* to see."

"Leave your mother in peace," Primigenia says, trying to usher Rufina away.

The sight of the beautiful slave woman comforting her own child makes Amara regret her outburst even more. She tries to deal with her churning emotions by pretending she feels nothing, turning instead to the woman from Verrecundus's store. "I'm sorry to have kept you waiting."

"Oh, no trouble," the woman replies, in the obsequious tone reserved for the rich. It makes Amara even more uncomfortable. She empties out Demetrius's money into her hand, then counts it back into the bag, so the woman can see the amount, all the while aware Philos is watching too. There is an awkward moment when Amara tries to hand the money bag over, but the woman has nowhere to put the bulky parcel containing the robes. Philos instantly steps forward to take it.

"No!" Amara exclaims, seizing the bundle before he has a chance. "I can manage." She clasps the wedding clothes to her chest, knowing she cannot bear Philos to have touched them, feeling dangerously close to tears. Britannica's words are in her head, only now they sound like a taunt. *He is loyal.* Philos steps back from her, his expression unreadable. Behind his shoulder, Amara sees Primigenia flick her eyes to the side in what looks like disdain. "Come on Rufina," Amara says with false cheer. "Let's show these to Auntie Julia and Livia. They are longing to see you in your pretty dress."

She makes her way back into Julia's house, weighed down by the parcel, Rufina skipping at her heels, chattering with happiness. Amara smiles until her cheeks ache, determined to wear a mask for her daughter, even though her feelings about marrying Demetrius grow more complicated with every day that passes in Pompeii.

In the heat of the afternoon the smell of cooked goat and spiced wine is overpowering. The small bar Amara sits in is completely open to the street, its shutters folded to the side, yet still the stench lingers. She can feel her face growing damp with sweat. The seat she is perched on is at the same spot where she once sat with Cressa, her friend and fellow she-wolf, whose bones now lie in Pompeii's harbor. There are times when every spot in this town feels haunted; yet Amara not only chose to return to this bar, she chose to buy it.

Philos is sitting beside her. She did not want him to come, but knew it would have been irrational to refuse his company. He is the one who always deals with her tenant Marcella, and he knows far more about the business than she does. They have left Rufina at Julia's in the care of Primigenia and Servius for the afternoon, their daughter still full of excitement about the clothes she had shown off to her doting "aunts." Amara couldn't help but notice how friendly Philos had been to Primigenia when they parted. She remembers when Philos smiled at her like that. It makes her doubt his protestation that there is nothing between them. Sexual jealousy is an unfamiliar emotion to Amara. She has never had cause to feel this way before, and hates the shameful fog of confusion it brings.

"There you go," Marcella says, setting down two cups of spiced wine on the marble countertop, before leaning on it herself, settling in for a chat. Marcella has aged in the five years since Amara first met her, her bright red hair even more obviously dyed. Their relationship did not get off to a promising start. Marcella was the very first debtor Amara found for Felix, and she ended up extorting the woman's family jewelry as repayment of the loan on her master's behalf. It has, unsurprisingly, taken a long time for Marcella to trust her. At first, she scoffed at the idea that Amara's proposal to buy the bar and pay her to keep running it was a means of making amends. It was only after seeing the contract drawn up by Philos, with its promise of keeping rent at a low level for ten years, that she grudgingly agreed. In return for the sale, Amara has invested in renovation and a better wine supplier. For the past two years, profits have steadily increased, though Felix is now making a small but unwelcome dent.

"What do you think?" Marcella asks them both, as Amara and Philos take a sip. "I added more honey."

"It's good," Amara says, truthfully. "How have customers been liking it?"

"Seems to go down well with the theater crowd," Marcella replies. "And we should do good business during the festival of Mars. It's always a busy time."

"I suppose it's not worth hiring a hawker before the festival?" Philos asks.

"No," Marcella agrees. "Though I'm thinking of getting in a boy for a day's trial, when the next performance is given."

Amara nods and sips more of her drink, watching two gladiators swagger past on the pavement, heading toward their barracks. They might even be men from the troop she sponsors. Besides Britannica, Amara is not familiar with all the other fighters. She leaves that side of the business to Stephanus. The entrance of the theater is just visible from her seat at the bar. The place always makes her think of Rufus. Her former patron brought her to the theater for their first evening together, and on many other occasions after that. She almost expects to see her former self walk past, in the white dress Pliny gave her. It had seemed an impossibly luxurious outfit at the time, though she now owns many clothes far grander. Amara steals a glance at Philos, who is making pleasant conversation with Marcella, complimenting her on the new fresco above the bar. He holds himself with such confidence it is easy to forget that he is still enslaved. That Rufus still refuses to sell him. The knowledge of how differently her fortunes have fallen than his, weighs her with guilt. She has no right to feel jealous about anything Philos does to make his life happier, even if it means loving another woman. Like Primigenia.

"*Mind if I join you?*"

The familiar voice is like a cold blade pressed to the back of her neck. Amara turns. Felix is standing on the pavement, smiling as if he were an old friend. He glances between her and Philos. "I hear congratulations are in order for your betrothal."

"Oh!" Marcella exclaims. "Are you getting married?"

Marcella has never met Felix before. Amara is aware that if Marcella knew he was the man who once extorted Marcella's dead mother's ring to pay a debt, a public row would follow. The last thing she needs are reminders of her life at the brothel being shouted across the public square. "My patron is a most generous man," she says, trying to hide the fact Felix has succeeded in disconcerting her.

"We should all drink to that!" Marcella exclaims, clearly delighted at the prospect of the wealthy Demetrius investing money in her business. She reaches for the jug of wine, gesturing at her slave girl to bring more cups.

"What an excellent idea." Felix moves to stand between Philos and Amara. Philos immediately steps off the stool to block him, physically shielding Amara, but making it look like an act of courtesy to Felix.

"I couldn't possibly sit in the presence of a freedman," Philos says.

"You've always had such *pretty* manners," Felix replies, taking his seat. Philos stares back, his expression indifferent, and Amara is surprised to see Felix look away first.

"You must tell us all about the wedding preparations," Marcella enthuses, enjoying the presence of two attractive men at her bar too much to notice the tension between them.

"Demetrius has forbidden me to discuss it," Amara lies, making the sign of the evil eye. "He believes it brings bad luck."

"Ah well," Marcella agrees. "Fortuna is a fickle goddess. Always best to placate her."

"Though no goddess is greater than Venus." Felix smiles at Marcella who blushes. He raises his cup. "The beloved patron of our town." Amara knows Felix also means to remind her of her life at the brothel, when she was subject to Venus, but does not give him the satisfaction of looking perturbed.

"The great goddess's temple is almost complete again," Marcella says. "What celebrations there will be when the work is finished! We should have hired our hawker by then."

Felix opens his mouth, perhaps to express interest in their business plans, or to compliment the wine, but he never gets a chance to speak. A massive jolt shakes him from his stool. At first Amara is so shocked she almost imagines it is a manifestation of her own anger. Then there is a loud rattling as the pots on the shelves skitter, one falling to the ground with a smash. Amara catches sight of Marcella's terrified face as the floor seems to pitch beneath their feet. It is an earth tremor. Philos grabs Amara, dragging her toward the door frame.

"*Down! Get down!*" They crouch low to the ground while Felix, Marcella and the slave girl dive behind the counter. Philos pulls Amara in toward him, so that her head is pressed against his chest as he covers her, instinctively protecting her body with his own. Amara closes her eyes, even though she cannot see anything with her face buried in Philos's tunic, her ears full of the sound of rumbling, screaming and the smash of roof tiles on the pavement.

The quake only lasts a moment, but it is still a while before people start to surface from their hiding places. When Amara stands the ground shudders briefly again, and she drops back down to the floor in fright. Philos crouches beside her, resting his hand on her shoulder for reassurance. Then the earth settles and he moves away. Amara experiences their physical separation as a loss. It felt so natural to be close to him again.

"Well," Marcella says, standing up from behind the counter and helping the slave to her feet. "So much for a quiet glass of wine!" Her bravado is obviously false, as Amara can see Marcella's face is ashen.

Felix also emerges, a hand pressed to his forehead. There is blood on his cheek. He must have been cut by one of the falling pots. Marcella exclaims in concern but he waves her away with a vicious, bad-tempered gesture, one Amara has seen him use countless times on Victoria. He catches sight of Marcella's surprised face and remembers the role he was playing. "It's nothing," he says, charming again. "Please, don't trouble yourself. But I must go to my family, to be sure they are unharmed."

He hurries off and is soon lost to sight in the milling crowds who have spilled out onto the pavement following the quake, many swearing and exclaiming, looking around at the debris now littering the streets.

"Rufina!" Amara exclaims, clutching Philos's arm.

"We will go back now." He presses her hand, and the fact his own is steady gives her confidence. "She will be fine, I promise." He lets go of Amara and walks to the counter. "Marcella, I have to warn you that the man we just met is not to be trusted. He might even be behind the demands that have been made against you."

"*Him?*" Marcella says. "But he seemed so friendly?"

"Looks can be deceiving." Philos glances at the mess in the bar, the smashed pots on the floor and a crack in the recently painted fresco. "I need to get my mistress back to the house, to her daughter. But after that I will come back to help you with this."

Philos offers Amara his arm and they make their way home. She tries not to clutch him too hard in her panic, pushing aside mental images of Rufina hurt, injured by a falling tile or worse. Their journey is slow, the streets are crowded and chaotic; people lean out of windows calling to friends and family below, everyone trying to check over their homes and businesses for signs of damage. Amara looks down, mindful of where she walks, not wanting to cut herself. Roof tiles lie scattered on the pavement like autumn leaves.

"It's not as bad as the last one, which hit just before you arrived," Philos says, picking his way through a heap of baskets that have scattered over the road from a shop front. "I'm sure she will be safe."

"I don't remember the tremors being as frequent as this."

"It's just how things are in Campania," Philos reassures her. "All my life they've come and gone. This is nothing unusual." He guides Amara past a partially collapsed wall. An old man stands in the midst of it, his face streaked with plaster powder, berating the unfortunate slaves who are trying to clear the rubble. "You must have been used to this in Greece too."

Amara shakes her head. "Not really. My parents lived through a severe tremor, but it was before I was born."

At last, they reach the home stretch of road. Amara has to restrain herself from running. The door to Julia's atrium is wide open, perhaps jolted that way by the tremor. Livia is with some of the servants, inspecting a crack in the ceiling that fans out from the window opening to the sky. "Darling," she says, seeing Amara's worried face, "Rufina is quite well. She is with one of the girls in the garden."

"Perhaps you would like to be alone with her?" Philos says. "I can return to help Marcella now."

"No," Amara replies, not wanting to break the intimacy that has returned between them. "Rufina will want to see that you are safe."

They find their daughter playing with Primigenia and Servius in the orchard, the two children running between the trees kicking at the fallen fruit, which must have been dislodged by the quake. Another slave remonstrates with them both, trying to gather the fruit into a basket, not wanting to waste the precious crop. He slaps Servius as the boy nips past, but lets Rufina be, knowing better than to touch a freeborn child. Rufina is uninterested in the appearance of Amara and Philos, shooing her mother away when she tries to kiss her, seemingly unconcerned by the tremor that just shook her small world. Amara glances up to see Primigenia and Philos smiling at the children; they look so completely at ease together, as if *they* were the parents. Amara feels a stab of doubt. Perhaps Philos protecting her just now in the quake meant less than she imagined. Perhaps he would have done the same for any woman. It doesn't mean he cares more for her than Primigenia. After all, he is naturally kind. To Amara's mortification, Philos catches her watching him.

"Do you need me to inspect any damage to the apartment?" he asks.

"Thank you," she replies. They walk back together to their home, which is also no longer their home as a couple, the awkwardness between them returning now they have recovered from the heightened anxiety of the quake. Amara waits downstairs while Philos checks each room. The worst damage is in the kitchen, where a cupboard has fallen open, leaving a number of clay pots and jars smashed on the floor beneath. Amara sees the red glazed lamp of Venus is broken, split down the middle. Philos starts to sweep up the shards, stopping Amara when she tries to help. It feels like a rebuke, a reminder of their difference in status.

"Will you speak to Britannica about Felix turning up today?" he asks.

"I can't. She is due in the arena in two days. I don't want to disturb her concentration. But I will send a message to Stephanus, asking Cosmus to keep a closer watch."

Philos finishes sweeping the shards into an unbroken pot, then stands, leaning against the wall at some distance from Amara. "It's concerning he knew about your marriage to Demetrius."

"That must have been from Victoria."

"*Victoria?* How would she know?"

"She followed me the other day, and spied when I bought the wedding clothes."

"Why didn't you tell me this?" Philos is annoyed, and although she knows it's wrong, Amara is relieved to see some crack in the calm indifference he always shows her. She says nothing, and the silence seems to anger him more. "I don't know why you would keep this to yourself, as if these things don't also affect me. How can I protect our daughter if I don't know what's going on?" He is speaking to her directly, as an equal, losing yet more of his reserve. "And this morning I might have been a monster, the way you snatched the parcel away before I could touch it. What did you think would happen? That I would somehow *pollute* the clothes you're wearing to marry him?"

"That wasn't it at all! And why would you even care? I thought you were relieved I was getting married!"

Philos throws up his hands in exasperation. "I *am* relieved. But for Rufina! Not for myself. I hate every part of this. I *hate* to think of you with him. How can you believe the idea of him marrying you doesn't make me jealous? When there was once so much love between us? I never even imagined I could feel like that about a woman again after losing my wife. And then I met you." Philos pauses, trying to get his emotion back under control. "I'd have liked to have taken that parcel and shoved it in the furnace under the baths to watch it burn, not meekly carry it off as a slave. But that's my role, Amara. One I'm forced to play to protect our daughter, who is the only person who matters now. I don't have the freedom to feel anything else, or to *be* anything else. Don't you understand?"

The feelings Amara has for Philos, all the tenderness and desire that she has tried so hard to stamp down, resurface as a wave of grief. She turns aside, not wanting to cry, but cannot stop herself. The truth confronting her is too obvious. Whatever security her marriage brings, she and Demetrius will never come close to sharing a love like the one she once knew with Philos. Nor will Rufina ever again know a love like the one her real father now gives her. Demetrius is cold, and all the money in the world cannot compensate her, still less Philos, for a life they will never live together with their child. Amara tries to suppress her sobs, longing for Philos to put his arms around her, even though she knows he won't.

"I'm sorry. I didn't mean to hurt you with what I said."

"You have nothing to be sorry for." Amara has a sick feeling in her stomach, knowing there can be no resolution from this that brings either of them any comfort. "I just wish so much that it were different."

"I know," Philos says. He waits as Amara collects herself. "I want to be here to protect you and Rufina from Felix before you go to Stabiae. But I imagine Rufus knows you are getting married?" Amara nods, miserable. "Then it is possible he will recall me before you leave, though I promise I will do everything I can to stay."

"Does he still rely on you as much in the business as before? Is there no way Julia might not persuade Rufus to let her buy you? He might find it harder to refuse her than me. And I *know* Julia would free you, if I asked her."

"Julia has already asked Rufus," Philos replies. "More than once."

Amara wipes her face, feeling ashamed. She should have known this already. Whatever loss she feels is absolutely nothing compared to the suffering Philos endures as a slave. "I'm sorry I cried like that, when things are so much harder for you. It was selfish of me."

"We don't need to compete over our apologies to one another," Philos says, raising his eyebrows and encouraging her to smile with him, but she cannot. After a moment's hesitation he goes to her. She thinks he is finally going to hold her in his arms, that there will be some relief from her longing, but he still keeps a distance between them, only reaching over to wipe her cheek with his thumb where it is still wet. "It's not your fault that I am enslaved and it never has been." She starts to cry again and he cups her face in both his hands. "Do you hear me, Amara? *It is not your fault.*"

"But Rufina," she cries. "I don't want you to have to leave her."

She sees his composure waver. Philos drops his hands. "I have known this would happen since the day she was born. If Rufina is safe and happy in Rome, anything either of us have suffered in our lives is worthwhile. I have to believe that." Amara reaches for him, but he steps away from her. "Perhaps you could leave me for a moment."

Amara understands that he does not want her to see his emotion. She finds she cannot speak but walks from the room as he has asked.

15

*"They must conquer or fall. Such was the settled purpose
of a woman—the men might live and be slaves!"*
—Tacitus on Boudicca, Queen of the Iceni, Annals 14

The trumpet blasts make it impossible to speak. Priests process around the arena, blowing on their enormous curved tubas in honor of Mars, treading a circle of sand that will soon become a theater of death. It is the twenty-third of October, the closing festival for the god of war, marked by games that also celebrate the end of the agricultural season. The walls that surround the marching priests are brightly colored, just tall enough to protect spectators from the action. From where she is sitting high up in the women's section, Amara can see painted lions and winged Victories, imaginary fighters frozen in combat, their weapons raised. Pompeii's arena, the pride of its citizens, feels tiny after the Circus Maximus. Amara can remember watching chariot races dedicated to Mars there from a luxurious balcony on the Palatine. And yet she never felt so much tension before a show as this.

"I'm sure she will do well!" Julia is almost shouting into her right ear to make herself heard over the trumpets. Amara is too stressed to reply. She knows that her three companions—Julia, Livia and Drusilla—are all willing Britannica to victory, but none with the same sense of love and fear as she feels. Amara scans the ranks of men in the seats below, wondering if Felix is watching too, hoping to see his enemy die.

Britannica will be the first act to appear. Stephanus has enough influence to ensure his most valuable fighter does not spend hours waiting. At first Amara was relieved, but now that the time is approaching, she wants to delay the moment Britannica faces danger. In her mind she pictures the monumental statue of Fortuna in Rome, whose impassive, androgynous face reminded her of her friend. The thought of Fortuna, that most pitiless of deities, no longer makes her smile. *Grant Senovara victory*, Amara prays, giving the goddess Britannica's real name. *May she live, I beg you.*

The priests have finished their procession and disappear into the bowels of the arena. Referees, swathed in white, are the first figures to appear, bearing the gladiators' weapons that they lay in the center of the ring. Then it is the turn of the fighters to enter. Celadus the Thracian is first. He jogs out onto the sand raising his arm to shouts of excitement. He is one of the older gladiators; Amara remembers him from years before, when he picked Victoria out from the crowd for a kiss. Britannica follows, to more jeers than cheering. She is dressed in a padded tunic and her face is painted blue, an imitation of the woad worn by British warriors. Amara wonders how Britannica feels about this parody of the real wars she must have witnessed. The Briton does not look up at the crowd, or search for Amara's face. Strangely, this brings Amara relief. All Britannica's focus is on winning; it has never mattered to her whether she is hated or loved.

Attendants busy themselves helping the two gladiators prepare for the fight, while a herald drones a panegyric to the games' sponsor, some rich man hoping for election. Celadus is now encased in armor, his face obscured by the helmet, his body protected by a breastplate. An attendant watches Celadus heft a shield on his arm, testing its weight, then hands over the sword. Britannica stands waiting, armed with nothing other than a trident and a net. Her head is unprotected, her red hair fastened back like a helmet's plume.

A priest strides forward to stand between them, bearing a tuba. The crowd hushes, waiting for the trumpet blast, and when it sounds, Amara jumps, even though she was expecting the noise. Drusilla takes her left hand and squeezes it.

Celadus and Britannica circle one another, sizing each other up. They must have fought, and watched each other fight, many times before. The crowd begin chanting Celadus's name, preferring the Italian man to the strange foreign woman. Perhaps spurred on by the admiration of his audience, Celadus takes a swing toward Britannica. She sidesteps him easily, returning with a jab of her trident. The pair carry on in this vein, neither coming too close. Some of the audience yell insults, eager for the real fighting to start, but the gladiators are too busy testing one another to rush to their death like fools.

It is Britannica who breaks the deadlock. She flings her net, its barbs sounding like hailstones as they strike the Thracian's shield, yanking it from his grasp. Celadus has the wit to let his protection drop rather than bend to retrieve it, or else he would have been skewered by the follow-up blow from Britannica's trident. He tries to parry but Britannica dodges, swinging the net at his calves. Celadus stumbles.

There is an uneasy murmur from the crowd. Nobody has any desire to see their favorite beaten so swiftly. But Celadus did not win fifteen fights in this ring by giving up. When Britannica jabs again, he swings upward at her trident, the force throwing her backward, although she manages to keep hold of her weapon. He seizes back his shield while she recovers, then attacks, forcing her onto the defensive.

Amara feels as if she cannot breathe, watching Britannica retreating, the crowd baying at the prospect of her defeat. Then as Celadus becomes more confident, Britannica sidesteps and he lurches forward. He swings again, trying to regain his momentum and again she slips from reach. Britannica stands still, watching Celadus as he circles, her head cocked to one side. This time when he swipes at her, she bends like a reed, swinging the net at his feet so he is forced to skip over it. The movement makes him look ridiculous, like a child playing. He tries again and Britannica makes the same movement. She is mocking him.

Few men like to be laughed at, especially in the face of death. Celadus hits back hard, trying to knock the trident from Britannica's grasp. She retaliates, jabbing his breast plate viciously with her prong. Celadus backs away, and now it is Britannica on the offensive. She moves so fast it is hard to keep track of her, darting in first with the net, then the trident, so that Celadus is forced to circle frantically, barely fending her off. The crowd is ominously quiet.

Then, just as it seems Britannica might be moving in for the kill, she suddenly turns and stalks toward the outer wall. She raises her arms to the crowd, shouting up at the highest part of the arena. People murmur, perplexed, and even Celadus seems wrong-footed, until he seizes the advantage offered by his opponent's madness and runs toward the Briton while her back is turned. At the last possible moment, Britannica whips around, scoring his arm with her trident, knocking him flying. Celadus staggers, his shoulder red with blood. Britannica screams again in her own language, this time her aggression directed straight at her rival, who quails at the sight.

Britannica circles Celadus, continuing her strange incantation of violence, and although Amara cannot understand the words, she understands that they are not a meaningless tirade. Whatever Britannica is saying is giving her strength, igniting the rage and ferocity that has always lit her from within. Watching her, Amara is no longer gripped by anxiety; instead she feels euphoria. Britannica has the strength, the fearlessness, the unbridled fury she has always wanted for herself, and unlike Amara, unlike every woman here, *this* woman has the power to make men feel afraid.

Without even fully realizing what she is doing, Amara jumps to her feet. Drusilla is standing beside her, arms raised, unrecognizable with passion. All around her, women are screaming, their lust for violence contagious.

Britannica no longer seems immune to the emotion of the crowd. She swings the trident in a giant arc, knocking the sword from Celadus's hand, before attacking again, forcing him to defend himself with the shield rather than retrieve his weapon. Britannica strikes repeatedly, her force increasing with each blow, filling Amara with both terror and excitement. Her friend no longer looks mortal, she has the savagery of a god, consumed by vengeance. And Celadus is no longer a man with the right to mercy—he is Felix, he is Thraso, he is every man who ever dared inflict violence and pain, and he must die. Britannica strikes again. The shield splits under the force of her trident. She whips the net around his legs dragging him off balance and Celadus falls onto his back. Before he can raise himself, she has leapt forward. Her foot rests on his chest and the lethal prongs of her weapon are at his throat. The crowd falls silent.

Amara can see Britannica's shoulders heaving. She must be breathing hard from the exertion of the fight, the blood lust coursing through her. She is saying something to Celadus, the words impossible to hear, and steps back off his chest though she does not remove the trident. The defeated gladiator removes his helmet, the instruction Britannica must have given him. Britannica shouts up at the crowd, repeating a single word that has no meaning to Amara: *Budeg.* Then she raises her trident above her vanquished opponent and brings it down full force. The violence of the movement is so extreme, so out of proportion to the man's supine position, that Amara breaks out of her trance, screaming in horror.

Then to her confusion, Britannica is raising Celadus to his feet, clasping him by the hand. The trident is still quivering, upright in the ground. Britannica must have driven the weapon into the sand a hair's breadth from his face. The two gladiators turn to face the master of the games, Britannica raising Celadus's injured arm into the air along with her own.

Britannica no longer looks like a goddess. She is a woman, smeared in dirt and blood, exhausted but still standing, made formidable by her own strength, determination and pride. Amara screams her friend's name, her voice joined with hundreds of others, Pompeii's arena erupting in celebration of this savage fighter from a foreign land.

16

"In difficult and desperate cases, the boldest counsels are the safest."
—Livy, *History of Rome*

The relief Amara feels after Britannica's victory is so overwhelming, she barely focuses on the rest of the games. Two men die, their lives extinguished before her like the light from a lamp, and she thinks nothing of it. She sits gossiping with Drusilla, sharing a snack of dried fruit and olives, while all around them women are shouting and cheering on their favorite gladiators. Toward the end of the entertainment another earth tremor strikes, rocking the awnings above the spectators. The interruption causes a moment of panic, but the awnings hold. It is not as severe as the quake Amara experienced in Marcella's bar and soon subsides; very few people bother to get up and leave. Amara looks to Julia for guidance, but her friend simply shrugs, undeterred.

When the last pair of gladiators have fought, Julia, Livia, Amara and Drusilla make their way out of the arena. It is a long process, nobody is in a hurry to move themselves, instead they dawdle, gathering their belongings. On the square outside, a thicket of stalls has sprung up like weeds, selling hot snacks, wine and souvenirs. Amara lingers at a stall for commemorative lamps. They are small and roughly made in terracotta clay, stamped with different gladiators, all selling for five sesterces. Amara picks one up that shows a netman, brandishing his trident; she can almost imagine it is Britannica.

"I will take this," she says, and the stall holder seizes it, tying it up in a scrap of fabric before she can change her mind.

Livia rolls her eyes. "*Really* darling, it's hideously overpriced."

"Rufina will love it," Amara retorts. "She was so annoyed not getting to watch Britannica today."

The women weave their way through the stalls and the crowds, eventually arriving at the back entrance to Julia's orchard, which is guarded by two of her slaves. Inside the walls of the garden, the hubbub of the marketplace becomes muted, the sound of voices, laughter and celebration more enjoyable at a distance. Amara tries not to look at the garden Philos planted as they head toward the house. She knows he has been working today to ensure Julia's bars facing the Via Veneria can handle the influx of people who will be there to celebrate Mars's festival day.

The blue dining room has been set out ready for their return, its couches heaped with cushions, while dates, figs and pomegranates are piled up on the tables. Julia collapses onto a couch with a loud sigh. "Well, that's better. It's good to be out of the madness." She turns to Drusilla. "I hope Ampliatus and Primus are joining us?"

"They will be," Drusilla says. "But Primus wanted to see the gladiators after the show, so the pair of them might not be here for a while."

Amara settles herself beside Drusilla, also enjoying the chance to recline. Water flows down the back wall over marble steps, before splashing into a pool that runs through the center of the room. Livia told Amara once that it was supposed to represent the Nile, a backdrop for the painted hippos, crocodiles and pygmies who cavort over the walls. One of the slaves has filled a floating bowl with cut flowers, and it bobs on the imaginary Egyptian river, a splash of color in all the blue.

"Amara tells us you were responsible for the recommendation to Verecundus," Julia says to Drusilla. "The gold in the fabric is exquisite. Demetrius will be delighted when he sees his bride looking so fine."

"Lovely touch to dress Fina too," Livia agrees. "I'm sure he will be absolutely taken with her, though we will miss the little creature when she goes to Rome."

"Perhaps we could all visit," Drusilla says, languidly holding out her glass for a slave to fill. "I should love to see the capital of the world."

"That would be wonderful," Amara says, imagining how much she will enjoy showing Drusilla Demetrius's house on the Vicus Longus, filling its rooms with their laughter. *And how Drusilla will gasp at the glittering glass mosaics.* "When I'm a wife, he can hardly refuse me. I shall insist you all come!"

Drusilla squeezes Amara's hand, giving her a look alight with pleasure and mischief. "And we will walk through Rome as two respectable married matrons."

The four women laugh, and Amara feels almost giddy with sudden happiness. *This* is where she will find some joy in her marriage. In the future she builds for her daughter, safe in the beautiful house on the Quirinal Hill. And if her husband himself is cold, she will be warmed by the love of her friends. Then the image of Philos comes to her, alone, trapped in service to Rufus, and she grips her glass tighter, not wanting to feel pain at this moment.

One of the servants arrives, leading Rufina by the hand. "Did Britannica win?" Rufina asks. "Did she beat the man?"

"Yes, my love," Amara says, scooping her up to sit between herself and Drusilla. "Look, I bought a lamp with her picture on it for you." Rufina unwraps the terracotta souvenir.

"That's Poseidon," Rufina says, pointing at the trident, frowning when the adults laugh.

The servant is still hovering near Amara, trying to catch her eye. "Yes?" Amara asks, not pleased to be disturbed.

"There is a visitor for you in the atrium. Philos says it is urgent."

Amara rises from the couch, trying not to show her alarm. "Excuse me, ladies." She bends to kiss Rufina on the top of her head. "I will be back in a moment, my love."

Philos would never disturb her unless something terrible had happened. Amara hurries to the atrium, her breathing quickening with panic. She sees him as soon as she walks into the atrium, standing beside a bench, one hand resting on the shoulder of a seated, huddled figure. It is Marcella, her eyes smudged with kohl from where she has been weeping. She does not get up as her landlady approaches.

Amara sits beside her. "What is it? What has happened?"

"The bar, the business, everything—it's all destroyed."

"What! But how?"

"Some men came, maybe three or four. They ordered wine, but seemed drunk already and a fight started between them," Marcella says, gabbling in her distress. "Cosmus was there, he tried to intervene, but one of them knocked him out. When I left, he was still unconscious. They ripped the place apart, Amara. I was screaming for them to stop . . ." Marcella breaks off, clasping a hand to her mouth, reliving the horror of the moment. She pauses to collect herself then continues. "At first, I thought it was just a fight, but then they were smashing things, someone set fire to the ladder that leads upstairs to my home. It was chaos. A couple of the neighbors came to help, but so many people were away at the arena, I had almost nobody to call on, and anyway, by then the bastards had scattered. It was impossible to understand who was attacking and who was trying to help . . ."

"Your home, is it safe? Did you put out the fire?"

"Yes, we managed to put it out before it spread upstairs, but it's still done so much damage." Marcella starts to sob. "I didn't know where to turn! I knew Stephanus and Britannica were at the arena, and with Cosmus hurt, there was nobody to protect me."

"Did you recognize any of the men?"

"No," Marcella shakes her head. "None of them looked familiar; I don't know who they were."

Amara thinks of Felix, of what she knows about the way he operates, and the sheer number of criminals he works with in so many different areas of his business. She remembers the night he forced her to act as a decoy when he burned down Simo's bar, how he chose men for the task who would not readily be connected to him.

"Is there any chance these were random drunks, that it wasn't a targeted attack?" Philos asks. Marcella and Amara turn to look at him with incredulity.

"Does it sound random to you?" Marcella asks. "After everything that's been going on."

"We won't let this go unpunished," Amara says. "I promise."

"I don't care about punishment," Marcella snaps. "I don't care about your fucking feuds. If it weren't for your past, I would still have a business."

"I will make sure the bar is repaired, as quickly as possible." Amara ignores Marcella's insult, knowing how distressed she is. "I promise you."

"There must be plenty of drunks on the streets today," Philos persists. "The games often lead to violence. It doesn't mean this was a targeted attack."

Amara turns on him. "Of *course* it was targeted!"

"But there's no rush to retaliate," Philos says, his voice low in case any of the other servants are passing. He grips her arm. "Think carefully about the timing. About *who* might be put at risk."

Amara knows that he is talking about their daughter and feels ashamed for losing her temper. "I need to speak to Britannica. And Stephanus."

"They won't be free for hours."

"Well, I can't wait here to hear what you decide," Marcella says, heaving herself to her feet. She looks unsteady with shock. "I need to get back to the bar."

"I will come with you," Philos says, moving swiftly to help her. "You shouldn't be there alone. And I can take a look at the damage."

"Be careful," Amara says, even sorrier that she was so impatient with Philos earlier.

Marcella thinks the warning is for her. "Bit late for that now!"

Amara stands alone in the atrium after they have gone. For a moment her mind is blank with fear. The promise Beronice and Victoria made only days ago is worthless. Perhaps her old master only sent them to lull her into a false sense of security. There will be no peaceful resolution with Felix, no means for her to escape the shadow of the brothel without violence. Amara understands this, yet she still dreads the thought of acting, of what it will mean.

The sound of laughter reaches her from the garden. She has to return to her daughter and her friends. Amara smiles, practicing the mask she will wear, then walks back to the dining room.

The three women are sprawled on the couches, their shoes kicked off upon the tiled floor. Rufina is paddling her feet in the water feature, the souvenir lamp beside her. Amara gives a shortened explanation for Marcella's visit, accepting their commiserations for the damage to her property while downplaying the extent of the destruction, inferring it was the work of drunks.

"It often happens around the games," Julia says, patting Amara on the shoulder as she reclines beside her. "I'm old enough to remember the riot that broke out twenty years ago. The senate itself got involved that time, the violence was so serious. More people died outside the arena than in it! Pompeii was banned from holding gladiator fights for ten years. Can you imagine! Just dreadful."

"So there you go, darling," Livia says to Amara, in her most mischievous tone. "You had better get Demetrius to intervene so that the senate—or maybe even Titus!—can punish whoever turned over your bar."

"Don't scoff!" Julia says, annoyed. "You weren't here that day. It was a truly hideous affair."

"Do you think you will continue with the gladiators and the bars," Drusilla interrupts, changing the subject. "After you and Demetrius are married?"

"I will ask him what he prefers," Amara says, wondering if there will still *be* a marriage after the street war she may be forced to unleash on Pompeii. "But I will have to pay to restore Marcella's business regardless. I can't abandon her."

"Yes, best to repair it. The place won't be worth much, otherwise, if you wanted to sell," Livia says, always the pragmatist.

"Enough about bars!" Julia says. "Tell us more about the wedding, darling. Do you think Demetrius will manage to squeeze out even *one* romantic sentiment at the celebrations? Or will I have to prompt him?"

The others laugh, and Amara pretends to join them. Soothed by the musical sound of the flowing water, she tries to lose herself again in the pleasure of the afternoon, although the shadow of violence lingers.

For a while, Amara is able to avoid thinking of Marcella or Felix. Drusilla's husband Ampliatus and her son Primus arrive, adding yet more noise and laughter to Julia's dining room. It seems as if the gathering might be a moment suspended in time, a bee caught in amber, if Amara only wishes hard enough. And yet hours still pass, shadows lengthen and the air grows chill. Britannica must be long back from the arena; Amara cannot keep delaying her next move, however much she might wish to. She asks to be excused and finds it easier to leave the party than she expected, with everyone accepting her promised sacrifice at the Temple of Fortuna as an excuse, their nonchalance aided by copious amounts of wine. Rufina is already fast asleep on the couch, and Livia promises to see her safely into bed. Amara glances back at her daughter one last time. Rufina looks so small and precious. And *safe*. It is hard to believe that a brawl in a bar could lead to her daughter losing her freeborn status.

Two of Julia's servants accompany Amara on her walk to the barracks, both burly men who usually work in the gardens. The first carries a torch to light the way, even though it is not yet dark, the painted red and yellow buildings still bright as sunset approaches. More people than usual are out on the streets, hurrying to evening celebrations of the festival. Amara passes one of the grander homes on the Via Veneria, the tall doors open wide enough to catch a glimpse of the courtyard inside, as guests arrive to celebrate. A large mosaic dog, picked out in glittering black-and-white, sits on the threshold and the sound of laughter drifts onto the street. It is hard not to think of the first gathering at a grand house that she and Dido once attended as entertainers, on the night of the Vinalia. Amara never imagined then that she would one day see the Imperial palace on the Palatine.

The barracks are almost empty when Amara arrives. After their day in the arena, most of the gladiators are either giving thanks at the temple or out drinking, enjoying a rare night of freedom after their public brush with death. Amara ascends the stairs to Stephanus's chambers, one of the slaves going ahead. She is admitted into his familiar study. Lying on the couch is a man Amara has never met before, but she knows it must be Cosmus. His brother, Stephanus, is sitting beside him.

"You came," Stephanus says, looking up at her. His eyes are red from weeping. "I remember Britannica said your father was a doctor."

Amara feels ashamed, knowing she came here out of fear for her own family, not for Cosmus, but she does not admit this, instead kneeling down on the floor behind the couch. Cosmus is deeply unconscious. Dark blood is caked around a wound on his temple, which is alarmingly concave. Amara has never considered Cosmus beyond his usefulness to her. She always knew that Stephanus could call on him for her protection, while turning a blind eye to the man himself, not wanting to have direct dealings with a criminal. Yet now his existence as a real man confronts her. She strokes his face, so like that of the brother who loves him.

"What do you think?"

Stephanus's voice has the same mix of fear and hope she remembers so vividly from her childhood. It is the voice of abject desperation people use to beg a doctor to save their loved one, even though they understand, in their hearts, that this is not possible. Amara wishes her father were here now. Not to save Cosmus, because this is impossible. But to comfort Stephanus.

"The next night will be crucial," she says. "But if he does not wake after that, it is less likely that he will recover."

"Can we do nothing for the wound now?"

"You are doing everything right," Amara says. "The best thing you can do is to keep him comfortable, and move him as little as possible."

Stephanus looks at her. Amara knows from the deep pain in his eyes that he has understood her. That he knows his brother is dying.

"Felix will pay for this," Stephanus says, not to Amara but to his brother. "I swear he will pay."

"Do you think . . ." Amara begins, but Stephanus cuts her off.

"This is no longer about your family. It is about *mine*."

Amara nods, both afraid and relieved. Whatever happens next, whatever lives are lost, she will not have to carry the weight of such a decision. "I understand," she says. "I only ask that you also protect my daughter. That your revenge ensures *all* Felix's secrets die with him."

Stephanus takes her hand, laying it over his own heart. He is no longer the grieving brother. Instead, Amara sees in his face something of the pitilessness that must have ensured his survival in the arena, for so many years. "It will be as if he never existed."

The Forum is busy, drinkers milling about the stalls, while street musicians play and people dance. The sound echoes off the marble, rising like hot air in the dusk. Amara and Julia's two men hurry along the narrow street that leads to the temple of Fortuna

Augusta, at the very end of the marketplace. The temple has drawn a small crowd of onlookers. A number of gladiators are gathered at the altar at the bottom of the steps, wearing laurel wreaths, giving their offerings of incense to the temple's priest, who burns them to the goddess. Britannica is not hard to spot. She stands a little apart from her fellows, waiting at the back. A few curious people are pressed up against the railings that surround the temple, and Amara joins them.

The priest's head is covered and he chants praise to Fortuna as he burns the incense. Amara watches the smoke rise, filling the air with its smell of laurel and verbena, when suddenly the hazy cloud veers off course, as if there is a wind, although Amara cannot feel a breeze. Then there is a low rumble and the ground shakes. People look around, uneasy, anticipating another tremor, but instead there is stillness, as the quake fails to materialize. The priest hesitates, then accepts the next gladiator's offering.

Britannica is the last to come forward. The priest averts his eyes as he takes her sprig of laurel but still places it upon the altar. The Briton is out of her fighting clothes, her face clean, dressed in a ceremonial red tunic for Mars. Her hand rests on a thread around her neck. Amara knows what it signifies. It is the necklace she and Dido bought for Britannica, a leather amulet soaked in a gladiator's blood, their gift for the Saturnalia when the three of them were enslaved by Felix at the Wolf Den. Britannica glances over at the crowd, sees Amara, and nods in recognition.

With the rites complete, Amara approaches the entry to the temple, asking for admission. She has brought fruit from Julia's garden to lay at the feet of the goddess. The priest admits her, though he obliges Julia's slaves to wait. Britannica walks with Amara, the pair of them ascending the temple steps, side by side. The interior is dim, but the gilded statue of the goddess illuminates the small space. Fortuna Augusta stands in a niche at the far end, flanked by columns, a fraction of the size of the giant Fortuna that Amara visited so recently in Rome. The lamps flicker, their light glimmering on the goddess's gold robes, while she holds her cornucopia of plenty. Amara lays down the pomegranates she has brought, and Britannica removes the wreath from her hair, adding it to the pile at the foot of the plinth. Statues of the Imperial family, who line the walls, stand watching the two she-wolves.

"Stephanus will not let this go unpunished," Britannica murmurs.

"I know," Amara replies.

"We strike quickly. With the goddess's favor perhaps not many will die."

"You mean to burn it?" Amara whispers, thinking of the Wolf Den, the hated building where they both suffered so much pain, but which is also the home of Victoria and her children. She does not allow herself to think of Beronice.

Britannica turns to Amara and although her face is shadowed, her eyes shine white in the gloom. "Not one stone will be left standing," she says. "I vow this to the goddess."

VESUVIUS

OCTOBER 24, 79 CE

17

*"It was not clear at that distance from which mountain the cloud
was rising (it was afterward known to be Vesuvius); its general
appearance can best be expressed as being like an umbrella pine,
for it rose to a great height on a sort of trunk and then split off
into branches, I imagine because it was thrust upward by
the first blast and then left unsupported as the pressure
subsided, or else it was borne down by its own weight so
that it spread out and gradually dispersed."*

—Pliny the Younger, letter to Tacitus on the
eruption of Vesuvius

Amara sits in Julia's garden, soaking up the warmth of the
midday sun. Above her the sky is blue and the dry lavender
bushes hum with insects. It is hard to imagine a more peaceful
scene, yet Amara is far from calm. Having felt so deeply conflicted
about marrying Demetrius, she is now terrified that the security
he offers her will be snatched away and her daughter's life ruined.
The possibility of violence and disgrace engulfing her family before
she can get Rufina to safety in Rome, fills her with dread. A message from the barracks this morning did nothing to allay her fear.
Cosmus remains unconscious. Her future now depends on how
rationally Stephanus reacts to his brother's inevitable death.

Her daughter's voice brings her back to the present. Amara glances over to where Rufina sits on the grass with Philos, spelling out words on a wax tablet. It is hard to believe, looking at them both, how much danger her family is in. Behind them, she catches sight of Julia stalking over from the baths toward her.

"Darling, it's too annoying. The water still isn't flowing!" Julia stops to stand at the pond with her hands on her hips. "We'll have to close for the day. Not what I need with a headache like this."

Amara thinks of all the wine Julia drank last night, but is too polite to tease her. "Is it working at the public fountains yet?"

"No! I've sent slaves up and down town. It's not working anywhere. We'll have to send a team to the river with buckets if this carries on," Julia says. "So tiresome."

"Perhaps you should have a lie down, to rest."

"I might do that," Julia agrees. She raises her hand, shading her eyes to look at the blue sky. The gold ring she always wears, with its carnelian stone of the god Mercury, glints in the sun. "Although it's a shame to miss this weather. It could almost be summer." Julia sighs heavily and walks back into the house.

Rufina darts up from the grass, to an exclamation of surprise from her father. Amara gets to her feet as their daughter runs alongside the pool, squealing at the flash of silver fish in the water.

"Rufina!" Philos calls. "We haven't finished your lesson."

Amara stares. The surface of the water behind Rufina is quivering. For one moment she thinks it is shaking to the pounding of her daughter's tiny feet. Then an explosion, louder than any sound she has ever heard, bursts overhead. Amara throws herself flat to the ground, terrified, as Rufina screams. The earth is trembling beneath her. Slowly, Amara raises herself onto her haunches, ears ringing, trying to understand where the noise has come from. She sees Philos clutching their daughter to his chest, his face stricken with fear. Then the light starts to fade, as if dusk is falling with unnatural speed. Amara looks up. Above the mountain, a black column has risen, is still rising, piercing the sky like a spear thrown from the kingdom of Vulcan, god of fire. Dark fingers spread out from its summit, reaching for the city of Pompeii, stretching out over the blue. Then the world turns gray as the sun is blotted out and it starts to rain—except this is unlike any downpour Amara has ever experienced. She brushes at her arms, confused. The drops are warm, leaving smuts on her skin. It is ash. Through the ringing in her head, Amara realizes people are screaming.

"Vesuvius!" Philos's voice reaches her, shouting above the chaos. "It's a mountain of fire." He seizes Amara, shaking her from her daze. "We have to get away from here!"

"Get away?" Amara asks, still in shock. "Where are we going? What are you talking about?"

Rufina is clinging to Philos, her arms around his neck, face buried in his chest, terrified into silence. Philos forcibly turns Amara to face Mount Vesuvius. Even through the ash rain, she can see its shadow, the black column exploding from its heart. She gasps, unable to believe what is so plainly before her. "Vesuvius is burning," Philos speaks slowly, to be sure she understands. "It's a mountain of fire, like Etna. We have to get as far away from it as possible."

"Would we be safe at Demetrius's estate at Stabiae? Is that far enough away?" Amara asks, but she can tell from Philos's face that he knows no better than she does.

Julia and Livia run out of the house. Livia is screaming and for the first time since Amara has known her, Julia looks afraid. "We have to get away from here," Philos yells at them both. "We're heading for Stabiae. Come with us!"

As he speaks, hail starts to fall on the roof tiles, in a loud angry drumbeat. Some of them bounce onto the ground and Amara sees they are not hail, but stones. Instinctively she covers her head with her arms, while Philos protects their daughter. "We should take shelter inside," Julia shouts back, her voice firm, even though she looks terrified. "Until the storm passes. It would be *madness* to leave in this. All of you, come now! Come inside!" She runs back into the house, but Livia stays, staring at Philos, her mouth hanging open.

"We can't take shelter here. The mountain is too close." He has to shout at Livia to make himself heard above the hail and the roaring of Vesuvius. "It's too dangerous. We have to escape!"

"You go ahead to Stabiae, take Rufina," Livia says, briefly clasping Amara's arm. "I will try to persuade Julia to leave and get the rest of the household together." She turns without saying goodbye, running back into the house. The garden is now full of people bumping into each other in the gloom. Tenants, slaves and customers all mill together like ants, but without the insects' instinct for order. Amara cries out in pain as a sudden flurry of stones pelt down.

"We need to wear something to protect ourselves," Philos says, grabbing her arm. "Quickly."

They hurry into their apartment, which is now pitch dark save for the faint glow of embers in the kitchen brazier. Philos sets Rufina down onto a stool, searching for oil lamps. He picks up the one stamped with a netman that Amara bought outside the arena only yesterday, and lights it from the red ashes of the morning's fire. "Britannica," Amara says, watching him. "We should go for her. It's on our way."

"Good idea," Philos says, handing her the first lamp and lighting another. "And we need to dress for protection. Cloaks and something to cover our heads."

Amara's heart is still racing with fear and confusion but Philos's tone calms her. She rushes to the storeroom, rifling through the bags and boxes from Rome. Rufina begins to cry, but aside from the briefest word of consolation from Philos, neither of her parents have time to comfort her. She sits in the kitchen, bewildered, watching them run around the house.

It is hard to see with the light from only one lamp. Amara begins dumping wads of fabric out onto the floor. She finds the rich red cloak she bought for Philos, along with cloaks and robes for herself and Rufina, bundling up the rest of the material so it can be shoved under their hoods. Then she grabs the box containing her most valuable possessions, the jewels and silver plate she brought back from Rome. Some of the rings and necklaces she shoves onto her fingers or winds around her neck, the rest she starts stuffing into a bag.

"There's no time for that," Philos says from the doorway, Rufina already in his arms. "What are you doing?"

"I'm not leaving everything I've worked for!" Amara shouts, on the verge of tears. "What if we never come back?"

At her mother's words, Rufina begins to sob too. "Julia! I want Julia!" It takes her parents a moment to realize she means the doll.

"Upstairs on the bed!" Amara says, and Philos hurries off to fetch the toy.

Desperation comes over Amara as she starts to realize how little she can take. She grabs the material she just bought for her wedding clothes along with the most expensive items, which will be light enough for her and Philos to carry, leaving behind the rest. She fills three bags. Most of the chests sit in the dark, unopened. In the corner is the strong box, containing all the valuables she has been collecting since her days with Rufus. Amara goes to it and heaves open the lid. She finds the leather pouch full of all the jewels her former lover gave her, which she never wears in Rome, and shoves it into one of the bags. The precious glass bottle, full of jasmine perfume, she leaves. It will smash too easily. The two priceless scrolls Pliny gave her are also here. Amara runs her fingers over them both, uncertain. She is fondest of his first gift, Herophilus's treaty on the circulation of the blood, a medical text her father once owned, but it is too bulky and would almost require a bag of its own. So instead she takes the scroll on the properties and uses of plants, Pliny's more recent gift, which Philos uses in the garden.

The hail of stones on the roof seems to be gaining in ferocity. Amara shuts the box, praying that she can come back for the rest. Philos is waiting in the kitchen with Rufina. They swathe their daughter in the expensive material that was supposed to be saved for her dowry, before wrapping her to Philos's body in yet more fabric, so that he has his arms free. Amara drapes one of the three bags she has filled over Philos's shoulder, then helps him into the red cloak, stuffing the hood with rolls of fabric to protect his head. Then she slings the other two bags over her own shoulders, wrapping herself in a similar cloak with a padded hood. They each take a lamp.

"Ready?" Philos asks.

Amara nods, although she is not. They run out into the garden, but the sight that greets them almost has Amara retreat, terrified, back into the safety of the house. Philos grips her arm to stop her from fleeing. One of the trees in the orchard is on fire, the flames quickly spreading. It is even darker now, and the fire is almost the only real source of light. Everything is covered in ash and stones, and part of the colonnade is cracked, the deadly rain collecting on the roof, weighing down the building. They head to the atrium, their progress slowed by debris that is now almost ankle-deep. Rufina cries, her sobs muffled by layers of fabric.

"Julia! Livia!" Amara shouts for her friends when she reaches the house. But there is no answer, only a crash, as a shower of roof tiles collapses in the garden behind them. Amara calls out again, but this time inhales a mouthful of ash, and doubles over coughing.

"Wait here," Philos says, helping Amara to a bench. "I will run into the house for them."

He disappears. Amara is left alone in the atrium, still gasping for air, looking around wildly. Scenes of Pompeii's forum surround her, but in the dark, her lamp only gives her glimpses of the frescoes, ghostly faces picked out in the gloom. It makes her think of the spirits of the underworld, gathered together, waiting to cross the River Styx. She looks up, desperate for Philos to return. Ash and stones are falling through the opening to the sky, pouring down into Julia's house, like earth filling a tomb.

Philos runs back into the atrium. "They won't come," he says. "Julia is completely adamant. Livia is never going to leave her, and the rest of the servants want to shelter rather than risk it."

"Are you *sure* it's not safer to stay here?" Amara says, feeling it would be much more comfortable to huddle together with Livia and Julia, and hope this passes, than to walk out into the terrifying darkness.

"I'm very sure," he says. "Please trust me." Philos stretches out his hand to her. After a moment's hesitation, she takes it and stands. They stare at one another, then he squeezes her fingers, and pulls her after him. He pauses at the door, yanking it open. Ash and stones fall inward, already building up against the wood. They step out into the city. The darkened street is full of people fleeing, all clutching lamps that burn in the swirling gray dust. Many, like Amara or Philos, have thought to tie fabric or pillows to their heads. Some are shouting or crying, others are silent, set grimly on the business of surviving. Philos pushes his way through the crush, Amara still clinging onto his hand so they do not lose each other.

Everything is chaotic. Shopkeepers have had no time to drag all their wares inside and Amara finds herself stumbling over a basket of olives, the oil drenching her legs as the slippery fruit spills over her feet. She almost drops her lamp, but Philos seizes her elbow, stopping her from falling. People around her shove and scream, and she is forced to keep moving, frightened they will be crushed in a stampede. It is hard to breathe in the ash-filled air, and the straps of the bags she is carrying weigh heavily. A steady drizzle of hot, falling stones continue to drop from the sky and Amara brushes them from her clothes, not allowing them to settle. Some are black and charred as if they have been burned, leaving soot on her fingers. Larger rocks also fall, one crashing onto a house further up the street, collapsing its roof in a violent explosion of tiles. As they approach the building, Amara averts her eyes. The body of a man lies half hidden by the rubble, while his desperate wife tries to drag him free. There is no way he can have survived.

Their short journey on a familiar street is transformed into a punishment from Hades, as they wade through the ever-deepening ash and stones. It feels like earth tremors are also starting to shake the city, but with the falling debris, the darkness, and the terrifying noise, it is hard to distinguish one horror from another. They arrive at the barracks to find the place unscathed, its doors gaping open. Amara feels certain that Britannica must have already fled. She lets go of Philos and runs into the colonnade, calling out for her.

"Amara!" Britannica's answering deep voice almost makes Amara sob with relief. "What you do here? Why you not shelter with Julia?" Britannica is standing, barely visible in the darkness, by the gladiator's cells. Amara realizes the room behind her friend is filled with people, a single, flickering lamp illuminating their frightened faces. "There was show at the theater," Britannica says, gesturing at the huddled group. "They hide here until it passes. We are helping."

"It's not going to pass," Philos says, grabbing the Briton's arm. "It's going to get worse. The mountain is on fire. We have to get as far away as we possibly can. Go fetch Stephanus and whoever else will come with us. Quickly!"

Britannica does not pause to argue. She runs to a nearby cell, where Stephanus is trying to calm the people taking shelter.

The colonnade provides some protection from the hail of stones as Stephanus tries to round up the other gladiators and persuade the theatergoers to leave. Then he disappears to his rooms to say goodbye to Cosmus. He is gone for some time. Amara starts to fear that perhaps Stephanus will change his mind and decide to stay beside his dying brother to the end. She looks out into the swirling ash. Vesuvius is no longer fully visible in the darkness, but she can hear it roar, the sound so loud it seems as if the mountain's rage will never be spent. She thinks of her friends, wondering how Drusilla is keeping Primus calm, and hopes they too are escaping.

When Stephanus returns, they set out again, joined by Britannica and three other men. Amara does not dare ask Stephanus about Cosmus, understanding from his anguished face what it must cost him to leave. The barracks is close to the Stabian Gate, and they join the crush of refugees trying to make their way out of the stone arch in the city's walls. It does not look like the same gate she and Britannica passed through just days ago. The road is jammed. Some people have loaded up carts, trying to support their elderly relatives or to take as much of their wealth as possible, but it is difficult to steer through the debris. Deserted wagons become yet another obstacle to navigate in the hot, poisonous rain.

Amara is sweating under the thick clothing, almost suffocated by the heat, her bags slowing her down, digging painfully into her shoulder blades. Britannica is at her back, pushing her forward as they fight their way along the road that leads south. A man leading a mule slung round with baskets, tries to shove the two women aside. Scrambling over the skittering stones, Amara is almost trampled under the beast's hooves, but Britannica grabs her and the pair of them cling to a tomb front, one of many lining the route out of the city. Amara screams for Philos, terrified she has lost him and her daughter in the rushing ebb and flow of people. She inhales more ash from shouting and is soon coughing, struggling for breath. Then Philos is beside her, pressing his forehead to her own, Rufina between them. She holds them both close, calmed for a moment. Their child is silent.

"Is she alright?" Amara asks, laying a hand on her daughter's small body, wanting to feel the rise and fall of her breathing.

"She's asleep," Philos says. "I think the stress of it."

"Where are the others?" It is Britannica talking to Stephanus.

"We lost them," Stephanus replies, gesturing at the road with its writhing sea of bodies, pinpoints of light from the lamps barely distinguishing one frantic face from another.

"We cannot stay," Britannica says, resting her hand on Amara's shoulder. "Come."

They continue on their laborious journey from Pompeii, avoiding the crush of wagons and mules in the center of the road, clinging instead to the tombs of the Necropolis, the dead aiding their escape. Stabiae is not far along the coast but at this slow pace, Amara suspects the walk will take hours. She starts to think of nothing beyond putting one step in front of the other, not allowing her mind to terrify her with the magnitude of what is happening. Sometimes she looks around, hoping to see her friends—perhaps Livia has already persuaded Julia to leave—but there is no sign of anyone she knows or loves.

They reach the bridge over the River Sarnus. Somebody has driven a cart straight into the water, perhaps losing control on the uneven surface of the road. The river brings a welcome breeze, lessening the suffocating warmth of swirling ash. Amara is afraid that people might shove or fight in the long queue to cross over, but a survival instinct seems to have gripped the crowd, and the wait is long but relatively orderly.

As they travel further out of Pompeii, the road rises steeply and the number of people thins. This is not a journey for the weak. Amara tries not to look at those who stop, wheezing by the roadside. Parents are forced to carry their children, slowed down by their weight, slipping in the debris. It is exhausting work scrabbling in the dark, pelted by the constantly falling stones. Even the light from Amara's lamp provides little guidance and it feels like yet another impossible task on top of walking, trying to protect the flame from going out.

"We survive this," Britannica says to her when Amara stops for a moment, pausing for breath, trying to quell the panic rising in her chest. "We survive."

"We have to keep going." Philos grabs Amara's hand, pulling her upright. He lacks Britannica's brute strength, but Amara realizes, seeing the determination on his face, that Philos possesses a ferocity she has not imagined before.

"Rufina?" Amara asks, unable to form more words than this.

"Breathing," Philos replies, his hand resting on their child's back. They are high enough up now to look back on Pompeii, and as they set off again, Amara turns to glance toward the homes they have left. She breathes in sharply. A trail of lamp lights snakes back to the city, glowing brighter where people must be bunched together at the bottom of the hill. In the darkness she can see the red rooftops, lit by myriad fires that have broken out across the city.

"No," Britannica says, roughly turning her to face the south. "We don't look back."

They trudge on, the road increasingly dangerous as ash and stones roll down the slopes of the hilltop above them, onto the road, and then down again toward the sea. A few people are swept off the path with the rolling debris, but nobody except their own desperate families stops to attempt a rescue.

After what must be an hour or more of walking, they stop for water. Neither Amara nor Philos thought to pack anything to eat or drink, but Stephanus, who is no stranger to surviving hostile odds, brought a leather bag filled with bread and two goatskin flasks of water. Philos wakes Rufina up to drink, but she refuses the food, nestling back against him to sleep. Amara tears into her portion, gulping down the bread. She had not realized how famished she had become. They rest their backs against a small farm building at the side of the road, its walls providing some protection from the increasingly alarming landslides that roll down the hill and crash into the waves far below.

Amara is about to hand the water skin to Britannica when the wall behind them cracks. For one terrified moment, Britannica and Amara's eyes lock, then they spring apart—Philos and Amara scrambling for safety in one direction, Stephanus and Britannica in the other. The building they were sheltering against is falling apart. Clouds of dust and ash, thrown up by the crash of collapsing rubble, create a scene of total confusion. People are screaming, calling on the gods to spare them. Amara's lamp goes out, and all she is conscious of is the grip of Philos's hand, dragging her further up the hill, away from the destruction. The debris that had piled up behind the small building's walls must have pushed it over, like a child kicking down a pile of wooden blocks.

They keep scrambling, as far and as fast up the road as they can, until the noise of the landslide subsides. Then they stop. People are coughing and weeping, trying to take stock of whatever now surrounds them, calling out for their relatives and friends. In the hot, dusty darkness, Amara feels suddenly cold.

"Britannica!" she screams. "Britannica!"

There is no answer save the crying of strangers.

18

"He gave orders for the warships to be launched and went on board himself with the intention of bringing help . . . He hurried to the place which everyone else was hastily leaving, steering his course straight for the danger zone."
—Pliny the Younger, writing on the rescue mission launched by his uncle Pliny the Elder during the eruption of Vesuvius

Amara does not know how long she and Philos spend searching for her friend, both of them calling for Britannica over and over in the darkness. Rufina is crying, and the sound of her daughter's anguish echoes that of Amara's heart. Philos has lost his lamp, and Amara's has gone out, making their search harder, until a man Amara has never met grabs her by the arm, holding her steady. Without speaking, he lowers his lamp to hers, reigniting the flame. His unexpected act of kindness almost overwhelms her; she wants to thank him, but by the time she has found the words, he has gone.

Even with the light back, movement is difficult. The stones slow Amara down, adding to her desperation. They push and scramble among the other survivors, seeing their own expressions of grief and disappointment reflected in the faces of those they meet. And all the while the ash falls. It is a nightmare without the hope of waking.

"We have to keep going," Philos says at last. "We're not going to find them. I'm so sorry."

"No," she cries. "I'm not leaving her. She isn't dead. She can't be." Amara thinks of Britannica in the arena, how she fought there, victorious, just one day ago, and screams her friend's name, willing her back into existence. Her voice breaks, hoarse from the dust and so much crying. It is impossible that Amara is still clutching the souvenir lamp, with its imaginary netman, yet Britannica herself is dead.

"Perhaps she *has* survived," Philos says, holding her tight around the shoulders. "But if so, we will have to trust her and Stephanus to look after themselves. We cannot keep looking for them here."

"I suppose they might have found some way to make it out into the open countryside." Amara seizes on the only hope that remains, not wanting to face the alternative.

"Yes," Philos says. "And Britannica will want us to continue, not wait here."

Amara knows this is true. Whether Britannica is living or dead, she would not want them to perish looking for her; she would want Amara to ensure Fighter's survival. The thought of Britannica's nickname for Rufina brings on a fresh flood of tears, but Amara cries silently, holding Philos's hand as they keep walking onward. Rufina cries more loudly, but neither Amara nor Philos have the strength to comfort their daughter. Eventually Rufina too subsides into silence.

All sense of time and place is obliterated by the disaster. Amara has traveled the route between Pompeii and Stabiae many times by carriage, taken in luxury to Demetrius's estate, but she cannot make out any landmarks in this changed, gray world. Her sense of grief deepens as they press onward; the pain in her chest at Britannica's death is a seeping wound, weakening her will to survive.

All she wants to do is huddle into a ball like her daughter, and close her eyes to the horror. She starts to resent the way Philos tugs ceaselessly at her arm, dragging her onward, when everything before them is as hellish as the scene they have just left behind. The dread builds in her mind, until it becomes overwhelming. She longs to slump to the ground, even though she knows if she does, she will never get up.

She stops abruptly. "I need to rest for a moment."

"We can't." Philos tugs at her again. "We have to get to Stabiae."

"I can't keep going." Amara feels as if she cannot get enough air to breathe. It is not only the ash—panic is drowning her, trapping her in darkness. "You will get Rufina to safety quicker without me. I'm too afraid, Philos. I can't do this. I can't."

Philos pulls her to the side of the road, so they are not buffeted as much by their fellow refugees. "Of course you can. Come on."

His determination only increases Amara's sense of powerlessness. It feels impossible to explain what the loss of Britannica means to her, that what she feels is not only grief but despair. Britannica's strength, her courage, the ways in which she was always so vividly and fearlessly *alive*—all these qualities made Amara feel that anything she suffered could be overcome, if only she too fought hard enough. Britannica's death is the death of hope. Amara begins to sob.

"No." Philos grips her by the shoulder. "This is *not* where you die. Think of everything you have already survived. You are one of the strongest people I have ever met." He puts his hand to her cheek, tilting her face toward him, his other arm wrapped around Rufina, who is half-hidden in his cloak. "It's why I love you. It is why I will always love you."

In the light of their single lamp, Philos's face is streaked with soot, his gray eyes fixed on hers. His earnest expression, and his tenderness, are completely at odds with the misery surrounding them. He is holding Rufina, the child she once hoped would set him free. The thought of their daughter jolts Amara out of her headlong descent. Britannica is dead but she still has Rufina to protect. She still has Philos. Her family is here. Amara does not think of the implications of what she is saying, only the truth of it. "I love you too."

"Then you will keep going?"

She nods, accepting the gift he is offering her, holding his hand more tightly as a promise that she will not give up.

The hail of stones lessens slightly the closer they get to Stabiae, or at least it does not grow worse. They struggle on, running out of the last of Stephanus's water, until eventually they round the bay to see the town's harbor far below. It is lit by torches as if it were nighttime, although it must only be late afternoon. Moored, or perhaps beached in the wide basin, are two enormous warships, dwarfing all the other boats that lurch up and down beside them.

"Those ships belong to the Roman fleet," Amara says, amazed. "Do you think the admiral is here?" For the first time since they lost Britannica, at the thought of Pliny, she feels something close to hope.

"If he is," Philos says, "perhaps we can escape by sea. It's a better chance than going to Demetrius's estate. Everyone must have fled there by now."

They scramble down the road that leads to the shore. A handful of other refugees join them, though most continue doggedly on the main road, heading for Surrentum. It is hard to get into Stabiae as they are walking against the flow of those escaping, and have to jostle their way through the crowd. On the streets they find people packing up wagons, blocking the pavements as they bolt their doors and shutters, preparing to flee from the mountain's rage. From the number of boarded-up shops, it looks as if many have already fled. Amara and Philos press on through the emptying town to the sea.

The warships tower over the port and have drawn a gaggle of people who must be hoping to board, although the waves whipping against the harbor look too ferocious for any ship to set sail. Amara squints at the soldiers from the Praetorian Guard who stand onshore, desperate to see Pliny among them. At first she thinks it is only her imagination that makes the man in the center look like the admiral, before relief hits her.

"It's him!"

They hurry toward the soldiers and Amara flings herself at the nearest guard. "Please," she begs, clutching the man's arm. "I am the admiral's freedwoman, Plinia Amara. Please take me to him!" The man looks at her, suspicious. "This is my . . . freedman, Philos. And my daughter Rufina. The admiral will know me, I promise you. He only brought me from Rome to Misenum a few weeks ago, after the emperor's funeral. And from there I went on to Pompeii. We have walked all the way here."

Her knowledge of his commander's recent movements seems to convince the guard. "Come, then," he says, ushering her through the crowds to where the admiral is standing. The soldier approaches Pliny who is talking to another man. At first Pliny looks irritated by the interruption but then his eyes fall on Amara. He stares for a moment, perhaps taking a while to recognize his freedwoman; Amara realizes she must make for a strange sight with her head swathed in fabric and her face blackened with ash.

"*Amara?*" Pliny asks at last. "Is that really you? How did you get here?"

The familiar sound of his voice brings the promise of safety. Amara takes Pliny's outstretched hands, almost crying with relief. It is all she can do to stop herself from kissing him. "We took the road from Pompeii," she says. "I wanted to get to Demetrius's estate."

"You walked in *this*? My dear girl, you must be exhausted." Pliny turns to his companion who seems not at all pleased by the sudden loss of the Admiral's attention. "Pomponianus, this is my freedwoman Plinia Amara. She is betrothed to our friend Demetrius, who I know you have met before."

Pliny's tone is one of absolute calm, as if this were nothing more than a regular social introduction. Pomponianus still looks fraught, but nonetheless bows to Amara, managing to recover his manners. "Then you must join us, Plinia Amara, at my house. We were hoping to leave by sea but will have to wait until the winds have died down." They all look toward the stranded warships. Judging by the black waves, currently hurling themselves at the harbor wall, their escape will not be any time soon.

"Not much of a rescue mission," Pliny says, sounding amused in spite of their dire circumstances. "My apologies to everyone. But I think at this stage our best hope is to shelter indoors and hope the storm passes."

They follow Pomponianus and his gaggle of servants, heading away from the harbor. Philos is no longer holding Amara's hand. She is conscious of him walking just behind her, resuming his servile role. It feels as if she has committed an act of betrayal, after everything that just happened on the road, but she cannot turn around.

Pomponianus's house is on the main street that leads to Stabiae's forum. It is an enormous building, and its height gives the illusion of strength. Whatever shops normally sit either side of its giant doors are shuttered up, turning their blank wooden faces to the road. They all huddle on the doorstep until the porter admits them, bowing to his master; Amara steps over the threshold— a beautiful black-and-white mosaic of two dolphins, swimming playfully with a Nereid.

Inside, the atrium is brightly lit with torches and oil lamps. Amara blinks, staring around at the painted walls, which are decorated with gilded frescoes of the hero Hercules. It is the first time she has been able to see clearly since she left Julia's house, and the light instantly lifts her spirits. A large courtyard and garden sit beyond the main entrance, open to the darkened sky above. From this distance, the steady fall of ash and stone could almost be mistaken for heavy rain, though the drumbeat as it hits the roof is too loud to be soothing—even the worst hailstorms do not sound like this.

"I'm sorry we have so many calling upon you unexpectedly for dinner," Pliny says to Pomponianus, raising his voice to be heard over the din. "Perhaps I might take a bath before we dine?" Everyone, including Amara, gapes at him. "Well, even if it *is* the end of the world," Pliny says, testily. "I don't wish to eat my last supper looking as if I spent the afternoon in Vulcan's forge. And you could do with washing yourself too, Amara, or at the very least clean your face. I can scarcely recognize you." He gestures at her, pursing his lips in displeasure. "You might have been down a mine."

"We should indeed, all take a bath before dinner," Pomponianus agrees, perhaps drawing strength from his guest's insistence on normality. He nods toward a man who must be the household steward, who in turn rushes to see that his master's bidding is done. Pomponianus and Pliny make their way to the back of the complex, keeping to the sheltered colonnade as they head to where the baths must be. A slave girl hovers by Amara.

"Shall I show you to your room?" the girl asks.

"In a moment, thank you," Amara replies. She turns to Philos, who is unwrapping the fabric that keeps Rufina tied to his body, waking her up.

Rufina starts to cry. "There now," Philos soothes. "You are quite safe. We are with your mother's protector, the Admiral of the Roman Fleet. In Stabiae."

"I want to go home," Rufina wails. "I want Julia; I want Livia."

The mention of her two absent friends crushes Amara's emerging sense of hope. It seems likely that yet more grief lies ahead, and she cannot face the idea of further heartbreak so soon after Britannica's death. She hauls the two heavy bags she has carried from Pompeii off her shoulders, letting them lie on the floor, and hurries to reassure her daughter. "I'm sure we will see them soon, my love," she says, as Philos lifts Rufina into her arms. She holds her daughter close, stroking her head; Rufina's small body is hot and damp with sweat. "Come with me to have a bath, you will feel better."

"Don't leave me," Rufina cries, leaning over her mother's shoulder to clutch at Philos's cloak. "I want you!"

"I will be right here with the other servants, little one," Philos reassures her, handing over the wooden doll, which must have been wedged uncomfortably against his chest for the entirety of their escape from Pompeii. "I'm not going anywhere, I promise." He catches Amara's eye, and for one mad moment, she nearly asks him to accompany them. It feels unnatural to separate.

Amara turns away from Philos, carrying off the still crying Rufina, and follows the maid into one of the rooms off the courtyard. "I don't know how much water I can bring you," the girl says, setting down her oil lamp with a shaking hand, obviously terrified of being sent out to the well in the raging, unearthly storm outside.

"Please don't disturb yourself," Amara says. "Just some water to drink and to clean our faces will be fine." The girl nods and leaves the room.

Rufina's cries have subsided into whimpers. Amara sits down at the dressing table, where the slave girl placed the lamp, gathering her child onto her knee, holding her close. "There now," she says. "I bet Julia is hungry, don't you?" She holds the doll upright, balancing her on the table as if she were standing. "I think we should take her with us to dinner."

"I need a wee," her daughter sniffs.

Amara gets up, leaving Rufina on the stool where she sits gazing mournfully at Julia, and searches for the chamber pot. It is not a task for a respectable woman, but she is in no mind to disturb the slaves, who must be wrestling with enough of their own terrors without having to cater to every need of Pomponianus's guests. A single lamp does not throw as much light as she would like, and the room is made gloomier by being painted in dark colors—pale cupids and flowers stand out against its black walls. Amara has to scrabble blindly under the bed to find the pot. After she and Rufina have relieved themselves, the slave girl returns with a large tray. It holds a silver jug, two expensive glasses, a pile of linen, and a large basin of water. If it weren't for the increasingly loud banging on the roof, it could almost be a homely scene.

"Thank you," Amara says, as the girl sets down the tray. Between them, she and Rufina quickly drink the whole jug of water; Amara's throat is parched and sore from the ash. She watches as the slave girl cleans her daughter's face and hands, dabbing the linen in the basin. Then it is Amara's turn. Rufina was largely protected by Philos's cloak, but the same was not true of her mother. Judging from the blackened state of the linen, Pliny's assessment of Amara looking like a miner must have been fairly accurate.

"Thank you," Amara says to the slave girl when she has finished.

"Will you come through to the dining room now?" the girl asks.

Amara follows her, balancing Rufina on her hip. Pomponianus's winter dining room is a large, elegant room, painted in green, with three enormous couches. Two women are already reclining inside, one in her fifties the other much younger. A slave washes Amara's feet before she enters, blackening yet more linen. Amara winces as the cloth rubs against her blisters.

"I am Volusia," the older woman declares when Amara enters, with the air of a hostess who is determined not to allow the impending destruction of civilization to dampen her dinner party. "Pomponianus's wife. This is my daughter Cornelia, who is visiting us from Surrentum with her husband."

Amara sits on the couch opposite, conscious of her dusty clothes, holding Rufina. "I am Amara, the admiral's freedwoman, betrothed to Demetrius. This is my daughter, Rufina. Delighted to meet you both." Unlike her mother, Cornelia looks frightened, hunched into herself on the couch. She barely manages to mumble a greeting in response. Amara looks around the room, trying to think of something more to say. "The painting work in your house is very fine. We might really be in the presence of Penelope and her loom; I have never seen her depicted quite like that before."

Volusia looks gratified. "Weaving is an accomplishment all women should take pride in. I make some of my husband's robes myself."

Amara is nodding politely, hoping she won't be asked whether she does the same for Demetrius, when Pliny arrives with their host, along with a younger man, who must be Pomponianus's son-in-law.

"You see," Pliny declares pleasantly, "I knew we would all have clearer heads after taking a bath." Everyone smiles, though it's obvious they feel the strain of keeping up the pretence. Two slaves enter with platters of food, setting them on the small tables that rest near the couches. Amara wonders how the pair of them feel, being obliged to serve at such a time. Pliny helps himself to a small roasted songbird and some boiled eggs. "Your hospitality is as gracious as always, Volusia."

Nobody else seems inclined to talk, but after a glass of wine, they all become a little bolder, if not quite matching the admiral's mood. "What hope do you think there is of the wind lifting?" Pomponianus asks.

"It doesn't look terribly hopeful," Pliny admits. "But tomorrow is a new day."

"We cannot wait until tomorrow, surely?" Cornelia cries. "Oh! How I wish we had never left Surrentum!" She starts to weep. Her husband Maximus, who looks equally miserable, pats her on the shoulder.

"Well, after dinner we might take a look outside," Pliny concedes. "To see what's happening with the weather."

They continue with their meal, although Rufina seems to be the only one present who has much of an appetite. Amara feeds her hungry daughter pieces of egg and fowl, while Volusia valiantly asks about her wedding preparations. Amara answers that it was supposed to be here, in Stabiae, around the Saturnalia. At that Volusia falls silent and everyone looks at each other, each wondering what Stabiae might look like in December. They carry on, forcing themselves to eat and talk, the conversation mostly driven by Pliny whose hearty attitude is a little grating. Amara keeps glancing at him, trying to divine if he is really as calm as he seems. His mask remains impeccable until a mild earth tremor shakes the house, setting the glasses rattling. It is only then that she sees concern, even fear, flash across his face.

"Perhaps we might go outside now," he says, "and see what is happening with the storm."

They all scramble up from their couches, their haste at odds with the veneer of calm. Amara holds Rufina tight in her arms as they head toward the gardens at the back of the house, taking shelter under the colonnade. Standing out here, the thunder of pelting stones is unbearably loud, and when Amara looks up toward Vesuvius, she gasps. The mountain is ablaze in the night, flames breaking out across its slopes with the vicious intent of a hostile army. Enormous clouds of smoke continue to belch from the mountain's summit, blasted upward from the raging forge at its heart, and as the column rises, it is riven by sheets of lightning and fire. The sight is so shocking, Amara cannot speak. Cornelia begins to weep, and even Volusia turns aside, hiding her face in her husband's embrace. Amara clutches Rufina, certain she must be terrified, but instead her daughter gazes at Vesuvius dry-eyed, mesmerized by the vision of flame.

"I think," Pliny says slowly, "some peasants must have left bonfires burning when they fled."

" *Peasants?*" Pomponianus declares, incredulous. "The mountain is on fire, man!"

Pliny skewers Pomponianus with a look, before flicking his eyes in warning toward the sobbing Cornelia. "Yes," he says firmly. "*Peasants.* Or perhaps some of the buildings were set on fire as people abandoned the district. At any rate, nothing that need unduly alarm us at this distance."

The two old friends stare at one another. "Maybe you are right," Pomponianus mutters. He clears his throat. "No need to cry so much, girl. The admiral says it's just a few house fires. Let's all go back inside."

The family leaves, but Amara remains standing with Pliny, who has now fished out a wax tablet from the folds of his robe. He opens it, staring up at the mountain before scratching down notes in his booklet, recording the extraordinary phenomena unfolding before them. "You don't think it's peasants, do you," Amara says when he finally snaps the tablet shut. It is not a question.

"That's very astute of you," Pliny says drily. "No, I don't think peasants set the whole mountain on fire. Vesuvius is clearly another Etna. Though an angrier beast than its Sicilian cousin." He bends to pick up one of the many fallen stones on the floor, and turns it in his fingers. "Look, you see, pumice. Full of holes. If it weren't so light, the weight of all this debris would have brought the roof down by now." He hands the pumice stone to Rufina, who pokes at it, her childish curiosity matching the admiral's own.

Amara cannot keep back the only question that concerns her. "Are we going to survive?"

Pliny looks at Rufina who is still peering at the pumice stone, her small face glowing orange in the unearthly light. He strokes the child's hair. "I have read many books but I've yet to find one that can predict the future." He smiles at Amara, and she feels intense affection for this strange, inexplicable man who has done so much to alter the course of her life. "Still, I came here to stage a rescue mission. And you know how I hate for my plans to be thwarted." He turns to leave. "Seems as good a time as any for bed, don't you think?"

19

"Elsewhere there was daylight by this time, but they were still in darkness, blacker and denser than any ordinary night, which they relieved by lighting torches and various kinds of lamp."

—Pliny the Younger, on the final day of
Pliny the Elder's rescue mission

Pliny is the only member of the household to go to bed, everyone else stays up throughout the night, gathered in the atrium. The slaves huddle on the floor in one corner, Philos among them, while the family and Amara sit on benches. As the night goes on, earth tremors begin rocking the house, slowly growing in intensity, reminding Amara of the birthing pains she once suffered. Rufina lies dozing on her lap. Her weight is heavy, deadening Amara's legs, but she could not bear to lay her child down to sleep in another room, out of sight. Rufina's soft, snuffling breaths are at odds with the tension of everyone else in the room. They all watch as the central pool is smothered by a growing pyramid of ash and stones, which rain relentlessly through the opening in the roof. As more stones fall, they start to spill beyond the edge of the pool, creeping over the tiles toward the living. The garden and courtyard are also filling up.

"If we stay here, we will be buried alive in our own home," Volusia says, breaking the silence. "Can the admiral not at least *try* to set sail?"

"You weren't at the harbor," Pomponianus snaps. "It's impossible."

Another tremor hits, and this time cracks fan out over the plaster on the painted walls, as if Hercules's lion is raking its claws across the hero's exploits.

"We're going to die," Cornelia cries, weeping into her husband's shoulder. Some of the servants are crying too. Amara looks over at Philos. He is gazing out at the garden, his face completely still.

"What is Pliny doing, sleeping through it? I can hear his snores from here!" Volusia exclaims.

"He has asthma," Pomponianus says. "I don't suppose all this ash is doing him much good."

"Then why don't we *leave*?" Volusia barely manages to get the words out before an especially violent tremor shakes the house. Several people scream. One of the marble pillars in the garden cracks, and the edge of the colonnade that rests upon it sags downwards.

"That's it," Volusia shouts. "I'm waking him. If we don't get him up now, we'll barely be able to open his door for all the ash in the courtyard." She gestures at the household steward, dispatching the man to wake the admiral. The steward hurries along the undamaged side of the colonnade, wading through the stones.

Pliny emerges a short while after. He rests his hand on the wall as he walks, and even at a distance, Amara can see his chest rising and falling with the exertion of breathing. "Well," he begins, but he is interrupted by a coughing fit. "Well," he tries again, "it seems things have become more uncomfortable." The earth shakes again, and this time, the cracked pillar collapses, bringing down the roof at the end of the garden, in a rush of brick and tiles. Cornelia screams, calling on the goddess Juno to save her. Amara instinctively bends over Rufina, as if somehow her own frail body might protect her daughter from the full force of a collapsing building. The rumbling of the quake and the pounding of her own heart are so loud in her head, Amara cannot tell them apart. Her daughter does not even wake. At last the tremor subsides.

"We can't stay here," Volusia says, getting to her feet, her hand against the wall as if somehow this will keep her steady. "The house is falling apart! We have to try and set sail."

"I'm not sure that will be possible," Pliny says. "But I agree the house will soon offer us little protection."

"Where will we go to be safe?" Amara asks, still hoping Pliny might know the answer to this unanswerable question.

"As far from the mountain as possible," Pliny replies. "Much as you had the good sense to do earlier."

The household readies itself to leave, everyone moving swiftly, even though the danger they face outside is hardly preferable to the danger of remaining indoors. Amara and Philos tie Rufina to her father again, although this time she squirms and cries, annoyed at being woken. Philos jigs up and down, trying to lull her back to sleep, while Amara loads them both up with their bags. Then they swathe themselves back into their now filthy cloaks with padded hoods. Amara is so tired from fear and lack of sleep, she is not sure if she is swaying on her feet from exhaustion or the constantly trembling ground. She feels Philos grip her elbow, helping her stay upright.

Volusia orders the slaves to bring all the pillows in the house to the atrium. When they are in a large pile, everyone steps forward to tie one to their heads, the freeborn taking protection first, the slaves taking what is left. After a heated exchange, Pomponianus refuses his wife's request to gather more of their valuables. "We don't have time," he declares. "Most of it's already loaded in the boat. That will have to do."

The steward hands out lamps and torches to the whole household, including to a number of small children who are dotted among the slaves, so that everyone will have some light to see by. Amara finds herself thinking of Primigenia and Servius, wondering if they are both still in Pompeii with Livia and Julia, and what Philos might have said when he tried to persuade them all to leave. She hopes they are safe; the disaster is too huge to leave room for jealousy.

When everyone is ready, the porter unlocks the doors, swinging them inward. He is rewarded by a heap of ash and stones that rush in over the dolphin mosaic, burying his feet, making him cry out in shock. The steward and some of the other slaves run forward to help, trying in vain to clear a path through the debris. Heaps of pumice have raised the level of the street, meaning everyone has to climb and scramble upward out of the house, as if they were scaling a steep hill. Volusia was right about the risk of them being buried alive.

Once they are outside, even more time is wasted by Pomponianus who insists on pulling the doors shut again, wanting to lock them in case of thieves. It takes several failed attempts, with the poor slaves struggling against the weight of the stones that stream into the house, before their master accepts the task is fruitless.

It is not possible to walk through the street, instead they wade. Amara's sense of claustrophobia grows as her legs sink deep into the ash and stones. She reaches instinctively for Philos, and they make their way through, hand in hand. Tremors are still shaking the town, the buildings surrounding them cracking and swaying. Amara knows that a pillow tied to her head will not provide any protection from a collapsing house, but the sheer multitude of terrors they are enduring means she is almost numb to fear. There is nothing to do but keep going.

Their journey is short but exhausting, and when they reach the open space of the port Amara experiences a momentary sense of relief. Debris has not piled up as deeply here as in the narrow streets, although the darkness feels more absolute. There are no buildings hemming them in to catch the light of their torches, instead their small gathering feels like it might be all that survives of Stabiae, the rest swallowed by black ash. Pliny is coughing so hard, Amara is not sure how he is still upright, but he insists on going to the shore to inspect the state of the waves. They follow him, slipping and scrambling their way to the edge of the harbor. Even though she cannot see far, Amara sees enough to know that the black expanse of sea offers no escape. Not only is the water too wild and dangerous to set sail, but the ships are also silted in with debris, the shoreline seeming to have retreated from the harbor. It's no less than they were all expecting but the disappointment is still crushing. Some small part of Amara had dared to imagine herself bundling Rufina on board, Pliny gathering them all together before commanding his men to set sail for the safety of Rome.

It seems everyone was clinging to the same fantasy. They stand in a gaggle, clutching their torches, looking to Pliny for reassurance like children leaning on a parent, as if somehow, against all odds, the admiral will have the answers. He opens his mouth to speak but instead starts to cough again, this time uncontrollably. With horror, Amara realizes his body is convulsing. He cannot breathe. A household slave catches hold of him, as Pliny gasps for air.

"The admiral is having an asthma attack," she cries. "He needs some space. He needs to rest."

"Out here?" Pomponianus cries, his face stricken with fear. "This is no place for him to rest!"

One of the sailors guarding the ships lays out a sheet and Pliny sits down, as if his legs will no longer support him. Slowly his convulsions subside. "Water might help," Amara says to the man, who takes out a flask for the admiral to drink from. Pliny seizes it, gulping down liquid between great wheezing breaths.

"Thank you," Pliny says to Amara, his voice unrecognizably hoarse. "I think it best," he continues, looking up at the terrified faces of his friends, "if you now get as far out of Stabiae as you can." Pliny stops, gasping for air, like a fish stranded on land. When he speaks again, he has to pause after every other word, suffering obvious pain. "My men will help you now. I will rest here and join you later."

"But we cannot leave you here alone!" Pomponianus cries. "How will you come after us?"

"Go," Pliny says, his chest heaving with the effort of speech. "Please."

"Do as he says," Volusia hisses.

Pomponianus starts to argue when a violent tremor strikes. Amara is flung to the ground, landing on the sheet beside Pliny. The warships sway crazily, their timbers cracking, and in the darkness she can hear the deafening roar and crash of buildings collapsing in the town behind. Heat hits them in a wave, the air carrying the tang of sulfur, and Amara finds herself choking in its acrid stench. The slaves begin to flee, heeding the warning of that ultimate master, Death. With a last anguished look back at the admiral, Pomponianus also turns and flees, running and sliding over the stones, following his family. Even the guards, either through fear or obedience to the word of their commander, are running away. Philos and Amara try to haul Pliny to his feet, but he is a dead weight.

"Please try and get up," she begs. "You have to try. Please. I can't just leave you here."

"*Amara*," Pliny gasps, and even though his face is drawn with pain, she can hear exasperation in his voice. "Don't squander the freedom I gave you. Don't . . ." Pliny coughs again, but this time when he tries to speak, he cannot—he is suffocating in the sulfurous air.

Philos kneels beside the admiral. "You don't have to stay here," he says. "If you put your arm around my shoulders, I can help carry you."

"Please," Amara begs again, pressing her face close to his. "*Please* try."

Pliny is now completely collapsed, and lies on his back, the ash raining down upon him. Amara tries to brush it from his face, but more falls. He is looking at her, desperation in his eyes, unable to find the breath to speak. Instead he manages to raise his arm, flinging it out and pointing in the direction the others fled, the gesture unmistakable. *Go.*

Amara wants to say something, to give Pliny some comfort in the darkness, but finds she has no words. Instead she bends and kisses him on the forehead, pressing her lips to his skin, so that his last human touch will be one of love. Then she takes Philos's hand, allowing him to pull her to her feet, and leaves Pliny to die alone on the shore.

20

*"A terrifying black cloud, split by twisted blasts of fire shooting
in different directions, gaped to reveal long fiery shapes,
similar to flashes of lightning, only bigger."*

—Pliny the Younger, on the eruption of Vesuvius

The darkness that engulfs them as they scramble out of Stabiae
is somehow more frightening than all that has gone before.
The loss of Pliny, immediately after the loss of Britannica, is so
overwhelming that Amara cannot even cry. Instead, she clings
tightly to Philos. His hand gripping hers is all that keeps her teth-
ered to the living world.

At first they careen blindly across the harbor, keeping away
from the buildings that sway dangerously in the now near constant tremors. The main road proves impossible to find in the
choking black air, and so they strike out from the harbor on
a track that runs along the shoreline. Philos carries a flaming
torch, much brighter than the oil lamp Amara took, the same
souvenir lamp she bought at the games in Pompeii, a lifetime ago.
The torch gives just enough light to see a step ahead, and they
often stumble, rocked by the shaking earth. Other lights on the
path pick out more refugees, both small groups, and lone stragglers. They are not the only ones fleeing this way, although this is

nothing like the crush of people on the road yesterday. Most of those they meet are vulnerable—the elderly, a heavily pregnant girl—people who perhaps had hoped to wait out the storm, until waiting became even more dangerous than fleeing.

They are not far out from Stabiae, when they hear a roaring, like approaching thunder. An old woman grabs at Philos as they try to pass. "The mountain! The mountain!" she cries, pointing back the way they have come.

Amara looks over her shoulder. She cannot see Vesuvius. Instead, in the far distance, there is a giant black cloud lit by flame and lightning. It is collapsing outward at speed, heading south. A hot wind blows, carrying the overpowering stench of sulfur. People on the path are screaming, and the old woman beside her calls on the gods, begging the immortals to intervene. Amara holds Philos tightly, Rufina crying between them. Without words, she knows that Philos too believes this is the moment life ends. He pulls her down to sit on the verge, hunching over so that he can protect her and Rufina as much as possible from whatever is coming. Huddled together, Amara places her hand on the sobbing body of her child. It feels incomprehensible that they will die like this. Amara is too shocked even for fear, her mind balking at the coming nothingness Pliny once described as death. They cower in the darkness, as the roaring gets louder.

Scorching hot air strikes, made more violent by the dust and debris it flings in its path. Amara is thrown forward, Philos too, and they cling to one another, trying to withstand the mountain's rage. Amara screws her eyes shut. She presses still closer to Philos, helping him shield Rufina, trying to protect her with their bodies.

They stay like that, too terrified to move, until at last the heat is less suffocating, and although the ash still falls, it is not with the same fury. People begin moaning and weeping again, the old woman is coughing, and Amara understands that they have survived whatever demon just passed. She and Philos sit upright, comforting Rufina, who is totally silent with fear.

Amara looks back toward Vesuvius. Fires burn on its slopes, and flames are dotted elsewhere across the still darkened countryside, but the giant cloud seems to have burned itself out on its torrent through Campania. Philos pats the ground, looking for their lights, which were extinguished in the blast. He finds the still smoking torch that Pomponianus gave him and blows on it until the flame rekindles.

"We should keep going," Philos says, the effort of speech making him cough, "in case Vesuvius has more to throw at us." They rise unsteadily to their feet, the old woman watching them from her place on the verge. "Do you need help?" Philos asks her, holding out his hand.

"My son and daughter-in-law," the old woman says. "I lost them in the darkness."

"Perhaps we will find them on the path?" Amara says.

The old woman looks around, eyes shining white in her ash-coated face. "I don't know where to look."

"Let us help you, then," Philos says. "Here, I can take some of your weight." With difficulty, Philos manages to heave the old woman to her feet, slinging her arm around his shoulders. "There now, that's not too bad. How long ago did you lose your son?"

"I don't remember," the woman says.

Their new companion slows their journey still further. Her presence makes Amara think of Pliny, and it upsets her that Philos is able to save this stranger, and yet the admiral is dead. A flood of rage hits her. *Why* did Pliny not even try? How could he give up like that? The thought of him lying alone in the dark, unable to breathe, makes her want to retch. Anger shifts swiftly into a quicksand of guilt. She should have stayed with him. Even if it was to do nothing more than hold his hand and watch him die. Amara knows that it doesn't matter that Pliny ordered her to leave, that all his other friends abandoned him, that there was nothing they could do to save his life—she will always be haunted by the loneliness of his death.

They rest a moment, Philos sharing their water with the old woman, whose name is Cassia. Her hands tremble when she takes the flask that Stephanus brought from Pompeii, which Philos thought to refill at Pomponianus's house. "I'm very sorry," Cassia says, handing the flask back to him. "But I'm afraid I'm not going to turn into the goddess Hera now to reward you for your kindness to a stranger."

The humor is so unexpected, it takes Amara and Philos a moment to understand the joke; the idea that Cassia is one of the Olympian gods in disguise, here to discover whether a legendary hero is capable of compassion. It makes Amara smile, in spite of herself.

"Well, I'm no Jason of the Argonauts, either," Philos laughs. "Though finding the Golden Fleece might be an easier quest than reaching Surrentum today."

"Did your family say where you should meet them in town, if you separated?" Amara says, suspecting that Cassia might be accompanying them the whole way.

Cassia shakes her head. "I would have thought we would have found them by now."

None of them raise the possibility that all must be considering. That her son is dead.

Philos helps Cassia to her feet again, smiling encouragement as she leans on him, giving no indication of the exhaustion Amara knows he must feel. Instead he acts as if Cassia were no burden at all. His kindness is a spark, illuminating so many of the memories Amara tries to keep hidden: the respect Philos always gave her when she was a nobody at the brothel, his gentleness with her as a lover, his selfless care for Rufina. Amara has always known that Philos is kind, but what she had not understood, perhaps until now, is how much strength lies behind his refusal to do what is expedient, when that's all that is expected of a slave.

"Shall I take the other bag for a while?" she asks, unable to think of any other way to let Philos know she understands the weight he is carrying.

"No, no, you're carrying enough. Don't worry."

They carry on walking along the path. The hail of stones has abated, but the ash still falls and their progress is painfully slow. Every now and then, they have to pause as the earth trembles. Cassia's presence slows them down, but she also gives them a purpose, a chance to focus on something other than their own fears and suffering. The flow of people is all in one direction, and so when Amara becomes aware of a flame approaching them, from a torch raised high, she points it out to Cassia.

"Could that be your son?"

It is hard to see far in the darkness, so they stop and wait.

"Yes," Cassia exclaims. "Yes, it's him!"

Amara watches the young couple approach with a feeling of intense relief, anticipating an emotional reunion.

"*There* you are!" the man says in annoyance, without greeting Philos or Amara. "Why did you wander off like that?"

"I'm so sorry," Cassia replies. "I lost sight of you."

"Your mother is having some difficulty breathing," Philos interrupts. "I think she might need more support."

The man gestures impatiently for Cassia to take his arm, while the woman beside him, presumably his wife, eyes Philos with suspicion. "Thank you for taking care of her," she says stiffly. "I'm afraid we don't have any reward to give you."

Philos stares back; his face, lit by the torch, is unreadable. "And I did not ask for one," he replies. He turns to Cassia. "Go well, my friend. Your company was a pleasure on the road." He stretches his hand out to Amara, who takes it, and they carry on walking along the path together, leaving Cassia and her ungrateful family behind.

Hours pass and they are so numbed by grief and exhaustion they do not notice at first that the day is getting brighter. Amara is so used to darkness, she dismisses it as an illusion, but soon it becomes undeniable. The sun is starting to break through the haze and the clouds of dust are dispersing. Philos turns to her, his hand resting on Rufina, and there is something close to hope on his face. They extinguish the torch, leaving it buried in the ash that lies piled around them, like filthy drifts of snow. The more the air clears, the more it becomes obvious how dramatically the world has changed. Everything is gray, heaped with ash and stones, leaving a barren, blasted landscape. Even the sea is not unscathed. Debris has pushed the land outward, and a murky foam breaks on the new, jagged shore far below.

Ash and stones no longer fall. After a while they risk taking off their hot, sweaty hoods. There is no room in the bags for the spare fabric and so Philos ties it all into a bundle to carry. His expensive red cloak is ruined, and his face is smeared and blackened by dust, while Rufina's hair is powdered white and gray, like an old woman. Amara knows she will not look any better; her hair is stuck to her forehead with perspiration as if she has been in the steam room of Julia's baths.

With the strengthening sunshine, Rufina starts to recover from her terror and becomes more alert. Amara is relieved to hear her daughter sound increasingly like herself—questioning where they are going, expressing her displeasure at the whole journey—but it is exhausting trying to keep her entertained. She and Philos take it in turn to tell Rufina stories, and Amara finds herself retelling fables she has not remembered in years, which were taught to her by her own mother. She is not as adept as Philos, who is gifted at making the different characters come alive, and Rufina soon orders her mother to stop, leaving the tiresome task entirely to her father. Eventually, lulled by the movement and the sound of their voices, Rufina nods off again.

In whispers, Amara and Philos begin to track the mountain's weakening impact by comparing the abandoned houses they pass. The level of ash gradually lowers, until whole front doors become visible again. These homes seem inhabited, the residents never having had to flee. They stop to drink from Stephanus's flask, which is getting low on water.

"We need to start thinking about where we will find shelter," Philos says, stowing the flask away.

Amara looks around, uncertain. "I've no idea where we are." The land here is not only gray, but steeper and craggier than the countryside surrounding Pompeii. She feels acutely aware of how friendless they are. The disaster has stripped away her social standing; she knows nobody and has become nobody.

Philos points ahead. "That looks like a town or fishing village. If we make for that, perhaps we might be able to get some food, or a bed for the night." He does not suggest what they should do after that, and Amara herself struggles to see further than getting through until evening. The safety and comfort of Demetrius's house seems impossibly far off.

She looks up and down the path, but nobody is close by. "I think we should say we are married," she says, taking the purse full of money from around her neck and handing it to him. "I don't want to be separated from you overnight. It's safer this way."

Philos nods, taking the purse but not meeting her eye.

The town, as they approach, turns out to be bigger than it appeared in the distance, since most of it was hidden by a steep gorge. They join the trickle of refugees making their way in toward the harbor; one of the women tells them they have reached Surrentum. Amara tries to think of anyone Demetrius has spoken of in the town, any name that might grant them access to shelter, but there is nobody. Without a connection to the elite, she and Philos know better than to seek help at the richest villas on the outskirts, where the inhabitants will likely fear them as thieves. Instead, they make for the more densely populated center within the city walls. It is impossible to know how long they have been walking and Amara is now almost delirious with exhaustion, unsure how she is managing to keep putting one foot in front of the other.

Surrentum is grimy in the aftermath of the ash rain. The buildings have suffered badly from the earth tremors too, but at least the town's people have not been buried alive by falling stones. Instead, they are out on the streets, trying to clear up the rubble and the ash, weeping and shouting. One old man is screaming from a top-floor window above a fabric shop, leaning out over the street as they pass, his spittle landing on Amara: *This is the punishment of the gods! Vulcan hasn't finished with us yet! We're all going to die!* A shopkeeper opposite, who seems to know the man, starts swearing at him, telling his neighbor he will bring them more bad luck. The two men screech curses at each other, until somebody inside the house grabs the old man from behind and yanks him away from view.

The noise in town is raucous compared to the near silent despair of the refugees on the road. Rufina is awake again and discontented, wriggling to see better, tugging at her father's neck, crying to be set down. Philos repeats reassurances to her over and over, until her grumbling subsides. They search for taverns where they might stay and instead find themselves wandering into the town's Forum. Part of the colonnade here has collapsed, and in the eddy of people moving across the square, an ornate water clock in the middle of the marketplace seems to act as a natural stopping point. People are gathered around it, pointing. Its cone has split, and the bronze figure of Saturn, who once marked the passing hours with his scythe, now hangs loose at an alarming angle. Perhaps it was a particularly well-loved local monument, given how upset people seem at its destruction. The sight of so much grief over a clock makes Amara feel irrationally angry. Surrentum's Saturn is just a useless lump of metal, easily replaced, unlike the beloved friends she has lost.

Philos approaches one of the bystanders, a burly man who is dressed like a freeborn citizen. "Can you help us, please?" Philos asks. "I escaped from Pompeii with my wife and child. We've walked for two days now. Do you know anywhere that we might get lodgings for the night?"

"No, I don't," the man says, shrugging Philos off. "We've got troubles enough of our own. Can't you see? And half of Pompeii seems to have turned up already!"

Amara is about to make a furious retort, but she is interrupted by another man, who was listening in. "There are lots of taverns and inns down that way," he says to Philos, pointing toward one of the narrow streets off the Forum. "You might find somewhere in that part of town, if you're not fussy about sharing a room and have some money."

Philos nods his thanks and they hurry off in the direction the man indicated. Amara hopes the mention of money was not a ruse to see if they were worth robbing, but they haven't walked far before she sees that the description was accurate. The street is packed with taverns and fast-food restaurants. The first few inns they visit are full, the rooms already taken by at least two families each. Amara trails after Philos as they enter each business, playing the part of the meek wife, feeling increasingly crushed by the refusals. On the corner of a side street, near the bottom of the road, they encounter a familiar-looking building; it is a brothel, with a sign outside detailing the women's names and prices. A lantern, which must have been hanging over the door, lies smashed on the street. Amara tries to quicken her pace, but Philos holds her back. "It's attached to an inn, look." Sure enough, down the side street is the opening of a packed bar. The people inside appear to be refugees, rather than customers, marked out by their filthy clothes and obvious exhaustion. On the wall above the door is an enormous fresco of a griffin, which must be the name of the inn.

Amara follows Philos reluctantly over the threshold. A metal wind chime hangs low over the entrance—a winged phallus for good luck. She avoids touching it, not wanting any fortune brought by this place. It is impossible not to think of Felix when they greet the sharp-faced man at the bar; Amara senses he is also the pimp. Even though the place is in serious disarray, with fresh-looking cracks in the wall, and a mess of smashed jars swept into a corner, the man is busy serving customers, clearly determined to make money out of the disaster.

"We've come from Pompeii," Philos says, when the landlord is free, speaking loudly to make himself heard over the noise of the busy bar, "and are looking for shelter."

The man looks them over. Even though their clothes are covered in dust, it is obvious the cloaks are not cheap. "Ten sesterces," he says. "And you'll have to share with another family. All my rooms are taken. Unless you want one of the girl's cells for the night."

He is staring boldly at Amara, enjoying his guests' powerlessness. It is like facing Felix. Fear prickles along her skin. She clutches Philos's hand, turning her face from the man's gaze.

"Well!" the man sneers. "Apologies if your woman is too *fine* for my establishment."

"We will take the room upstairs," Philos says, coldly. "But you will not speak ill of my wife, or mock her after all she's endured."

The man stares back, clearly planning a retort, but something in Philos's look of fury makes him change his mind. He shrugs in a half-hearted apology. "I suppose you'll be having something to eat?"

Philos glances at Amara, and she nods, understanding that to leave now would risk losing their shelter for the night. "Yes," Philos says to the innkeeper. "We will."

"I don't like it here," Amara whispers, when they have finally managed to squeeze around one of the remaining tables. "I don't want to stay."

"I know, but that's why it still has room. We will move on tomorrow."

"He was a *horrid* man," Rufina pipes up loudly. "I hate him."

"Hush," Philos says, trying to soothe her into silence, although he looks amused. Amara glances over at the counter but the landlord is too busy barking orders at one of his slaves to notice what a small girl has to say.

"The rooms aren't too bad," says a voice from the table next to them. It is a man, accompanied by what looks like his household: a woman, two children and three younger men in poorer-looking tunics, who Amara guesses must be household slaves. A large dusty bag is resting on the man's lap, his arms clamped around it, while other bags sit at their feet. "And we can all look out for each other."

"Where did you flee from?" Philos asks.

"Stabiae," the man replies. "We lost my wife's father in the escape. We're hoping he might still find his way here. He knew we were going to Surrentum."

Amara realizes the man's wife is weeping silently to herself. Two small boys—perhaps aged seven or eight—are huddled beside her, so similar they might be twins, and unnaturally quiet for children their age. One of them stares at Rufina, who Philos has set down on a stool. Rufina notices and before her parents can stop her, she has slipped onto the floor, and is pressing herself between the other children. "This is Julia," Rufina declares, holding out the doll to one of the boys. "She's named after my auntie Julia, who lives in Pompeii. We will be going home there soon. She has a very nice big bath and a garden and I get to play in all of it."

"Hello, Julia," says the boy, politely patting the doll.

A slave girl weaves her way to their table from the kitchen, carrying a tray. It contains three bowls of stew and a lump of bread, together with a jug of water. She sets it down in front of Philos. Rufina toddles back to join her parents, without saying goodbye to her new friends, and scrambles up onto Philos's knee. He feeds her the tepid vegetable stew while also eating his own. Amara is so hungry that the soggy vegetables taste better than any meal she can remember. All around her is a hubbub of voices. People are reliving the horror of their escape, speculating on what might have happened. Disconnected strands of personal tragedy weave themselves into her consciousness as she spoons up her stew: *I hear Pompeii was totally destroyed; there's nothing left of it, the whole place buried or burned. . . . It was the wrath of the gods. People say it was the mountain, but I saw Zeus himself, wielding the fire. . . . When can we go home? I don't want to be here; I want to go home. . . . He will turn up, my darling, don't cry. We have to trust he made it to safety . . .*

Amara starts to find the bar oppressive, with its murmuring weight of grief and uncertainty. She thinks of Britannica, Stephanus and Pliny and wonders what happened to Drusilla, Primus, Julia and Livia, hoping desperately that at least some of her friends managed to survive. The magnitude of loss leaves her numb; none of this feels real. It is a waking nightmare.

"Maybe we could go to the room?" she says to Philos when they have finished eating, wanting to escape the bar. He nods, and they get up, saying goodbye to the other family beside them, who have just been served with wine. The woman is no longer weeping but is busying herself with the two boys.

"That little girl obviously loves her father," the woman says, nodding at Rufina.

Amara freezes, not daring to look at Philos. "My father is very *important*," Rufina declares, repeating the word Julia always uses to describe Rufus: *your father is an important man in Pompeii.*

The family laugh, amused by such filial devotion, and Philos and Amara pretend to join in, before hurrying toward the counter where the landlord is watching them. "We will take the room now," Philos says.

The landlord jerks his head at a harassed looking slave girl, who ushers them toward a dark stairway. It is painted in the cheap black-and-white geometric design used for servants' quarters, which does not fill Amara with hope for the state of the rest of the place. On the top floor, the girl pushes open a door. It reveals a small room, painted with tiny griffins in blocks of red and white. At least two families are huddled onto a large bed, bags strewn all around it. The people on the bed look at the newcomers, blinking fearfully. There is absolutely no space for anyone else to fit onto that mattress.

"You'll have to hand over the pillows and blankets for them to sleep on the floor," the girl orders the collection of strangers. "You've got the bed and it's softer."

The frightened refugees do as they are told, and the girl tosses the pillows and blankets into a pile in the one corner of the room that's not covered by bags. Philos begins talking to the other families, holding Rufina up in his arms, while everyone introduces themselves, when Amara realizes that she is not only tired but absolutely sick with exhaustion. It has been two days and a night since she slept and if she does not lie down immediately, she will collapse. "I can't stay awake any longer," she says. "I'm sorry."

She huddles onto the floor, taking one of the pillows and lying on the blankets, not even bothering to remove her cloak or the two bags still slung over her shoulders. Within moments she is asleep.

21

"We attended to our physical needs as best we could, and then spent an anxious night alternating between hope and fear. Fear predominated, for the earthquakes went on, and several hysterical individuals made their own and other people's calamities seem ludicrous in comparison with their frightful predictions."

—Pliny the Younger on the aftermath of the eruption of Vesuvius

When Amara wakes, it takes her a moment to remember where she is. Rufina is nestled against her, fast asleep, and on the other side of her daughter is Philos, so close to her their three bodies are touching. Philos is already awake, watching Rufina. When he sees Amara stir, he reaches out to touch her shoulder. Her confusion grows. This room is dimly lit, and she can hear strange voices. Then understanding hits and, with it, a wave of horror. Amara begins to cry, wishing she could go back to sleep, wishing she could blot out whatever sorrow is coming next.

Philos continues to stroke her shoulder, murmuring reassurance, and Rufina wriggles. Amara tries to stop crying, not wanting to wake their daughter, but her body shakes at the effort of containing her grief. She takes Philos's hand, pressing it against her own cheek, wanting to calm herself but she cannot. Then she sits up, drawing her arms around her knees and sobs. Her eyes are screwed shut, but the self-imposed darkness reminds her of the terror of Vesuvius, and she opens them, looking wildly around the room. It is dingier than she remembers from yesterday. A heap of strangers is on the bed. One of them, an old man, is also crying. There is a young couple bickering in whispers, three children tangled together like puppies, who are somehow managing to sleep through it all, and a shapeless mound on the edge of the mattress that must be the prone form of one or two more people. Amara does not want to be here in this cramped, smelly room, trapped with people she does not know. She wants her family—she wants Julia and Livia; she wants to be at home. But the thought of how that home last looked—drowned in ash with its hellish, burning orchard—fills her with panic. Nowhere is safe. Not unless she makes it to Rome.

Rufina is waking. Amara watches as her daughter takes in the unfamiliar place, before her small face crumples with distress. "I'm hungry," she wails. "I want to go home! I want to go home!"

Amara and Philos drag themselves to their feet. As she moves, Amara realizes her whole body hurts. She is stiff everywhere, in pain from sleeping on the wooden floor and from so much walking. Her feet are covered in blisters. Philos is picking up the bags, packing together their belongings, and Amara swings them up onto her shoulders, which are already raw. They make their way downstairs, Rufina still crying, and head into the bar. The landlord is at the counter, chatting to one of the slaves. He looks up at his guests, his face unfriendly, eyeing the wailing three-year-old with distaste.

"It's another ten sesterces to keep the room for tonight. If you don't pay now, I will give it to someone else. I've had plenty come in asking this morning."

Philos and Amara exchange a look. She watches Philos pay the landlord their money, hating the man for his greed.

They step out onto the street. The road is packed with ash, bringing it level with the raised pavement, and everything looks dirty. The shop opposite the brothel is boarded up, the owners not feeling able to resume normal life. Philos lifts Rufina to sit on his shoulders, and he and Amara join the stream of dusty, bewildered people who are wandering about outside. They walk until they reach a bakery, which is remarkably serving customers, and cram themselves into one of the small tables. Rufina eats her bread, looking like a beggar child, with tear lines streaked down her dusty face. Amara resolves to find a water fountain after breakfast.

"When do you think we should go back to Pompeii?" she asks, keeping her tone light for Rufina's sake, although the thought of getting closer to Vesuvius again terrifies her. "Do you think it might be safe now?"

"I don't know," Philos answers. "But I don't think any of us are strong enough to walk that far, so soon."

"Could we perhaps take a boat back?" Amara suggests. "We could ask at the harbor."

"I want to take a boat," Rufina says. "I want to go home to Auntie Julia and Livia."

They ask the baker for directions to the harbor, and set off after they have paid for their breakfast. The road slopes downwards, the air feeling fresher the closer they get to the sea. At the very outskirts of the town, before they hit the steepest part of the descent, is a temple to the Sirens. The vast structure looks unscathed by the quake, and Amara thinks of Pliny, of the time he told her that Surrentum was the ancient home and namesake of the infamous sea creatures, half-bird and half-woman, who lure sailors to their doom. She tries to picture Pliny as he was then, standing on the deck of his quadrireme in the sunshine, speeding toward Misenum, while she, Julia and Livia listened to his stories. But instead, she sees him lying alone on the dark shore as the ash fell. Her eyes fill with tears, and she blinks, willing the grief away. Amara does not think there will ever be time enough to cry for all that has been lost.

The blue of the sea, when they reach the harbor, feels like it belongs to an earlier, more innocent time. A sickly haze still discolors the sky, but it cannot prevent the water from catching the light, and threads of silver shimmer through the shifting tapestry of waves. Amara dares to look toward Vesuvius. The mountain's pointed summit is missing, and instead its peak is now concave, perhaps blasted off in the explosion and scattered across the towns at its feet. Smoke billows from the mountain's shrunken form, but the only fires she can see smolder on its blackened slopes, rather than rise from its heart. Out in the bay, facing the mountain, sits the island of Capri, which Demetrius once promised to visit with her.

A crowd is gathered by the harbor wall. Amara and Philos are not the only refugees wanting to go home by sea. They are walking toward where the boats are moored, breathing in the fresher air, when another tremor strikes. There is nowhere to take shelter out here in the open, so instead they crouch down on the ground. Amara turns her face to look toward Vesuvius, dreading another explosion, but it only continues to smoke as the ground shakes beneath her. One of the statues perched high on the colonnade around the harbor smashes loudly to the ground. People scream in terror.

"Have the gods not punished us enough?" Amara hears a woman cry. *"When will it end?"*

"Fuck the gods!" someone else yells, before being shouted down by people screaming at him to hold his peace lest the immortals grow even angrier.

Eventually the shaking stops and people get back on their feet. Many, including Rufina, are still weeping and afraid. Everyone's nerves are shredded; people from Campania may have taken quakes in their stride in the past, but not now.

The tremor has made the survivors waiting for the boats more restless. Sailors are walking up and down, asking people where they want to go, while those who are not picked shout for attention. Amara and Philos are jostled into the sizable crowd of refugees who want to get back to Pompeii. She scans the faces of those waiting, hoping desperately to see Britannica or Livia, but there is nobody here she knows. They wait nearly an hour, people growing increasingly agitated, before three sailors gather them around. One of the men seems to be in charge. He is a large, tough-looking fisherman, and it is hard to tell his age, as his face is so lined and weather-beaten.

"There's not room for everyone today," the man says. "Some of you will need to come back tomorrow. And the price is a denarius for a family of five, going up by another denarius if there's more in your household than that."

"What if we don't have the money?" one woman cries.

"Then you get to the back of the line, and perhaps someone will take you at the end. Or you walk home."

"You're getting rich while we suffer," the woman retorts. "You should be ashamed!"

"Do you think anyone *wants* to go sailing toward Vesuvius?" the man shouts in the woman's face, making her quail back. "What should we fucking do? Not feed our families and take you all for free?"

"You don't have to charge so much," one of the other refugees says, a man in an expensive looking cloak. Amara suspects he's someone who is not used to being ordered around. "We don't know what we're going home to. Some of us might have lost everything."

"Not my problem," the fisherman shrugs. "Those are our prices—take it or leave it."

Amara and Philos know better than to argue, instead they press forward, trying to be among the first to be picked. The pushing and shoving soon degenerates into actual fighting, with people hitting and shouting to get to the front. On her own, Amara might have sharp-elbowed her way through, but she and Philos are too frightened for Rufina's safety to risk it. The most determined, aggressive refugees make it onto the boats, those with smaller children are left stranded. Amara stands at the harbor wall, watching the boats leave, crammed with their desperate human cargo, dipping low in the water.

"I don't like it here," Rufina says, high up on her father's shoulders. "I don't like this place."

Philos reaches up to take Rufina's hand, but neither of her parents reply, too heartsick to offer more comfort than this.

The steep roads of Surrentum, descending sharply to the sea, are more winding than the streets of Pompeii. Amara comes to know the brightly painted main road that leads to the harbor better than she would like, as one day in the town ekes into two and then three, with no space becoming free on the boats. Her sense of desperation grows every time they are sent away. Rumors start to spread about Pompeii; people whisper that it has been destroyed, that it is now home to vengeful giants from the mountain, that it is still on fire. Every tale makes Amara both afraid of returning yet even more eager to go back, longing to find that it is all untrue, that her friends have survived and the town is still standing.

There are moments, as they trudge through the streets, that Amara almost feels she must have died on the journey here—so many people in Surrentum stare through her as if she were a ghost. Her friendlessness reminds her of when she was enslaved. It is a shock to return to a state of not mattering, to have people turn their faces to the side, rather than address her as if she were someone of worth. She is so used to having status through belonging to Demetrius, it has become part of her identity, but here she is unmoored. The townspeople are too busy dealing with their own damaged homes and businesses to care much for the refugees, while the more unscrupulous exploit their captive customers. Each day the price of everything rises—for the newcomers at least. Philos and Amara spend time searching for somewhere else to stay, eventually leaving the brothel for a better inn that is also closer to the harbor, but the cost of having their own private room is considerable.

The money in Amara's purse steadily dwindles. She is determined not to pay for cheap necessities by handing out priceless jewels—as she has seen some of the richer refugees do—and so spends an afternoon with Philos visiting gem stores, trying to sell her bronze ring set with an amethyst. It is her favorite, but also one of the few pieces she bought for herself, which means she knows the price, and Amara has always placed survival over sentimentality. After discussion, she and Philos agree that he will be the one to do the negotiating. This is one of the other strange reversals in Surrentum—Philos has become more visible than her and while Amara's star has sunk, his has risen. Now that he has shed his enslaved status, the borrowed identity he wears as a married freedman—even a displaced one—is giving him a confidence Amara has never seen before. Or perhaps it is only that his quiet self-assertion, which he always possessed, is now reflected back in the respect others give him.

They walk from store to store, Amara carrying Rufina, watching Philos speak to every gem dealer they manage to find. Most of the conversations are brief; Philos's experience in running Rufus's business means he is able to spot time-wasters quickly. Eventually his tenacity pays off, and they find a man honest enough to buy Amara's ring for something close to what it is worth. The exchange is such a relief that after they have left the shop, she cries in the street. Philos takes Rufina from Amara's arms and holds them both close, shielding them from the impatience and indifference of those pushing past on the pavement.

That night is their fourth in Surrentum. When it is dark, they sit together in the overpriced room, the shutters closed against the cold breeze blowing from the sea. The night sky is finally clear enough of ash to see the stars, but Amara finds their light gives her little hope. Rufina is snoring, flung out like a starfish on the edge of the bed, while she and Philos again count through the possessions they brought from Pompeii, before packing them back into the bags. She misses not having to worry about money. The cold room makes her long for Demetrius's luxurious house: the bath suite where she could soak off the dirt of their ordeal, the comfort of servants to bring her food, the peace of her own room with its familiar paintings of Athena. But the intense longing she feels for the place is not extended to Demetrius himself. It is not that she does not care for her patron, only that Amara knows she cares for Philos so much more. She glances over at where he stands by the window. He has opened the shutter a crack to look outside, his face watchful and still. The night air he lets in is cold, but also fresher than the smell of roasting pigeon and coriander that rises from the kitchen below. Amara wonders what Philos is thinking, as he gazes out at the night sky. The sight of him, lost in contemplation, makes her feel calm. She thinks of his determination when they fled Pompeii, his strength of will that reminded her of Britannica. If it were not for Philos, she knows she would never have survived. He has not told Amara he loves her since that desperate moment during their escape to Stabiae. Now she is uncertain whether he truly meant what he said, or if they were only the words of a man facing death.

Amara walks over to the window. Philos smiles at her, moving so that she too can look out. "You see the moon?" he says, quietly. "It's much clearer tonight. Almost how it used to look."

"Artemis-Diana," Amara murmurs, remembering the offering Britannica left to the lunar goddess at the shrine outside Pompeii. Grief wells again in her heart. She stares out onto the dark street, unable to take any of it in. Instead, she is conscious of the warmth of Philos's body, so close to her, yet not touching. Loneliness is a chasm, so deep and vast, she cannot move for fear of falling, even though she longs to reach across it. The loss of Britannica, of Pliny, of perhaps all her dearest friends, is a pain Amara cannot imagine learning to bear alone. Her vision blurs, the orange buildings and black sky bleeding together. She feels Philos put his arms around her. He holds her lightly, not too close, allowing her the space to move away if she wishes.

There is no hesitation in Amara's choice. She turns around and kisses him, pulling the weight of his body against her. The longing she feels for Philos is not only born of love and desire, but also the overwhelming need to feel alive, to feel close to another human being. Philos responds with the same passion, kissing her back as if he too were starving, scarcely able to let go of her long enough for them both to get undressed. Neither say a word, perhaps afraid speaking will oblige them to confront the risk they are taking. Instead, they stumble their way over to the couch where Philos has been sleeping alone, leaving their daughter to lie undisturbed on the bed, and make love with silent, frantic desperation. Afterward they remain wrapped around one another. Amara presses her face to Philos's chest, feeling the rise and fall of his breathing, the warmth of his skin on hers.

"I have missed you so much," she whispers, the first words either of them has spoken.

Philos holds her tighter. "I missed you too."

"I can't leave you again. I can't."

Philos kisses her on the forehead. "Don't think of all that now, my love. Just surviving is enough for today. Let's not look further ahead than we have to."

In the past, Philos's fatalism did not comfort Amara. She always felt the need to scheme for more, determined to control the future, to force Fortuna to do her bidding. But now, with so much uncertainty hanging over them, she only sighs, and tries to do as he asks. Philos strokes her shoulders, the way she remembers him doing whenever she felt afraid at the house with the golden door. They lie like that awhile, until she starts to kiss him again, and desire takes over. They make love more slowly this time, and with greater tenderness, although the grief feels closer too.

The thought of Rufina waking to discover them lying together finally obliges them both to move. Amara finds it difficult to pry herself away, instead wanting to fall asleep in her lover's arms. She slips on her shift, getting into bed alongside Rufina, leaving Philos to the less comfortable couch. The room is dark as they do not want to waste money on keeping an oil lamp burning. She stares up at the black ceiling, wondering how she is going to spend the rest of her life without Philos, when even a single night feels too long.

Amara is woken the next morning by Rufina who knees her in the stomach, treating her mother's body as nothing more than an obstacle to be scaled in her quest to reach the couch where Philos is sleeping.

"Tell me a story!" Rufina demands, speaking straight into her father's face, jolting him awake.

Philos sighs, lifting Rufina up onto the couch. "Good morning to you too," he says, a hint of laughter in his voice, "even if you don't have any manners."

Amara slips out of bed, while Philos patiently regales their imperious child with yet another fable and washes her face in the basin on the table. Her hands shake as she splashes the cold water on her skin. From the pale light seeping through the shutters, she guesses it cannot be long past dawn.

Her clothes are in an undignified jumble on the floor, and she picks them up swiftly, cheeks burning. It is an even harder task to unspool all the painful emotions now tangled up in her chest, though one thread runs clear through the labyrinth: guilt. It tugs at Amara's heart, and she cannot see any way to loosen its grip. She feels guilt at betraying Demetrius and shame at the thought of him ever discovering her behavior last night. But the thought of living without Philos is even worse. How can she possibly leave him now, after all they have been through together, or expect Philos to go back to being enslaved? The idea is unspeakable. Yet the thought of leaving Demetrius is also terrifying. Amara closes her eyes, trying to calm herself. From the moment she told Philos she loved him, she has known that if they survived, she would have to face the implications of what that love means.

Amara pulls the tunic over her head, covering her body. She knows herself too well not to acknowledge her least sentimental, most selfish motives. Last night in Philos's arms, she could think of nothing more agonizing than being separated from her lover again, but this morning she is confronted with the stark reality of what it would mean to abandon her life in Rome. The complete loss of high status, wealth and power. She would have to give up all the security she has worked so hard to achieve, and which has shone these past days like a lamp, promising her a way out of the darkness in Surrentum.

"Another story!" Rufina cries, her shrill voice interrupting Amara's thoughts. Amara watches Philos bounce their daughter up and down, marveling that he is not completely exasperated at the constant demands on his attention.

"It's time for you to get dressed," Philos says, "or we will miss our chance of a boat."

Rufina clutches onto Philos's knees, still begging him for a story, trying to stop him from moving. Amara turns away, unable to look at them both. It is not only security for herself Amara will be giving up if she leaves Demetrius to go on the run with a slave. Her daughter has the chance to live a life of untold luxury in Rome. Yet seeing Rufina with Philos, Amara cannot decide what degree of wealth would ever be worth the price of wrenching her child from the person she loves most in the world: her own father.

Getting ready does not take them long; everything is packed. Amara stands by the door, anxiety making her fumble with the fastening of her cloak. Philos walks over to help, and she averts her face in embarrassment, unable to meet his smile. He fastens the clasp, then rests a hand on her shoulder. "You know," he says quietly, "I didn't assume anything from last night. I know you are betrothed to Demetrius." He lets go before she can reply, and Amara's distress is heightened rather than allayed by the fact that Philos knows her scheming heart so well.

The walk to the harbor is dispiritingly familiar. They join the crowd waiting for a boat, a huddle of displaced strangers, shuffling and restless. Misery has leveled down everyone's status, but it is still possible to tell who the richer refugees are. Amara is grateful now that she bought Philos the ostentatious red cloak; it makes his status as a freedman go unchallenged. Rufina sits on his shoulders, and they both try to keep her occupied by telling stories about Odysseus and the Sirens.

The crowd has thinned considerably compared to previous days, but the wait has been so interminable, Amara is still surprised when the sailor finally points at Philos, gesturing at him to bring his family. Panic grips her. She steps back, overwhelmed by a sudden, irrational urge to flee. Surrentum holds no future, yet returning to Pompeii also feels frightening. The sailor gestures at her impatiently, and Amara feels Philos's hand on the small of her back, guiding her forward.

They have no time to collect the money they left as a deposit for another night at the inn; the sailors are in no mood to wait. Instead, they are forced to scramble aboard the waiting fishing boat immediately, helped in by the crew. The small vessel is nothing like one of Pliny's warships. It stinks of fish and rocks alarmingly as everyone squashes in. The sailors watch the boat sink low into the water, before deciding to call a halt to the number of refugees. They push off from the harbor, watched by the disappointed stragglers left behind. Amara sees Surrentum's Temple of the Sirens rise higher above the town, the further they sail from the shore.

"We're going home," Rufina shrieks excitedly. "We're going to see Julia!"

"What is it like in Pompeii?" Amara asks one of the rowing fishermen.

"I've not been into the town," he replies.

"But you must have seen it from the shore? I've heard rumors it was destroyed. Have you been able to see?"

The man says nothing, and Amara's sense of unease grows. She looks out at the coastline they are passing at a painfully slow speed, amazed she and Philos ever walked so far. At first the gray is punctuated by signs of life. She can make out trees that have survived the ash fall, turning green again after the passage of several days, and there are villas on the cliff tops, still standing. But the further along they travel, the worse the landscape looks. Drifts of ash become denser, heaps of stone burying the trees and the houses, until only their upper floors and highest branches and upper stories show. Growing slowly closer, too, is Vesuvius, the monstrous giant still smoking from its mutilated summit.

Wanting to distract herself from the endless churn of anxious thoughts, Amara turns her attention to a refugee who is talking loudly to Philos. The man's name is Modestus. He owns a bakery in the town, and it turns out that almost all the other passengers in the boat belong to his household: his parents-in-law, his wife, his teenage son and four of his slaves. Modestus is a large man, with burst veins spread across his nose from too much wine. Like them, his clothes are dirty, but would once have been fine. Amara thinks he seems pleasant enough, if over-fond of his own voice.

"When did you decide to flee?" Modestus is asking. "We left early. I had to abandon half the bread in the oven! Not that I suppose one more fire in the town would have made much difference. Almost all the slaves upped and ran as soon as the mountain exploded. They went north, I suppose, as that was the nearest gate. We had to get to the south end of town, to pick up my parents. Who knows if we will *ever* manage to round up all the lost slaves up; it's going to be like Spartacus all over again, with the little shits camping out in the countryside. Which household are you from, did you say?"

"The household of Julia Felix," Philos replies. They are being careful how much information they give away. Amara does not want to tell too many lies, but equally she has no desire to be seen as an isolated, unmarried female, traveling with nobody but a child and a slave. She tells herself it is safer, until they find proper protection, to keep letting people assume she is a wife.

"The Venus baths!" Modestus exclaims. "Very fancy. You're a freedman?" Philos nods, the lie coming more easily with practice. "My father was a freedman, so you're welcome here. I'm no snob." At that the woman beside him, presumably his wife, snorts. "No need for that, Petronia. I know I'm ambitious. But that's different." He hesitates, a flicker of fear showing beneath the bombast. "I hope *some* of the business has survived, though I realize there will be a lot of repairs needed. We'll no doubt have to rebuild. But we did that after the earthquake, a decade or so ago. And we're still here! We have family in Ostia, if the worst comes to the worst. Though I'd rather not go begging."

"We stopped for a while in Stabiae on our escape to Surrentum," Philos says. "When we left, ash was burying the place."

Modestus shudders. "The journey was terrible, wasn't it? The darkness. I don't think I will ever forget it." His forced jollity slips again, and Amara realizes why the man is talking so much. It is a way to keep the fear at bay. Modestus notices Rufina watching him, perched solemnly on Amara's knee. "That's a nice doll," he says kindly.

"This is Julia," Rufina replies. "She's named for my auntie. We are going home to her now."

The adults exchange glances. "Julia Felix did not come with you?" It is Modestus's mother this time, addressing Amara.

"She wanted to shelter at home until the storm passed," Amara says. "But we are hoping she changed her mind." Nobody replies, each silently contemplating the alternative.

Too many hours pass for even Modestus to keep up the flow of conversation. Instead, they try to keep each other's spirits up by singing songs, but when they reach Stabiae, their voices peter out. Even from their position at sea, it is obvious the town is in ruins. Landslides of gray ash and stones have drowned its streets, with only the upper floors and pinnacles of the temples poking through, and the harbor has all but collapsed, a new gray shoreline silting up the bay. Amara wonders if Pliny is buried underneath the ash, or if his friends went back to fetch his body. The thought brings a lump to her throat. Petronia, Modestus's wife, starts to cry.

Modestus puts his arm around her and addresses one of the fishermen, pointing toward the ruined town. "Is Pompeii like that?"

"Pretty much," the man says, although Amara thinks he looks shifty. "But the army is there, trying to reunite people with their families and their property. You will be looked after."

"Is the army based *in* the town?" Amara asks. "Or camped outside?"

The man only shrugs, and looks away from her, making it clear he is not open to more questions.

The weather turns on the final stretch of their journey. It is not rough enough to be described as a storm, but the waves are uncomfortably choppy, and the darker sky makes everyone fearful, reminding them of the horrors they so recently suffered.

Rufina is sick over the side, her small body heaving as Philos holds her, and they are all soaked through with the drizzle. The gray rainfall makes it harder to see the land, and Amara does not at first realize that they are heading in toward Pompeii. She looks for the harbor's distinctive column of Venus, but cannot find it. The goddess must have been felled by the tremors, and is now hidden beneath the waves.

The land draws nearer and Amara realizes the gray haze is not only from the rain—it is smoke. Dread tightens its grip on her heart. More people in the boat begin to cry as the reality before them becomes inescapable. Amara would weep too, but the pain in her chest is so great, it is choking her. Vast drifts of smoking ash and stone are heaped before them, growing taller the closer they get. Pockets of flame burn on these new ugly, misshaped hills that stretch back as far as she can see. She squints, desperate to make out a familiar shape, some half-buried landmark, anything she can recognize. But the gray here is not pierced by the red of terracotta tiles—there are no upper floors poking through. Pompeii is not a ruin, like Stabiae; it has been obliterated.

22

"[Emperor Titus] chose commissioners by lot from among the ex-consuls for the relief of Campania; and the property of those who lost their lives by Vesuvius and had no heirs left alive he applied to the rebuilding of the buried cities."
—Suetonius, *The Lives of the Caesars*

There is no surviving harbor to moor in, and so the fishermen find what space they can on the new shore, scraping the hull as they beach their boat on the stones. The refugees sit bunched together, shocked into silence. A number of other boats are already anchored in the same spot. Amara recognizes vessels from Pliny's fleet, moored high above them. Looking up, she can just make out some of the crew, standing on the deck. She thinks again of the admiral, and his death not only brings her pain, but also a sense of hopelessness. One of her most powerful protectors is gone.

"This is it," the fisherman says. His passengers gaze up at him, eyes round with fear, nobody showing any eagerness to leave. He points impatiently to what looks like a mass of tents much further inland. "That's the relief effort over there. That's where you need to go."

His tone does not invite argument, although Modestus tries. He remonstrates with the man, angry that he did not warn them of the state of the place, demanding a return trip or their money back, but the fisherman refuses to take anyone back to Surrentum. The small group of survivors are obliged to gather up their bags and step out onto the soaking dunes and drifts of blackened pumice that buried their city. Rufina does not want to get out of the boat. She sobs and screams, pounding on Philos's back, demanding to be taken home. "This is not home!" she cries. "No!"

Amara and Philos try to console her as the fishermen push their vessel off from the shore, starting the long return journey to Surrentum. "Where is it?" Rufina wails. "Where's Pompeii?"

"It's gone, my love," Amara says, her own voice breaking. "I'm so sorry."

"It can't be gone. It can't be." Rufina begins to howl, no longer sounding like a child; the heartbreak in her cries is guttural, unbearable to hear. Philos hugs her close, his hand covering her small head, and Amara sees that his face, too, is wet with tears.

"Perhaps it's not as bad as it looks," Modestus says, trying to sound cheerful although his voice is hoarse with emotion. "Rome's soldiers are here, and the fleet. I suppose they know what they're doing." He encourages his parents to start walking, and together the survivors pick their way across the dunes. Several of the slaves are crying, while Modestus's teenage son looks terrified, gulping back his tears. "Perhaps part of the town has survived." Modestus sounds even less certain than before. "Perhaps there's a way back in. It might not be as bad as it looks. You never know."

"Stop it!" Petronia shouts, beside herself with grief. "Stop treating us like children! Do you think the streets nearest Vesuvius somehow escaped? We're ruined. The place is gone. Our home. It's all gone." She sinks toward the ground, sobbing, but Modestus gathers her up before she can fall.

"Hush now," he says, close to tears himself. "Hush, hush."

Somehow, they keep walking, trudging over the ash and pumice—it's not as if they have any alternative. No one has the strength to speak. Rufina's sobs subside into silent misery, and Amara grips Philos's hand. She feels numb with shock. The walk is endless, their feet often sinking into the ash, their strength sapped by despair. It soon becomes clear that the tents are both much further away and also more numerous than they looked from the sea. They draw closer, and Amara realizes an animal-hide city has sprung up near the grave of the real one, and that even though Pompeii is dead, hundreds of its people seem to have survived. The thought is both heartening and alarming. She has greater hope of finding her friends yet no idea how everyone is being fed, sheltered and given water, or what conditions she is bringing her daughter into. The bags she has been carrying since she fled this place, bump against her hips as she trudges over the uneven ground. In her mind's eye she pictures the chests of wealth she left behind at Julia's house, now buried under the frightening, smoking gray hills that tower above them. She pulls on the straps of her bags, drawing them close, clutching her remaining belongings more tightly. Mentally she runs through what is inside: the silver plate, the jewelry, the precious ornaments. Even the expensive fabrics that she and Philos used to protect themselves from the eruption should be salvageable. Her three bags contain more wealth than many people manage to amass over a lifetime. *And Demetrius will be generous*, she tells herself. *If I go home to him.*

The stench of excrement, cooking and unwashed bodies reaches them before they reach the camp, as does the noise of voices. There are crowds of people. Some mill about the encampment, whose ground is churned up into gray sludge from the rain, others sit slumped outside their tents, while a few are cooking over open fires. Amara eyes the flames with alarm. A few soldiers, perhaps some from Pliny's own fleet, are also patrolling, doing their best to fend off desperate petitions for help from those they pass.

Modestus hurries toward the nearest guard, without even bidding Philos and Amara goodbye, the remains of his household trailing after him. The soldier does not stop but keeps on walking, the baker and his family trotting to keep up. They are soon lost to view.

Amara and Philos stare at the camp, increasingly bewildered. The place looks filthy and on the verge of chaos. "What do we do?" Amara whispers.

"You need to declare who you are," Philos says. "Maybe Pliny's men will grant you and Rufina some protection."

They start walking through the camp, looking out for anyone they know from Pompeii. The faces of the people Amara passes are ash-stained and gray; some stare keenly back at her as if they too are hoping to find someone, while others are listless. A noisy group of refugees, crowding outside a tent, signals the presence of a soldier. The man is trying to stop himself from being mobbed, swatting people away like flies. Amara pushes herself to the front, elbowing her way without shame. Please," she says. "I am Plinia Amara, freedwoman of the late Admiral of the Roman Fleet, Gaius Plinius Secundus. We've just arrived. I need to find Julia Felix, to find out if she is still alive. She was one of the leading citizens of Pompeii. Where might I find a record of her?"

"A freedwoman?" The man asks, ignoring or unimpressed by a ragged stranger's claim to know the admiral. "We are counting freeborn citizens first. When they are all registered, we will get to you."

"But that doesn't make any sense," Amara says. "Can't you at least tell me if Julia Felix is registered? So I know where to find her?"

The guard ignores her question. "If I were you, I would go get food and shelter. It's at that end of the camp." He keeps walking, trying to shake off the people who follow him.

"I don't understand," Amara says. "Why don't they just register everyone as they come along?"

"Presumably so the richest can be taken away somewhere nicer, or get better supplies," Philos says, with the acuity of a person who is always used to being at the bottom of the pile.

They walk in the direction the guard commanded. The place is not hard to find. In spite of the filth, there is a semblance of order here, the tents staked out in straight rows, following the grid of a regular Roman town. At the center, the soldiers have created a camp within a camp, with yet more guards stationed outside it. Amara and Philos are admitted as one household and told to make for the supply tent. There is a long line outside. Those waiting look exhausted and withdrawn, while some of the smaller children waiting in line cry and complain. The only sound of joy comes from two young boys who shriek with excitement, as they chase each other up and down, their legs splattered with mud. One of the soldiers smiles at the children, pretending to start a chase, and the boys shriek even more.

Rain starts to fall again and Amara huddles closer to Philos, both of them trying to shield their daughter. Rufina shows none of her usual curiosity or spark. She clutches her father, back in the fabric wrap, her gray eyes wide with grief and fear. By the time they get inside the tent, Amara is shivering with cold. The interior is gloomy and smells of wood smoke and tallow. Two harassed-looking guards are handing out supplies of bread and water, batting away pleas for more. Supplies are severely rationed, due to everything being brought from out of town. Amara thinks gratefully of the food Philos thought to stock up on before they left Surrentum: bread, a roll of cheese and some smoked boar are stowed in one of their bags.

Another, more officious guard, is in charge of shelter. Their family is too small to be assigned their own tent, so they are bundled to the side and combined with two other households: a widow and her son, and an elderly couple with two slaves. The couple look relatively wealthy, which Amara hopes will mean there is less chance of their tent-mates robbing and murdering them in the night.

The soldier explains how to set up the shelter and sends them on their way. Philos, the two slaves and the widow's son carry the posts, rope and heavy rolls of goat-hide outside, back into the main encampment. They are reluctant to travel too far from the soldier's camp, hoping that it might prove some protection, but dusk is falling and it is hard to find a spot to pitch on. Rain makes the thick ash and debris even harder to walk through, and the only usable spot they can find is tiny, squashed in between two tents. Philos and the other men begin the difficult process of setting up, which proves impossible without knocking into the hide of the tent beside them. Some of its occupants come out into the rain, and Amara is expecting a row, but instead the strangers silently start to help. She clutches Rufina in her arms, watching the men work together, unable to stop crying.

Once it is up, the interior of their tent is dark and damp. The roll of goat's hide rolled out onto the ground barely protects them from the filth below it, but still they all pile in, waiting for the rain to pass. The guard handing out food told them latrines have been dug at the edge of the camp, but from the smell seeping from the floor, Amara suspects not everyone has bothered to tramp that far. It is painfully cramped inside, too. The slaves are forced to take the wettest position by the opening, while Amara and Philos are stuck in the middle.

"Not much room is there?" the widow says, from her place wedged next to Amara. "We only came back to see what was left of the place. I really hoped we might be able to salvage something. But I think we'll be off in the morning."

"Where will you go?" Amara asks.

"Back to Neapolis," the widow replies. "That's where we fled when the mountain exploded. It's hard; there are lots of refugees in town, but it's much better than being here—I can tell you that for nothing."

"You should be careful," says the elderly man, at the back of the tent. "I've heard all the ruffians are headed that way. Slaves passing themselves off as freedmen and all sorts."

The widow tuts to herself. Philos and Amara stay silent. Rain falls more heavily, beating onto the hide above them, and it is dark. After they have eaten their bread, and with nothing else to do, the small group of survivors bed down for the night, trying to sleep in the filthy tent as best they can.

Amara wakes early. She did not believe that any bed would ever bring her more misery than her cell in the Wolf Den, but back then, when she dreamed of nothing but escaping Felix, she could not have imagined being crushed into a stinking tent, pitched on the bones of a dead city.

She nudges Philos, and they clamber over the slaves huddled at the entrance into the pale pink light of the dawn. Rufina sleepily opens her eyes, then closes them again, burying herself against her father, not wanting to face the day. They load themselves up with all their belongings, not trusting to leave anything behind, and trudge to the edge of the camp, to the latrines. The stench from the gaping trench is almost unbearable.

"We can't stay here," Amara says. "We have to leave."

"Do you want to make for Neapolis?" Philos asks. "You could try and send word for Demetrius from there."

"I want to try and find Julia and Livia first. Or Drusilla. There must be a way of finding them here, even if we have to ask at every tent."

They walk back through the camp, which is only just stirring into life. Rufina clings to her father's neck, and her small face is pressed to his, gray eyes wide and watchful. The pair of them look so alike, it tugs at Amara's heart. She knows that her escape depends on declaring herself, but she cannot bear to give up the pretense of being a family. Not yet. "Until we find out what's happened to Julia," she says. "I think we keep things as they are, and tell people we are freed members of her household. It's just safer."

Philos glances at her, his expression sharp. "Very well," he says.

"Perhaps we had better start looking for Julia." Amara stops, staring at the tents surrounding them, hardly knowing where to start. It feels like they have reached the edge of the world. Behind them stands the still-burning remains of Pompeii. She realizes now that the gray hills follow the shape of the old town walls, and that they must be camped on what was once the shore beyond the harbor to the south of town. Amara squints. A peak, poking from the smoldering mass of the buried city, is just recognizable as the Temple of Venus, and towering beyond that is the dark outline of the vengeful mountain. A blue haze hangs over the new, makeshift town, and it is impossible to tell if it is wood smoke from campfires, or the remnants of ash blown up by Vesuvius. Perhaps it is both. Amara feels as if she will never get the stench of burning from her hair or clothes, or the choking smell of sulfur from her nostrils. Sometimes she doesn't know if her senses can still be trusted—if the smell is even real or a reimagined horror.

At first, it is difficult to intrude on strangers, to call loudly into tents where people lie sleeping, but soon Amara loses her shame, driven on by desperation. They walk all morning, tramping up and down the length of the encampment, searching for Drusilla, Primus, Julia, Livia, and also for Philos's friends, the men he has worked alongside for years. Sometimes they stumble upon half-remembered faces—the dressmaker from Verrecundus's store, the man who used to sell pots at the Forum—but Amara does not find those she loves, whose faces she longs so much to see. Philos is more fortunate. On their first foray down the main track, they discover his old friend Vitalio, a slave from Rufus's household. The two men embrace, almost weeping for joy, but Amara is terrified they might find her former lover here too, that Rufus will lay claim to Philos as his slave. She interrupts the men's affectionate reminiscences, demanding to know where Rufus is. Vitalio takes her aside, out of Rufina's earshot, to break the news that he fears the family perished after Rufus's father Hortensius insisted they all take shelter in the house. Amara clasps a hand to her mouth, not sure if the pain in her chest is grief, or guilt at feeling so relieved.

Rufus is not the only survivor she fears. Calling into each tent, her hope that Drusilla or Julia might answer competes with her dread that she will instead find Felix. Amara has no doubt that in the lawlessness of the camp, her former master would think nothing of robbing or even killing her family. Yet Felix, too, is nowhere to be found. Neither are Victoria, Gallus or Beronice. It is as if none of the people she knows ever even existed. Britannica's vow to burn the Wolf Den to the ground lingers in Amara's mind, along with an irrational thought that the two vengeful she-wolves are somehow responsible for bringing down the violence of the mountain. After all, Fortuna is a fickle goddess, who might take pleasure in destroying not only her acolytes' enemies but everything else besides.

By midday Amara is forced to accept that if her friends survived, they are not here. She and Philos make their way wearily back to the central encampment, but the closer they get, the livelier the place becomes, with far more soldiers than Amara remembers a short while ago. Guards are clearing people outward, forcing them back to the edges of the tent city. She clutches Philos's hand tighter, uneasy about what might be coming, as the way is soon blocked by row upon row of soldiers. The men stand in a fat, shining phalanx. Amara is reminded of Vespasian's funeral, although the white stones of the Via Sacra are from a different world to this grimy track.

"What's happening?" Philos asks one of the guards.

"Pompeii is honored," the man replies. "The emperor is visiting Campania."

"The Emperor Titus is here?" Amara exclaims, in total amazement. "But I know him!"

She is greeted with laughter. The idea of a ragged refugee being familiar with the ruler of the world's greatest empire is too absurd. "Well," the solider says, indulgently, "I should hope you *have* heard of him. I should hope everyone has."

Amara understands that now is not the time to insist she is betrothed to one of Titus's imperial freedmen, or that she is on friendly terms with his one-time concubine, Queen Berenice of Judea. She will not be believed. "Will the people be able to petition him?"

"Not all of you," says the guard. "A few families have already been chosen."

"Is there no way I might see him?" she asks. "*Please.* Our patron is in his service."

The soldier looks from Amara to Philos to Rufina—who is as filthy as a beggar child—and Amara's heart sinks, anticipating his answer. "The petitioners have already been chosen," he repeats, his voice kind but firm.

The wait they endure is almost as long as that Amara and Saturia once experienced at the funeral procession in Rome, but it is much less comfortable here. Rufina wails with hunger, and Philos gives her most of the bread they are carrying. After an age has passed, they finally hear the deafening blast of trumpets, and a murmur of excitement ripples through the crowd. Some survivors begin crying, others cheer loudly, shouting the emperor's name, making a din that competes with the trumpets. Rufina clamps her hands over her ears, hating it all. Amara stands on tiptoe, trying to lift herself as far as she can in the mud, and sees the Roman standards, held high above the crowds, along with what might be a glimpse of Titus on his white horse. Then the standards disappear into the greater safety of the central encampment, taking the emperor with them.

The wait goes on for another hour. Everyone is kept at bay while Titus hands out bread to the chosen few, before another blast of trumpets and cheers signals that he is leaving the camp, presumably to board whichever vessel must have brought him here from Rome. Amara wonders if Titus will stay at Misenum, at his friend the admiral's house. The thought of the beautiful villa, empty of Pliny's presence, makes her feel unspeakably sad.

The soldiers disperse, meaning everyone is finally free to move where they will. As they walk through the camp again, Amara realizes the atmosphere feels different; she can hear laughter and people look more hopeful. Even if all the waiting was tedious, the attention from Rome shows they are not forgotten. At their own tent, she and Philos find the widow and her son are busy packing up their belongings.

"There are ships ready, taking people to Neapolis and Ostia," the widow explains. "All you have to do is register before you get on, so there's a record. If you want to leave, now's your chance."

"We should go," Amara says, gripping Philos's arm. "There's nothing for us here. And perhaps we will find Julia's name on the register. Perhaps she has already left!"

Philos looks at her, and she sees the hesitation on his face, instantly understanding its meaning. To sign an official register is to sign away his freedom, to return to being enslaved. She lets go of his arm. Amara has been dreading this moment, and now it is crashing down on her before she is ready, before she has worked out what to do. Philos is a slave, and nothing has changed. Then the thought she has kept buried rises to the surface of her mind. *Unless we keep on lying.*

Amara thinks of the wealth that sits in the bags they carry. It is enough to start again. Not as a rich woman, not as a powerful courtesan, but as an ordinary wife and mother, married to a man who knows how to run a business. A man who would support and care for her every day of his life. Who deserves the chance to be free.

She walks away from the tent, too distracted to say good-bye to the widow, and Philos follows her, Rufina perched on his shoulders. "What is it?" he asks, unable to keep the concern from his voice.

Amara's heart is pounding. She knew deep down that this choice was coming, even though she wanted to pretend to herself that she would never have to make it. "I don't want to leave you," she says, almost too choked to get the words out. "And maybe I don't have to." Philos does not ask her what she means. There is no point pretending he has not imagined what she offers. It is the life they promised each other, years ago. The life Amara promised him, when she swore to do everything in her power to buy his freedom. "This is our chance, Philos," she says, her eyes welling with tears. "To take some happiness from all this. To live as a family. To be . . . somebody else."

"Do you understand," he says, taking her hand, "I mean, *really* understand, what this choice would mean? All that you would give up and all that you would risk? This is not something I could ever demand of you, Amara. You don't owe me your life. You never have."

"I know," Amara replies. "But I love you." Philos stares at her, his lips parted, and her sense of certainty grows. "I love you," she repeats. "And what else truly matters, in the end?"

Philos is about to reply, to tell her he loves her too, but Rufina is bored by the intensity of all the hushed voices and interrupts. "*I* love him," she exclaims, flinging her chubby arms around her father's face. The three of them laugh, but it is a laughter close to tears.

"Perhaps we should go for that boat, then," Philos says, taking Amara's hand. He looks at her, and the emotion between them is unlike anything Amara has ever felt. "I love you, Plinia Amara," he says. "And I will always try to deserve you."

23

"Love dictates and Cupid points the way as I write
I'd rather die than be a god without you"
—Pompeii graffiti

On their walk back to the shore, Amara is still warmed by the love she feels for Philos, and yet at the same time, the magnitude of the choice she has just made feels unreal. It does not seem possible that she will never again set foot in Demetrius's house, or relax in his beautiful gardens, or have the protection of untold wealth at her fingertips. *She will never see Demetrius again.* That last thought brings a painful lurch to her stomach. Amara tries to squash the guilt before it takes hold. She tells herself that Demetrius does not love her, not like Philos does, and yet she knows, in her heart, that Demetrius loves her as much as he is capable of loving anyone. That her loss will pain him beyond measure, and leave his final years darker and lonelier through her absence.

"What names shall we give to the register?" Philos asks, his voice low, even though they have deliberately distanced themselves from the other refugees walking this way. Rufina is tied back in the wrap, and is mercifully fast asleep.

"I will be Timarete again," Amara says. "At least it's true."

"I can't go back to being Rufus," Philos says, referring to the name given to him by his first master, before he was renamed. He raises his eyebrows at Amara, amused. "Why don't *you* choose something?"

"I can't name you!" Amara is aghast.

Philos shrugs. "Well, if I don't like it, I won't take it."

Amara thinks for a moment. "Fidelius."

"*Fidelius?*" Philos laughs out loud. "Is that a request or a command?"

"It's an observation."

Philos stops, pulling her in for a kiss. "Fine. Fidelius it is."

His amusement is contagious, pushing away some of the guilt Amara feels for the patron she is leaving behind. She kisses Philos back, allowing herself to enjoy the thought of what it will mean to spend her days with a man she loves and respects, to be a family with Rufina at last. Before she met Demetrius, this was everything she wanted, after all.

They join the queue for the boat to Neapolis, nodding in greeting at the widow and her son, who are already standing further ahead in the line. Amara is struck again by the unreality of her situation. Here she is, about to discard her former life like an old cloak, leaving it buried in the ruined city behind her. Can it really be this easy? She looks back at the dark, smoking hills, remembering what the baker Modestus said about runaway slaves. *It will be like Spartacus all over again.* Fear chills Amara. Her choice is not only one of personal sacrifice: it is a crime. She grips Philos's hand more tightly, suddenly anxious about being discovered. It would be a loss so severe it is almost laughable, if she were to give up a wealthy life with Demetrius, only to lose Philos to the authorities too.

"Are you alright?" Philos looks at her intently, as if trying to read her mind, and she can see the effort his next words cost him. "You don't have to do this, if you are having second thoughts. I would understand."

"No." Amara leans over to kiss him again, loving him more for asking. "This is what I want."

They arrive at the front of the line. The soldier registering them looks for Julia Felix's name, and even though Amara is not really expecting him to find her, it is still crushing when the man shakes his head. "You are both from her household?" the soldier asks.

"Yes," Amara replies, not remembering that as a married woman, she should let her husband speak for them both.

The guard looks at Philos as if he has not heard her. "Names."

"I am Fidelius, this is my wife Timarete and my daughter . . . Fidelia. Julia Felix is our patron."

"As her freedman you are entitled to a portion of her wealth, if she is not found alive. This is what the emperor has decreed."

"No," Amara bursts out. "We can't take her money!"

The soldier looks at her, eyes narrowing with suspicion. Nobody, who has nothing to hide, turns down a handout. "If you don't want what you are due, you can raise the issue with her niece, Livia Balbina."

"Livia is alive?" Amara gasps, clapping her hands with joy, not thinking of the sudden danger. "Oh, thank goodness!" She hugs Philos, overcome with emotion at learning one of her dearest friends has survived.

The soldier motions at another guard to take them aside. "Livia Balbina is indeed alive. And she gave us a list of her household, which I have here." He pauses, letting the words sink in. "None of you are on it."

✦ ✦ ✦

There is no chance for Philos and Amara to decide in private what they will say to Livia, or to discuss how they will prepare her for the lies they have told. The guard who takes them back to camp does not give them a moment alone. Ash and stones spill over their feet as they trudge again along the gray dunes, and the closer they draw to the dead mound of Pompeii, smoldering above the tents, the worse Amara feels. It seems its shadow was not so easy to escape, after all.

When they reach the tent city, the noise wakes Rufina, and her childlike excitement on learning she will see her auntie Livia again, softens the guard's attitude. He grows noticeably kinder toward them all, explaining that perhaps in her great distress, Livia Balbina simply forgot to write everyone's names down. Knowing the truth, Amara is not completely reassured. In her heart she cannot believe Livia would ever wish harm to come to her, but harm might be unavoidable if Livia does not understand the deception in time. They head into the central encampment, where Livia is stationed. It seems Philos was right in guessing that the wealthier freeborn citizens were given greater protection. No wonder they could not find her. Amara only hopes they do not also bump into his master, Rufus.

The soldier speaks to some of his fellows, working out where to go, then ushers them toward a tent, holding open the flap. Amara rushes inside ahead of Philos and Rufina, before the guard has a chance to announce them.

"Livia!" she cries.

A hunched figure, unrecognizable from the vibrant woman Amara knew in Pompeii, rises from the center of the floor. Livia stares at Amara, as if she is seeing a ghost. "You're alive," She looks behind Amara to see Philos, carrying Rufina. "You're *all* alive." Livia lets out a howl, and Amara rushes to embrace her. They hold one another, sobbing, their tears not only from relief at finding each other, but also from the loss of Julia. Only now, seeing Livia alone, can Amara truly accept that Julia is dead. Eventually, they break apart, and Livia holds Amara's face in her hands, pressing fervent kisses to her forehead.

"Well, that was a happy ending," the guard is saying to Philos, his tone apologetic. "I am sorry for the suspicion." He approaches Livia. "Your freedman Fidelius and his family, returned to you."

Livia gapes at him, uncomprehending. "*Who?*"

"Your freedman, Fidelius," the guard says slowly, pointing at Philos, obviously thinking Livia is too emotional to take in what he says. "His wife Timarete. And their daughter."

Livia continues to stare at Philos. "Fidelius," she repeats. "And his daughter."

"Yes," the guard says patiently. "They weren't on the list."

"No." Livia stares at Philos. "They weren't." She turns to Amara. "But now they are here, and that is all that matters." Amara begins to cry again, both in gratitude at the protection Livia is giving them and shame at having lied. Livia kisses her, smoothing the hair from Amara's face. "My darling, there is no need. Julia always said she had her father's eyes." Livia gazes at her, with the faintest trace of a smile. The two women stare at one another, the unspoken stories of their lives passing between them. Amara understands then that Julia must have known her secret, just as Amara had long since guessed Julia's—that Julia loved Livia, not only as a friend, but as a wife. "You know everything that she meant to me," Livia says, her voice inexpressibly sad. "There is nothing we did not share."

"I know," Amara replies. "I know exactly what Julia meant to you." Livia cries again, holding Amara, perhaps relieved to have someone who recognizes the true extent of the loss she is suffering. Comforting her, Amara finally becomes aware of the other people huddled in the tent. With dismay she realizes that several members of Julia's household are here, watching their display of grief. Primigenia is sitting with her son Servius. So too are the porter, steward, and any number of slaves who know who she really is. Livia feels Amara's body stiffen, and looks up, following her gaze. Livia gives a slight shake of her head. It would be too suspicious to dismiss them all, in front of the guard. They will have to brazen it out.

Livia straightens her shoulders, taking on her former, more confident persona, and ushers Philos toward her. She lifts Rufina from his arms. "My darling girl," she says. "How brave you must have been!"

Rufina hugs Livia, clasping her around the neck. "Where is Julia?"

"Dear little one," Livia says. "She is not here."

"Will I see her later?" Rufina persists.

"Maybe," Livia replies, her voice faltering. She turns to Philos, speaking to him as she hands Rufina back into his arms. "We left several hours after you. I finally managed to persuade her to take your advice and flee. But things were much worse then, and part of the roof collapsed as we were trying to escape."

"I'm so sorry," Philos replies. "I cannot imagine how terrible it must have been."

"I couldn't even find her," Livia says, starting to cry again. "She was buried so deep underneath it. I had to leave, I couldn't do anything, I couldn't save her."

Amara takes Livia in her arms again, thinking of Pliny. "There was nothing you could do," she says firmly, the words as much for herself as they are for Livia. "You had to leave. She would have wanted you to live. You know this."

"Thank you darling," Livia whispers.

The guard interrupts, perhaps not eager for yet more tears. "Mistress, I am needed at the boats. I told your freedman that he is entitled to a portion of Julia Felix's estate. But he declined. I imagine because they will now be staying with you? In which case, I will head back to the shore."

"No, you mustn't decline Julia's gift," Livia says quickly, turning to Philos. "She would want the three of you to have something. And I know you cannot stay with me. The disaster has only hastened our separation."

There is so much more Amara wants to say, but she does not dare speak openly in front of the hovering soldier, who is clearly keen to take them back to the ship. "Where will you go?"

"I have family in Rome. A distant relative of Julia, who is also a cousin of my late husband." Livia tries to smile. "So I will live out my days as a dutiful widow. Which is what every woman does, after her love has died." Amara takes both Livia's hands, wishing there was some way she could acknowledge her friend's loss, to tell her she understands the emptiness she is facing. "My darling," Livia whispers, drawing Amara closer so that their faces are almost touching. "There is something else. Have you seen my dear friend Amara?" Silence stretches between them. Amara is unable to say anything, too shocked to speak. "That is very sad," Livia continues, her voice even lower, so that none of her household can hear. "I suppose she must not have survived. I am asking because her patron Demetrius sent a messenger here, in the emperor's company, hoping to find her. I believe he is distraught to have lost her." Amara clasps a hand to her mouth, as if that might somehow contain the terrible guilt Livia's words have provoked. *Demetrius is looking for her. He is desperate to find her alive. And she is abandoning him to his grief.* Amara tries to stop herself from crying, hunching her shoulders over to hold in her distress. She looks up at Livia, but finds no judgment in her friend's face, only pity. "I hope you understand that I had to tell you, darling. I did not think you would have seen her. But you never know."

Amara tries to regain control of herself, not even daring to look at Philos, wishing he was not a witness to her intense regret for her patron, which she will never now be able to hide. "I know that Amara would not wish Demetrius to darken his life with mourning," she whispers, hesitating over what to say, knowing this is the only message she will ever have for the man she promised to marry. "I know that she loved him. And she was incredibly grateful for everything he ever did for her."

Livia presses a hand to Amara's shoulder, then turns to Philos. "I hope you understand your wife's value, Fidelius. And that you will always look after her."

"Always," Philos says. "I promise you."

"Not that she has ever needed much looking after, I suppose," Livia smiles at Amara, and even in her sadness, there is a hint of her former mischief. "Julia always said you were the most determined woman she had ever met. That you had the tenacity of a *wolf*, and would make a success out of anything, however unlikely. So live your life, my darling. And don't prove her wrong."

NEAPOLIS

DECEMBER 80 CE

24

"Here is Vesuvius that until recently was green with shady vines. Here did the noble grape load the vats with juice . . . Here was Venus' seat, that she favored over Sparta; this spot was famous for its Herculean name. All lie sunk in flames and dismal ash. The gods themselves must have wished this was not in their power."

—Martial, *Epigrams*

The air is sweet with the scent of fennel and lavender as Amara grinds the herbs on the marble countertop. The light and sounds of the street fill the small shop, which is open to the road. She can hear the laughter of their next-door neighbor, Eumelia, as she stands on the pavement doing business, persuading another woman to buy extra dried fruit for the Saturnalia. Beside Amara, Fidelius is talking in Greek to a customer, advising the man on treatment for his daughter, who has a fever.

"A tonic of garlic and honey, made into a tea," he says. "Drunk twice a day, morning and evening. And it would be best to add some ginger. My wife will be able to make up the remedy for you."

"Ginger is expensive," the man grumbles. "I imagine the fever will simply burn itself out before the festival even starts. But my wife insisted I come here. She won't leave the house; she's just sitting there weeping. Wouldn't even trust a slave with the medicine."

"Your child is very young," Fidelius says, ignoring the suggestion his customer is here under duress. "We wouldn't need to add a lot of ginger. My wife Timarete is skilled at preparing the draught. Her father was a physician in Attica."

"How much?"

"Fifteen sesterces."

The man sighs heavily. "Very well," he says without looking at Amara.

Fidelius gently touches their daughter on the shoulder; she is sitting behind the counter on his other side, weaving a wreath for the Saturnalia. "Could you fetch the honey and garlic for your mother?" Fidelia puts down a handful of fir and holly, and her father picks up the stool she was sitting on, walking with her to the other side of the shop. He sets down the stool, so that she can stand on it and reach the shelves herself, then waits while she chooses the correct jars, spelling out the letters of the ingredients. Amara knows why Fidelius does this. It is to make sure their child has a chance to read as much as possible during the day.

"Thank you, my love," he says, as Fidelia hands over the jars of garlic and honey.

Amara gets the vial of expensive ginger from its hidden place behind the counter, while Fidelius brings her the rest. He moves differently now he is no longer Philos. It still surprises Amara just how much his current life has changed him. He seems somehow taller, and even though his calm manner is the same, it now naturally commands the respect that was always denied him as a slave.

Their customer watches Fidelia, as the little girl returns to her wreath. "You taught your daughter to read?"

"She reads Latin and Greek," Fidelius replies. "Both languages are necessary for our trade. She is already able to make up simple remedies herself."

"Where in Attica is your wife from?"

"Aphidnai." Fidelius says, answering for Amara. She is used to being silent in front of new customers. They live in the Greek district of Neapolis, and although most of their neighbors' families have been in Italy for generations, some of the attitudes toward women remind her of her hometown. Amara herself is granted more latitude, thanks to her Italian husband.

"But you are not Greek," the man continues, stating the obvious given Fidelius's accent. "You are Campanian, no? You freed her to marry her?"

Amara continues crushing the garlic, its scent bitter. She and Fidelius spent a long time perfecting their story. That he was granted his freedom first, then bought hers. It is the safest option when it comes to her sexual honor, implying that even as a slave, she was—morally if not legally—married.

Fidelius inclines his head in agreement, resting his hand on the small of Amara's back. "Her value to me is incomparable."

The truth is a tale that would bring nothing but disgrace. It is unthinkable that Amara was once a brothel slave who rose to become a powerful concubine, acquiring riches through her body and her wits, who deceived both her patrons with the enslaved man now acting as her husband. And that after using the terror of Vesuvius to reinvent their lives, these two cunning liars continue to make their fortune like foxes from a fable, determined to create a better future for their child whose freeborn status is also a lie, stolen from a man who was not even her father. Amara starts to spoon the nosy customer's tonic into a jar. She can never reveal who she is; she does not wish to. And yet, the total erasure of her past life still causes her pain. Perhaps this is why she does not yet feel like Timarete, why she is still Amara inside, while Philos has become Fidelius without a backward glance.

Amara hands the jar to the man, looking directly into his eyes. "Give your child a spoonful of this in each draft," she says in her deep, strong voice, tired of being spoken about as if she were not present. "Mix it in a cup of hot water so that everything dissolves, then let it cool before your daughter drinks. And pray to Pallas-Athene for her return to health."

The customer listens to Amara, then looks at Fidelius to address his reply. "For that price, I hope it works."

The man leaves the shop and Amara reaches for Fidelius's hand. He holds her briefly, kissing her on the forehead, before they step apart. "I had better take this to Irene," Amara says, gesturing at the crushed fennel and lavender. "She is due any day now."

"Of course. Take as long as you need." He turns to their daughter. "You can help me with the shop, can't you?"

Fidelia nods at her father, gazing at him with wide-eyed devotion. He will always be her favorite parent. She took little persuasion to see "Philos" as her father, given he had always been the most important person in her life, while Rufus barely registered on her consciousness. But even though Fidelia is starting to forget her life in Pompeii—the sharp edges of it rubbed smooth like a pebble washed by the sea—her mother's unremembered absence in her earliest years still leaves its mark.

Amara leaves as another customer comes into the shop, making sure the veil covering her hair is secure before stepping out onto the street. She nods to her neighbor, Eumelia, who raises a hand in greeting, then walks briskly along the pavement. The streets here are painted in the same vivid reds and yellows of Pompeii, and the air has the same seaside tang. And yet Amara could never mistake one place for the other. Neapolis is a bigger town, and its long, narrow streets run up and down steep hills, some of them ending with a hazy view of the glittering blue sea. And now all the refugees whose homes were destroyed by the mountain are expanding the town's streets still further. The Emperor Titus is pouring money into building new districts for Neapolis—one of which is named for the destroyed seaside resort of Herculaneum—as well as new baths and a bigger arena. The incessant sound of hammering, the endless movement of carts and masonry, all make the place busier, more crowded and more chaotic than Pompeii. Sometimes, it almost reminds her of Rome.

At the corner of the street, Amara pauses. She reaches up to touch the base of the shrine on the wall, a small corner altar for Pallas-Athene, writhing with snakes. A brightly painted statue of the goddess stands in her niche, looking out along the road, sharp-smelling incense rising from a smoldering offering at her feet. This Athena is nothing like the precious glass statue that Amara remembers from her parents' house, yet it is still comforting to find Attica's patron goddess here, so close to her new home. The Greek district where she lives is older and more dilapidated than the new businesses and homes being built in Neapolis, but Amara and Fidelius took the first rental opening they could, not wanting the wealth she acquired as a concubine to dwindle. There are times it grips Amara with panic, the relative precariousness of their lives, the knowledge that she will never again make back the vast wealth she once possessed. But the sight of Vesuvius, rising over the rooftops, oddly quells this anxiety. Mortality sits on her doorstep and Fortuna will turn her wheel, whatever plans Amara makes. Today, she has her family, she has love and she has a living. May this be enough.

The street starts to descend as she turns left, walking in the direction of the harbor. If she were to go as far as the sea, she might catch a glimpse of Misenum. A new admiral of the fleet lives there now. Amara holds the jar of tonic more tightly, hit by a familiar wave of grief. The dead are with her constantly, yet she cannot reach them. Pompeii has been destroyed as if it never existed, buried beneath hills of ash, but in Amara's mind it is still painfully alive. Its streets and houses exist in her memory, and she walks them, daily. She can still step over the threshold of Drusilla's door, into the house Drusilla owned before she married Ampliatus, and there she will find Primus, playing with his mother, frozen forever as a child, while Amara's own daughter grows older. She can watch Julia welcome guests into the Venus Baths, filling the space with her inimitable laughter, while Livia smiles. She can travel further back, performing music with Dido, watched by a man who would change her life: Pliny, the Admiral of the Roman Fleet, who she last saw on the dark shores of Stabiae. But above all when Amara thinks of Pompeii, she thinks of its arena, of Britannica raising her arms in savage victory, impossibly powerful and alive.

She presses a hand to her eyes, aware that she is crying. People do not stop to ask her what is wrong. Tears are common here in Neapolis. It is a city being built on the foundations of loss, in the shadow of a monster they barely escaped. Amara continues down the street, taking deep breaths to calm herself, until she reaches the potter's shop where Irene lives. It is similar to Amara's own home: a square space for the shop and a smaller room with a single window above, reached by a ladder at the back. But where Amara and Fidelius have a tiny courtyard that they use for growing plants, Irene and her husband use a second property next door, which houses the kiln.

The front of the shop is already wreathed in greenery, a few days early for the Saturnalia, and tables of small clay figures are set out, ready to be bought as gifts. Kallias, Irene's handsome husband, is charming a customer as Amara walks in, trying to sell a painted figurine of Saturn. He breaks off from his sales patter to greet Amara.

"Timarete!" he exclaims in his sonorous, Athenian accent. "How well you look as always. Irene will be so pleased by the visit. She is just having a little rest upstairs. Please thank your dear husband Fidelius, from me, for sparing you."

Amara smiles, genuinely pleased as always to see Kallias. The irony of their friendship makes her laugh inside, even though Kallias's arrival in their apothecary shop earlier this year was one of the most alarming moments she and Fidelius have encountered in Neapolis. Fear of discovery still haunts Amara. Every day she finds it hard to relax at the counter, half expecting to see Felix, or some other hated ghost from her past, step over the threshold of their shop. And the moment Kallias walked into their store, she recognized him. He is Menander, her first love, the potter's slave, who she once left for Rufus. Kallias instantly recognized her too, and in his shock, had called her by her former name.

It had been a hideous moment, as all three of them understood what had happened. Fidelius had stepped in front of Amara, shielding his wife from whatever the stranger intended, but fortunately for them all, Kallias is no more a freedman than Fidelius. He apologized profusely for his "mistake," explaining that he is a potter from Pompeii, who thought he recognized a former customer from his shop. Since then, the two runaway slaves have bolstered one another's stories by providing a false, respectable past for each other. Amara is beginning to suspect that perhaps many of the "freed" Pompeiians she meets are slaves, and some of the "freeborn" are freed, everyone deciding to take the chance to step up the social hierarchy in the confusion left by the disaster.

Amara climbs the ladder up to the living quarters above the shop. There is very little space, much of it taken up with casts Kallias is working on. He and Irene do not own or rent the business they run, but are employed, one step down from Amara and Fidelius, a distinction Amara dislikes herself for noticing.

"I'm so glad you came," Irene says. She is sitting on the bed in the corner, her feet up on the mattress, hands resting on her huge, pregnant belly. Irene is Greek too, like Amara and Kallias. Back in Pompeii, she was also enslaved. In certain lights, her cascade of curls reminds Amara of Victoria, though Irene has none of her old friend's bitterness, or her heartbreak.

"It's as much a treat for me," Amara says, embracing Irene warmly. "I'm so happy to see you. Also I just had to make up a tonic for some pompous old fool who resented spending money on his own daughter, so I can't say I'm sorry to leave the shop."

"I'm sure Fidelius charmed him," Irene says.

"Well, *I* wasn't going to," Amara replies, and they both laugh. Irene did not know Amara in Pompeii, yet she knows who Amara once was, which is perhaps why Irene has become her closest friend in Neapolis. It is a relief to have someone besides Fidelius who understands her past, and still loves her. She hands Irene the jar. "To be drunk as a tea, as often as you like. It helps with relaxation."

"I'm a bit nervous," Irene says, stroking a hand over her swollen abdomen. "Can you feel where he is lying?"

Amara had very little proper training from the expensive midwife who delivered her own child in Pompeii, but puts what knowledge she gleaned into practice, feeling the taut skin beneath Irene's ribs. "I think that's the feet. Which means the baby is facing downwards, ready for birth." She does not refer to the child as a boy, disliking the custom of assuming her friend is carrying a son.

"Kallias is so excited," Irene says, lowering her voice. "As well he might be! It's not him risking his life."

"I know it's very frightening. But you are strong and you will endure it, I promise." Amara squeezes Irene's hand, remembering her own fear before her daughter was born.

"Have you and Fidelius made a decision yet?" Irene asks, lowering her voice still further so that their conversation has no risk of being overheard in the shop.

"We have decided to stop using the contraceptive," Amara replies, thinking of all the late-night agonizing that led to this point. "So we will see. But you should try and avoid another pregnancy for at least a year after this one. My father once told me it is safest not to rush headlong into one childbirth after another." She does not add that the method she learned to avoid pregnancy came from her fellow whores at the brothel, rather than her respectable father, but suspects Irene will have guessed this.

"I hope the baby doesn't arrive right in the middle of the feasting," Irene says. "The midwife might be drunk."

"Well, I won't be," Amara says. "Not even one glass of wine until the baby is here. Virgulla taught me enough for me to keep an eye on things, or to step in if I have to. She was the best midwife in Pompeii."

"Thank you," Irene replies. They sit in silence a moment, perhaps both thinking of all the people and all the knowledge that has been lost. "You know they have managed to tunnel into the Forum?" Irene says, not needing to explain which town she is talking about. "Teams are stripping the Temple of Venus, and even the stones from the marketplace, to get hold of the marble. So I suppose we will see parts of Pompeii again, here in Neapolis. People have been breaking into some of the houses too, or that's the rumor Kallias heard. Do you think you will go back, like you did this spring, and try to get into the Venus Baths again?"

"I don't think so," Amara says. "It was impossible last time. That part of the town is completely buried; I can't even work out where the arena is." Amara does not add that she is not sure she could bear to go back, to walk again over the baked ruins with Fidelius, desperately hunting for signs of where they once lived, knowing that crushed beneath her feet are so many of the people she loves, and all the wealth she worked so hard to acquire. "People die all the time trying to tunnel back into Pompeii for their belongings," she says with a shrug. "We escaped with our lives and enough to start again. It's not worth the risk. Fidelia has a dowry, and she needs both her parents alive."

Irene nods. "It feels so strange that this one"—she strokes her belly—"will never know the place. Though I can't say I'm entirely sorry. It never felt like home, did it? And it's awful to say so, but I'm much happier now. There are times I think of the old shop, of all I suffered there, and I'm glad it's gone." Amara knows what Irene means. There are nights she imagines the Wolf Den consumed by flames and ash, obliterated by the rage of Vesuvius, and it brings her a savage sense of retribution. Britannica got her wish after all. A sudden image of her dearest friend, fighting in the arena, catches Amara off-guard, and she puts a hand to her mouth, not wanting to cry. *Britannica.* Of all her losses, Britannica's death hurts the most. Irene puts an arm around her. "I'm so sorry, I didn't mean to be unkind. I know you lost a great deal more than me."

Amara hugs her back. "No, it wasn't what you said. Honestly, I feel the same about the place. It wasn't home. And I hated much of it. But many of the people I lost there were like family."

Irene kisses Amara on the forehead. "We are family now. Our children will be cousins."

There is such sweetness to Irene in that moment, and such innocence, that Amara is reminded of her love for Dido. The thought of Dido brings with it an intense fear of loss. She sends up a silent prayer to the goddess of childbirth. *So many women die in labor, let Irene not be one of them, please let her live, Great Artemis, deliver her safely, I beg you.* Amara holds Irene close, crushing the spark of terror in her heart, smothering it before the flames can catch. In her mind, she hears her father's calm voice: *Thousands of women give birth every day.* She lets Irene go, smiling to hide her anxiety. Love always pains Amara like this. She cannot cherish anyone it seems, without a long shadow of fear trailing after.

"I suppose I had better get back to Fidelius," Amara says. "Salvius isn't coming in to help until much later."

"I had better go downstairs too," Irene sighs, heaving herself off the bed.

Amara goes down the ladder first, keeping an eye on the shop while Kallias goes up the ladder to help his wife safely down. Watching them together, and seeing Kallias's obvious care, Amara feels intense affection for them both. She is glad Menander has found the love he always deserved, as Kallias.

"See you at the temple tomorrow," he says, his arm around Irene, as Amara leaves the shop. She steps out onto the pavement, into the noise and chaos, and makes her way back up the steep hill toward home.

Amara and Fidelius keep their shop open until dusk falls, not wanting to lose the money from a single customer during the short winter days. Salvius, the slave boy they hire in the afternoons from Eumelia next door, trudges out to the well to bring the water in for the night, and to sweep up. Then Fidelius releases him, and he, Amara and Fidelia, lock up, drawing the wooden shutters across the entire shop front, plunging it into darkness.

They take an oil lamp and leave through the small door cut into the side, heading to the cook shop opposite for dinner.

Laughter and light spills out over the threshold and into the darkened street. The place is painted bright yellow, with portraits of roosters, rabbits and fruit, all looking more vibrant than the real hot meals on offer, which sit in steaming bowls on the marble counter. It has been one of the biggest changes to Amara's life, the return to eating out, rather than relaxing in the comfort of a private dining room. She sits at a small table, Fidelia on her lap, while Fidelius orders for them at the counter. Fidelia is humming to herself, playing with Julia the doll, whose features have almost worn off. Amara will have to get them repainted. She strokes her daughter's hair, warmed by the intensity of the love she feels. Fidelia no longer cries every night for her friends or asks to go home. She seems to be adapting to her new life, even if she is a more subdued child than before—although Fidelia still surprises her parents from time to time by demanding that her father take her to see Britannica fight.

The couple at the next table laugh loudly, and Fidelia frowns, snuggling closer against her mother, annoyed by the noise. The cook-shop is loud and hot, making private conversation difficult. Memories of the restaurant Amara once visited with Rufus, with its luxurious rooftop, return to her. Such an evening would not be a wholly impossible expense for her and Fidelius, if they chose to spend their hard-earned money that way, but she knows she will never again walk into a magnificent house like Pliny's in Misenum, to be waited on by slaves, reclining on a couch next to eminent guests. Guests like Demetrius.

Guilt stings her, sharp as a knife. Even though she tries so hard to avoid thinking about him, Demetrius still haunts her. They would have been married a year this Saturnalia, if Vesuvius had not erupted. Her wedding dress was the first item she sold in Neapolis—it had pained her beyond words to look at it. Everyone's favorite winter festival is doubly tainted for Amara; first by Dido's death and now by the knowledge of her own betrayal. Demetrius did not love her like Fidelius does, but still, Amara knows that he cared, and knows that he will have grieved her loss deeply. He did not deserve the distress she caused him, or to be abandoned in his old age.

"Are you alright my love?" It is her husband, returning to the table.

Amara looks up. Fidelius is a strikingly attractive man, and in the lamplight even more so. He is looking at her with so much kindness and concern in his gray eyes that Amara smiles, wanting to reassure him. "Everything is well," she says, as he sits down beside her.

Fidelia scrambles off Amara's lap, wanting to wedge herself between her parents, to be close to both of them. Guilt starts to loosen its grip. Amara tells herself she faced an impossible choice, one that was always going to inflict pain, yet in the end, she does not regret the love she chose. She rests her hand on her daughter's shoulder and leans over to kiss Fidelius on the cheek. "Everything is as it should be," she says.

25

"This alone is certain, namely that there is no such thing as certainty."
—Pliny the Elder, *Natural History*

The goddess Fortuna Redux sits on the wooden platform, carried by temple priests. Her hair is red, and her face gold. In one hand she carries the cornucopia of plenty, in the other a ship's rudder, a symbol of the danger she has steered them through. A marble veil falls over her curls, and the drapes of her robes are painted blue, gilded with images of the merciless wheel that she turns without a care for those who drop to the bottom. Musicians surround this most fickle of gods, celebrating her procession, as she is carried around the Forum.

The crowds are quieter than Amara has ever known in a street celebration like this, the sound of Fortuna's trumpets blasting out with little competition from peoples' chatter. She pulls the thin veil down lower over her face. Beside her, Fidelius has their daughter on his shoulders, so that she can see the goddess. Kallias and Irene are also here; Amara and Irene hold hands to avoid being separated in the crush. Amara does not stare about too much, not wanting to be recognized. It is dangerous to be in this crowd, where it is possible someone will know who they really are, but to have stayed away would have caused even more suspicion. The Forum of Neapolis is packed full of survivors: refugees from Pompeii, Herculaneum, Stabiae, Oplontis, along with unknown villages whose names are already dead and buried. They are here to give thanks for their own salvation from Vesuvius and to see the town's Temple of Fortuna rededicated to the goddess in her form as *Fortuna Redux;* the one who delivers mortals from danger and brings them home from a perilous journey.

Amara thinks of the Temple of Fortuna Redux in Rome, a massive edifice near the Circus Maximus, whose dedication day is shared by this new Neapolitan upstart. She looks up at Fidelia, at her small, solemn face, rapt with attention, and wonders if her daughter will ever see Rome. Most likely not. Instead, she will live the life Amara's own parents intended for their daughter, staying in her hometown, marrying into a respectable family, never encountering anyone as brutal as Felix or as intelligent as Pliny. Nor will she meet a woman as unique or forceful as Julia, her namesake clutched in Fidelia's hand, still loved. Although memories of her real auntie Julia are fading, a thought that brings Amara both relief and sadness. She and Fidelius have yet to decide exactly how much of their own lives to tell their daughter, when she is grown. They will need some explanation for the priceless jewels in her dowry, after all.

Fortuna has reached the steps to her temple, and slowly she ascends. It is a difficult journey for her priests, making sure the heavy goddess does not tilt from her platform. Framed behind the temple's pointed roof is the sunken summit of Vesuvius, and behind that the sky, as blue as the goddess robes. A haze of smoke rises from the mountain's broken peak, its slopes no longer green with the vineyards Pliny once pointed out to Amara, but black. She feels surprisingly little fear, watching the sleeping monster. It is not that she trusts in the goddess to save her—rather that Neapolis has escaped destruction once already.

The trumpets ring out as the statue is set down at the top of the steps, flanked by decorated columns. There Fortuna sits, looking out over her new home, her golden face implacable. The priests busy themselves at the altar for the sacrifice, and Fidelius takes their daughter down from his shoulders so she will not cry at seeing the bull killed. Beside Amara, Irene sways slightly on her feet. It is a long time to be standing with the baby due so soon, but they cannot insult the goddess by leaving now. They wait. Then there is a bellow from the bull as its lifeblood is spent, and the musicians blast again on their trumpets, signaling the sacrifice is over. People start to move—some pressing closer to see what omens might be left on the altar, others milling toward the stalls where small clay mementos of Fortuna are being sold, along with hot snacks. Amara wrinkles her nose, the smell of roasted nuts and fish turning her stomach. It's not the first time this week she has felt queasy. She places her hand over her flat belly. It is too soon to tell, but the thought she might be carrying a child gives her a sense of intense expectation, neither wholly good nor bad, much like all Fortuna's gifts.

"We must be getting back to the shop," Kallias is saying to Fidelius. "And get some business in before the festival. But I look forward to joining families at the Saturnalia. Perhaps there will even be six of us then!"

The two men embrace warmly and Amara feels a little irritated by their enthusiasm, knowing how afraid Irene is about the birth. "See you in three days," Amara says to her. "And I am sure the baby will hold out until after the feast."

She and Fidelius head for the street that leads back to their home, their daughter between them, holding both their hands.

Amara feels intense relief the ceremony is over, and that she did not see the face she dreads above all others. *Felix is dead*, she tells herself. *And the Wolf Den is destroyed.*

Salvius looks anxious when they return to the shop. He is a slight boy, perhaps sixteen or seventeen, with the air of a startled rabbit. Like many slaves he does not know his exact age, having lived without a mother since he was small.

"A man came in and was difficult," he says to Fidelius, cringing as if expecting a telling-off. "I didn't mean to insult him, but I didn't know which remedy he was talking about. I think he might come back. I'm sorry if I lost you business."

"Never mind," Fidelius says, his voice kind. He has a soft spot for the boy, perhaps born from guilt at the enslaved status Salvius unknowingly shares with him. "I'm sure you tried."

Salvius slips gratefully from the stool behind the counter, hurrying to finish hanging up the evergreen wreaths. The shop is looking especially pretty for the Saturnalia; holly and fir sit well in an apothecary. Amara and Fidelius have worked hard to build this business; the small courtyard at the back is full of brightly colored pots, not only resting on the ground but fixed up the wall, using every possible scrap of sunlight. A tiny pool, barely more than a puddle, sits in the center, just deep enough to store rainwater for the plants. Inside the shop, the painted walls are faded, but shelves cover most of the space, crammed with jars of dried herbs, flowers and even a few more exotic remedies, which they collect when they can afford them. Never one to miss a chance to make money, Amara has branched out into cosmetics, as well as medicine.

The most prominent position is taken up by Pliny's scroll on the uses of plants, which is shelved on the wall behind the counter, rolled open slightly to reveal a beautiful illustration of silphium, the rarest and most precious of herbs. It is displayed to advertise their professional credentials. The story they tell is that it was left to them by Amara's father, which she supposes, is almost true. Whenever she sees it, Amara feels as if the admiral is still looking after her, even though, deep down, she knows that Pliny, were he alive, would have been appalled by her choice to leave his friend Demetrius.

They currently rent the shop from the family who live in the grand house behind, but Amara's wealth and the bequest from Julia's estate were enough to set them up in business, and as long as they continue to do well, it is possible they might eventually be able to buy a space in the newly built part of town. Amara misses the luxury of her life in Rome, but she has not given up on all ambition for herself, or for her family.

"Do you think you can spare me?" Amara says to Fidelius, who is leaning against the counter, going through their accounts. "If so, I might go now to the harbor to see if it's true they have brought some cinnamon in."

"Of course," Fidelius says. "Do you need to take Salvius with you?"

Amara is always the one to buy the rarer and more expensive herbs. Her early life preparing medicines for her father means there is a smaller chance of her being cheated with false substitutes. "I am fine." She smiles, knowing that a gangly boy would not provide her much protection in any case. "I will try not to be too long."

She sets off, feeling lighter now the dedication to Fortuna is over, although she cannot shake off a creeping sense of being followed. Amara turns around. The street stretches back up the hill, empty of familiar faces. She dismisses her fear. It's not the first time her mind has played tricks on her. Sometimes she thinks the past will never let her go. There are so many people from Pompeii she longs to see again—Britannica, Drusilla, Stephanus—yet still more that she dreads. It is not only Felix. She fears encountering any of her old friends from the Wolf Den, or even worse, Rufus. Livia's word as a woman, vouching for their freed status, would not count for much against a man of his class.

It is cold at the harbor, and Amara's breath clouds the air in huffs of smoke. She glances over at the colonnade that lines the seafront. The fine houses here remind her of the beautiful mansion Drusilla once lived in at the port of Pompeii. It must lie buried now, under mounds of ash. Grief tugs at her, threatening her composure, and Amara comforts herself with the same story she always repeats whenever she thinks of her lost friend: *Drusilla and her family escaped by boat as soon as the mountain exploded. They did not die in the disaster. Somewhere out there, Drusilla is still alive.*

Amara does not look over the silver water toward the shoreline that hides Misenum, but concentrates instead on finding the trader whose ship is said to have come in from India. The soothing sigh and slap of the waves, the call of gulls and sailors reminds her again of the harbor at Pompeii, but she pushes the memory away. She walks up and down, finding the ship without too much difficulty, as the trader has set out stalls on the dock. Amara looks over the tumbled range of goods. There are sacks of spices, together with statues of strange gods and goddesses, wholly unfamiliar and alien. One has the face of an elephant.

"He will remove obstacles from your path," the man at the stall says, noticing Amara staring at the statue. He gestures at the elephant god with an ingratiating smile.

"I was looking for cinnamon," she replies.

The trader yells for a slave, who hurries over. The two men exchange a few words in Punic, a North African language Amara recognizes, as it was Dido's mother tongue. Then the slave scurries up the gangplank onto the ship behind, swiftly disappearing below deck. The trader watches Amara, who keeps her expression neither friendly nor unfriendly, her eyes fixed on the ship, as if waiting for the slave. She still has the poise she learned in Rome, a confidence that she has found repels some of the worst male attention.

The boy hurries back to his master, clutching a small bag. The man snatches it, then hands it to Amara with a bow. She looks inside. Immediately, the sweet, rich scent takes her back to her father's house. With great care, she lifts one of the rolled sticks, turning it in her fingers. The cinnamon is real. "How much for ten of these?"

"Sixty denarii," the man replies.

Anger flashes across Amara's face. "Do you take me for a *complete* fool?" she snaps. "My father is a physician. Cinnamon is not worth that much. How would we ever recoup the cost of the medicine?"

The trader holds up his hands. "You are very fierce, Mistress. For you, I can do forty."

"Ten," Amara replies, and it is the trader's turn to look annoyed.

"Thirty."

"Twenty."

"Twenty-five," the man says, folding his arms, and Amara senses she is close to his bottom price.

She looks again at the precious stick in her fingers. Twenty-five denarii would not grant them much profit from the sale, but it would not be a loss, and the boost to their reputation is likely worth the price. Amara puts the stick carefully back into its container. "Twenty-two. Or nothing." She hands back the small bag of spice.

"Done," the trader replies.

Amara feels a pang, seeing how swiftly the man accepts the deal. Perhaps she should have stuck to twenty. She watches as he counts out the ten sticks, wrapping them in the square of fabric that she hands over. Whatever the cinnamon's real value, she consoles herself, she has at least not miscalculated the amount she can add to the resale price.

"Thank you," Amara says, using one of the only Punic phrases Dido taught her, as she gives him the money.

"May the gods protect you," he replies in Greek, laying a hand over his heart.

Amara hurries away from the harbor, eager to be safely home now the deal is done. Fidelius will be delighted her trip was not in vain. From the corner of her eye, she sees a shadow. A man, following her. She turns sharply, but he has gone. She starts off again, telling herself not to be foolish, her heart beating faster, when a familiar voice stops her dead.

"Not lost the gift for haggling, I see."

Amara does not turn around, as if by pretending she has not heard, she can deny the reality of who is speaking, and prevent the horror that will come.

"I wouldn't keep walking, Amara," the man says, closer behind her now. "You don't want to cause a scene."

She turns. It is Felix.

They stare at one another. Amara has dreaded this moment for so long, she feels as if she has conjured the figure before her out of her own fear. Her old master is at once the same and different. He has lost none of his sharp-eyed cruelty, the sense of bunched muscle and barely contained rage, but he is no longer a commanding presence. Felix, who she only ever saw sober, sways slightly on his feet and reeks of drink. Amara takes a step back.

"You have mistaken me for someone else," she says coldly.

"I don't believe so, *Plinia* Amara." He jabs a finger toward her. "I wonder what your betrothed would say, if he knew you were living in Neapolis, whoring yourself out to a runaway slave."

"Get away from me," Amara hisses. "I don't have to listen to this slander!"

Felix leans in, breathing wine fumes in her face. "You will listen to me in private, or I will shout your real name to the entire harbor."

He is too close to her, threatening her physical space in a way that no man has dared for years. It is a lifetime since Amara endured Felix's violence in the Wolf Den, and yet the memory of it now is as painful as if it were yesterday. She knows he will not hesitate to hurt her if she disobeys. "I can only spare you a moment," she says, aiming for a tone of disdain but unable to keep the tremor from her voice.

Felix bows. "You are too gracious."

Amara walks alongside her old master, who makes for a narrow street off the harbor, into a less reputable part of town. The buildings are tall, blocking out the light, and there is a stench from all the waste dumped in the road. "Where are we going?" she asks, trying not to sound frightened.

"Just for a walk," Felix replies.

They reach a tiny square with a tavern. It reminds Amara of The Sparrow in Pompeii, the inn near the brothel where she used to drink with the other she-wolves. There is a poorly painted fresco of three wine jugs on the wall outside, with their prices underneath. The place is cheap. "I'm not going inside," Amara says, folding her arms.

Felix rolls his eyes. "Wait here," he says. "And don't even think of running away. I know where your shop is, where you and *Fidelius* live." He walks unsteadily into the dingy bar. Other drinkers are loitering outside, some of them looking over at the surprising sight of a respectably dressed woman. Amara pulls her veil closer over her face, hunching her shoulders to make herself smaller. It is not likely anyone here will recognize her, but she doesn't want to take the risk. Felix comes back out again, clutching a cup of wine. He leans against the wall beside her, his body far too close to hers. She wants to move away, but at least at this proximity nobody is likely to overhear them.

"Why is it, I wonder," Felix asks, "that I lost *everything*, but here you are, living like a well-bred matron, with a stolen family and business?" Amara says nothing, not wanting to add anything to Felix's store of knowledge about her. "My boys and my wife. Dead. My business. Gone. I have nothing. And here *you* are, living life just as you please."

Victoria is dead then. Amara suspected as much, seeing him alone, but even amidst her fear the loss still hurts, not least because it surely makes Felix more dangerous. "I am sorry about your family," she whispers.

"Gone," Felix repeats. "It wasn't the ash but the fucking earthquake that killed them. A building we sheltered in on the way to Neapolis collapsed." He looms closer, eyes red-rimmed with alcohol and grief. "Do you have any idea what it's like to search for your children in rubble, in the dark, only to find them dead?"

Amara thinks of the two boys she saw at the Wolf Den, remembering Victoria with the baby in her arms. If Felix were a different man, her heart would break for him. "I'm sorry," she says again.

"No, you're fucking not," Felix snarls. "But I will *make* you sorry, you fucking little Greek whore. Let's see how brave you are, now the British bitch is gone."

"Why are you doing this? Nothing you do to me will bring them back."

"No," Felix says. "But it will give me immense satisfaction to expose you for the liar you are."

"Look at yourself," Amara says, almost spitting with contempt. "You're a penniless drunk who used to run a brothel. Nobody is going to believe anything you have to say about me." She pushes away from the wall, making as if to leave, but Felix seizes her wrist.

"Don't you fucking dare walk away from me," he says, all the more menacing for not raising his voice. "Do you know what I do for a living now, Amara? I track down lying slaves who are using Vesuvius to exploit the emperor's generosity with their false names and their false lives. You would be surprised how much money the authorities pay for runaway property."

"I'm no runaway slave," Amara says. "And Livia herself vouched for the freeborn status of myself and my husband. We are officially registered." She feels some satisfaction at his obvious look of surprise.

"Well, that hardly matters. Your patron is still alive. The one you abandoned. I suspect *his* word would count for more. Imagine how he might react, discovering the woman he offered to marry, to share his name and his wealth with, left him for a *slave*. The shame of it, and the disgust." Amara has indeed imagined this scenario, many times, in the dead of night. She has never deluded herself that whatever love Demetrius had for her would be strong enough to counter his hurt pride at such a betrayal. She swallows, not wanting to show Felix how close she is to tears. "Do you know how runaway slaves who pose as freed are punished, Amara? Do you know what they would do to Philos? Or your daughter? Perhaps I might buy her myself. To stop her starving on the street after her parents' punishment."

"You have no evidence he is not freed. Livia swore to it."

"He is branded. Victoria told me, when she saw you naked together. Marked straight across his chest. How often is a branded slave freed? And besides, it is *your* identity that betrays him. Why else would the admiral's freedwoman lie about her own name, give up all that wealth, if it were not to hide who her lover really is."

"Victoria lied," Amara says. "There is no mark on him."

"Really," Felix sneers. "Maybe tell the crowds that when I demand he takes his tunic off before the magistrates in the Forum." Terror is tightening its grip on Amara, her vision darkening, the roar in her head louder than Vesuvius in its rage. Felix catches her by the arm, to prevent her from fainting. "Of course," Felix says, soothingly, "there are alternatives."

"What do you want?" Amara is shaking. She cannot even pretend to hide her fear anymore.

"You will give me a cut of everything you make. And I fancy setting up my old business again. Your *husband* will lend you to me, while I save up for some more girls. I'm sure that will make for a happy marriage for you both, knowing men pay me so they can fuck you, as the price for his freedom."

"What if we refuse?"

"I don't think that would be very wise, Amara, do you?"

She shakes him off. "How long do I have to give you an answer? I need to discuss this with my husband."

"You will meet me here tomorrow at noon with your answer and a first payment of five denarii," Felix says. "Otherwise I will go to the authorities."

Amara shakes him off. "Very well. I will be here."

Felix watches her, eyes narrowed in contempt. "Would you like me to walk you safely home?"

"Don't fucking touch me," she snaps, swatting away his hand.

"No," Felix says. "You're right. I will save that until tomorrow." He turns his back on her, with an unsteady wave of dismissal. "Sleep well, Plinia Amara."

26

"Timarete scorned the duties of women and practiced her father's art."
—Pliny the Elder on the Greek artist Timarete, famous
for her painting of the goddess Diana

Amara tries to collect herself on her way home, to rebuild the façade of genuine happiness she once felt at finding the cinnamon. She walks the steep street up from the harbor, barely noticing her surroundings, buffeted by other passersby on the pavement. Her world is gray, leeched of life and vitality. Felix's threats have cast a terrifying darkness over her family's future, as lethal as the ash cloud that once fell from the mountain.

The shop is mercifully busy when she gets back, people buying what they might need before the holidays. Tomorrow is the last day they have to trade before everything closes for the Saturnalia. She barely has a chance to show Fidelius the cinnamon before getting back to work, making up the list of remedies he has written out for her, all of which are due for collection.

From behind the counter, she can see her daughter. Fidelia sits on a wooden chest in the far corner of the shop, practicing her letters on a wax tablet. Her new life as the child of shopkeepers means Fidelia is often obliged to keep herself quietly entertained. She is perched on top of her own dowry, small legs dangling over the side of the chest. Locked inside the chest are many of Amara's remaining treasures from Rome and Pompeii. The fine fabrics, the silver plate, the ornaments. Upstairs, in another box, are the last of the jewels Demetrius and Rufus gave her. It is the final remnant of her security. They have already spent all the money gifted to them by Julia to set up the shop. Amara looks again at Fidelia, at the frown of concentration wrinkling the small brow above her perfect gray eyes.

Perhaps I might buy her myself. To stop her starving on the street after her parents' punishment.

Felix knows where she lives. He knows who Fidelius is. He has seen their shop, and now he threatens her daughter. The enormity of it makes Amara feel nauseous and she hurries to the back of the room, out into the small courtyard, pretending to be busy with one of the plants. She tries to calm herself. Felix is a drunk. The authorities will see she is registered and not even listen to him. And yet he is telling the truth, and the truth, once scented, can become harder to hide.

Amara thinks of Irene and Kallias, and the child they are about to bring into the world. It is not only her own family at risk. Fidelius and Kallias have bound a fabric of lies so tightly to one another, creating a false, freed past, that she has no doubt suspicion would fall on her friends too, and on the motives they had to hide another's slave status. Then there is Demetrius. Amara closes her eyes. The thought of her former protector discovering her betrayal is one of unendurable humiliation. She has little doubt that his love would be destroyed by bitterness at what she has done. How could he ever forgive all the pain and grief she knowingly inflicted by leading him to believe she had died?

She returns to the counter, going back to grinding the ingredients for a poultice one of the neighbors has ordered. Fidelius glances over at her, frowning in concern. He looks so much like their daughter.

"Are you feeling well? You look pale."

"I will be fine," Amara murmurs, not looking up from her work.

The rest of the afternoon passes interminably. She both longs to share her burden with Fidelius and dreads shattering their lives. Once she has told him, she knows nothing will restore his peace. Felix will have invaded every part of their relationship, leaving everything tainted. At dinner in the cookshop, she is barely able to eat, but when Fidelius again asks her what is wrong, she only shakes her head, glancing toward their daughter to show she cannot speak.

Fidelia sees the movement and is instantly alert. She is a quieter child since the eruption, but she is still sharp. "What is it?" she asks, looking between her parents. "What's wrong?"

"Nothing, my love," Amara reassures her, kissing her daughter on the top of her head. The thought of Felix hurting Fidelia is a pain she cannot even begin to fathom. "It's nothing," she repeats, as if saying the words will make it so.

"It's not the mountain, is it?" Fidelia turns anxiously to her father.

Fidelius shakes his head, his smile warm and reassuring, then lifts his daughter onto his knee. "Not the mountain, no. But do you think Julia might like to be repainted for the Saturnalia?"

Fidelia holds out her doll, and the pair of them regard Julia solemnly. Normally the sight of them both would make Amara smile. Now she is simply relieved to have Fidelius turn his attention to their child for the rest of the meal, as it takes some of the strain out of her pretence that all is well. When they have eaten, she takes her husband's arm as they cross the darkened street back to their home. She glances down the road toward the dimly lit shrine to

Pallas-Athene. How long has Felix been watching them all? Might he be out there now? With a sick feeling, Amara realizes she will never feel safe again.

Fidelius unlocks the small side door cut into the building's wooden shutters, and lets them in. Guided by his oil lamp, they all climb the ladder to the single room that they share above the shop. The ceiling is soft and green; a swaying curtain of herbs hung up to dry, making the small space smell sweet. The room below is in total darkness as they settle Fidelia in her cot, the light from the lamp dancing on the walls. Fidelius softly tells his daughter a story, then joins Amara to sit on the edge of the bed. They draw the curtain between Fidelia's cot and their own bed, listening to their child's snuffling breaths, waiting for her to drift off.

"Something happened today, down at the harbor," Fidelius whispers. "What was it?" Amara cannot speak and instead starts to cry. He opens his arms to her, and she sobs silently onto his chest, while he holds her tightly. "Whatever it is, please tell me."

"I think I'm pregnant." They are not the words Amara intended, but they are nonetheless part of the reason for her distress.

"But that's not so terrible is it?" Fidelius says, and she can feel his body relax. "Isn't that what we were hoping for?"

"But what if something happened to you? What if you got taken away? Or Fidelia? What if we lost everything? What if . . ." Amara cannot continue but begins crying again.

"My love, you can't worry like this," he says, stroking her shoulders. "You've been through so much. But it doesn't mean that suffering is destined to go on and on forever. Sometimes there's an end to it. And nothing is going to happen to me, I promise you."

They lie down, facing each other on the bed. Fidelius gazes into her eyes and he is so calm, so certain that he can protect her and take away her pain. Amara cannot believe, looking at him, that she has wasted any time in Neapolis missing the wealth and luxury of her life in Rome. In this moment, she wants nothing more than the chance to live peacefully, to see her daughter grow up, to see Fidelius grow old, to live long enough for the desire she feels for him to mellow and lose its intensity, because with each passing year, he will become safer and more familiar. "I love you," she says.

"I love you too."

She kisses him, drawing him closer, driven by both fear and desire, wanting to blot out the horror of the next day, wanting to forget that soon it will not be his hands on her, but hands belonging to Felix. The thought makes her stop, suddenly cold, but Fidelius mistakes this for anxiety about their daughter. "She's asleep," he says, pushing himself upright on the bed and picking up the oil lamp. "Listen."

Amara slips out of bed to look behind the curtain. Their child is sprawled across the cot, an arm flung over her head, oblivious to the danger that stalks her. Fidelius sets down the lamp and pulls off his tunic, the shame he once felt in front of her at the branding on his skin long forgotten. Amara undresses too, her hands shaking slightly. She climbs back into the bed, and Fidelius catches hold of her waist. She kisses him, taking his face in her hands. His body is warm as she leans against him, wanting to be even closer. Amara closes her eyes. She will not tell him about today. Some burdens are not lightened by sharing. She will pay Felix, and do what she has to do to protect her family. Nobody else needs to know.

It is easy enough to tell Fidelius that she needs to go out to buy more stock, that the trader yesterday had reports of a delivery of silphium, the rarest and most precious of herbs. She even manages to lighten the story with an anecdote: that Pliny once told her there had only been a single sighting of the plant in his lifetime.

"It's probably nonsense," Amara says brightly, "but I ought to go and check. Imagine if we did find silphium, here in Neapolis!"

She does not walk directly to the inn by the harbor; first she visits a clothing shop in another, unfamiliar district of town, buying a thick, poor-looking cloak that she wears over her own. It is winter, and there is nothing suspicious about a woman being muffled up in a hood, hiding her face. If she is going to have to endure shame and horror to protect her family, she will at least try to protect her reputation. Amara takes a circuitous route to the inn, avoiding her own district entirely, arriving a little late in the square outside. Felix is already there. He is drunk.

"You came," he says, looking her up and down.

Amara does not answer. She follows him down the narrow lane to another inn. It is a large ramshackle building with the reek of manure wafting from the stables. They walk into the bar, which is almost empty. The landlord gives Felix a surly look from behind the counter. "Make sure you pay what you fucking owe me," he shouts as they pass. "Don't be spending my money on whores!"

The blood is beating loudly in Amara's head as she climbs the narrow stairs, following Felix along the corridor to his room. He opens the door, and then they are shut inside. She looks the place over quickly. It is filthy and smells of stale wine. There is a bed and a table by the window. Felix leans against the table, watching her.

"Do you think you can keep up the disguise? That Philos won't discover how you pay me?"

"I don't want my husband to ever know about this." Amara wraps her arms around herself, wishing time could jump forward an hour, that she could erase what she will be forced to do.

Felix watches her tug anxiously at her cloak, fastening it more tightly. "I don't know why you're bothering with that—you can't keep it on," he smirks, grabbing hold of her wrist and pulling her closer. "But give me the money first."

Amara reaches under the clothes, as if searching for her purse. Then she brings her hand up swiftly, hitting Felix in the stomach. He looks down in surprise. Amara's fingers are clasped around a knife, buried deep underneath his ribs.

Strike first

Britannica's voice is in Amara's head. Her dead friend is beside her, so close she can feel the whisper of her breath against her ear. Britannica was denied the chance to kill Felix, and it was Amara who denied her that chance. But no longer.

Always remove your weapon

Amara yanks out the knife and Felix staggers forward. His eyes lock with hers, wide with shock and pain. Horror grips her then at what she has done, but she cannot turn back now, she only has a heartbeat before he recovers himself. The old Felix would have recovered himself already. Britannica's voice is louder this time, filling the room, impossible to be denied.

The second blow is the hardest

Without pause, without waiting for compassion to destroy her, Amara allows the rage that burns in her heart to catch fire, consuming everything in its path. She raises her arm in a lethal arc, bringing down the knife with full force, driving it into Felix's unprotected throat.

The power of the blow throws his body against hers. Warm blood spills out over her hand, but she does not dare remove the blade. Within moments Felix will be dead. They both know this. Amara's eyes fill with tears. She holds Felix, almost with tenderness, as she lowers his body to the floor. She might be back at the house with the golden door and this is only practice, this is only a lesson Britannica is giving her, and the knife is blunt and made of wood.

But remember it is him or you

Felix is lying on the floor. He opens his mouth, wanting to talk, but only blood comes out. All this time, Amara has said nothing. She knows now that her face is the last thing he will see, her words the last he will hear. Felix's eyes are fixed desperately on her, perhaps hoping to hear the love as well as the hate she has always felt for him. And yet it is not her own words she speaks, but Britannica's.

"And when you are dead, you are nothing."

The room is silent and cold. Britannica is not here. Amara is alone, and she alone killed Felix. His dead eyes stare upward, fixed on the last point he saw her. She knows that grief lies on the other side of her anger, but she cannot allow herself to feel it. Gently, she presses down his eyelids, then lays her hand on his chest, over his heart.

"Take back the name you gave me. Take it with you to the underworld. May Amara never be spoken in this life again."

From the purse around her neck she takes a coin, then places it under his tongue. It is his fare for Charon, the demon who ferries the dead across the River Styx.

"I am Timarete, daughter of Timaios, blessed by Pallas-Athene, patron goddess of Attica. You will not haunt me, Felix. I have granted you safe passage to the underworld." She stops as tears well again in her eyes. "I do this out of respect for your wife Victoria, whose heart you broke and whose love you never deserved."

Timarete rises. She has no more time to waste on the dead; she needs to escape, to protect her family, or else she just destroyed her soul for nothing. She grabs some of the grubby sheets on the bed, wrapping them around Felix, hoping they will soak up the blood and stop it pooling through the floorboards into the room below. Carefully, she pulls the knife from his neck, hoping the risk of her being sprayed red has passed. The blood is already congealing, but she still stuffs fabric around the wound to be safe. The corpse does not distress her. This body is no longer Felix; his shade will be on the banks of the River Styx now, clamoring for passage to Hades. In all senses, Felix has gone.

Timarete wipes the knife clean on the sheet, removing the blood. She gets to her feet and searches the room, hoping for a jug of water. One stands in the corner by the bed. It is half empty, but she dips in the hem of the cloak, soaking up enough to rub her face well with the damp fabric, in case any blood has sprayed onto her skin. Next she immerses her hands, darkening the water. Timarete inspects the thick cloak she bought earlier. There is a large blood stain upon it, where Felix fell against her. She curses, taking it off, wrapping it up so that the blood is hidden. It would have been better to leave in the cloak she came into the place wearing, but at least her own cloak underneath appears unmarked.

She slips from the room, without looking back at the body, and shuts the door behind her. The corridor is empty. If she has to, she will leave by the bar, but it would be better not. She walks to the far end, where there is another staircase. From the smell, it seems to lead to the stables. Timarete walks down quietly, praying to Athena, the goddess of strategy, that the place is empty. The large, melancholy eyes of a mule are fixed on her as she passes his stall and slips out onto the street.

It is hard to resist the temptation to run. Timarete walks slowly and deliberately from the inn, her cloak pulled up to her face, taking the opposite route that she came, hoping she can find her way back to the harbor. The pavements are crowded, people out doing their last day's shopping for the Saturnalia. Nobody pays her much mind. She presses her back against a tall basket outside a fullers, which is already filled with washing to be laundered, and drops the cloak on top, hurrying on rather than waiting to make sure it is hidden.

The port is easy enough to find. She follows the smell of fresh air and the noise of the harbor. Timarete steps out from a narrow street, into the large public space, walking along the colonnade. Only now does she begin to relax. She glances out to sea, visible above the bobbing masts of trading ships and fishing vessels. The day is gray today, the water dull as stone, the sky lowering with clouds. She pauses a moment. *Felix is dead.* The words sound in her head, but the guilt and panic she expects to follow, do not answer. Instead she hears Britannica again. *Remember it is him or you.*

As Amara, she dreamed so many times of avenging herself on Felix, of the satisfaction she would feel. But now, as Timarete, she feels relief. Nothing more. She looks out across the bay, to where she knows Pliny's villa still lies in Misenum. In her mind, she walks once more through the admiral's gardens, and sees Clytemnestra painted on the wall, drenched in blood. Again, Timarete waits to feel afraid, but does not. Felix was a pimp, not the King of Mycenae, and nobody is coming to avenge his death. The past is buried and she is finally free.

Timarete turns from the sea, and takes the main road home, passing Kallias and Irene's shop. She glances in without entering, seeing her friends together at the counter, Irene with her hand resting on her belly. Timarete keeps walking. At the corner of her own street, she passes the shrine to Athena and lightly touches the snakes on the wall. *Take his death as an offering,* she prays, *and let my family now live in peace.*

Eumelia, her neighbor, smiles as she approaches the shop, which is hung with evergreen for the festival. When Timarete walks over the threshold of her home, Fidelius is dealing with a customer and their daughter is sitting on the countertop playing with a figurine of the hunting goddess Diana—an early present for the Saturnalia.

"Ah, my wife is back," Fidelius says as she approaches. "I am sure she can help you. Her father was a physician in Attica." He beckons her closer, his gray eyes warm with affection. "My love, the gentleman wants to know the best remedy for sleeping disorders. He is plagued by bad dreams. I have suggested a few, but I am sure you will know better."

Timarete slips behind the counter to stand demurely beside her husband, the image of propriety. She glances at the man in front of her, swiftly sizing up from his clothes how much money they might charge. Then she gives her customer the same hard, inscrutable smile she once learned from a dead man in Pompeii.

EPILOGUE

April 81 CE

"Fortune favors the brave"
—Words spoken by Pliny the Elder, on his rescue
mission during the eruption of Vesuvius

Their ship is turning into the harbor of Neapolis, getting closer to shore. The heaving sigh of the waves and creak of timber is steadily drowned out by the shouts of sailors, the crash of masonry being unloaded at the dock. But it is not the busy town that holds Senovara's attention. Her eyes are fixed on Vesuvius. The mountain is black, still charred from the force of its rage. She touches the tattered amulet around her neck. A gesture of respect for the only being she has ever encountered whose violence outpaces her own.

"Not afraid are you, Britannica?" It is Stephanus, his tanned face crinkled in amusement.

Senovara grins, baring her gap teeth. She punches him on the arm, a playful blow but still hard enough to hurt. "Why afraid? I not fight the mountain."

Stephanus shakes his head, laughing, and Senovara feels a fierce rush of affection. She will never love him, not the way that he wants, but he is her brother. This man has walked beside her as she traveled from town to town, even going with her to Rome, his loyalty never wavering throughout all the long months she has been searching for the child she swore to protect. Fighter, Amara's daughter. Senovara refuses to accept that the girl is dead. Her small spirit was so fierce; she knows she would have felt the loss if Fighter had passed to the underworld. And she has not felt it.

The crew steer the ship into dock. The two survivors of Pompeii heave all their bags up onto their backs, joining the other passengers waiting to clamber ashore. Senovara knows people are staring and pretends not to notice, but her indifference is an act. She is always more watchful than watched, aware of every small movement around her, alert to the possibility of danger or attack.

They have arrived at the start of the Cerealia—the harvest festival in honor of the goddess Ceres-Demeter—and are forced to weave their way through the piled baskets of grain being unloaded at the harbor. Campania's own fields have not recovered enough from the eruption to produce all that its people need for bread. Flashes of white mark out the presence of women in the crowded marketplace; they are all dressed in honor of Ceres, making Senovara stand out further, in her plain, dark tunic. Her hand rests lightly on the hilt of her dagger, hidden in the folds of her clothes.

Stephanus asks a group of merchants for directions to the forum, while Senovara looks over at the slave market where people are on sale, left to stand naked in the blazing sun. Anger burns in her chest. She sends up a familiar curse to Andraste the Indestructible, asking the goddess to destroy the men who killed her family and enslaved her. *May their bones already rot unmourned.*

The walk to the forum is up a steep, brightly painted road that stretches from the sea. At least they will have a bed tonight, rather than have to camp out in the fields. They have enough money for several nights at an inn, thanks to the generosity of Livia. It took Senovara many months to find Amara's old friend in Rome. After the landslide that nearly killed her and Stephanus on their escape from Pompeii, they were swept far off course and forced to abandon their journey to Stabiae, instead fleeing north toward Neapolis. Since then they have survived by staging fights at the forums of small towns, sometimes even managing to win a slot in the arena of bigger cities, like Ostia. Senovara had been so certain that she would find Amara in Rome that the disappointment when they finally discovered Livia, alone, was devastating. Even now, she cannot be certain that Amara has survived. Only Livia's parting words, urging them to stop searching, give her some hope: *if she lives, perhaps she does not wish to be found.* And so Senovara is not searching for her friend. She will not endanger Amara by giving her name at every port. Instead, she is determined to make herself known in as many towns in Campania as she can, so that Amara might find *her*, the fighter Britannica.

Stephanus finds them an inn on a side street off the forum. They take a room, heading up the narrow wooden stairs together. It is a small, hot cupboard of a space, with only one bed. Senovara grunts, setting down her bag. She is not worried about Stephanus asking to lie with her. He asked once, which was forgivable, as one man cannot see into the heart of another, but now he knows her answer, she trusts him not to try again. Besides, her reply was crushing enough the first time.

"Do you want a rest, before we try out?" Stephanus asks, dumping his own bag on the bed.

"Maybe some bread," she replies. "No need for rest."

Stephanus gets out the bread they bought at Ostia, along with some olives that have turned dry and sour. They share his flask of water between them in companionable silence. "If we aim for a booking on the last day of the Ludi Cerealis," he says, "there should be time to have some graffiti put up, advertising your fight."

"We write it everywhere," Senovara says. "If she lives, she see my name."

Their meal over, the two former gladiators unpack their equipment, including the precious weapons they have earned in various fights. Senovara ties her hair back in a horse's tail, daubing blue paste along the lines of her cheekbones. Then they head out again, making for the public square. The town's large forum is already set up in preparation for the festival games; Neapolis's vast amphitheater is still under construction, meaning all entertainments must be held here. That should make it easier to book a slot, at least. People in the milling crowds stare at Senovara and Stephanus as they pass, stepping aside to let them through, this strange foreign woman clutching a trident, alongside a scarred, tough-looking man with a wooden sword.

It is not hard to find where the entertainers are gathered. A group of women in elaborate white robes, their hair decorated with crowns of wheat, are gathered together near the Temple of Fortuna Redux, rehearsing their dance to reenact Ceres-Demeter's search for her daughter Persephone. Stephanus catches the arm of one of the women, asking to be taken to the *lanista* of the gladiatorial games. She points him toward a gathering of men idling in the shade of the colonnade, under a painting of Jupiter. The person they want is called Proclus.

Stephanus approaches the men, Senovara walking beside him. Around his neck he has hung the wooden sword granted to him when he was freed from his service as a gladiator, a symbol any true fighter will understand. He approaches Proclus, who eyes him with suspicion.

Stephanus lays his hand over his heart in a formal gesture of sincerity and respect. "It is my honor to meet you, Proclus. I am Stephanus, *lanista* of the Venus troop of Pompeii, and I have come to offer you Britannica, the greatest gladiator of that dead city, to perform in your games."

"If Pompeii's greatest gladiator was a woman, no wonder it's dead," one of the men scoffs. The rest of the group laugh.

Proclus smiles at the joke but still addresses Stephanus with courtesy. "I have heard of you, Stephanus. We do not have space here for a woman, but you yourself would be welcome to perform. It would be an honor."

Stephanus bows. "I will perform only if Britannica is also given a fight, and her name written across town before the games."

At this Proclus joins in the laughter. "That's a bold request. Are you proposing to fight each other?"

"No, we are never matched together."

The men exchange smirks, some looking Senovara up and down, assuming Stephanus won't fight his woman because he is fucking her. She is used to this, calmly meeting the eye of any man who dares to stare at her directly, remembering his face for later. Proclus shrugs. "Then I don't think we can help."

"If you only give my gladiator a trial," Stephanus continues, undaunted by the mockery, "you will understand why you should take her for your games. She is one of the great warriors of the lost Iceni tribe of Britannia, and served their notorious queen."

"A little young to have fought for Boudicca, isn't she?" Proclus folds his arms.

"I was child," Senovara says, her harsh voice ringing out like a challenge. "I serve her." The crowd laughs again, disbelieving. *Let them*, she thinks. Her memories are no less true for their ignorance. In this country she is no one, a savage slave without a past, but among the Iceni she was once held sacred. Held aloft in the arms of Bouddica herself, after the goddess Andraste's hare ran toward her on the eve of battle. Senovara eyes the men before her with contempt. None of them have seen war, as she has, or fought to defend their people. She turns to Proclus. "Give me your strongest fighter for trial. If I defeat him, you take me."

"Very well," Proclus says. "It's your funeral."

Senovara's heart is beating hard as she walks out onto the public square, to the section set up as a fighting ring. She catches Stephanus's eye as she passes and he winks, his face creasing in a smile. This is also why she loves him. Even if Stephanus fears for her, he never shows it. The gladiator Proclus has selected to fight her is complaining as he walks ahead, telling Proclus it is shameful for him to face some drifter's whore. She hears Proclus's irritated reply. *"Then just disarm her quickly and have done with it."*

Senovara watches her opponent striding aggressively in front, taking in every detail. He is well built, heavy even, which means he may not be so light on his feet. There is no other obvious weakness she can spy. She will have to wait to see him move. Stephanus and Proclus discuss the terms, agreeing that their gladiators will have a short practice first, and that the fight will not aim to kill. Senovara steps into the ring, aware that some curious people in the forum have drifted over to watch, but she does not pay them attention. One of Proclus's men brings her the net she is to fight with, dropping it at her feet rather than handing it over. She picks the net up, flicking it to gauge its weight, before practicing the feints and jabs she will use with her trident. She defeated the weapon's previous owner in one of her quickest ever fights. That man underestimated her too.

Senovara's opponent does not wear body armor, and she has no padded tunic, both of them matched with a lack of protection.

She watches him put on his helmet before taking practice swings with his sword. There is great power in his movements, but as he thrusts and turns, she spies his second weakness: he is too much in love with the admiration of the watching crowd.

They warm up for a few minutes longer, until Proclus claps his hands, impatient for the gladiators to begin. Senovara does not think of Amara, or Rufina, or anything else that rests on this fight as she steps in front of her opponent. Nothing exists except her will to win—it is a fire that burns within her, as terrible as the mountain that destroyed a city. Her opponent turns his head, rolling his eyes at one of his watching fellows, laughing, and it is there that Senovara sees his greatest weakness. The man's disdain for her. It is the gift she has been given so many times before. Her opponent's defeat is written in the lack of effort he has put into studying her movements, and in his complacency she sees her own victory, if she only strikes hard enough, and fast enough.

Senovara raises her trident, murmuring the words she says before every fight, the words her brother taught her so many years ago. It is the prayer to Andraste, a vow to survive the battle.

And as Senovara speaks, she knows the words are true. *This is not where it ends.*

ACKNOWLEDGMENTS

Writing this book—and concluding the trilogy—has at times been a total joy, at others a task that seemed nearly impossible. When it comes to thanks, nobody has done more for me this past year than Juliet Mushens. You are an incredible agent Juliet, but it is your friendship that has made the most difference to my life. Without your love and support, *The Temple of Fortuna* would not have been written. Thank you for this and for so much more.

Thank you to my fabulous American agent, Jenny Bent, and to the entire team at Union Square & Co., my US publishers. Thanks especially to Barbara Berger, also to Emily Meehan, Amanda Englander, Lisa Forde, Melissa Farris, Elizabeth Lindy, Kevin Ullrich, Kevin Iwano, Michael Cea, Chris Stambaugh, Jenny Lu, Daniel Denning, and Chris Vaccari. Thank you to the whole team at Head of Zeus and Bloomsbury in the UK: Madeleine O'Shea, Sophie Whitehead, Dan Groenewald, Jo Liddiard, Amy Watson, Kathryn Colwell, Nick Cheetham, Anthony Cheetham, Clemence Jacquinet, Katrina Harvey, and Matt Bray.

Special thanks to Holly Ovenden for the trilogy's beautiful cover art: you have brought Amara's story to life in each book with your stunning illustrations.

One of the highlights of last year was visiting Rome for the Piu Libri Piu Liberi book fair and spending time with the team at Fazi who publish the Wolf Den in Italy. Thank you Francesco Fazi, Valentina Bortolamedi, Livia Senni, and Debora Pisano for making me so very welcome. It was wonderful too, to meet the team at Calmann Levy in Paris. I am truly grateful to all the co-agents, publishers, and translators who have taken Amara to so many countries, in such beautiful editions, and in the UK I owe a massive thanks to Liza DeBlock at Mushens Entertainment, who has worked tirelessly on this.

A big thank-you too, to Rachel Neely at Mushens Entertainment, who has been phenomenal, also to Kiya Evans, Catriona Fida, and Alba Arnau Prado.

Booksellers, reviewers, bloggers, and fellow authors continue to be an amazing source of support for my work, and I am so very grateful for this. It has been a real pleasure to meet many booksellers doing events in the UK, and I have been touched beyond measure to see online posts from booksellers abroad promoting the trilogy in the US and beyond. You are the reason readers pick up my novels and I can never thank you enough for all that you do.

Closest to my heart, thank you above all to my dearest son Jonathon: I love you so much and am so very proud of all that you are. How lucky I am to be your mum. Thank you to my own mother, Suzy Kendall, who has always been incredibly supportive of my writing, to my father, Sandy Harper, my siblings Eugenie Walker and Tom Harper, and my fabulous nieces Eadie Young, Mia Walker, Isadora Harper, Rosa Harper, and Chloe Walker. And to our darling Ruth, Tom's beloved wife and Eadie, Dora and Rosa's irreplaceable, devoted mother: we all miss you so very much.

I am incredibly grateful to my friends, for all their love and support. Thank you to Samira Ahmed, who came to Rome with me and who is endlessly inspiring. Thank you to Claire McGlasson for always being there, to Susan Stokes-Chapman for putting up with my nonsense, and to Jennifer Saint for sharing so much of the writing journey. Also thank you to Kristina Holt, Lingling Hu, Jo Jacobson, Jason Farrington, Sophie Hay, Dan Jones, Alice Reynolds, Jane Johnson, Vasiliki Alexandridou, Trilby Fox-Rumley, Bethan Francis, Anna Sahalayeva, Mita Patel and Kate Appleton. Special mention to Seth Patrick-Mushens for being the cutest baby—what a wonderful mum and dad you have in Juliet and Den, I can't wait to see all that you get up to.

And thank you to my forever-friend Andrea Binfor. Years ago, we sat in the park together as seventeen-year-olds, pondering what sins it might be worth going to Hell for, what books we loved, and many other earnest things besides. We got (slightly) less earnest over the years, but you have been there with me through it all: the dreams, the laughter, and the grief. Mainly laughter, though, because that's what we do. Mate, this book is for you.

TOPICS AND QUESTIONS
FOR DISCUSSION

1. The Amara we see in *The Temple of Fortuna* has been through a great deal since we first met her in *The Wolf Den*, which is set five years earlier. Think of all the ways in which she has remained the same, and the ways in which she is different. What do you think of who she has become? Is she more or less admirable than before? If you disagree with her behavior, what do you think you might have done instead, when faced with her options?

2. Toward the end of the book, Amara is forced to make a life-altering choice, from which there is no return. In the end, she gives up wealth and security to live under a "false" identity with her family. She is also making a choice between two men, Demetrius and Philos. What did you think of these men? What are their good and bad qualities? Which life—and which partner—do you think you would have chosen, and why?

3. Amara's choice has major implications for the life of her daughter, Rufina. Did she choose wisely on her child's behalf? How different might Rufina's life have been, growing up in Rome? Would this life also have carried risks, and if so, what are they? Amara felt obliged to leave her daughter in order to protect her at the end of *The House with the Golden Door*. How does Amara cope with this separation? What do you think of her as a mother?

4. The epilogue is written from the point of view of Senovara/Britannica. In what ways did this deepen your understanding of her character? How do you think Britannica has changed over the course of the trilogy? If Britannica finds Amara, how do you think this might affect both women's lives?

5. The other surviving women from the lupanar—Victoria and Beronice— meet Amara again in this book. Have your feelings for those two women

changed? How has the relationship dynamic between the three of them changed? Amara and Victoria's friendship has been destroyed by Victoria's betrayal, which puts Amara's entire family at risk. Do you think Amara might have saved their friendship by treating Victoria differently in *The House with the Golden Door*? Or was it always inevitable Victoria would return to Felix?

6. Felix is Amara's nemesis throughout the trilogy, and in this book, she finally hopes she has freed herself from him. Have there been any moments where you felt sympathy for Felix? In what ways do you think Amara and Felix may be similar? Amara asks Felix not to "haunt" her—do you think she will ever manage to put her former master behind her?

7. In *The Wolf Den*, Amara is enslaved, but after she is freed, she herself owns or uses other enslaved people. This was very common in the Roman world, where freedmen and women would often go on to enslave others. Amara notices how her own attitudes have changed, when she realizes she has become like Rufus, and does not "see" those who serve her. Did you notice this change through the books? How uncomfortable did this make you feel as a reader? Now that Philos is "freed," Amara notices that he seems different—but she cannot tell if he has truly changed, or if it is because the way that people treat him has changed. Which do you think it is?

8. Fortuna was an important figure to the Romans: in his *Natural History*, Pliny writes that "We are so subject to chance that Chance herself takes the place of God; she proves that God is uncertain." In *The Temple of Fortuna*, we see Fortuna being worshiped in various guises: as the luck of the present day and as the good fortune of being saved from disaster. How do you think the Romans' idea that chance is the most powerful force influenced the way they saw life? How do the different characters view Fortuna?

A CONVERSATION WITH ELODIE HARPER

In the Wolf Den trilogy, Elodie Harper draws extensively on the archaeological discoveries at Pompeii and writing from Roman times to tell her story. Here, she explores ancient accounts of the eruption and its aftermath, and the rediscovery of Pompeii and Herculaneum.

We have a surviving eyewitness account of the eruption of Vesuvius in 79 CE. Who was it by and what does it tell us?

Gaius Caecilius Cilo—later known as Pliny the younger—was seventeen years old and living at Misenum with his mother, Plinia, and his uncle Pliny the Elder, when Vesuvius erupted. To avoid confusion, I will refer to him here as Cilo and to his uncle as Pliny, as in the novel. Cilo wrote his account to the historian Tacitus in the form of two letters, many years after the eruptions. In the first, we learn that Pliny and his family became aware of a strange cloud rising over the mountains in the early afternoon of August 24 (later believed to have been miscopied from October). Pliny wanted to investigate this strange natural phenomenon and was preparing to set sail when he received a message from his friend Rectina, who lived close to Vesuvius, begging him to rescue her. At this point, Pliny realized the severity of the threat and launched the fleet on a rescue mission.

Cilo remained in Misenum but drew on the accounts of Pliny's friends to describe what happened during the mission. The hail of ash and pumice, and the strong winds, forced Pliny to dock at Stabiae, where he met his friend Pomponianus and stayed overnight at his house. Many of the details of this—such as Pliny's cheerful insistence that the fires on Vesuvius were lit by peasants, his decision to take a bath and go to bed early, the increasing earth tremors and the whole household's escape wearing pillows on their heads and carrying torches—are in my book. (All the Stabian characters in this book besides Pliny and Pomponianus, are however, invented.) As well as his uncle's mission, Cilo also describes the course of the eruption in some detail, including his famous comparison of the Vesuvian explosion resembling an umbrella pine: a tall column rising from the mountain's heart, with a giant cloud expanding overhead. Volcanic eruptions of this type are today referred to as Plinian in honor of his description.

The account of Pliny's actual death is confusing, but it seems that either just before or after he had collapsed from what seems to have been suffocation, Pliny was left by his friends, who fled in terror from a sudden rush of heat and sulfurous fumes. This may have been a less intense version of one of the pyroclastic flows of boiling gas that killed everyone who remained in Pompeii on the second day of the eruption. Although Cilo's account suggests two servants may have been with Pliny when he died, it is difficult to see Pliny's death as anything other than abandonment in a moment of chaotic terror. Cilo says that Pliny's friends returned a day later to find his body lying undisturbed, as if asleep.

In his second letter, Cilo records what happened in Misenum to him, his mother, and a Spanish guest. From this we get Cilo's account of people fleeing and battling their way through constant earth tremors, before the collapse of the volcanic ash cloud that plunged everything into darkness, causing absolute terror. Cilo also writes of the darkness finally dissipating, leaving the landscape buried in ash as if by drifts of snow. The tremors continued into the next day, after the eruption.

Your book does not end with the eruption, as might be expected for a story about Pompeii. What made you decide to concentrate on the aftermath of the volcano?

Firstly, as this is a trilogy, I thought people would feel short-changed not to have proper resolution for the various characters: if it all ends with a bang, we don't know what happens to everyone! Also, although the Vesuvius explosion is very famous, for people living at the time, the aftermath of the eruption was in many ways even more significant. It was a huge ongoing humanitarian, economic, and political crisis and I wanted to explore this less well-known aspect of the disaster. It was a collective trauma for the Roman world that lasted generations. The historian Cassius Dio, writing over a century later, claims that the volcanic dust traveled as far as Rome, darkening the capital's skies. Even for people living in Italy in 79 CE who had no direct link to the towns of Pompeii and Herculaneum, news of their destruction would have been a profound shock.

How did the Roman state respond to the eruption?

We have two famous accounts of what happened written by the Roman historians Cassius Dio and Suetonius, who both tell us the disaster was treated as a priority by Emperor Titus. They both praised his swift action, recording that Titus gave to the relief effort all the wealth left by those who died heirless. Dio further adds that the emperor himself toured the affected area twice, as well as appointing former consuls to supervise the rebuilding efforts, which were considerable. Campania had been damaged not only by the mounds of ash and stone but also by the eruption's accompanying earthquakes. Towns across the entire bay, far from the scorching pyroclastic flows, were shaken. Mementos of this horror still remain: in Sorrento (Surrentum) an inscription praises Titus for his restoration of the citizens' beloved town clock, which had been damaged in the earth tremors of 79 CE.

We have fewer recorded details about what happened in the immediate aftermath. Those first days and weeks must have been unspeakably distressing for survivors. It would also have created a refugee crisis of displaced people. The burned remains of a Praetorian soldier on the shore of Herculaneum suggests that Pliny dispatched the fleet to multiple locations during the rescue mission, and so I imagined (perhaps optimistically) the fleet and the army playing a role in the immediate days that followed, even building one of the military encampments that the Roman army was famed for as a makeshift refugee shelter. What is more certain is that people fleeing the disaster would have swamped nearby towns in their desperate quest for shelter. Although Vesuvius killed many of Pompeii's inhabitants, some of whom are visible there today in the plaster casts made of their hollowed-out remains, it is believed still more managed to escape. They eventually resettled close to their former homes, predominantly in Neapolis or Puteoli, modern-day Naples and Pozzuoli.

Do we have any record of how the people of neighboring towns responded?

I tried to imagine this in Amara and Philos's arrival at Surrentum. The whole area was suffering, so helping the survivors may have brought communities together, but equally it may have increased tensions too. In the longer term, the refugees brought with them an influx of investment and jobs. New public baths, an amphitheater, roads, shops, and houses were built in Neapolis, funded by the state's relief effort. Amara and Philos are fortunate to go straight into a new business in my book—this option would most likely only have been available for those who had enough money or relevant skills. Others may have been obliged to live for a long while in refugee camps or more makeshift homes. I imagined Philos, Menander, and Irene using the disaster to reinvent themselves as free. Again, this is optimistic, but it was also not unknown for runaway enslaved people in the ancient world to do this, in spite of the dire punishments that awaited those who were discovered—or those who harbored them. It is hard to believe that such a massive upheaval did *not* result in at least a few enslaved men and women seizing the chance to forge a better life. Others who had been higher up the social hierarchy perhaps tried to replicate the communities they had lost. Three centuries after the eruption, an entire district of Naples was still named after Herculaneum, suggesting many refugees not only survived, but kept the memory of their dead town alive, too.

Why did the Romans not dig up the buried cities and rebuild them?

Digging up Pompeii would have been more time-consuming and expensive than simply expanding districts of existing towns. In their fascinating book *Four Lost Cities* (2021), the writer Annalee Newitz also suggests that Pompeii and Herculaneum were simply too dangerous and toxic to unearth, given the volcanic debris that smothered them. The buried cities were not wholly abandoned, though. After the ash had cooled, some areas of Pompeii were likely salvaged as part of the relief effort, with the forum and theater being stripped of much of their marble for reuse. Some of the survivors must have tried to tunnel back into their homes to retrieve their wealth, and so too did looters. Graffiti reading "*house tunneled through*" suggests some of this work—whether by the authorities or thieves—was fairly systematic. It was also dangerous. Among the bodies discovered by archaeologists are those of people who are believed to have died in their attempt to break back into Pompeii.

When and how was Pompeii rediscovered in more modern times?

The eruption of Vesuvius and the destruction of Pompeii were remembered for hundreds of years. The exact location of the once-prosperous Roman town, now buried not only by pumice and ash but also by earth and fields, was forgotten, yet rumors of its existence, sunk deep beneath the landscape like a lost Atlantis, refused to die. It was not until the eighteenth century, however, that Pompeii was rediscovered.

Herculaneum resurfaced first. A medieval town, Resina (renamed Ercolano in 1969), had been built over the ancient site, and in 1709 a well shaft penetrated deep into the Roman theater. Within a few years, excavation in the region had picked up steam, although those early forays had more in common with the methods of the looters of antiquity than the painstaking work of modern archaeologists.

While Herculaneum began to give up its secrets, the location of Pompeii remained unknown. The sunken form of its amphitheater was identified in 1748, but it was thought to be Stabiae, not Pompeii, and digging there yielded few results. Then, in 1755, a farmer discovered an ornate pillar while plowing a field. Locals had been making such finds for generations, but now the Roman past had piqued royal interest. The engineer Roque Joaquín de Alcubierre, who had been put in charge of the excavations by King Charles VII in Naples, started digging in the same field in April of that year. This time they struck gold. His men unearthed priceless statues and mosaics, as well as incredible, vivid frescoes—some of which were hacked off the walls to be carted back to Naples, while others were simply destroyed along with anything else the men found uninteresting. Alcubierre realized the place where they were digging was a grand villa, the first such Roman house to be discovered in the region. In 1756, he learned the name of its owner from a carefully written inscription. He had dug up the home of Julia Felix.

The excavation—and preservation—of Pompeii continues to this day. Whole sections of the town remain buried and are yet to be uncovered. Modern methods of archaeology are significantly improved from those of the past, and the hope is that as the science continues to advance, so too will our understanding of how people in the ancient Roman town lived and died.